Praise for

Lilies in Moonlight

"Flappers and family. Baseball and cosmetics. War and wealth. Give Allison Pittman those threads, and you have the rich tapestry that is *Lilies in Moonlight.* Lilly Margolis is an off-the-charts heroine that will have you fumbling to turn the pages to keep up with her. But it's the honesty in Lilly and the entire cast of characters that is Pittman's greatest gift to us in this compelling story."

—MONA HODGSON, author of *Two Brides Too Many* and *Too Rich for a Bride*

"In *Lilies in Moonlight,* Allison Pittman offers a fine mix of sin, redemption, and history as an unflappable flapper takes a poignant ride through Prohibition-era Florida. From the homes of the wealthy to a backwoods tent revival, hard times and harder truths chase a wild girl and a war-wounded man into the arms of a love that won't let them go. By turns both heartbreaking and flat-out fun, this story is a gem."

—MEG MOSELEY, author of *When Sparrows Fall*

"*Lilies in Moonlight* transported me to a world radiant with the bold, jaunty spirit of the Jazz Age. I was completely absorbed in the story of Lilly, an unsinkable flapper who turns the pain of her past into a drive to live her life to the fullest. Allison Pittman's novel is vastly entertaining, romantic, and deeply spiritual: a sparkling, fun read that also brought me to tears of sympathy for the characters. Beautifully written, this is a rich story of overcoming, hope, and love that surprised me in a wonderful way with every turn of the page—truly in a league of its own."

—ROSSLYN ELLIOTT, author of *Fairer than Morning*

"*Lilies in Moonlight* is a tender story full of mercy and grace. When two scarred souls meet in God-orchestrated circumstances, Mrs. Betty Ruth Burnside makes it her mission to meld them together. Her son, Cullen, has no desire to fellowship with a flapper. Yet Lilly Margolis has such magnetism, and she's drawn to the Burnside's elegance and wealth. How could such an unlikely match work?"

—Eileen Key, author of *Forget-Me-Not*

LILIES IN MOONLIGHT

Allison Pittman

MULTNOMAH
BOOKS

Lilies in Moonlight
Published by Multnomah Books
12265 Oracle Boulevard, Suite 200
Colorado Springs, Colorado 80921

ISBN 978-1-60142-138-8

ISBN 978-1-60142-336-8 (electronic)

Cover design by Kristopher Orr.
Cover photo by Joel Strayer.

Published in association with the William K. Jensen Literary Agency, 119 Bampton Court, Eugene, OR 97404, bill@wkjagency.com.

Published in the United States by WaterBrook Multnomah, an imprint of the Crown Publishing Group, a division of Random House Inc., New York.

Library of Congress Cataloging-in-Publication Data
Pittman, Allison.
Lilies in moonlight : novel / Allison Pittman. — 1st ed.
p. cm.
ISBN: 978-1-60142-138-8 — ISBN 978-1-60142-336-8 (electronic)
1. Nineteen twenties. 2. Self-realization—Fiction. 3. World War, 1914–1918—Veterans—Fiction. I. Title.
PS3616.I885L55 2011
813'.6—dc22
2010043876

Printed in the United States of America
2011

10 9 8 7 6 5 4 3 2

For Mom

Oh, how I delight to be at your feet!

OTHER BOOKS BY ALLISON PITTMAN

Nonfiction

Saturdays with Stella

Fiction

The Bridegrooms

Stealing Home

Crossroads of Grace Series

Ten Thousand Charms

Speak Through the Wind

With Endless Sight

1

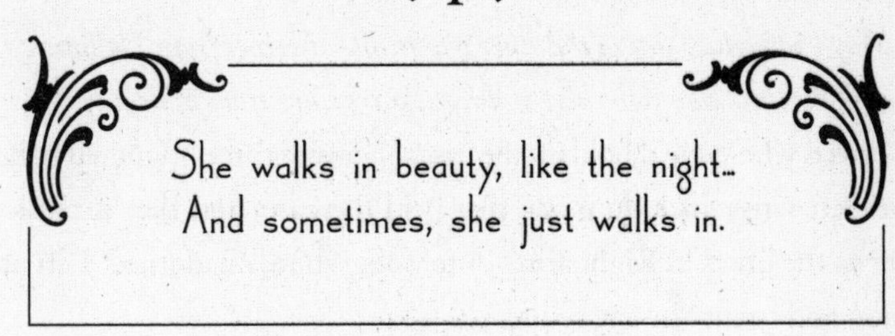

October 1925

Just ten o'clock in the morning, and already Lilly Margolis could feel the trickle of sweat sliding between her shoulder blades.

Head up. Big smile, chin out, she silently rehearsed.

Good morning, madam. Are you the lady of the house?

Pause, two, three, four.

Allow me to introduce myself. My name is Lilly, Lilly Margolis. But Lilly's not just my name. It's also the name of the fabulous new body crème from Dalliance Cosmetics. Lilies in Moonlight. I use it myself.

She held out her arm, focusing on the creamy silk of her skin against the dark wood of the door.

Makes my skin smooth as silk and irresistible to the touch. At least that's what my boyfriend says.

Wink, wink. She didn't really have a boyfriend, but every man who'd ever touched her said she felt like satin. Or cold milk. White and soft and pure. She, of course, didn't use Lilies in Moonlight body crème. She couldn't afford it. Nothing but Ivory soap from the five-and-dime and maybe a dab of Jergens lotion.

May I introduce you to the other irresistible offerings from Dalliance Cosmetics? This little case right here is a regular treasure trove of beauty.

This is where she'd hold up the case. She wore three bright red bangles on her left wrist, including one that held the case, and they'd clank together as she lifted it. Right arm? Pure, soft, white, unadorned. Left arm? Fashion and beauty in one grip.

Lilly Margolis was everything—blond, bobbed hair, perfectly plucked eyebrows, bright red lips—all wrapped up in the perfect porch-sized package. What would Mama say if she could be on the other side of that door? No great mystery there. She'd say Lilly looked like a tramp, that God would condemn her for cutting her hair. To her, Lilly's smooth skin meant that she was lazy, pampered, indulged.

Lilly banished such ugliness behind what she knew to be a dazzling face. Her mother might not approve, but the rest of the world sure did. Men most of all. And if she got lucky, the woman behind this door would too. Resolved, she touched her painted fingertips to her hair, doubled her smile, and rang the bell.

"What do you want?" The woman on the other side of the door wore a faded housedress. Her hair was mostly piled on top of her head, though tendrils floated around her face.

Smile. "Good morning, madam! Are you the lady of the house?"

"Oh, for the love of Pete."

And Lilly faced the door again.

She relaxed her posture, letting her shoulder stoop with the weight of the tan leather case, getting no satisfaction from even the clank of her bangles. She turned and walked down the front steps. Those potted flowers looked a little less lovely than they did when she first walked past them just a minute ago.

"Should've opened with the flowers." Next door, she'd know.

Back on the sidewalk, she assessed the next house. Trim lawn, roses in bloom at the corner.

Chin up, big smile, shoulders squared, she strode up the walkway, looking confident lest the lady be looking out the front window at that moment. At the door, she shifted the leather case from one hand to the other, bangles rattling as she raised her fist to knock.

The door opened and this woman looked much like the previous one, but her hair was a little neater, her dress less faded.

"Good morning, madam. Tell me, are you responsible for those beautiful roses in bloom?"

"Why yes, I am." The woman touched her fingers to her throat, as if shocked to be greeted with such a compliment.

"Well then, it won't surprise you to learn that the delicate rose petal is a key ingredient in Dalliance Cosmetics's Rose of Sharon hand crème. Just a dab worked in at night, and your hands will be as soft as the petals on your lovely flowers. May I offer you a demonstration?"

"Oh, I don't think so, dear. Jergens works fine for me."

A softer closing of the door this time, but a closing nonetheless. Back on the sidewalk, Lilly looked up the street. One house after another, all of them small and square. In some ways, no different from the row of clapboard shacks she left behind in Miresburgh. But here there seemed to be a sweetness to the smallness. Maybe it was the trim green lawns, the varied gardens, the short white fences. Who knows? Maybe her own street would take on life and beauty if it were bathed in this relentless Florida sun. Still, small houses meant small lives; small lives meant small dreams. Green grass or not, when she looked down the street all she saw was one closed door after another.

"Never gonna sell nothin' in this lousy neighborhood," she muttered under her breath. Still, she wasn't about to cry over it. After all, it could be worse. She could be one of those women all wrapped up in a housedress with nowhere to go. Why, they might be looking out of their windows right now thinking, *What is that stunning vision of beauty doing on our humble little street?* Lilly herself had been inspired by the beauties she'd seen in the movies and magazines.

Mindful of her purpose, she smiled sweetly at the young woman pushing a pram, followed by two sticky children. Half a block behind Lilly was a park. She'd planned to stop there and sit on one of its bright red benches to eat the cheese sandwich that was wrapped in wax paper and nestled among the bottles and jars of Dalliance Cosmetics in the tan leather case.

She turned around and followed the woman and the pram and the sticky children, who took turns looking back at her. Lilly stuck out her tongue and they did too. The mother never glanced over her shoulder even once.

Once in the park, the sticky children ran to the swing set; the mother settled on a bench and pulled the baby out of the pram to settle it on her lap for a gentle bouncing.

"Cute baby." Lilly chose the bench on the opposite side of the little walking path that stretched around the park.

"His name's John." The recollection of the name seemed an exhausting endeavor.

"I don't have any children myself." Lilly crossed her leg and admired her shoe. White patent leather with a wide sea-foam green ribbon. She'd have to sell ten jars of Lilies in Moonlight to pay for them. "I'm a salesgirl for Dalliance Cosmetics. It's highly rewarding."

The mother smiled weakly, then hollered at the sticky children—June and Teddy—telling them to play nice and take turns.

"Of course, motherhood is its own reward." Though truthfully, Lilly could think of nothing worse. Besides the disaster a pregnancy would bring to her perfect planklike figure, she'd grown up knowing exactly what kind of inconvenience it could bring to a girl's life. "But I bet you like to take yourself a long, hot bath at the end of a day."

Baby John began to fuss, bucking straight back in his mother's lap.

"Or on a hot day like this, maybe a nice cool one. Not too cold—that can be shocking. But tepid. Just enough warm to take off the edge. So when you dip your foot in, you can't hardly tell where the air stops and the water starts, except for the wet. And then, when you lift yourself out, no matter how hot it is, you get this breeze that just chills—"

"Look, lady. I don't usually have time to take a bath. I got three kids."

"Haven't you got a husband?"

"He's a manager down at Parson's. Sometimes he works late."

"So you never have time to bathe?" Lilly widened her eyes, creating an image of innocent incredulity.

"'Course I do." The mother set baby John back in his pram and handed him a bottle of milk, a veneer of resentment on her smile. "Just nothing long and luxurious is all."

Lilly pouted. "Poor dear." She lifted the tan leather case and set it beside her. Two clicks of the brass latches and she had a wide-mouthed jar—frosted pink glass with a silver-painted lid. "There's no reason you can't pamper yourself with even the shortest dip. It's not the length of the soak but the quality of the soap, that's what we say at Dalliance Cosmetics."

"I use Ivory—"

"As well you should, what with the little ones and all. But how about something like this?" Lilly rose from her bench and crossed the path, carrying the wide-mouthed jar aloft like a treasure. Slowly, holding the jar just under the mother's nose, she twisted the silver lid, wincing a bit at the glare from the bouncing sun. "Bath salts. Lavender. Here, just take a whiff."

The mother closed her eyes, revealing thin lids with tiny blue branching veins. Perhaps it was the shiny silver lid that caught the attention of the now sticky and sweaty children, because they abandoned their swings and ran pell-mell toward their mother.

Lilly stopped them in their tracks with nothing more than a kohl-eyed glare. "Scram, kids. This is for your ma."

The mother opened her eyes again, transformed. Soft and content. "Very nice."

"Not bad for a nickel, is it?"

"A nickel? You're kidding."

"Well, the whole jar is a dollar thirty, but there's enough in here for at least twenty-five baths, so that works out to about a nickel a bath. Don't you think at the end of a day you deserve a nickel's worth of bath salts all to yourself?"

Perhaps some innate protective sense had taken over the children, because once again they abandoned their swinging and were running—more cautiously this time—toward the benches. Now the mother, with her arms crossed, looked at them with narrowed eyes.

"Teddy and June! You two go play or I'm going to give you a spank right here and now and another when we get home!"

Teddy and June obeyed, taking sulky backward steps so their selfish mother could gaze upon their sweaty, sticky, grubby faces for as long as possible.

The mother scooted an inch or so away from Lilly. "Put that lid back on. I haven't got a dollar thirty to spend on bath salts."

"Don't forget about the beauty of the jar itself," Lilly said, grasping to close the deal. "When you've finished with the lavender, you can always refill it with something from the five-and-dime, and none of your friends need be the wiser. With this beautiful Dalliance Cosmetics jar on your powder-room shelf, you'll be the envy—"

"I don't have friends who visit my powder room." The mother lifted baby John out of the pram again and held him close, resting her chin on top of his bald little head.

Teddy and June would not be denied a third time. They scrambled onto the bench, wedging their way between the two women.

Lilly leaped to her feet, barely snatching the pretty pink jar from the grimy clutches of June.

Once again the mother's manner softened. What sternness she had dissolved like so many bath salts as her children peppered her with silly questions. Who was this lady? What was in the jar? Could they have a Coca-Cola with their lunch when they got home? And could the lady come have lunch with them? And wasn't she pretty?

With gentleness Lilly couldn't have imagined, the mother answered each child. Yes, the lady was pretty, but no, she was far too busy to come home for lunch. This response was given with a wary eye across the top of Teddy's grubby face, but Lilly just smiled and winked.

It was enough that they thought she was pretty.

Lilly checked to be sure the silver lid was screwed on tight. Then, as the little family debated whether they should play on the swings or the slide, she reached inside baby John's pram and nestled the lavender bath salts within his blankets. She quickly closed the latches on her leather case and lifted it off the bench.

Before she could get away, however, the mother called out, "Hey! I told you I can't afford that."

Lilly waved a hand behind her, bangles clanking. "Forget it. You qualify for the free sample of the day."

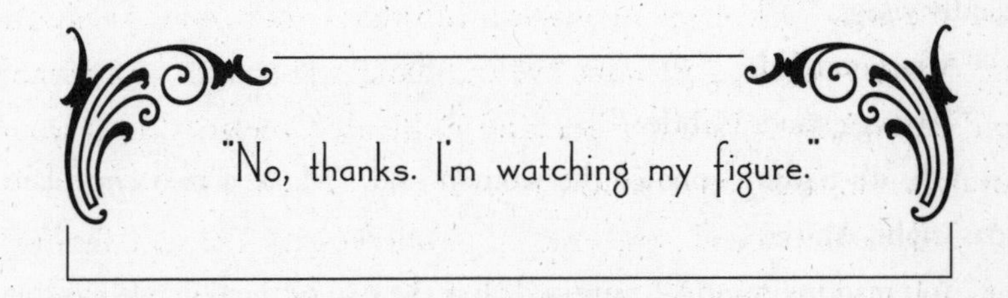

Three blocks later Lilly sat down again—this time at a drugstore counter—and filled out a sales slip. She thought back to the nearly empty powder box on the washstand in her room at Mrs. Myrtle's Hotel for Women. She had a little more than three dollars in there—two of which were meant for next week's rent. A couple of big sales would make up the difference, but she'd need to find better hunting ground.

"Hey, lady." The man behind the counter wore a blue-and-white-striped shirt and blue suspenders. His gray hair was thick and curly; the glasses on the bottom of his nose gave a kindly effect absent from his voice. "This isn't your office. You going to order something?"

Lilly dug into her little beaded purse and pulled out a dime. "Two Coca-Colas." One for later tonight with the supper included in her two-dollar-a-week rent.

The man behind the counter popped the top off one of the bottles before swiping the dime across the polished wood. Lilly quietly unwrapped her sandwich, keeping it hidden on her lap as she tore off one bite at a time, chewing slowly and washing it down with sips of the cold, dark, fizzing soda.

Behind her the bell rang, and though she didn't know another soul in this part of town, Lilly spun on her stool to see who walked in. Two women, probably in their fifties, wearing identical gray dresses, white aprons, and ugly brown shoes.

Maids.

"Afternoon, ladies." Now the man behind the counter lived up to his friendly visage.

"Afternoon, Ed."

"Two egg salads? Coffee?"

"Oh, it's payday," one of the women said. "Make it two chocolate sodas, right, Annie?"

"You read my mind," Annie said, and the two of them giggled as if it were truly funny.

"Sounds good," Lilly said. She imagined herself part of their conversation, but they responded with a dismissive glare. The few bites of sandwich sat heavy in her stomach, and she wished for just a minute she were sharing a sticky table with little June and Teddy.

Deciding these women weren't worthy of her smile, she drooped her face into an exaggerated pout and twirled back to her sandwich, giving the women a view of the back of her neck, imitating the pose she'd seen on the cover of the *Vogue* magazine on the newsstand in the corner.

She continued with her sandwich and soda and sales-ticket book, all the while listening to Annie and her friend. Apparently their mistresses were at a weekly country club luncheon, meaning somewhere within walking distance there was a neighborhood with money.

Lilly tore her sandwich into smaller and smaller pieces, making it last long enough for Annie and her friend to finish their egg salads and chocolate sodas. Ed was not fooled for a moment; he'd come close to catching her midbite several times, but every time he asked if she wanted to order something, Lilly smiled her brightest and said no, thank you, she was watching her figure.

At ten minutes to one, the maids slurped the last of their sodas and bid Ed good-bye. Lilly swigged the last of her Coca-Cola—warm and flat by now—and carefully folded the square of wax paper to put back in her leather case. It would wrap tomorrow's sandwich.

"See ya, Ed." She gave a little salute, bangles clanking, and set the door's bell ringing.

With the women in gray about twenty paces ahead, Lilly straightened her shoulders, refreshed her grip on the case's handle, and took a determined step. Fortune could not be far away.

2

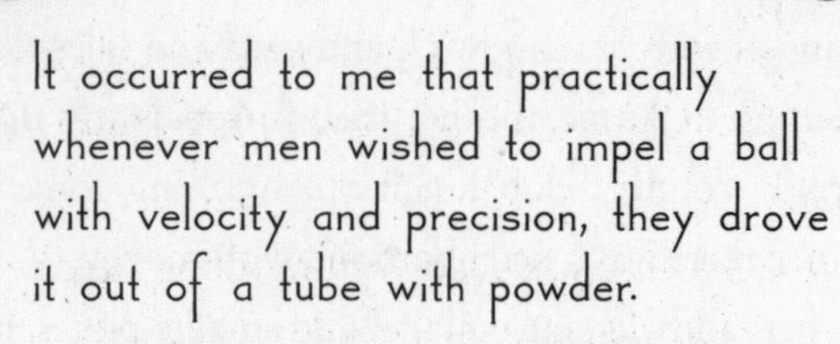

It occurred to me that practically whenever men wished to impel a ball with velocity and precision, they drove it out of a tube with powder.

—Charles Hinton, inventor of the pitching machine

Cullen Burnside reached into the bucket and took out another brand-new baseball. Stainless white leather, smooth as skin. Bright red stitching. He turned it over and over in his hand, just as he had since he was a kid. Like this for a fastball. Like that for a curve ball. Change-up. After a couple of soft tosses straight up and down, loving the feel of it landing in his open palm, he gripped it tight in one hand and grasped the barrel of the cannon steady with what remained of the other.

"A little to the left, Eugenie." He gestured with the ball to accompany his voice, which wouldn't carry all the way across the yard.

Through the pitching machine's scope, he saw the figure in the maid's uniform and starched white apron. She had one hand on her hip, impatient, most likely because his mother waited inside with some urgent need. But it was essential to get the position just right. After all, she was the same height as Cullen—within an inch at least—and her feet were roughly the same size.

He stood straight, taking his eyes away from the cannon's scope. "Bat up." He manipulated his own body, and she hers, until they made a mirror image. His arms up, her arms up. His back bent, her back bent. He couldn't help the fact that her face maintained its familiar mix of irritation and frustration.

"Choke up." His final instruction before taking another look through the scope. Perfect. He tightened the bolts and loaded the ball into the top tube leading down to the cannon's barrel.

"You shoot that thing at me, and you'll wish you died in France." Eugenie made this same threat every day. It had lost its sting.

He ran his finger along the tube that fed the gas into the cannon and checked the powder level. After attaching a wire leading to the remote trigger, he dropped in the ball.

Eugenie remained in position until he reached her. In one seamless motion, he placed his hands over her hands on the bat and stepped into her place as she let go. The doorbell inside the house rang.

"Oh no. That means Mrs. B is going to open that front door herself."

"Go ahead." Cullen stared straight down the barrel of the cannon. "We're finished here."

Giving no thought to what or who might be at the front door, he settled into his stance. He'd never get used to batting left, but he knew plenty of fellows who came back from the war with no right arm at all, so no use complaining about not matching the stats on the back of a baseball card.

"Batter up," he barked, gambling that he'd still have enough breath afterward to swing the bat full around. He stared down the barrel of the cannon, unblinking.

Why couldn't it have been a gun, Lord? Why couldn't I have been shot instead?

The trigger sat in perfect position. He could keep his heel dug in and rotate his foot to depress it. He did this now, his toe hovering over the switch. He closed his eyes, replacing the mounted machine in the middle of the yard with the image of a mound of dirt and a man upon it, all wound up and ready to fire. Maybe a young Babe Ruth. Or Carl Mays.

The scents of cut grass and flowers faded behind the imagined ones of sweat and dirt and beer. In his mind, the roar of a crowd overtook the quietness of his upper-crust neighborhood. His name over a loudspeaker: *Now batting for Pittsburgh, Cullen Burnside.* No nickname. That would come later.

He didn't want to open his eyes, but if not, he'd never swing the bat. Never hit the ball. So when the echo of his name faded into the darkness of his mind, he once again stared down the barrel of the pitching machine.

Three, two, one.

His toe hit the trigger. Simultaneous with the explosion was the image of the red-stitched projectile hurtling straight toward him. Cullen stood, fearless and ready in its path. In the time it took for the ball to cross the distance between the barrel and the bat, his mind moved far away from the tranquility of a baseball field. Now, he saw men fallen all around him, steam rising from torn, bleeding bodies, limbs and guns and endless, endless mud. Finally, the engulfing yellow cloud that robbed him of his life.

What had he to fear from a five-cent toy?

He swung. The muscles remaining in his right arm screamed with the effort. They screamed, because he couldn't. He channeled all his strength into the bat, bracing for the desired impact between the bat and ball. But if he'd miscalculated, or Eugenie had grown taller, or the ball slid across some imperfection in the barrel and the ball collided with him, what loss could there be?

And then, the sound. Wood connecting with leather. His eyes closed again at that second—a habit he'd never been able to break. But he could feel a good hit. When he opened his eyes again, he saw it, long and low. Line drive to right field, or at least into the hydrangeas. The flowers quivered with the impact. At any field in the country that would be a single. But he didn't run. He didn't have to. He needed all his strength to return to the bucket to take out and load the next ball.

3

Our girl Lilly finds herself at the home of Betty Ruth Burnside, wife of railroad tycoon Davis Burnside, one of the richest families in Pensacola...

Head up, shoulders back, bright smile.

Good afternoon. Is the lady of the house at home? Because this was not the neighborhood to have ladies answering their own doors. The houses sat on either side of a broad street with a wide green manicured strip—interrupted by a tree every so often—stretched right down the middle of it.

She stood in the shade of the first tree at the top of the street, pinching the fabric at the back of her dress, fanning the sweat dry. By now the kohl around her eyes was smeared, and she'd nibbled her lipstick away with her cheese sandwich. The weight of the case had left her shoulder numb, and there was no disguising the half-moon stains under her arms.

She surveyed the houses. *How to choose, how to choose, how to choose.* Several had discreet signs directing servants to a back entrance. She wouldn't choose any of those. Lilly Margolis might be a penniless girl from Miresburgh, Pennsylvania, but she was nobody's servant.

One house called to her. Tall—three stories—and white, with six columns across the front porch. Imposing and inviting at once, with a whimsical coral-colored path winding from the sidewalk to the front steps. The front door an enormous stained-glass window framed by dark cherry wood. A high stone barrier jutted out from either side of the house, extending to the back, with an iron gate marking the entrance to a wide side drive. But the lack of a fence around the front yard made the place seem that much more welcoming. A small brass plaque dangled over the doorway: 711.

"Seven-eleven." Lilly snapped her fingers. "What could be luckier than that?"

She made her way up the coral pathway, hoping if nothing else to be given the opportunity to come in and sit for a spell. Her shoes might be cute, but they weren't meant for walking all over Pensacola.

Up close, she could make out the images in the stained glass. A breathtaking scene of a train winding through a mountain pass, beginning on one door and carrying over to the next. She could have stood staring at it for the rest of the afternoon, admiring the tiny bits of glass in place as wildflowers and sleeper-car windows. Instead she took a deep breath and rang the bell. Twice. Just as she was about to turn away, figuring not even a seven and an eleven together could bring her any luck, half of the train swept away.

"Well, land sakes. Look at you! Such a vision, such a vision."

The door had swung open to reveal a woman hardly bigger than a child, yet she held herself with the dignity of a queen. She wore an old-fashioned dress—long sleeved and high necked, even in this heat—and her hair was a swirl of cinnamon and gray swept up into a Gibson girl style that she must have been wearing for the last twenty years. She had bright blue eyes and rosy cheeks—like some kind of grown-up lady doll.

Lilly's opening line stuck in her throat.

"You might just be the first genuine flapper who ever made a visit to my house. Come in, come in, darling. It is so hot outside. Will this heat never end? Come on in here for a cool drink of lemonade."

"Good afternoon, m'am," Lilly said, undaunted by the stream of welcome pouring over her. "Is the lady of the house at home?"

The woman opened the door wider, ushering Lilly in. "I'm the only lady of this house, unless you want to count Eugenie. Which I don't. Oh, she keeps it clean enough, but that's what she's paid for, after all. Wouldn't have her at all but my son..."

The woman prattled on, but Lilly heard nothing. She stood in a foyer of polished wood, gleaming walls, and a perfect little marble-topped table with an ornate gold mirror hanging above it. A glimpse confirmed her suspicions that her dress was drooping and her face and neck were blotchy red from the sun. Should have worn a hat.

"You have a lovely home here." Her voice echoed.

"My Davis saw to every detail. Every detail." The woman closed the door behind them, and the *click* of the latch echoed too.

"Well," Lilly got her thoughts together, "a woman with such fine taste will surely want to have the very best in her beauty regime."

But the woman was not listening. She simply walked through the house, beckoning Lilly with a ring-encrusted hand to follow her. "Right in here, the front parlor."

Lilly found herself in a room full of light. Two elegant white sofas faced each other, with an oblong table in between. The wallpaper appeared to be a series of twisting ribbons in alternating rose and green; the longest wall was covered with a series of small paintings—still-life in various fruit, bowls, pitchers, and wine. "Davis has a fine work by Thomas Nast in his study which I would much prefer to showcase here—better light, you know. Much better light. Glorious Gettysburg battle scene. But he says it's much too controversial for a front parlor."

"These are lovely." Lilly tried to sound as if she had a cultivated eye for art. "I can see you have a taste for fine things. That's why you'll find the very jars and bottles—"

The woman shouted, "Eugenie!" before extending a gracious invitation for Lilly to sit on one of the white sofas.

Within minutes, a tall woman in a black dress and crisp white apron appeared in the front parlor doorway, her hat slightly askew. The woman herself was gray. Her hair, her skin. All muted shades without a speck of color to be found. She had a face made of features—eyes, nose, mouth—all with a lack of distinction.

"Yes, Mrs. B?"

"Can you please fetch us a pitcher of lemonade and—are you hungry, dear?"

"Oh no," Lilly answered, too quickly to be believed.

"And a tray of sandwiches I think too. Not cucumber"—she turned to Lilly—"I don't know who ever thought a person could fill themselves up with a cucumber sandwich. Chicken salad, if we have any. No, make it ham."

"Now, Betty Ruth Burnside," the maid said, her voice as gray as her skin, "you know you've already had your lunch."

"But the world is full of people who haven't, Eugenie. We'd do best not to forget that. And cookies. Do we have any of those pink ones with the lemon icing?"

"I think your son might have left a few."

"Then bring those too." Her face transformed with childish delight, she clapped her hands and turned to Lilly. "They really are the most delicious treat!"

"Thank you." Now Lilly knew the woman's name was Betty Ruth, and possibly the most wonderful creature she'd ever encountered. "Pink cookies sound delicious. In fact, pink is the signature color of Dalliance Co—"

The rest of the word erupted in a scream as the sound of gunfire rattled the paintings on the wall.

"Oh dear." Betty Ruth smoothed her skirt and sat on the sofa next to Lilly. "That was a loud one."

"Wh-what was it?"

"My son. He is in the backyard, playing that foolish game of his. I expect the telephone will ring any minute."

As if on cue, the gilded white phone on the corner desk jangled.

"Eugenie, darling! Be a dear and answer that in the kitchen? Tell whoever is on the other line that we are not at home. Not at home." She reached over and patted Lilly's leg. Three of her fingers bore rings—a jumble of diamonds, rubies, sapphires, and gold. "It'll be a few minutes before the next one, and they aren't all that loud. Sometimes I don't hear anything at all."

"Is it safe?"

Betty Ruth cocked one perfectly arched brow. "Did you come here to talk about my son? Because he is very particular about the women with whom he keeps company."

For a moment, Lilly forgot exactly why she came here at all, but then she noticed the details of Betty Ruth's powdered face and caught a hint of expensive perfume as the woman removed her hand. Lilly looked around the room—marble tabletops, silk drapery, antique furniture. All of it belonged to this woman dripping in jewels, whose dress, though dated, was impeccably tailored. Lilly had come here with a leather case full of cheap lotions and powders and scented water. All of it together worth less than the single drop on Betty Ruth's wrist.

Lilly was about to excuse herself, apologize, and leave without trying to sell a single jar when two things happened. Eugenie arrived carrying a silver tray stacked with perfect little sandwiches, and the pistol or gun or cannon or whatever it was exploded again, startling the seemingly unflappable maid, causing her to stumble into the room and drop two tiny sandwiches to the floor.

"Let me get those," Lilly said, but at that moment a jingling sound heralded the arrival of a beautiful blond cocker spaniel. The dog swept the sandwiches off the carpet and swallowed them down in one gulp.

"That's my crazy Mazy." Betty Ruth reached down to pat the dog's head now on her lap. "And goodness, doesn't she look just like you? Big brown eyes and your hair waves just like hers. Of course you have a much more elegant nose. What my mother would have called 'patrician.'"

"Well, thank you. I never thought being compared to a dog would be so much of a compliment."

"You are a beautiful girl." Betty Ruth patted Lilly again, with every bit as much affection as she showed the lovely Mazy. "And I do so envy your style. So modern."

Eugenie made a noise—not an approving one—as she set down the tray.

"Oh, you just ignore her." Betty Ruth handed Mazy another sandwich. "She's old-fashioned."

Without comment, Eugenie handed Lilly a small china plate painted with a pastoral design and edged in gold leaf. At Betty Ruth's insistence, she loaded it with two sandwich triangles, a small bunch of green grapes, and two of the aforementioned pink-frosted cookies.

Betty Ruth ate nothing but a cookie, and Mazy was dismissed to follow Eugenie back to the kitchen.

"So nice to have a young person come visit." Somehow Betty Ruth managed not to get a single pink crumb in the corners of her lips, while the entire front of Lilly's dress had a dusting of bread and cookies. "Have you already told me your name?"

Lilly finished a sip of lemonade. "It's Lilly. Lilly Margolis."

"Lilly Margolis. Why, that sounds just like music, doesn't it? Lilly Margolis. Just like music."

"Thank you." Lilly'd never heard that before.

"And what brings you here, Lilly Margolis?"

Lilly nudged the tan leather case with her toe, embarrassed at its contents. Still, she couldn't claim to have simply dropped by unannounced for lunch. "I am a representative of Dalliance Cosmetics."

"Oh, a salesgirl! How glamorous."

"Some days more than others."

"And I suppose you would like to sell me some of your products."

"Oh no," Lilly said before realizing just how ridiculous that sounded. "I mean, I can tell you are a woman of fine taste, but I'm sure you already have a lovely array—"

"Nonsense. What kind of a salesgirl do you ever hope to be with that attitude? Come, come. Finish up your lunch and show me what you've got in there."

She savored the last bit of pink cookie as Eugenie came in to clear the tray. Soon after, Lilly carefully set the tan leather case on the marble-topped table and opened the latch, quickly snatching the wad of wax paper and the bottle of Coca-Cola while Betty Ruth occupied herself cooing at the recently reappeared Mazy. The case opened at the top and the sides, creating a blue velvet-lined display of bottles and jars, each held in place with a matching elastic band.

Betty Ruth clasped her hands. "How lovely! It's just like a little store."

Emboldened by the older woman's enthusiasm, Lilly reached for the largest, most expensive jar. "This is Lilies in Moonlight."

"Lilly! Just like you."

Lilly smiled. "Yes, and look at my skin. Just as smooth and white as the moon's reflection."

"Why, you make it sound like poetry. I'll take a jar."

"Oh," Lilly said, surprised at a new reaction to the familiar line. "It's really more of a coincidence that the cream and I have the same name. I didn't invent it or anything."

"Well, of course you didn't. I would hardly mistake you for a chemist. But I'll take it just the same."

"I'm afraid it's rather expensive."

"There you go again. Why, if you were my salesgirl, I'd have thrown you out on the street." Betty Ruth looked shocked at her own words and leaned forward, whispering, "That's not what happened to you, is it? You didn't do so badly they threw you out?"

Lilly laughed straight out loud, a sound that, unlike her name, had never been likened to music. "No. I sell door to door."

"And you have all this? Why, you haven't sold a thing."

"That's not true." The defensiveness in her voice prompted both Mazy and Betty Ruth to raise a brow. "I sold a jar of bath salts this morning. Besides, I've only been at it for three days." Four and a half days actually, but the first day consisted of training, and today was only half over. And she hadn't actually sold that jar of bath salts—she'd given it away, but still it was one item gone from her case.

"Well, I will buy all of it." Betty Ruth bounced her finger off several jars and bottles in the case. "Yes, one of everything you have."

"Really, you can't, Mrs.—"

"My name is Betty Ruth Burnside, wife of the late Mr. Davis Burnside, who can well afford to buy whatever she pleases."

"But you don't know—"

"Shall I call your supervisors at—what was the name of the company?"

"Dalliance." The name itself sounded cheap.

"My, what a provocative name. *Dalliance.*" Betty Ruth offered a comical, exaggerated shudder. "Sounds just like an adventure, doesn't it? Like an absolute adventure. Now, please add up my purchases and tell me what I owe you. In the meantime..." She perused the contents of the case and finally settled on the jar of Rose of Sharon hand crème.

Lilly took it from her to untwist the lid and handed it back. Betty Ruth sniffed its contents and smiled.

"Just a dab." Lilly opened her sales-ticket book. "It's quite thick."

The scent of roses filled the small distance between the two women. Betty Ruth extended her hand to Mazy, who seemed unimpressed. The sound of her bell-encrusted collar as she trotted out of the room accompanied the soft scratching of Lilly's pencil on the pad of sales tickets. Carefully, Lilly listed each product in the case, consulted her price list, and wrote the figures in the right-hand column. She clicked her tongue quietly as she added the numbers—three times—before hesitatingly writing the total at the bottom.

"Well? What do I owe?"

"Really, it's too much."

"I will be the judge of that." Betty Ruth snatched the entire ticket book from Lilly's lap, holding it first close to, then far away from her face, focusing.

"It's twenty-seven dollars and fifty cents," Lilly said finally.

"What a bargain, what a bargain." Betty Ruth handed the ticket book back. "Will you be able to make change for thirty dollars?"

Lilly shook her head. "I haven't got any money with me."

"Then we shall have to consider it a gratuity. Do you receive a commission on the sale?"

"Yes. Ten percent."

Betty Ruth clucked her tongue. "Robbery, after coming out in this heat and working so hard. Now, wait right here." Just like that, Betty Ruth was gone.

Carefully, with shaking hands, Lilly released each jar and bottle from its elastic belt, setting them on the small tabletop. She needed to move the case to the floor to make room for them all, and the frosted-pink glass that looked so elegant in the other neighborhoods looked unimpressive in this room.

She was placing the final bottle on the table when another explosion erupted from the backyard, leaving in its wake a tinkling of broken glass as the bottle slipped from Lilly's hand. The aroma of Garden Delights invaded the room.

"Oh no, no!" But it was too late. She had nothing with which to mop up the spilled toilet water, and her first attempt to stem its flow resulted in a gash in her hand, adding her spilled blood to the mess.

She looked around, panicked, and in desperation grabbed the crocheted doily covering the arm of the sofa. The mess on the table was a hopeless loss, so she wrapped the doily around her hand, hoping to stem the flow before adding to the already spreading stain on the carpet. Not to mention her new cute shoes.

Somewhere, off in another room, Betty Ruth's lilting voice called for Eugenie to identify the location of the family's household cash box, followed by Eugenie's less-than-engaging reply that Betty Ruth wasn't to make any kind of purchase without getting permission.

Without another thought, Lilly grabbed the tan leather case, not bothering to close and latch the compartments, and dragged it clumsily through the foyer and out the front door.

Somehow, it seemed a fair trade.

4

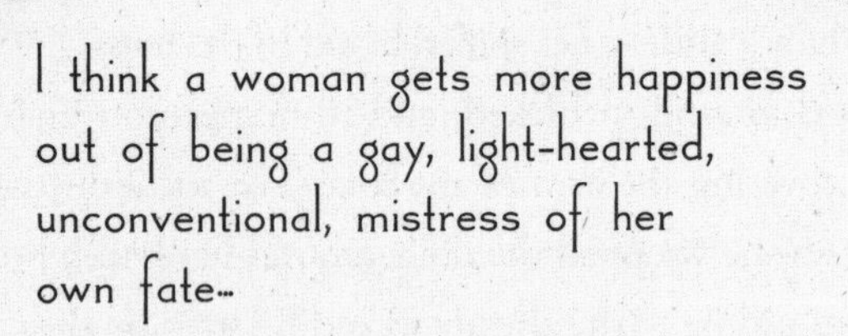

I think a woman gets more happiness out of being a gay, light-hearted, unconventional, mistress of her own fate...

—Zelda Fitzgerald

Mrs. Myrtle's Hotel for Women had one telephone in the front hallway, and it was ringing again. Lilly sat next to her open window, desperate for the breeze coming through, wearing only a satin slip and turquoise blue kimono-style robe. The robe had just been added because she knew the phone call would be for her. Sure enough, Mrs. Myrtle's voice droned from the other side of the door.

"Phone for you, Miss Margolis. It's that man again."

"Coming." She didn't bother to slip her feet into the kimono's matching mules before opening the door.

"Put some clothes on," Mrs. Myrtle hissed, satisfyingly shocked.

"The man's on the phone." Lilly drifted right past the diminutive landlady. "It's not like he can see me."

Lilly shared the house with five other boarders, and three of them—middle-aged women whose names she'd never bothered to learn—sat at the dining room table playing their endless game of canasta. They, too, seemed shocked at Lilly's appearance. Not disapproving, exactly, just surprised. It tweaked her nerves nonetheless. If she'd wanted to face huffs and scowls every day, she could have stayed home with Mama. Pretending to ignore them, Lilly shrugged one shoulder, opening the silk kimono robe a little wider, before picking up the phone.

"Hello?"

"Miss Margolis?"

"Yes. Who is this?" As if she hadn't had this conversation every day—sometimes twice a day—for the past several days.

"This really cannot go any further."

"Ah, good morning, Mr. Eggleston." She slouched, just like she'd seen the girls do in the magazines, licked her lips, and dropped her voice an octave. "How are you this morning?"

"Miss Margolis, when you signed on with Dalliance Cosmetics, I made it very clear to you that salesgirls were to check in every three days for inventory replenishment and to turn in sales receipts."

She aimed for something between innocent and stupid. "Every three days? Why, I could have sworn—"

"Now, we do appreciate that you were able to sell the entirety of your stock—"

"I—what?"

"Mr. Burnside's check arrived in the mail today, totaling the exact amount of your inventory minus…let me see…"

"A dollar thirty." She clutched at her kimono, drawing it closed, as if Betty Ruth Burnside could see her.

"Yes, exactly. Now, this is most unusual for Dalliance Cosmetics to receive payment directly from the customer. And I'm certain you have a fascinating tale as to how this happened."

"Well, it started—"

"Which you can tell me when you come in to replenish your supply. Not to mention collect your commission." His voice turned to something like syrup. "You *do* want to collect your commission, don't you, Miss Margolis?"

"I—I suppose so."

"Minus the dollar thirty, of course."

"Of course."

"Unless you happen to have a receipt for that. But it wouldn't be the first time one of the girls took a little nip from the basket. Is that what happened? Did you take a little nip?"

"No sir." Lilly draped herself in the wooden chair next to the telephone table, exhausted by the battle between relief and guilt. Not about her little nip—she wouldn't take that back for anything—but the trouble she caused for that sweet Mrs. Burnside.

"...later this afternoon?"

"I don't know, Mr. Eggleston. I've got quite a few things on my plate."

"Well, I suggest you do some rearranging, Miss Margolis. We may be square as far as the products are concerned, but there is still the matter of the case."

"Oh, the case."

"Fine leather, velvet lined." His words held the quality of a man in love. She could picture him—all five feet of him with his slick black hair, thin mustache, and blue-striped suit—running his thin fingers along the leather and velvet, positively cooing. "The value of this case far exceeds what is due to you in your sales commission. I assume you wish to continue your employment with Dalliance Cosmetics?"

Lilly glanced over her shoulder to see Mrs. Myrtle leaning against the wall, arms crossed. Her telephone, her business.

"Yes sir, Mr. Eggleston. Of course I do."

"Then I can look forward to seeing you within the hour?"

"More or less."

"Then let's make it less. I'm a busy man." And the line went dead.

Lilly set the earpiece back in its cradle and took a deep breath. "That was my boss at the cosmetics company." She tightened her sash. "I need to get to the office right away on some urgent business."

"Is it the kind of urgent business that's going to give you rent money?" Mrs. Myrtle asked. "Because you're three days late, you know."

"I know, and I'm sorry. There was a little mix-up with my commission, see, but I've no doubt I'll be square with you this afternoon." She reached for the woman's arm and offered a quick, friendly squeeze. "Perhaps I could ask Mr. Eggleston to throw in a little something to make up for the confusion he's caused. What would you like? A nice bath powder, perhaps? Or a scented soap?"

Mrs. Myrtle had a face that, in her youth, was probably quite plump and pretty, but in her old age had the appearance of cake batter run over the edge of the pan. Her nod to vanity consisted only of the flakes of white powder trapped in its folds.

"No, thank you." She touched the side of her head where thinning once-auburn hair was drawn back into a sensible bun. "I don't indulge in such fripperies. Cash will do. And, really, I must insist on not only last week's amount but, as we're already well into this week, the next in advance. Because I simply cannot work with this sort of irregularity."

"Of course not." Behind her warmest smile, Lilly frantically calculated. Last week, this week, next week—six dollars. Not a chance. "It's the least I can do." She made a slow and deliberate exit, just like Eleanor Boardman in *Souls for Sale.* Once back in her room, she closed the door behind her and leaned against it, exhaling the breath she held all the way up the stairs.

"Within the hour."

She opened the armoire and surveyed the row of dresses, finally deciding on a pretty green cap-sleeved dress—slim and straight. She hung it in front of the open window, letting the breeze air it out a bit while she filled the wash basin in her room with cold water from the pitcher placed outside her bedroom door every morning.

Rather than dry her hands on the towel hanging from the washstand, she ran her wet fingers through her hair to tame the frizz. Once damp, the bobbed hair took on perfect waves, and she wished she could just go around wet headed all day.

Luckily she bought a new hat just two weeks ago that would go perfectly with the green dress. *Bought* might be a generous term. She'd simply had the four-dollar cost added to her account. And thank goodness she had the foresight to do so; she needed to look her best today.

Both the kimono robe and the slip fell to the ground as she stepped into a clean pair of cotton knickers and a camisole. Her figure hadn't taken on a single inch since she was fifteen years old. If anything, she was slimmer, a fact that she was thankful for every time she tried on a new dress. No girdle or lacer for her. A man once told her she had the body of a gazelle, and she'd spent the night running from his clutches to prove him right.

She took her best stockings—the ones with the delicate vines snaking up the calves—and pulled them on, rolling them down to the knee, then sat on the side of her bed while she fastened the buckles on her tan patent-leather high-heeled shoes.

Now, to attend to all things above the waist.

She lit a candle and held her kohl stick in the flame before leaning close to the mirror and lining each eye. Next a quick dust of powder and lipstick. She puckered and pouted, stepped back, and angled her face, staring deep into her own brown eyes.

"Good afternoon, Mr. Eggleston. Might I talk to you about an advance on my commission?"

She held the pose as long as she could, deeply impressed with the height of her cheekbones, before trying something else. Eyes wide, she turned her mouth into a perfect little pucker and blinked furiously, willing herself to innocence.

"My goodness, Mr. Eggleston. I must have misunderstood. Are you sure there's nothing I can do to convince you to advance my next commission?"

Sighing, she resolved to rob a bank if neither tactic worked. But they would. They always did. She had a closet full of clothes and a box full of baubles to prove it. She wasn't vain, and she wasn't proud, but she was smart. She moved to take the green dress off its hanger.

"Lilly!"

The voice came from the sidewalk below, and without giving a thought to her present state, Lilly propped her elbows on the open windowsill and leaned out to see her latest best friend standing on the sidewalk, eyes shielded against the afternoon sun.

"Dina!" She knew in that instant something far more entertaining than an afternoon visit with Mr. Eggleston was about to be proposed. "Come on up!"

"Nah, those Mrs. Grumbies give me the heebie-jeebies. I'll wait down here."

"What for?"

"You'll see."

The way Dina Charlaine said "you'll see" always made Lilly feel like she was headed somewhere between adventure and arrest. Right now, anything seemed like a welcome diversion.

Lilly lifted her arms through the green dress and tugged it down over her shoulders, shimmying until the skirt fell just to her knee. It had a pretty keyhole at the neckline joined by a length of green ribbon, which she tied as she clambered down the stairs. Her new hat was gripped under her chin so she could barely mutter "good-bye" to the ladies playing cards before she ran out the front door.

"Well, don't you look the bee's knees," Dina said. By now she had a cigarette clamped in the corner of her mouth, and it bobbed as she moved her head up and down to take Lilly in.

"Thanks." To get a compliment from Dina was quite the achievement, as the girl always looked like she just stepped out of a fashion page herself. Today she wore effortless white, with a long chain of green beads. Her hair was sleek and short and raven black and perfect, but she carried herself as if all of this was nothing less than necessary.

"Did you already get word?" Dina asked.

"Word about what?"

"Fabulous goings-on tonight. Somebody's son just made partner in somebody's firm, and somebody's father wants to go all out with champagne and roast duck and caviar and whatever other goodies he can pull out to impress all the other somebodies."

The two fell in easy step with each other, hips thrust slightly forward, backs almost uncomfortably bent.

"And which of these somebodies do you know?"

Dina's thin red lips slashed into a smile. "I know the somebody who's catering the food, and I know the address he's bringing it to. Plus, I know there isn't a somebody around who doesn't want to have a couple of extra pretty girls at his party."

"Do you actually have an invite?"

Dina stopped in the middle of the sidewalk to strike a dramatic pose—one arm akimbo, the other held high allowing the smoke from her cigarette to ribbon up and away. "Darling, we *are* the invite. Get yourself all dolled up and I'll be by to get you around nine."

"Aw, you know Mrs. Myrtle has a thing for late nights. I gotta be in by nine thirty or she locks me out."

"So sneak down the back stairs, then slip in for breakfast. Don't tell me you never snuck out of a house before."

Lilly laughed. "Yeah, but that's when I was a kid. I'm twenty years old now. Thought my sneaking days were behind me."

"You just got to get yourself a real place to live." By now Dina's cigarette was down to her fingertips; she dropped the butt to the sidewalk and ground it in with her shoe.

"I can barely pull in the dough for this place."

"All the more reason to go tonight. Find yourself a rich daddy. Let's go shopping for something irresistible to hook him with."

"I got something I have to take care of first. With my job. You can come with me if you want."

Dina's nose wrinkled the way it always did when the subject of employment came up. "Nah, I have something new and blue. I'm just going to pick up some stockings at Woolworth's, then head home for a beauty nap."

"All right." She'd only known Dina for a month since arriving in Pensacola, but already she'd grown used to the girl's shifting moods. Often her attention didn't last the span of a cigarette. "So I'll see you tonight?"

"You're coming?"

"I'll work something out. But don't pick me up at the house. Get me at the corner."

"Attagirl!" Dina delivered a playful punch to Lilly's arm before the two exchanged a friendly kiss on the other's cheek. Well, not a *real* kiss, as that would leave a lipstick mark, but a nice smack in the air just above the surface.

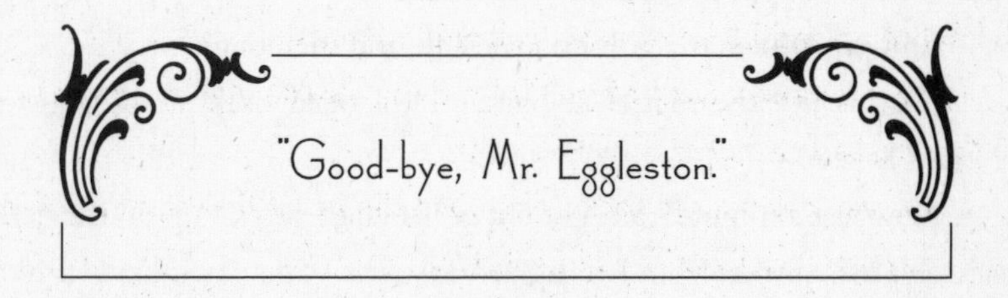

One hour later, Lilly stooped to repeat the gesture, landing a quick kiss just above the smooth, shiny face of Mr. Jules Eggleston.

"Ah, the lovely Miss Margolis. Come. Sit."

Lilly obeyed, folding herself on one of two high-backed wooden chairs. She gave her dress a discreet little hitch and crossed her legs, twisting her calf to better display the pattern on her stocking.

Mr. Eggleston was clearly considering sitting in the matching chair beside her, until she dropped her hat and pocketbook on it. His eyes even flickered quickly to the worn leather sofa against the back wall, but in the end he cleared his throat, ran his small hands over his hair, and made his way to the creaking seat behind his desk.

"Not quite so fancy back here, is it?" She turned her head and twisted her body, presumably to take in the dull colorlessness of a storefronts back office.

"Well, very few of our customers have the opportunity to see the business end of beauty." He made a show of opening the large leather check ledger. "Now, I believe you have a healthy commission coming to you?"

"Yes." Lilly moved her foot in a small, obviously mesmerizing circle. "About that. I was wondering if there was any way I could get a bit of an advance on my salary."

Suddenly, her leg lost its appeal. "Now, Miss Margolis, you know when you signed on with Dalliance Cosmetics that you would be working strictly on commission. None of our girls draw a salary until they've been with the company for at least three months."

"And just how many girls ever stick around that long?"

"That is not the matter at hand." He looked back at the register. "Now, I believe—"

"Now just a minute." She got out of her chair and sat up on the desk, her thigh mere inches from Mr. Eggleston's pinky ring. "I pulled in a great sale from that Mrs. Burnside, didn't I? If I'm going to make more deals like that, I got to dress the part. I figure you advance me ten, fifteen dollars—"

"Ten or fifteen dollars!"

"—and I can get myself a couple of nice things to wear door to door. Right now I'm wearing the best that I got, and I can't let them society ladies see me in the same old thing day after day trudging up and down their street. Why, they'll call the cops and have me hauled out."

"Miss—"

"You don't have to give me the cash right out, you know. You could just write me a letter of credit. I can take it to Hattie's or someplace. They could send the sales slip right to you so you know that I'm not blowing your dough on anything frivolous like silk stockings or negligees." She leaned in a little closer as she said the word *negligee,* causing Mr. Eggleston to drop his pen.

"I'm sure you have very nice things already."

His hand inched toward the pen, which had rolled right up next to Lilly's thigh. He couldn't touch one without touching the other, so she snatched up the writing instrument and dangled it right in front of his nose.

"Don't be so sure of anything." Lilly dropped the pen on the blotter and hopped off the desk, planting her palms on either side of the checkbook ledger and bringing her face within inches of his. "I'm just the poor kid down from Miresburgh, looking for a new life in a warm place. I sell a whole case of your lousy stuff, and that won't even get me enough to pay my rent in some lousy boardinghouse. How do you think that makes me feel, Mr. Eggleston? Tramping up and down the streets only to end up living on them? Because that's what's going to happen, you know. My landlady wants six bucks tomorrow, and I don't have a chance earning it if I have to walk around town in this, this—*rag!*"

She turned from him and buried her face carefully in her hands, just like she'd seen those weeping, desperate women do in the movies. Sure enough, a creak came from his chair and she felt his little hand gently touching her bare arm.

"Now, my dear, I think you look quite pretty."

"Well, of course I do today, but what about tomorrow?"

"I'm sorry, but it simply wouldn't be possible for me to open a line of credit at Hattie's."

"You're probably right." Lilly made a show of swallowing unshed tears. "Cash is probably best. That way I can shop around—"

"Nor can I extend you cash outright." He walked away and settled himself back behind the desk. "However, based on your exemplary sales record, I am prepared to raise your commission from ten to twelve percent. That's quite unheard of for someone who has been with Dalliance for such a short time. Will that do?"

She thought carefully before answering. Slowly, she turned to face him, imagining herself in black and white, framed in a dark cinematic circle, and batted her eyes. "Four dollars, Mr. Eggleston. That's all I ask. A four-dollar advance."

His brow furrowed as he scratched the pen across the check, and the ripping sound of the perforated paper bounced off the wall.

By the time Lilly took the paper from his hand, her chin was quivering, and she kept her eyes wide open to hold back the tears. She didn't want to look.

Three dollars.

"As you can see," Mr. Eggleston said, noting the amount in the ledger's margin, "I did not deduct the dollar thirty. I hope that will be somewhat helpful."

"Thank you, sir." She swallowed her disappointment along with her pride, folded the little slip of paper, and then dropped it in her pocketbook.

"Now"—he got up from his desk and crossed over to the office door—"if you'll meet me in the stockroom, we'll arrange your new inventory and you can work that Margolis magic again."

"Yes sir." She pulled out her powder compact and made a great show of checking her face. "I'll be right in there."

"Very well."

The moment she was left alone, Lilly fished the check out of her pocketbook, unfolded it, and laid it flat on the table. She took the cap off Mr. Eggleston's pen and drew a line through her name. Above it, copying his handwriting to her best ability, she wrote "Mrs. Beatrice Myrtle" and brought the paper to her lips to blow the ink dry.

"Miss Margolis?" he called from the stockroom.

As she left the office and stepped into the store with pink-and-purple laced windows, she spied a glimpse of him through the open door. The lovely leather case gaped, already half-filled with a new supply of jars and bottles and shiny silver foil boxes. Just looking at it brought the familiar ache back to her shoulder.

She mouthed the words *good-bye, Mr. Eggleston* but made no sound, not even as she carefully opened the door and stepped into the street.

5

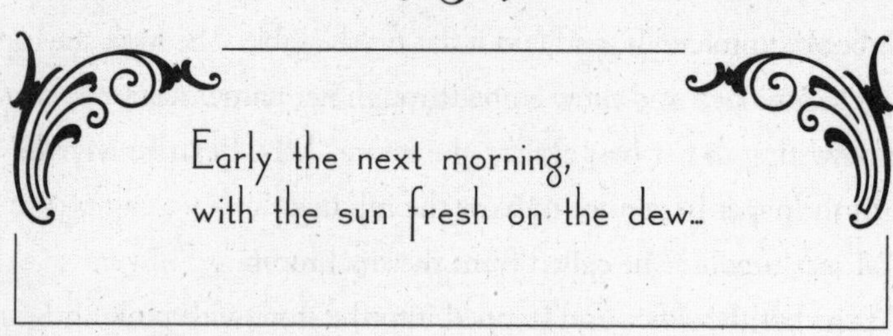

Cullen sipped his coffee, scowled, and then reached for the sugar.

"No more of that," Betty Ruth said. "It'll make you run crazy."

He wanted to say that *she,* in fact, made him crazy, but he'd been raised better. Still, without apology he closed the tiny silver clamp around a sugar cube and dropped it into the hot black coffee.

"Plum crazy." She sat at the opposite end of the long dining room table, well out of reach of the coffee service, but hers was already a perfect caramel-colored mixture of coffee and cream, three sugars, lukewarm. Cullen had mixed it just moments ago, delivering it to her along with a brief "Good morning, Mother" kiss to her temple.

He ignored her now. This early in the day, it was hard to know what would dissolve after a bit of harmless banter and what would throw her into a fit. After a second sip, he wished he'd dropped in two lumps of sugar. He picked up the newspaper folded to perfection beside his plate, but his mother interrupted him before he could take in the first headline.

"You need to turn to the society page. See if they have anything about the Owens boy."

"I don't need to check the society page, Mother. I know very well they had a blowout party for him last night."

"Were you there? Was it wonderful?"

"No, Mama. I was here last night with you, remember? You beat me at canasta."

"But I heard the music." She launched into a high warbling rendition of some jazz tune, including a rhythmic snapping of her fingers.

"Everybody in the neighborhood heard the music last night, Mother. Didn't stop until after three this morning."

"Oh, you young people, with your fun and your dancing. What fun, what joy. Tell me, was it wonderful?"

"I'm sure it was."

"What was that, darling? I didn't hear you. Speak up."

He cleared his throat. "I said I'm sure it was wonderful."

"Well, later you can tell me all about it. All about it. Don't leave out a single detail."

In order to prepare, Cullen opened the paper to page eight, where the great doings of Pensacola's most influential people had their exploits reported. There it was, in the bottom left-hand corner, a photograph of his neighbor Bill Owens shaking hands with the mayor, grinning as if becoming a partner in his own father's law firm was some big trick.

The Journal had other pictures too. One shot of the Owenses' massive backyard, complete with a swimming pool and fountain, dotted with people in various stages of drinking and dancing. Then another of the senior Mr. Owens, whose wire-rimmed glasses nearly disappeared in the folds of his face. His smile was broad and proud as he stood next to his son, one hand firmly on the younger man's shoulder, the other holding a cigar smoked down to a stub, as if a measure of the celebration.

He and Cullen's father, Davis Burnside, had been close friends; the invitation to share in the festivities sat on Cullen's desk for two weeks before he finally sent his regrets.

And then one more photograph at the bottom right-hand corner. A scene that seemingly had little to do with one man's advance in a law firm. Four women outlined against the starkness of the midnight sky. They were dressed in white, what little of them *was* dressed. Each wore light frocks anchored to slim white shoulders by thin straps. Two of them wore dresses so full of fringe not even the stillness of the camera could disguise the movement.

Slender legs created a repeating pattern captured midkick in some dance. Their lips were dark against pale faces, and three of them had their heads thrown back in what must have been laughter. But the fourth, the one second from the left, stared out, her eyes meeting the camera with a surprised expression, her lips puckered into a perfect O.

The caption read: "Four lovely ladies add to the merriment of the moment." No names, of course. One had to be somebody to get one's name printed on page eight of *The Journal.* But a pretty picture nonetheless.

He stared for a while, enjoying the image of the lovely ladies from the top of their bobbed hair to the bottom of their high-heeled feet; then he sighed and turned the page to see if there were any other such lovely surprises in the paper.

He was lost in the story of the high school's new natatorium when he heard the scream. He looked over the top of the paper to see his mother's placid face at the other end of the table spooning sweetened grapefruit into her otherwise blissfully still mouth.

"Did you hear that?" Cullen asked, risking confrontation.

"Hear what, dear?"

The scream pierced the peace again.

"Sounds like Eugenie," Mother said, her voice calm and dreamy as she scraped the fruit's rind. "Must have seen a mouse in the kitchen."

But the screams were not coming from the kitchen. They were fainter than that, coming from outside. From the backyard. Soon they were not merely screams at all but a shrill, focused command.

"Mr. Cullen! Mr. Cullen!" Then Eugenie's usually stoic gray face poked through the dining room door. "Come quick! There's a dead body in the yard!"

In an instant Cullen was up on his feet. Mindless of the napkin tucked beneath his chin, he ran from the table with only the briefest glance over his shoulder to see that his mother had reached across the table for the newspaper.

Just as well, for there was no telling how she would react to whatever scene awaited him. In fact, he wasn't quite sure how to prepare himself. He could hear his own blood pounding in his ears, and the last sip of sweet coffee turned to soil on his tongue.

His feet slowed behind the steps of the swift-moving maid, as if he were running through rain-induced mud rather than newly cleaned carpet. When they came to the sunroom, he flinched from the wall of light that flashed in front of him and ran straight into the middle-aged woman who had been leading him.

"See there." Eugenia pointed through the window.

Reluctantly, Cullen moved closer, peering through one of the glass panes. "I can't—"

"At the far wall. By the garden."

His eyes tracked across the pink stone patio, over the emerald lawn, and stopped when he came to the canvas-covered pitching machine. "I still don't see anything."

"Keep on."

He placed the tip of one finger against the window and strolled along the wall, tracing the intermittent glass and frame until he came to the door that opened to the patio. He turned the handle, walked across the pink flagstone, craned his neck, and saw it—saw *her*.

That's when he realized he'd been holding his breath since he fled the breakfast table. With every step he'd carried familiar, terrible images. Men torn to pieces, covered in mud, or, later, lying still under bloodstained sheets. But none of that prepared him for what waited for him in the garden.

"Who is she?" he asked, assuming Eugenie had followed him.

"Didn't get close enough to tell," the woman answered from the threshold of the open door.

Cullen turned around. "Do not allow Mrs. Burnside to come out here. Do you understand?"

"Should I call the police?"

"Not yet. Just go back inside and see if you can get Mother talking. Distract her."

Eugenie looked like she'd rather take her chances with the body, but Cullen's glare reinforced his request.

Alone again, he made his way slowly but purposefully across the yard, never taking his eyes off the body in the garden. The whiteness of it—of her—brought a fear-fueled tightness to his throat that war-torn khaki and red never could.

Odd how just two steps away, she didn't seem to be any bigger than she had been when he was on the other side of the yard. He walked a semicircle around her and crouched close to her head, to where she lay, half of her face buried in the grass, the other hidden behind short matted blond hair.

Lord, let her be—

And then he saw it. Faint but certain, her lips moving. Breathing.

"Miss?" He reached out, intending to move the hair away from her face, but stopped short. His eyes filled with the image of his own hand, scarred and discolored, his fingers melted and molded into some new thing against the backdrop of this woman's milky white bare shoulder.

Coolness emanated from her skin. The desire to touch her raged as fierce as any he'd ever known, but he dared not. He hadn't touched a woman since he sailed for France, with only a select few before that. And never a bare shoulder.

His eyes traveled the length of her, trying to keep the same dispassionate air he had moments ago when he studied the photograph of the four lovely ladies. In fact, she might well be one of those ladies, only now the thin white dress was as motionless as the woman who wore it. No curve of her body could hide beneath its thin fabric. For the sake of his soul, he tore his eyes away from that place where this skirt rose higher than any he'd ever seen before.

To his relief she muttered something. No real words, just a *"mmphrmph"* noise, but enough to reassure him that she was, indeed, alive, allowing him to tear his attention away from thoughts no Christian man should have in such a moment.

"Miss? Miss, are you all right?"

With what appeared to be great effort, she struggled to lift her head and repeated her earlier noise, only this time with a much more interrogative air.

"Miss? Do you know where you are? Do you know how you got here?"

If she heard or saw him at all, she gave no indication. Instead she dropped her face back into the grass and, bending her thin, pale arms, began a new endeavor to lift her entire torso. This, too, failed, prompting a muffled wailing sound from the woman whose face was now completely planted in the grass.

At this point, to leave the lady unassisted was something his mother would deem ungentleman-like. Bracing his mind against what he might see on the other side, he tried to imagine her as something more like a wounded soldier than a half-naked woman facedown on his lawn.

Carefully, he slid his left arm under her waist, his other just above her knees. He cringed at the thought of his burned, scarred flesh against the cool smoothness of hers, imagining how much more would she if consciousness were to revive her at that moment. Then after one swift, sure motion, he turned her onto her back. The repositioning brought her skirt even higher and revealed the full white expanse of her leg.

He took a deep breath before pinching the impossibly thin fabric between the thumb and functioning fingers of his hand and pulling the skirt down to what he hoped would be a more respectable length. He couldn't be sure because he averted his eyes, turning his head to look at her face.

"Well…"

It was her. The girl from the picture, second from the left. Only now there was no sweet, surprised puckering to her lips. No happy, healthy glow to her skin. Instead her mouth hung open and slack. Her breath carried a sour, unfamiliar smell. A large abrasion bisected her forehead, and pale lavender bruising surrounded one eye. All of this, and like an angel she was.

Not knowing exactly what to do, and knowing he'd never again have a chance to touch such beauty, he traced one tentative finger along the bridge of her nose, snatching it away the moment her long pale lashes began to flutter against her grass-stained cheeks.

"Deedle?" she said, or rather muttered. She smacked her lips; thick, white, pastelike spittle gathered at the corners of her mouth. "Deedlebug? 'S that you?" She swiped her mouth with the back of her hand.

He watched, breathless, knowing her eyes were seconds away from opening up to him and this would be the last time he'd ever be this close to such beauty—however flawed.

"Dina?" Her voice was clear now and insistent. Her hand shot straight up and out and would have grazed his nose had he not backed away. He was just regaining his balance when his mother's shrill voice pierced the quiet moment.

"Is that her? Cullen, darling? Is that the girl?"

The girl's face crunched into a grimace at the sound, but still her eyes remained closed.

Cullen turned around and held a finger to his lips, hoping to stem the tide of his mother's inevitable chatter, but it was no use.

"Eugenie told me all about her. All about her, that she was dead. But

I told Eugenie that was nonsense. Utter nonsense. Young women don't die in backyards. Simply doesn't happen. I—oh my land!" She came to a stop right at Cullen's elbow and steadied herself on his shoulder as she bent to look closer. "Cullen, darling, do you know who that is?"

"She's the woman in the paper," he said, his voice nearly lost in the whisper.

"Doesn't surprise me. She's a marvelous businesswoman. Simply marvelous." By now Mother was crouched by Cullen's side, and she reached out to take the woman's hand. "Lilly?"

Cullen looked at his mother. "You know her?"

"I knew she'd come back. We didn't have a chance to finish our talk." She patted the woman's hand. "Lilly, darling? It's me, Betty Ruth Burnside."

At that, the woman's eyes gave one final struggle and opened, looking straight at his mother.

"I'm so sorry—" And then she seemed to notice Cullen's presence, because she stretched her neck to look up and back at him.

How he hated this moment, those seconds when somebody saw him for the first time. Instinctively he ducked, turning his head to try to conceal the worst of the scarring. After all, the entire left side of his face and all of it from the nose up was nearly normal. It was the right side, the cheek, the jaw, his neck, that was nothing more than a mass of hardened blisters.

But he wasn't quick enough. She saw him—he knew this by the look in her eyes. Like everybody he met, she could not contain her reaction: her eyes grew wide with shock. But unlike most others, this Lilly made no attempt to hide it. Slowly she focused her eyes on his mother, then back to him.

"I'm so sorry—" she repeated again before she heaved and turned her head to throw up in the grass at his feet.

6

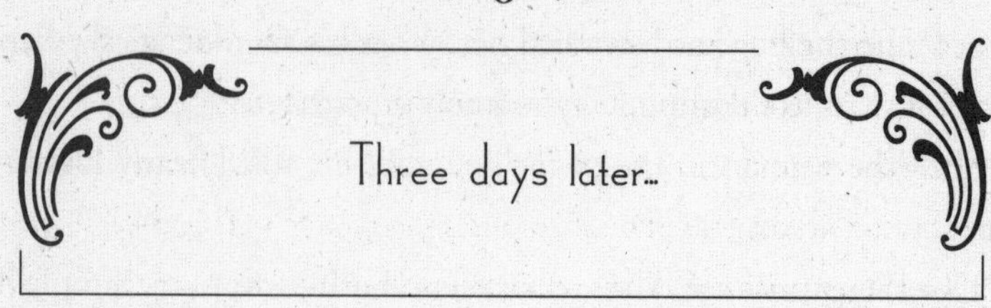

Three days later...

Lilly woke up to the sound of a snapping window shade. She yawned and stretched, arching her back and moving her legs to find the coolness of the sheets. The soft cotton grated against her wounded knees, but a cautious rotating of her ankle produced no pain. What a pleasant surprise to wake up to—almost as pleasant as the bright morning light streaming through the window, and much more pleasant than the woman who brought it.

"Good morning, Eugenie." Lilly smiled hard, using her elbows to push herself into a sitting position.

"Good morning, Miss Lilly." Even at this hour, Eugenie's voice carried the weariness of a day's labor, having brought not only the sunshine but also the breakfast tray sitting on the small lace-covered table by the window.

"Pardon me," Lilly said, smoothing the sheets around her, "do you think you could bring the tray over here? The coffee smells wonderful."

"You don't think you could manage the four steps over here to get it?"

"Oh no. The doctor said for me to stay off my feet for a few days."

"A few could be two."

"Or"—Lilly's smile stiffened—"it could be three."

Lilly had no idea who should have the upper hand at this point—the penniless guest or the maid. Eugenie, it seemed, had no such confusion. She picked up the tray and, counting under her breath, walked the three—not four—steps to the side of the bed and dropped it. The coffee cup rattled in its saucer, and the eggs, a little runnier than Lilly would have preferred, sloshed across the plate. Orange marmalade still jiggled in its dish long after Eugenie slammed the door behind her.

"Thank you!" Lilly called out, undaunted.

She was about to take her first bite of toast when she realized her magazine—*Saturday Evening Post,* no less—was over on the same table where Eugenie first set the tray. Now it was a matter of waiting until Eugenie came back, unless...

"Well, what do you know?" Her first careful step out of the bed produced absolutely no pain in her ankle.

She walked all the way to the table and returned to the bed, empty-handed, testing to see if maybe she'd just missed it. Then back to the table. Nothing, not even a twinge. She danced a slow Charleston, just to be sure. The raw, tight skin across her knees protested at the slightest bend of her legs, but her ankle felt fine. Gritting her teeth, she continued a little faster, waiting for her body to react to the joy of dancing again.

She crossed over to the breakfast tray, took a slice of crisp bacon off the plate, and clamped it in the corner of her mouth like a cigar. It tasted salty and perfect, too delicious to be a prop, so she chewed it down bit by bit, all the while keeping her feet in perfect rhythm.

She was midstep with a sloshing cup of coffee when Betty Ruth walked in.

"Oh, what a sight! What a beautiful sight is youth in bloom!" She immediately fell in step, pausing at the bed just long enough to pick up the pitcher of cream as her partner.

Lilly couldn't help but laugh and kick her leg a little higher to match Betty Ruth's enthusiasm. They might have danced all morning if not for the unannounced presence of Eugenie in the doorway where she stood, thick arms folded. The sight of her brought Lilly to a sudden, shocked stop, but Betty Ruth danced right up to her, jeweled finger twirling in the air.

"Come on, Eugenie. It'll make you feel young again."

"I'm as young as I need to be, Mrs. B, and you're nowhere near as young as you think you are. Now, are you going to stop that dancin', or do I need to call Dr. Dewers?"

Betty Ruth pouted, giving the impression of a graying toddler. Her petulance extended to her shoes.

Eugenie gave a long, slow look to Lilly, her pale eyes taking in every inch, lingering at her bare, still feet. "And looks to me like you're feelin' a world better."

"Oh yes." Lilly lifted her foot off the ground, giving it a slow circling twirl. "It's like some kind of miracle."

"Let me see."

Lilly moved to the wing-backed chair next to the window. Its upholstery depicted forest scenes and spotted deer, quite simply the most beautiful chair Lilly had ever seen. She sat down, set the coffee cup on the lace-covered table, and lifted her foot for Eugenie, who knelt on the floor. The woman's hands were dry and chapped, and they wrapped around Lilly's ankle like bands of straw.

"Swelling's gone down." She moved her hand down until it surrounded Lilly's foot, the touch too confident to tickle. "That hurt?"

"No."

"How about your knees?" She lifted the gown and touched a finger to the sores.

Lilly winced. "That stings." She looked down at the angry, bright spots right on top of the bone. Both had the shine of being something between scab and skin. "But not as much."

"Won't be doing much praying for a while, that's for sure." Eugenie gently poked at the wound.

"Nonsense," Betty Ruth said. She still danced, but slower now, with smaller steps. "A body doesn't have to be on her knees to pray. She can pray where she pleases. Wherever she pleases."

Eugenie gave Lilly a look that seemed to question whether Lilly ever prayed at all.

"And if the ankle has healed, then she must come join us downstairs for breakfast."

"You had your breakfast nearly two hours ago, Mrs. B."

A now-familiar cloud passed across Betty Ruth's face. "Well, I meant luncheon, then. Of course, after you get dressed, you'll have to come take lunch with us. Me and my son, I mean. Cullen. Have you met my son?"

"Yes." Something in Lilly tightened at the memory. His face, the scars. His voice, like the words were being scraped from his throat. And her behavior—so much of it a blur. What had she said? Something awful, that much she remembered. "Yes, I met him the other day. He was quite the hero, helping me like that." His touch, that twisted remnant of an arm balanced against her waist, helping her to stand. "But maybe it might be best not to impose—"

"Impose? Such a lovely young thing as you? Nonsense. Not a bit. Is it, Eugenie?"

"I wouldn't know, Mrs. B. I've never taken lunch with you myself."

"Well, it isn't. So wash up and get dressed in something pretty. One of those pretty dresses you young girls wear. Oh, if I had the figure..."

"Now, Mrs. B., you know you'd catch your death of cold in one of them dresses." Eugenie began to gently herd the older woman out of the room. "You just worry about your own self and leave what's young to the young."

"Oh, I'm not so very old as that." She fell in step with the maid. "Why, my little boy's only—how old is he now?"

"Goin' on thirty years old. He's a full-grown man."

"Thirty? Well, that's just nonsense. Why, just the other day..."

The conversation faded behind the door, leaving Lilly alone, staring at the magazine and chilled coffee sitting on the lace-covered table. This wasn't the first time she'd heard Betty Ruth lapse into forgetfulness. For a while, Lilly thought the woman might have two sons, or more. Sometimes Cullen was the baby only Betty Ruth could hear; sometimes he was the boy due to arrive home from school. Other times he was the star of his high school's baseball team, knocking home runs into the stands every Saturday afternoon. But never, not once, was he the wounded, twisted, whispering man who didn't quite have the strength to help a lady to her feet.

Lilly had asked her once, on that second morning, what had happened.

"To whom?"

"To your son."

"My son?" And she jumped up, panicked. "What's happened to my Cullen? Davis!"

She ran from the room, screaming for the husband Lilly had yet to meet, and it was Cullen who caught her in the hallway. Lilly could see the two of them through the crack of the open door, the diminutive woman slumped against her son's chest, his good arm wrapped around her quivering shoulder.

"Thank God you're all right," she said, sobbing.

"Of course I'm all right, Mother. Why wouldn't I be?"

"She said you were hurt."

"Who said?"

"That woman." Betty Ruth, never leaving her son's embrace, pointed right at Lilly's door. Cullen looked over his mother's head, straight at Lilly, his eyes narrowed in dislike.

"I'm not hurt." He held her at arm's length. "Look at me."

She stepped away, lifted her head, and placed her small hand on his scarred face. "Of course you are. Of course you are. So handsome. Just like your father."

"Do you feel better now?"

"I feel fine, absolutely fine."

"Why don't you go down and see if Eugenie will make you some tea."

"I think I will." She gave his cheek a little pat. "And then you can tell me all about your day."

She'd walked away, humming something sweet and high. Cullen, never taking his eyes off Lilly, reached inside her room, grabbed the white porcelain knob, and pulled the door shut.

Lilly hadn't seen him since.

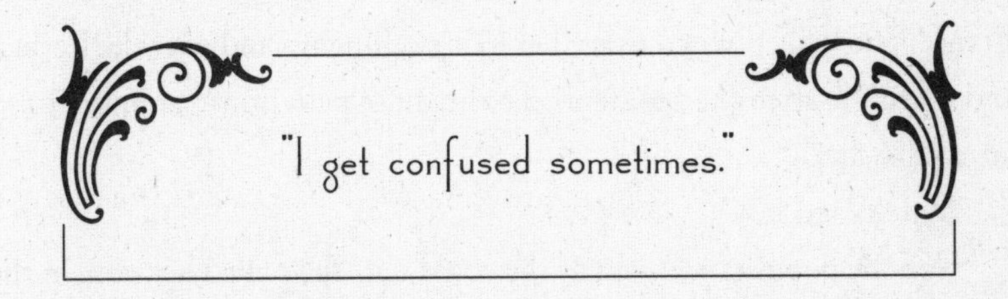

After a quick bath, Lilly stood, wrapped in her blue silk kimono, surveying her dresses. They all hung neatly in an enormous walnut armoire, having magically appeared one day. She'd stayed in bed and watched Eugenie hang up each and every one. What seemed such glamour in Mrs. Myrtle's rented room lost its luxury here. They might represent nearly twice as much money as she'd ever earned in her life, but there was a cheapness sewn into their very seams.

She took one out and held it up to her chin. Too short—her skinned knees would look ridiculous just under its hem. The next, too yellow. The next, too pink, unless they were planning to take lunch out in the garden. Which would be lovely. Her mother would stew herself silly if she saw her brazen, worthless daughter taking lunch in a millionaire's garden. Just the possibility of it brought Lilly's heart to settle on the pink dress after all. The neckline stretched from one thin shoulder to the other. Her skin was flushed pink from the bath, making it hard to tell where the dress ended and her flesh began. She'd skip the stockings, cringing at the idea of stretching even the softest silk across her wounds.

Her hair curled tight, damp from her bath, and she ran her fingers through it, creating waves that fell just to her earlobes. She took a length of pink satin ribbon from one of the tiny drawers on the other side of the armoire and wrapped it around her head, tucking the ends in and securing them with a hairpin. Her face was scrubbed clean, and she chose to leave it that way.

Last she slipped one foot into her favorite shoe, but when she attempted to slip a shoe on the other foot—the sprained one—she met resistance. She looked down to see her foot swelling up and over the leather. And when she attempted to stand, a remnant of pain from her injury cried out, as did she.

"Barefooted it is."

Nobody downstairs, as far as she could tell. She poked her nose in the front parlor and the dining room. She stood at the door of the kitchen but didn't dare go in. Instead she was drawn to a room full of light—a full wall of windows looking out onto the lush velvet green lawn. She glanced down at her raw red knees. How could something that looked so soft and inviting cause so much pain? Then again, such things were meant for a sweet stroll, not a soft landing.

She followed the line of windows to the door that opened out to the flagstone patio and stepped outside. The stones were warm and smooth on her bare feet. She walked to the place where the green grass met the pale pink stone and stepped out, thrilled to feel the soft blades between her toes. She closed her eyes and inhaled the fragrant breeze. Roses—real ones. And a host of other flowers, none of which she could name. They lined the fence surrounding the yard—great bushes and beds of blooms. They drew her like a bee. Maybe she should have worn the yellow dress after all.

She looked up and saw the window to her room. She remembered sitting at that window, watching Betty Ruth on her knees in the garden. Pruning, weeding, digging here, and planting there. Cutting those flowers that would find new homes in vases and bowls throughout the house—even in her own room. There wasn't a weed or a hint of one to come, every plant pruned to its intended glory.

And then, the scar. A great gash right in the middle of what might have been gardenias. The plants were flattened, blooms ripped from their stems. The soil dispersed. Lilly remembered the pain of those tiny grains of soil as Eugenie picked them out of her ruined skin. What a sight she must have looked, facedown in the midst of so much beauty.

"Oh my! Look what an absolute flower you are. Just a bloom of beauty." Betty Ruth stood on the patio. She wore a broad straw hat and green canvas gloves, a basket of tools hanging from her arm.

"You have a lovely garden, Mrs. Burnside. Really, the prettiest I've ever seen."

"God's imagination at work, I always say. Shows He knows how to love women. He gave flowers to women and women to men. We tend to the flowers and—if we're lucky—the men tend to us. My Davis did. Oh, how that man loved me."

"Do you—?" Lilly paused, not knowing exactly how to ask what she wanted to know. "Do you know where he is?"

Betty Ruth gave her a curious, insulted look. "What do you mean 'Do I know where he is?'? He's my husband; I hope I know where he is. He's in heaven, that's where he is."

"Oh," Lilly said, oddly relieved. "I wasn't sure."

"Well, where else would he be?"

"I don't know. Anywhere, I guess."

"Anywhere?"

"I didn't know that he was—that he'd passed away. Sometimes, when you talk about him, it's like he's just stepped out. Like he's going to come back."

Betty Ruth tugged her gloves a little tighter. "I get confused sometimes, I guess. That's what Cullen says. We loved each other so much, Davis and I. It's hard to remember that he's not coming home." She looked up, tears sparkling in her bright cobalt blue eyes. "But he's not. He's in glory. Why in the world would he come back to this old place?"

"I love it here. It's the most beautiful home I've ever known. Not that, you know, it's *my* home—"

"Of course it is." Betty Ruth reached for Lilly's hand and gave it a squeeze. "For as long as you need it to be."

She couldn't help it, couldn't wait another minute. Lilly stooped, wrapping her arms around the little woman's waist, and planted her head on Betty Ruth's shoulder. "Thank you, oh thank you."

"Well, my goodness," Betty Ruth said, and that's when Lilly noticed that her embrace was not returned. She wasn't rebuffed or pushed away, but at no time did she feel Betty Ruth's frail arms wrap around her.

Embarrassed, Lilly pulled away. "I'm sorry."

"You're an odd girl, Lilly Margolis." Betty Ruth made a show of straightening her barely rumpled dress. "A charming, wonderful girl, and I hardly know what to make of you."

"I think you're charming and wonderful too."

"And I think you're both going to fry like eggs if you stay out here much longer."

Lilly recognized his voice, of course, and faced him now for the first time since he'd discovered her in this very spot three days ago. He was taller than she'd remembered, broader shoulders too. His hair the color of cinnamon butter.

"Cullen, darling." Betty Ruth set her gardening basket on the ground and looped her arm through her son's. "Have you had the chance to meet our darling Lilly?"

"*Our* Lilly, is she?" His voice sounded like dry leaves skittering across a tin roof, making it hard to know if there was any hint of teasing warmth behind the statement. The scars at the corner of his lip left his smile incomplete, and his eyes were protected behind smoky gray lenses. "Yes, we have met."

"Not under the best of circumstances, I'm afraid." Whether from instinct or some desire to ingratiate herself, Lilly held out her hand. "Nice to meet you."

There was a moment suspended between them while Lilly's hand remained extended and empty. Cullen lifted his own, and for two full, horrible seconds, both of them looked at it, as if wishing the gesture would disappear. But it was too late.

Lilly braced herself, moving her eyes up to where his hid behind the lenses, and froze her smile. Then she felt it, their hands intertwined. His thumb and first finger seemed completely unharmed, but the other three twisted within her palm. The skin had a warm waxiness to it she'd never forget. When they released their grips, she wondered who felt the greater relief.

"You're feeling better, I see?"

"Yes, thank you so much. You've all been so kind."

His nod was barely perceptible but completely dismissive as he turned his attention to his diminutive mother still tucked up to his side. "And do you know why Eugenie is setting up luncheon outside?"

"Why to celebrate, of course. Lilly's finally able to leave the bed."

"So, it's a send-off?"

Betty Ruth swatted her son's wounded arm, causing Lilly to flinch. "Don't be rude, Cullen Burnside." She turned to Lilly. "He's teasing, of course. He has a wicked streak of humor. Positively evil."

"The devil himself," he said. "Now, can we eat? I have a meeting at two."

He escorted his mother back to the patio. Lilly followed. Watching the two of them together, the way he tilted his head to catch whatever soft comment Betty Ruth had for him, made her feel, for the first time, like an interloper. Their shoulders rose simultaneously, and she knew they were laughing. How could she be this close, yet so distant, from whatever had amused them? For a few terrifying steps, she feared they were laughing at her—her rough talk or cheap clothes. Her very arrival was fodder enough.

She began to make her plan: as soon as they started eating lunch, she'd excuse herself, run up to her room, grab what she could carry, and be gone before they'd think to look for her, if indeed they ever would. But as she stepped back onto the pink flagstone, she noticed the small round table set for three and hated the thought of an empty chair.

Then Cullen pulled out her chair, like a gentleman would for a lady, like few men ever seemed to do, at least not for her.

"Thank you." She glanced up and found herself inches away from the scarred flesh along his jaw and neck.

He said nothing, only moved to repeat the same gesture for his mother before taking his own place.

"It's chicken salad," Betty Ruth said. "I remember you saying you had a fondness for it."

"Did I?" Lilly couldn't remember ever having chicken salad before. "It looks delicious."

Cullen cleared his throat. He was sitting with his hands extended. Lilly, following the lead of mother and son, joined her hands to theirs, feeling guilty for her gratitude to be sitting at his left. She bowed her head when they did, but her eyes remained open, seeing nothing but the perfect mound of food on her plate—shredded chicken and walnuts and grapes on a bed of green lettuce. She hoped her companions would lead by example to show her just how to eat it.

"Gracious heavenly Father," Cullen prayed, "we thank You for this day, for the food we have to eat, and for the new friend to share it. Amen."

"Amen, amen." Betty Ruth gave Lilly's fingers a little squeeze before releasing them; Cullen did not. Still, it was the single best prayer she'd ever heard in her life.

Lilly took a slice of bread off the plate Cullen offered her and watched carefully, mimicking Betty Ruth's every move as she tore a corner off the bread, placed a bite of salad on it with her fork, and popped it in her mouth.

"Delicious," she said, her words muffled by food.

"Tell us," Cullen said, his own fork suspended over his plate, "how long do you intend to stay?"

Lilly swallowed—nearly choking. "I...I haven't thought—"

"She'll stay as long as she wants," Betty Ruth said. "She is my friend."

"Well"—he turned to his mother—"if I may be permitted to ask"—then back to Lilly—"is there anyone you should inform as to your whereabouts? Any family?"

"No."

"Friends?"

She couldn't bring Dina here. "None."

"Surely you have some people, dear." Betty Ruth smiled.

"No, I'm...I don't. Have people, that is. None who I'm in touch with."

"No parents?" Cullen asked.

It was time. "If you'll excuse me." Lilly pressed her napkin to her lips the way she'd seen heroines do in the movies. "I think I'm not used to so much sunlight. Feeling a bit weak, you know? I think I'll go lie down."

She began to stand, but one word from Cullen, "Sit," anchored her to her chair.

"I have a mother." She stared at the bowl of purple flowers in the middle of the table. "In a little town about thirty miles from Pittsburgh, Pennsylvania. I haven't seen her in three years."

"Pittsburgh!" Betty Ruth chimed. "Did you hear that, Cullen? Pittsburgh." She turned to Lilly. "My son plays baseball for a team in Pittsburgh."

"Not now, Mother." There could be no mistaking the authority in his voice. "How did you come to be here?"

Lilly picked at her food. "I went to a party—"

"Not *here,*" he interrupted, inclining his head toward his mother. "Here in Florida."

It occurred to her to come up with a perfect answer—something about the warm weather, the new possibilities, maybe even an imaginary relative. In short, everything she'd told Mrs. Myrtle and Mr. Eggleston and even her friend Dina. But none of her stories came to mind. Something about the fragrant breeze coming from the garden and the sound of Betty Ruth's bracelet against the china plate made her reluctant to make up a new one.

She looked at him, straight into his eyes, which were now unveiled. With these people, she would always tell the truth. "I ran out of road."

7

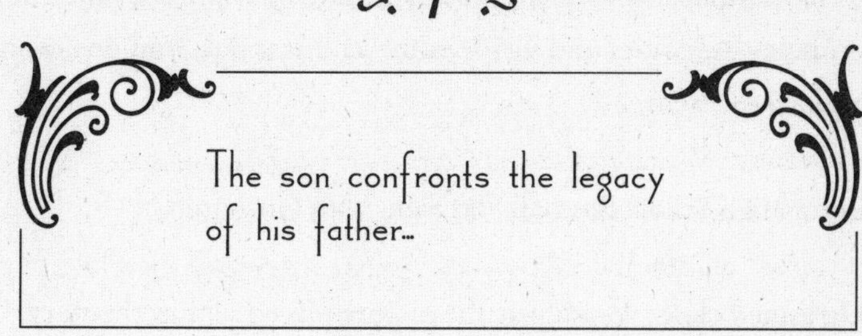

The son confronts the legacy of his father...

The next day, at precisely one thirty, Cullen slipped his dark glasses into his breast pocket and tugged his driving cap low on his brow. It was still too warm for a car coat or scarf, but his fresh linen suit felt crisp and cool. Some would say October was too late in the season for linen, but he wasn't bothered by such details. Nothing felt worse than wool against his skin. Life offered few moments of comfort; he could at least feel good in his own clothes.

He stood in what used to be his father's home office. In some ways it would always be his father's office even though Davis Burnside was long dead, leaving Cullen to manage the family fortune. Whether he wanted to or not.

There was nothing of Cullen in this room. The walls were dark-stained wood, lined with photographs of his father, a pictorial tribute to the man's rising fortune. His college graduation portrait. His first day working in the land office. Then a series of framed titles and deeds. Land, railroads, banks, buildings. An entire row of groundbreaking and ribbon-cutting ceremonies. His father standing next to John D. Rockefeller. His father as a young man shaking hands with Cornelius Vanderbilt. A handwritten note from Theodore Roosevelt, thanking him for some box of cigars. Newspapers in which Davis Burnside was both the headline and the footnote—charities and victories, never a scandal. And one centered on a wall all by itself:

Local High School Baseball Star Signs with Pittsburgh

He leaned closer, looking at the picture placed within the story. Cullen himself at seventeen, never mind that he'd played four inauspicious years of baseball at Yale. His hair combed back, he wore a suit too big for his narrow shoulders and an expression too serious for his youth. The day the paper came out, Cullen complained to his father about *The Journal*'s choice of picture.

"Why didn't they use my team picture?" The one where he stood, bat balanced on his shoulder, looking twenty feet tall.

"Because this is who you are," his father had replied, drumming his square finger repeatedly on Cullen's printed face. "My son."

Cullen hadn't questioned further. Who knew better than his father how to preserve a legacy in pictures? The photographs of him on the office wall spanned nearly thirty years, but his face was unchanging. Piercing eyes—blue, like Cullen's own; blond hair; clean-shaven face, even when every other American millionaire covered his triple chins with whiskers. Then again, Davis Burnside had no triple chins. He was five foot ten, one-hundred-seventy-five pounds in his college graduation photo, and he weighed exactly that the day he boarded the train to Arizona, where a converted tuberculosis hospital served the needs of soldiers who'd suffered the burns of mustard gas. The room was dark, but enough light came through the window to allow Cullen to see a hint of his reflection in the glass covering the newspaper. There he was, both faces, the innocence of his youth and the tragic relic of war. He took little satisfaction in the fact that he now filled out his suit with broad shoulders, at least one of which was strong.

What would that young man have done if a girl like Lilly landed in his backyard? Then again, twelve years ago there were no girls like Lilly. Maybe that was for the best.

An enormous mahogany desk, polished to a liquid shine, dominated the back of the room. On it sat a crisp green blotter, a sterling silver pen set, and a Tiffany lamp. Here, too, were what Cullen knew to be his father's most treasured photographs: a teenaged Betty Ruth, looking flirtatiously over her shoulder; an older, more serene Betty Ruth, wearing her bridal gown; and, years later, Betty Ruth sitting on their front porch, a chubby bundle of Cullen on her lap.

A black telephone sat on the corner of the desk, and it jangled, tearing Cullen away from his musings. He picked it up on the third ring, instantly recognizing his driver's voice.

"You ready for me to bring the car around, Mr. Burnside?"

"Yes, Miles. I'll be out front."

He replaced the receiver in its cradle and picked up the soft leather briefcase sitting on the chair by the door. His mother was upstairs taking her after-lunch nap, meaning the rest of the household help were somewhere similarly resting. Not napping, of course, but relaxed, knowing they were, for an hour at least, outside of the range of his mother's demands.

On any other day this was his favorite time, when he was guaranteed uninterrupted silence to read through a *Life* magazine and imagine what his own life might be like had he not walked off a ball field and onto a battlefield. Had he ever had the right to choose? Where would he be if he had been content to learn the family business under his father's watchful eye?

But he hadn't, and today was Wednesday, board-meeting day, and duty called. He paused at the mirror in the entryway and faced himself, loathe as he was to do so, slid his glasses out of his shirt pocket, and settled them on the bridge of his nose.

"Does the sun bother you?"

Sudden noises still startled him, and he jumped at the question, automatically reaching for an invisible gun as he spun around. His breath caught in his throat, throwing him into a coughing fit that echoed against the marble.

"Oh, I'm so sorry!" Lilly held her hands to her face, unsuccessfully stifling a giggle. "I didn't mean to scare you."

"You didn't scare me. You startled me. There's a difference." He might not have much dignity left, but he was bound to keep what he had.

"Either way... So, does the sun bother your eyes?"

"Somewhat." Where was that car?

"Mine too. It was one of the most difficult things to get used to, living down here. The sun."

"There's sun in Pennsylvania."

"Not like here."

"True enough. Now, excuse me." He gripped the doorknob, prepared to leave.

"Where are you going?"

"Downtown. To my father's office. I have business to attend to there."

"Oh." She looked down at her feet and so did he. He tried to ignore the blatant display of her knees and legs and concentrate on her feet. She was barefoot. Nobody had ever been barefoot in his home in the middle of the day before. "Sounds important."

"It is."

"Can I come?"

Once again, in less than a minute, she'd managed to knock him off balance, to take his very breath away. "To my father's office?" He barely had the breath to fully express his incredulity.

"Well, it's your office now, isn't it?"

According to legal documents, yes. But in the eyes of the shareholders, questionable.

"And what would you do in my...my office?"

She clasped her hands behind her back and traced a semicircle on the marble with her toe. "I got nearly three weeks of secretarial school."

"Are you looking for a job? According to my mother, you're a heck of a salesgirl."

"Not so much anymore. Wasn't my cup of tea."

"And you think you're better suited to secretarial work?" He thought of the secretary he'd inherited along with his father's fortune. Hilda Meyers, all starched cotton from her chin to her heels. The woman was born with a pencil behind her ear.

"What do you think?" She cocked her head to one side and thrust her shoulders back. Almost like she was flirting with him. But that was impossible. This vision and he—

Thankfully at that moment, the front bell rang, announcing Miles with the car. He'd long ago given up the disrespect of honking at the curb.

"I already have a very capable secretary, thank you." Cullen opened the door. "If Mother wakes, please inform her that I'll be home by three."

He greeted Miles, a diminutive dark-skinned man with a chalk white beard and full, square teeth.

"Afternoon, Mr. Burnside." Miles touched his cap.

Both men were halfway down the steps when the front door opened behind them.

"Hey!" Lilly's voice compelled them to turn around. "I guess that kind of makes me your secretary at home."

"If you like," Cullen said.

She winked. "I like." The door closed again.

If Miles had any questions, they remained unspoken, though his dark eyes twinkled as he held open the car door for Cullen to slide in.

"She's a friend of Mother's," Cullen said once the man slid behind the wheel.

"Wish my mama had such a one." Miles sent Cullen a wink in the mirror before pulling into the street.

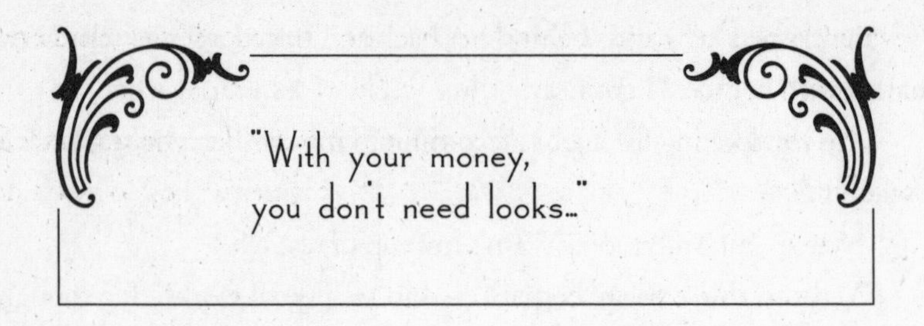

The office building downtown had a side entrance that Cullen preferred to use, as it spared him the long walk through the ornate lobby where people still greeted him as if he were shadowed by the ghost of his father.

"Back in an hour, Mr. Burnside?" Miles held open the car door, his smile near smirking.

Cullen checked his watch. "Yes. And if you wouldn't mind, I have some suits that need to be picked up at the cleaner. Eugenie has been otherwise occupied—"

"Say no more, sir. It'll be my pleasure."

"Thank you, Miles."

Once inside, Cullen headed straight to the elevator in the corner of the lobby. He remembered when it had been installed, what a thrill it seemed to ride this swift magic box all the way to the fourth floor in less time than it took his youthful legs to climb even a single flight of stairs. Later, once the novelty wore off, his father declared it a lazy man's conveyance; father and son would race up and down the stairs, with the elder Burnside winning as often as not.

On Cullen's first trip to the office after the war, as healed as he was ever going to be, he tried to take the stairs, his good hand firmly gripping the winding wooden banister with each step. But the effort left him weak and exhausted, doubled over at every landing. What a spectacle he'd made, breathlessly reassuring everybody he was fine, he didn't need a chair, he didn't need a drink of water, and, yes, he did know there was an elevator. When he'd finished his day's business, he rode it down, and every day since.

"Morning, Moon." The same man had operated the elevator since its construction, and he greeted Cullen with the nickname he'd borne since high school.

"Good afternoon, Mr. Toretta."

"My apologies. Easy to lose track of time stuck inside all day."

"Not at all." Cullen walked inside the cage. "Fourth floor."

"Of course." The unspoken agreement between the two guaranteed that Cullen would never ride the elevator alone.

Mr. Toretta slid the door closed and pulled the handle. Once the initial rattling roar set the two in motion, he turned to Cullen, rubbing his hands together. "Game one today."

"Yes."

"Who do you like for the Series?"

"Pittsburgh." Cullen leaned forward, bringing an air of confidentiality to the already private conversation. "But I'm hardly impartial."

Mr. Toretta laughed, revealing two gold teeth on the upper-right side. "I guess that's right, but we shall see. You goin' to any of the games?"

Second floor. No stopping. "No, not this time."

"Boy, if I had your money..." Mr. Toretta let that thought drop and allowed a brief moment of silence. "Say, Moon, you still know any of them fellows on the team?"

"No more than you do, Mr. Toretta. I had one season eight years ago. I'm surprised I even got a card."

"But you did, didn't ya? Oh, I remember your pa handin' them out all over."

"He was quite proud."

"Yeah, well, he would have been real proud to see you now too."

Cullen looked up to check the elevator's progress. Between three and four. "Thank you."

"I think about my boy. What he'd be if he had made it back."

Tony and Cullen played high school baseball together. "I think about him too."

"You don't know how blessed you are, you know? How good you got it." He cleared his throat as he opened the door. "Fourth floor."

"Thank you." Cullen stepped over the threshold, right across from where Burnside Enterprises, Inc. was written in bold black paint on a pane of frosted glass. He heard the inner door of the elevator closing and turned around. "Mr. Toretta?"

"Yes sir?"

"I could get you tickets, if you'd like. To the Series. Whichever team you want. Train fare too. And hotel. Pittsburgh, Washington. You let me know."

"Ah, thanks, Moon, but I got responsibilities here. Who's gonna run this box if I'm gone?"

"I'm sure we'd find somebody."

"You know what?" He beckoned Cullen closer, until the two men's faces nearly touched the metal gate. "Some of them buildings in the city? They got girls working the elevators. Can you imagine?"

Cullen thought of Lilly. He could, indeed.

"Think about it. Some gentleman such as yourself, all alone for maybe ten, twelve floors. Who knows what could happen?"

"You'd better watch yourself," Cullen said, surprised at his own levity. "Put ideas in my head, and I just might have to find someone pretty to take your place."

"Are you kiddin'? I got enough trouble with the secretaries trying to get fresh with me."

They shared a laugh. "You let me know if you change your mind about those tickets."

"Yes sir, Moon. I will."

Cullen hesitated for just a moment before opening the door; once it was open, there'd be no going back. He stood, absorbing the soothing sound of a dozen typewriters and the comforting smell of leather and paper and expensive furniture.

"Good afternoon, Mr. Burnside." The young woman at the first machine wore a crisp white blouse, her long hair secured at the nape of her neck.

"Afternoon." He began the walk down the aisle between the desks. The ritual was repeated as young, perfectly pleasant women glanced away from their pounding fingers long enough to acknowledge his presence. How many weeks of secretarial school could it possibly take to learn to do that?

Hilda Meyers waited for him at the conference room door, pencil firmly tucked above her ear.

"I'm afraid everybody's running late." She checked the little watch pinned to her blouse.

"Perhaps I'm a bit early."

"Perhaps. May I bring you anything? A glass of water? Tea?"

"No, thank you, Hilda."

"All the reports are there for you, sir. Call me if you need anything."

It was, by all standards, one of their warmest conversations.

Inside the conference room, the long oval table was set with a cut-glass pitcher of water on a tray at the center. Eight chairs—three along both sides and one at each end. He took his place at the head of the table, where a fat portfolio waited, and sat down, ready to face the endless numbers and charts and reports that represented his father's empire. He'd long ago given up the idea that he was any kind of a necessary cog in this machine. There were vice presidents and managers and accountants by the dozens. Cullen's was simply the hand that signed the name on the papers that mattered.

For a while, the only sound was the constant tapping of the typewriters in the front and the heavy ticking of the clock on the wall. Then something else joined the mix. Whistling. Cullen recognized the tune and supplied the lyrics in his head: *If you knew Susie, like I know Susie…*

Soon the office was filled with the boisterous, larger-than-life presence of Bill Owens, newest partner in his own father's firm and lately assigned to the legal dealings of Burnside Enterprises, Inc. He dropped his whistle and walked in singing, *"Oh, oh, oh, what a girl!"* He may as well have been twirling a cane and sporting a straw hat, his entrance was more that of a vaudevillian than a lawyer. He paused, obviously inviting Cullen to join in, but the song ended there.

"Afternoon, Bill."

"Good day, Burnsie." Only Bill Owens lacked the self-consciousness to call him that. "You still in the black?"

"So far as I can tell."

"Feel like raising my retainer?"

"You need a new car?"

"Always." He took his place at Cullen's right and drummed his thick fingers on the table. "I was looking for you at the party the other night."

"I sent a note with my regrets."

Bill waved him off. "Julia takes care of all that. You missed a wild time."

"So I heard. Literally, until three in the morning."

"Ah yes, great band. The Dalton Foster Orchestra. Next charity shindig you throw, you've got to get them."

"I'll keep that in mind."

"And the girls. Burnsie, I'm telling you, there's no better time to be alive."

"Is that so?"

Bill hunched over the table, looking every bit the linebacker he'd been all through high school and college. His was a head made to wear a leather helmet. "Think about it. Girls today, they're just so…accessible." His hands clutched in front of him like great, grabbing claws. "I'm telling you,

you see a pretty girl, nice set of legs... Why, if girls looked like that back before—"

"You were married?"

"What a waste. Should have held out. Stayed a bachelor. But I can look, can't I?"

"Apparently so."

"And there were some honies at the party."

"So I saw. Picture in the paper. Were they friends of Julia's?"

Bill let out a long, low whistle. "If Julia had friends like that, I might go to her stupid garden club. That's what I'm telling you—you missed out. Book a band, pop a few bottles of champagne, and they come running. And then"—he wagged his eyebrows—"they start dancing."

"I assume the liquor was legal?"

"From Pop's private stock. Some of those bottles been in our cellar since before the war."

"Really?"

"That's what the labels said."

Cullen didn't pursue the topic. "Next time, perhaps."

"Make that a promise. Look, I know it's got to be hard for you with the"—he gestured to his own face—"but with your money, you don't need looks. Girls today, they don't care. They want good music, good booze, and a good time."

"I'll keep that in mind. So tell me, those girls at the party, the ones in the paper. You say you don't know where they came from?"

"They were like dancing angels sent from jazz heaven."

"I assume they had escorts. Dates?"

Bill shrugged.

"And that somebody saw them safely home?"

"One of them caught your eye, huh? I can probably find out a name..."

"No." Part of him wanted to tell Bill the whole story; rather, have Bill tell him the whole story, assuming he'd know how Lilly Margolis went from dancing at a party in one backyard to falling on her face in another, but he was seized with an overwhelming sense of protectiveness.

"Wait a minute." Bill was looming again. "I've known you for twenty years. You don't ask questions for no reason. She's with you."

"She who?"

"It's making sense. There was talk about some girl running off. Disappearing. Then my maid said somebody's got a trollop sleeping in the guest room."

"She's not a trollop."

"Oh no. She's a beauty. And if you're interested, she has this friend—"

"She's a guest now. In my home."

"A guest?" Bill chuckled. "Is that what they're calling it now?"

"Careful, friend."

Bill held up his hands, surrendered. "How long is she going to stay?"

"Not long." Cullen stood and walked to the conference room doorway, then summoned the first person he saw walking by. Minutes later, Hilda Meyers was at his side, notebook at the ready.

"I need you to find an address for me."

"Yes sir."

"A Mrs. Margolis. Miresburgh, Pennsylvania."

"First name?"

"I don't know that yet. See what you can find. I'll bring you in later to dictate a letter."

After stepping aside to allow the first of the arriving board members to make their way past, Hilda gave a curt nod and left. Sometime during the first chatter of greetings and light business, Bill pulled Cullen aside.

"What's with the mystery?"

"Booze and music and 'good times' are no life for a young girl."

"So?"

"So I'm sending her back to her mother."

8

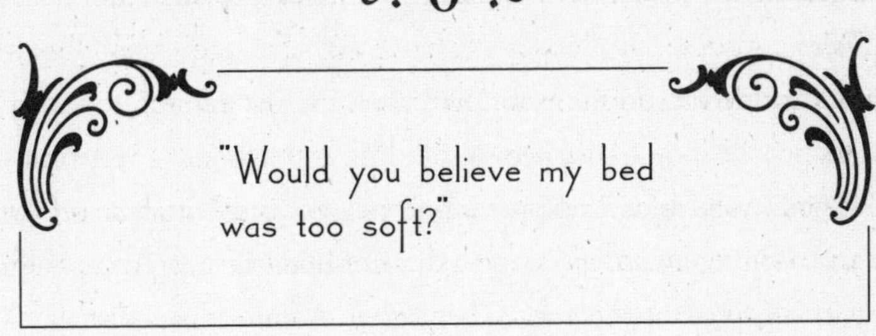

"Would you believe my bed was too soft?"

Lilly put her ear against the door and listened. Nothing. She turned the knob and peeked inside, whispering, "Mrs. Burnside? Betty Ruth?"

Drawn curtains brought near darkness. Once Lilly's eyes adjusted she could just make out the sleeping form on top of the bed—Betty Ruth, her shoes still on her feet, her bejeweled hands folded gracefully across her stomach. They rose and fell with her heavy breathing, and the perfumed air resonated with her soft snore.

Lilly sighed. Yesterday she would have been doing the same thing—a long, leisurely nap after lunch—but today she fairly buzzed with stored-up energy. Wound up like a top, her mother always said. Spinning and spinning without a thought to direction. She turned in a slow circle, wondering what to do. Where to go. She couldn't shake the fear that a step outside the house might mean never being let in again. And, oh, how she wanted to stay. Thankfully, there were enough undiscovered corners within its walls.

The second floor jutted out in two directions from a wide, generous landing. To the left was her room—what she'd come to know as her room, anyway. Betty Ruth's, where she now stood, was in the opposite hallway.

There was only one other door, tightly shut. Must be Cullen's. She grazed her fingers across its surface. What would a full-grown man's bedroom look like?

She intended to do no more than peek in, just enough to satisfy her curiosity, but she soon found herself standing at the foot of a very neat, very narrow bed. Solid blue bedspread, one pillow. Small nightstand with a lamp and a Bible, a window open to the afternoon breeze. An upholstered chair with a pair of slippers tucked beneath it. A four-drawer dresser, its top completely bare save for a framed photograph of a much younger Betty Ruth standing next to the late Mr. Burnside. And nothing else. She'd been in cheap hotel rooms with better décor. There wasn't a single painting on the wall, no sentimental cross-stitch about the joy of a son. No mirror.

She teetered on the edge of pity, though she'd never known a soul more deserving of pity than she was. Scarred face and all, he still had money. And a home. And a mother. If Cullen wanted to live like a monk that was his business.

Still, a certain sadness lurked in the very corners. The stark colors and sharp edges reminded her far too much of that little house in Miresburgh. She didn't belong here any more than she did there. As if to reinforce that fact, something—the breeze coming through the window, perhaps—caught the door and slammed it. The sound made her jump, and a curse flew from her lips before she could bring herself to stop it. She whirled around, and while relieved to find herself still alone, her heart pounded hard enough to shorten every breath.

"Giving myself the heebie-jeebies," she said, comforted by the sound of her own voice.

The slamming door revealed more than her unease as she realized the wall behind her held a set of shelves, and on those shelves were a series of perfectly aligned magazines. Lilly walked over, rose to her tiptoes, and wedged two fingers in to retrieve one. Soon she was looking into the handsome, smiling face of a man in a red cap. *Baseball Magazine,* August 1919.

And another, *Who's Who in Baseball,* with the grim, flat face of Ty Cobb on the cover.

She perused a dozen more, all the same. Nothing interesting. Nothing about fashion or movies. No *New Yorker* or *Saturday Evening Post,* which might have something interesting to read. Like one of those great flapper stories by F. Scott Fitzgerald. One after the other, baseball, baseball, baseball.

Too late, she realized she'd lost track of where the magazines she'd pulled belonged on the shelf, and it didn't take a genius to realize Cullen Burnside had a system. They didn't seem exactly chronological, but by now her calves ached with the strain of stretching, so she took her best guess and wedged the issues in.

A small card came fluttering out and down, landing squarely on her bare foot. Satisfied that the magazines looked just as straight as they had before she disturbed them, she bent to pick up the card and saw herself staring into a very familiar face. It wasn't a photograph but a sharp likeness nonetheless. Cullen, broad shoulders stretched beneath a Pirates uniform. The artist perfectly captured the piercing blue of his eyes and the narrow aquiline nose. His attractive face was positioned so he stared at something far and away. Wistful. Not quite a profile, but not full on either. And while she knew the portrait intended a handsome symmetry to his face, the part that was now a mass of scars remained hidden.

"What are you doing?"

If the slamming door had startled her, that voice—*his* voice—nearly brought her heart straight through her skin.

"I—"

"This is my room. You're in my room."

"I'm sorry." Lilly pinched the card between her fingers, wishing she'd thought to stash it behind her back. She stared at the face in front of her, trying to gauge his reaction. Angry? Hurt? Actually, with his eyes wide and his mouth slightly agape, he seemed almost afraid. Little by little she relaxed, her breathing slowed, and she draped her spine into a slouch. "Would you believe my bed was too soft?"

His eyes narrowed. "What are you talking about?"

She twirled her hair and pouted. "Like I'm your Goldilocks." If she hadn't been clutching the card she might have walked her fingers up his chest, claiming him to be her Baby Bear. That usually did the trick. Like when *Alice and the Three Bears* was the cartoon at the picture show, she called her date Papa Bear, necked with him a little, and got three new hats on the walk home. But Cullen seemed immune to the same charm.

"Get out."

"I just—" He hadn't noticed the card, so she eased it behind her back. "I wanted to explore a little. It's such a beautiful house—grander than anything I've ever seen—and I couldn't resist. I was only poking around. No harm done."

"Go."

"I wasn't even sure this was your room. The door was open and I—"

"It's open now." In fact, he stood in the middle of the open doorway. He moved aside, making a sweeping gesture with his wounded arm.

What could she do but leave? Working her hips with all the sway she could muster, Lilly walked past, brushing the front of his shirt with her elbow. She had one foot over the threshold when she felt the baseball card, still held tight behind her, being pulled from her grasp. The snatching of it brought his hand in contact with her skirt, and she paused long enough to send Cullen a saucy wink over her shoulder.

"What do you think?" She placed her hand on her hip and stopped to strike a pose. "Would you say this one is just right?"

"I'd say Goldilocks better be careful, or she'll find out that the sidewalk is too hard."

"My goodness, looks like Baby Bear is turning into the Big Bad Wolf before my very eyes." She gave him no time to respond to her flirtation but immediately turned and made her way slowly down the hall.

Her skirt was a series of sharp, thin pleats, and she felt them skimming rhythmically against the back of her knees. This time there was no slamming of the door. In fact, she was halfway to her room before she heard the soft *click* of its closing.

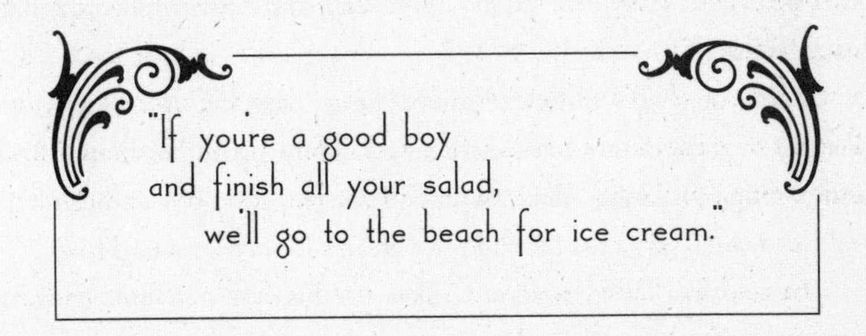

Dinner that night was to be a cold salmon salad, served on the patio, where Betty Ruth hoped to capture the last refreshing breeze of a summer day.

"Honestly, Cullen dear, it is so hot. So hot. Don't you think it's dreadfully hot, Lilly?"

It was. She crossed and uncrossed her legs, moving forward in her seat and resisting the urge to peel her dress away from her back. "The breeze feels wonderful."

Betty Ruth was not satisfied. "Not as wonderful as it would on the beach. Can we go to the beach? We could get ice cream. Or an Italian ice. Oh, Lilly, there's a little stand there that has the most wonderful Italian ice. Cullen, couldn't we go after supper?" Her gaze bounced back and forth between the two, and she looked every bit the small child at the table, right down to her imploring, sparkling eyes.

"It's late, Mother."

"Late! We'll have hours of sunlight left. And if the sun goes away, we'll have the moon. Oh, how I love the water in the moonlight." She placed her hand, still clutching a fork, on Lilly's arm. "You have a bathing costume, don't you?"

"Yes."

"I'll bet it's one of those scandalous ones. Is it? With the bare arms and legs? Just like the men wear? Scandalous."

Lilly glanced over at Cullen, who seemed lost in the noodles on his plate. "They're not so scandalous anymore. Not since Miss America started wearing them anyway. But I don't have a cap, and I just washed my hair this morning—"

"Then you shall wear one of mine. Eat up, now. Eat up!" Betty Ruth took two or three dainty bites and chewed, bouncing on her chair, then a healthy swig of iced tea. "And, darling, if you're a good boy and finish all your salad, we'll go to the beach for ice cream. Does that sound fun?"

Once again Lilly glanced at Cullen, but his eyes remained fixed on Betty Ruth. In his expression she saw a tenderness like nothing she'd ever seen before in a man. His face looked soft, his jaw slack, his eyes too empty for tears. He cleared his throat and wiped his mouth with the corner of his napkin. Standing, he placed a soft kiss on the top of his mother's head.

"That sounds fine, Mother. I'll bring the car around in ten minutes."

Betty Ruth reached up and absently patted the twisted hand resting on her shoulder.

Lilly had to look away.

It was, in fact, twenty minutes before the three of them piled into the car. This wasn't the same automobile she'd spied driving away earlier when he left for the office. No, this was sleek and red, a ragtop roadster with camel-colored leather seats and shining silver chrome.

"Say, that's spiffy." Lilly ran her finger along the door. "Mind if I get shotgun, Betty Ruth?"

"Do I what?"

"Mother prefers to ride in the front seat." Cullen came just short of pushing Lilly out of the way. He held the door open until Betty Ruth was settled in the seat.

"Very well, then," Lilly said. "I'll drive!"

She waited half a breath, giving Cullen the chance to play along, before running around the back of the car. He, in turn, stepped lively around the hood, and the two met at the driver's side door, its handle a prisoner of both their hands.

"After you." He stepped aside, not offering to open the door as he had for his mother.

"Don't mind if I do."

"Of course you'll need the keys."

"They're in the ignition, dear," Betty Ruth offered helpfully. She looked up at Lilly. "Do you really know how to drive an automobile?"

"Sure," Lilly said. "But it's impolite to do so without the owner's permission. Mr. Burnside? May I drive your car?"

The corner of his mouth twitched, almost as if he were considering the possibility. Almost. "Next time."

It was the closest thing to a promise she'd heard from a man in a long time. She let go of the door's handle. "I'll remember that." Then, in a move she'd perfected with a sweet college boy's breezer, Lilly planted her hands on the top of the door and, encouraged by a "whoop!" from Betty Ruth, swung her body over the side, landing with a bounce on the springy backseat.

"Charming," he said, and then with a roar of the engine, they were off.

9

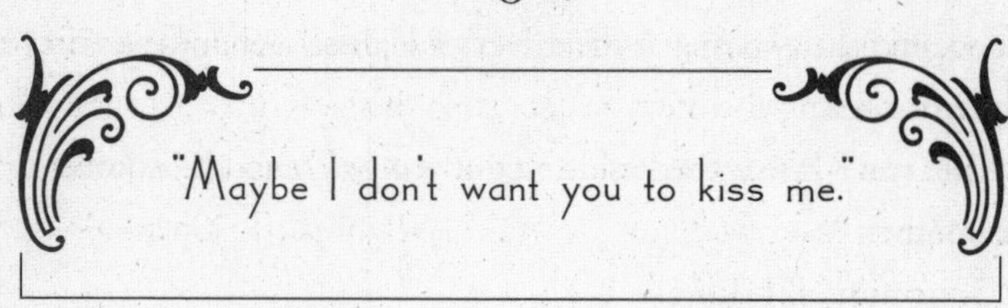

"Maybe I don't want you to kiss me."

Betty Ruth emerged from the small black-and-white-striped changing tent, and Lilly just had to laugh. Not a mean, teasing laugh, but a bubbling of pure delight at the vision of the woman in the old-fashioned bathing dress, wool stockings, ruffled cap, and all.

"I haven't seen one like that in years."

"Well, I'm not as young as you are, dear. I'd never get away with wearing one of those new suits. Never, never. But you look lovely."

"Thank you." Lilly wore a sleeveless black tank suit with a swirling turquoise wave design that stretched from hip to hip. She struck a pose like she'd seen in the magazines. "My friend Dina gave it to me. Her hips were a little too wide. Now, you probably have a terrific figure under all that fabric. You should let me take you shopping."

Betty Ruth reached up and tugged Lilly's chin. "One of the great joys of getting old is being able to hide your figure under great amounts of fabric."

"At least, maybe take your shoes off? And stockings. Don't you want to feel the sand between your toes? Come on." Lilly took Betty Ruth's hand and began heading for the cluster of wood-slat chairs by the water's edge. "Just give it a try. You can always put them right back on."

Falling short of consent, Betty Ruth followed. Few people remained here at the end of the day—two families packed up cranky, red-faced children and picnic baskets, and a group of high-school boys wearing track costumes ran along the water's edge. Each of them turned a moppy head to give Lilly an appreciative look, and one was bold enough to holler, "Hey, blondie! Ditch the grandma!" To which Lilly replied, "Swim along, tadpoles! I'm waitin' for a frog!"

The boys laughed together—never missing a single stride—and one of them muttered something vulgar enough to make Lilly want to cover up the ears beneath Betty Ruth's cap, but the woman seemed oblivious to the entire exchange.

"Here, now." Lilly eased Betty Ruth into a chair and knelt at her feet. How small Betty Ruth's feet were—not a bit longer than Lilly's hand. The shoes were of the finest, thinnest leather Lilly had ever seen, with a ribbon stitched into the side that wound midway up the calf. She untied the ribbon and eased off the first shoe, then the next, while Betty Ruth gazed out over the top of her head.

"Look, your toes are wiggling already. Doesn't that feel better?"

"I suppose." Betty Ruth held her feet directly out in front of her.

"Want to try the stockings too?"

There was a brief curling of tiny toes before Betty Ruth said, "Oh, why not?" This bit she took care of herself, looking over her shoulder before reaching up to the point where the top of the stocking slipped under the elasticized leg of her bloomers and then rolling it down and off her foot.

Lilly gave a long, low whistle. "Well, look at that. I'll make a flapper out of you yet."

"Oh no. My Davis would not approve. Not at all." But there was a bit of the devil behind Betty Ruth's grin. "Now, shall we walk?"

Lilly stood and held out her arm. "We shall, indeed."

The sand was warm and loose between her toes, less so with each step toward the water. Then damp and warm. Then damp and cool. The breeze came off the ocean, cooling her little by little until, as the first small wave lapped over her bare foot, Lilly lifted her face to the salty air and breathed in deep.

"This was a great idea, coming out here."

"I have a few left." Betty Ruth drew her hand away and took a few splashing steps into the water. "And this"—she stomped up and down, sending splashes up to dampen the hem of her sailor-blue dress—"was a wonderful idea too!"

"I knew you had a little wild streak in you."

"Don't tell my son. He thinks I'm a saint."

They waded out farther, until the water was well up to their knees, then entered into a frenzy of kicking, creating loud, crashing waves that playfully battled between them. The salty spray dampened Lilly's hair. It would be an unruly, frizzy, mushroom-shaped mass by the end of the evening, but she didn't care. The salt stung the still-torn flesh on her knees, but she ignored the pain. Right now she was laughing with an innocent, hearty abandon like she couldn't remember ever enjoying before. With each kick they exchanged roles—mother, daughter, daughter, mother. Instinctively she knew, somehow, that this was a moment worth treasuring.

"There he is!" Betty Ruth stopped midkick. "There's our boy."

Lilly let the disappointment settle and ultimately disappear when she saw Cullen standing on the shore. From this distance, the rapidly lessening light obscured his features, and she could only make out the pinpoints of his gaze. He wore a bathing suit too, and she could see firm, strong thighs and a narrow waist, but he also wore the same starched white shirt from earlier in the day, robbing her of any other observation. He was, in short, masculinity—devoid of all the slick and shine so many men fell to.

Stray hair blew across his forehead, bringing her to notice her own, wet and cold, slapping against her eye. She smoothed it back, tucking what she could behind her ears, and felt grateful for the stinging pain on her knees. It was the only proof she had that her legs still existed.

"Mother," he said once they were within earshot, "be careful. You'll tire yourself out."

"Oh, now, a little dip won't kill me."

"You know what the doctor says."

"If that doctor had any sense at all, he'd tell me to be here every day."

"We'll ask him about that next week."

Throughout this conversation, Lilly felt like a waste of a trim body in a cute suit as Cullen never once looked at her. He handed his mother a paper cone. "Italian ice."

"Lemon?"

"Of course." He turned, almost reluctantly, to Lilly. "I wasn't sure what you wanted, so I got the same."

"Thank you." She took the cone from him, chilled by the mere touch of the ice within. A tall spoon fashioned from thin balsa wood stood upright in the ice. She pulled it out and, at the first taste, felt the inside of her mouth draw. "Oooh, it's sour!"

Betty Ruth's face was all puckered too. Cullen looked from one to the other and chuckled. "That's why it's plain vanilla for me." A generous amount of ice cream mounded over the top of a pastry cone, and he took a long, winding lick, looking quite satisfied.

"Ever since he was a boy," Betty Ruth said, her ruffled cap shaking with mock disappointment. "Doesn't know what he's missing."

The three moved to the chairs where Betty Ruth's stockings sat on the sand. Betty Ruth sat in one chair, Cullen in another. Lilly opted for the sand. The only sound was the lapping of the waves and, in the distance, thin strains of music.

"We should have brought the Victrola," Betty Ruth said.

"Next time," Cullen replied.

Lilly quietly ate the lemony ice, letting her tongue press the wooden spoon into the contour of her mouth. There again, *next time.* She imagined the Victrola sitting atop Cullen's spiffy red roadster, the sound of the needle scratching at the end of each record. To her, that was almost as relaxing as the music of the ocean. Constant and scratchy. Come to think of it, Cullen's voice had that very quality. Maybe that's why she felt this lulling sense of security every time he spoke. Or, even now, when he didn't. When nobody did. This was nothing like the countless hours she'd spent in silence back home. Her at the table, Mama lost in the steam of her iron.

Every now and then, their silence was punctuated by the crunching sound of Cullen's ice cream cone, and each time that happened, Lilly looked over her shoulder. The moon was full out now, and at the first crunch, she'd turned to see him gazing straight at it. The second time, he'd been looking out over the water, and the third time, he was looking straight at her.

"They used to call him Moon when he was in high school, you know." Betty Ruth's voice felt as distant as the moonbeams, just as fragile and thin.

"Did they?" Lilly clamped her teeth on her spoon and let go. "Because he was always mooning after all the girls? Or because they were mooning after him?"

"Don't be so forward." While reproachful in nature, Betty Ruth's tone held the same light, airy lilt it always did, sending a new chill down Lilly's skin. "It's not becoming."

"It's a baseball term," Cullen said, almost in rescue. "When you hit a ball high and long, it hangs in the air. Seems like forever. Looks just like that." He pointed the remains of his cone to the sky. "Guys call it a moon shot."

Lilly twirled an unruly lock of hair. "And that's good, right?"

"Can be. If it goes over the fence or hits the wall. But if it's too high, it can fool you. That means there wasn't enough power in your swing, or you didn't hit it in the right spot. And then it can drop right into some guy's glove. And you're out."

"That's why you've always got to run." Betty Ruth looked at the sky.

"That's what his father used to say. If you don't have strength in your swing, have faith in your feet. If you're out, you're out. Just don't let 'em catch you standin'."

"You must have had a lot of strength in your swing," Lilly said. Finished with her treat, she placed the empty paper cone on the ground beside her and leaned back on her elbows.

"I had my moments," he said, sounding shy and pleased.

A gust of wind blew by, sending the paper cone tumbling down the beach. It also caught the edge of Cullen's shirt, blowing it open, exposing the twisted, folded skin of his shoulder and below. She tried not to look, but too late. His shyness turned to shame as he clutched at the fabric, wrestling one-handed with the buttons.

"Oh my." Betty Ruth wrapped her arms close around herself. "That is a chilly wind."

Cullen stood. "Let's get you home."

"Nonsense. The moonlight is just beautiful, isn't it? Beautiful. Let's stay a little while longer. There's a blanket in the car."

"Or you could get out of that wet suit. Get dressed—"

"Or *you* could indulge your old mother and get the blanket from the car."

Lilly was sitting up straight now, startled. Never had she heard Betty Ruth speak this harshly. But as swiftly as the woman's temper flared, it softened.

"If you don't mind, dear. I'd like to stay. Just a little while."

"Of course, Mother. No hurry." He reached down to take her empty cone and reached one long leg out to trap Lilly's wayward one beneath his bare foot before stooping to pick it up.

"And take Lilly with you."

"I can manage."

"Ah yes, but how often do you get the chance to walk on the moonlit beach with a pretty girl?"

"Very well." Cullen held out his hand, still holding the crushed paper cones, to Lilly, who grasped his forearm and allowed him to help her stand.

"Golly." She dusted sand from her backside. "That's the kind of flattery that could make a girl's head explode." But Cullen was already halfway to the car, and while he might have wanted her to hang back, she trotted ahead, easily matching his stride once she caught up to him.

"Your mother's a wonderful woman."

He stared straight ahead. "I've always thought so."

"I think she really likes me." Lilly looked up, and he indulged her with a glance.

"She does, very much."

"How about you?"

"Oh, she loves me."

They were at the car; she leaned against it, enjoying the feel of the warm metal against her bare back. "I mean, do *you* like me?"

"You're not without charm."

Lilly cocked an eyebrow but didn't spend long pondering. Instinct took over—the same instinct that had been guiding her since she left home. Men were men—rich, poor, handsome, hideous. She knew one way to get what she wanted, and what she wanted was night after night just like this. She sprang into action, wedging herself between him and the car.

"Lilly—" He attempted to reach past her.

She arched her back, bringing herself closer. "So, tell me. Cash or check?"

"I beg your pardon?"

"You know. To kiss me?" She hazarded a quick look back to the chairs. "Do you want to kiss me now? Or later?"

He laughed. "I don't want to kiss you at all."

"I don't believe you."

"Well then"—he gently pushed her aside—"maybe I don't want you to kiss me."

Speechless, she stood aside and watched him open the trunk, retrieve a blanket, and hold it out to her. "Are you cold?"

She shook her head.

With a curt nod he closed the trunk and prepared to make a wide berth around her to begin his way back to Betty Ruth.

"Wait." Lilly grabbed the sleeve of his shirt. "They're not nearly as bad as you think, you know. After a while, you hardly notice them." She reached up and gently touched his face, one hand on his smooth jaw, the other against the waxy, hardened skin. She felt her own breath, sweet and cooled by ice and lemon. This close, she knew he could feel it too.

"Did it ever occur to you," he said, no part of him moving but his lips, and those just barely, "that I have better things to do with my money?"

Nothing, not even the stiffest ocean breeze, could cool the burning of her flesh. Her face felt hot, and a tingling ran from the top of her head to the base of her neck, spreading across her shoulders, causing them to droop beneath the weight of it, and bringing her hands to drop, lifeless, to her side. Her thoughts swam in vain, looking for a witty retort, but Cullen would give her no such opportunity. The minute he was released from her embrace he sidestepped her, beginning his purposeful stride back across the beach.

"Now wait a minute..." The full possible range of his remark took hold. He thought she was cheap. Easy. Some two-bit vamp just out for his gold. Never mind that she liked him. That she felt safe and homey. And she loved his mother. Why, if she could have her way, she might skip him over all together and spend her days curled up with one of Betty Ruth's books in her hunting-scene chair.

How could Lilly know he wouldn't want to kiss her? When's the last time a fellow didn't want to kiss her? It's what people did. It's how you got to know a person. What was a kiss between friends? Or between strangers? She'd necked with countless—sometimes nameless—men in dark corners and backseats. Didn't mean a thing.

Doesn't mean a thing. One way or the other, he can consider this bank closed.

She was about to express the same sentiment out loud when she noticed something had changed. Up by the water, Betty Ruth was slumped over in her chair.

And Cullen was running fast in the moonlight.

10

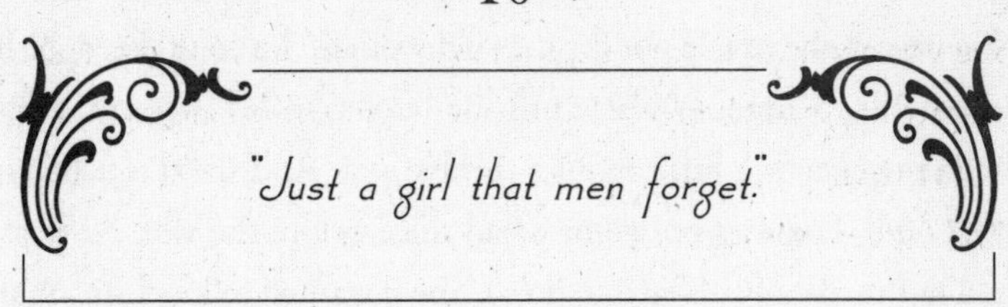

"Mother!"

He fell to his knees and grasped his mother's hand, his fingers wrapped around her wrist.

"Cullen, dear?" Her eyes fluttered open. "I must have worn myself out."

"How do you feel?"

She gave a reassuring smile and pat on his cheek. "I just dozed off, that's all." Her eyes closed again, but her pulse was as strong as her snore was soft, and Cullen sat back on his feet, relief washing over him.

"Poor little thing." Lilly stood right behind him, holding the blanket he'd dropped in his rush to his mother's side. She unfurled it now and draped it across Mother's peaceful sleeping form. "I guess it's time to leave."

"Yes." He remained rooted, not wanting to look at Lilly. It took some time these days to recover from even the simplest shock or fright, and within the space of a minute he'd been sent reeling by two. "Sit here with her, would you? While I go get dressed."

He strode back to the changing tent, each step a new, furious question. Why didn't he insist they leave the minute his mother took chill? Why did he continue to bow to her childish whims? What grown man devoted as much of his conversation to "Yes, Mother" and "No, Mother" as he did?

He passed the car. If not for that old woman, he could be right here, the lovely Lilly Margolis in his arms. Better yet, in his backseat. Because Lilly certainly knew a little about a rumble seat. And she'd touched him. *Touched him.* The way no woman had since before the war. At least, no woman not medically obliged to do so. She'd wanted to kiss him. Wanted him to kiss her. And that was real. Of course, he knew why. Kissing him gave her another foothold in their home—one in his mother's heart, the other in his flesh. He wished he didn't care. He was wounded, yes. Burned, scarred, weakened in breath and body. But he was still a man.

It was dark inside the changing tent, and he stood still, waiting for enough moonlight to filter in and adjust his sight.

Oh, Lord. Just a kiss. No harm in that.

But he knew with Lilly it would never be just a kiss. She wouldn't stop him from taking her completely, and chances were he wouldn't stop himself. That—stopping—took all the strength of his youth. When he was whole and, as the girls said, handsome. When even the good girls gave in to letting him nuzzle the softness of their pulsing throats and touch them here and there. Always, no matter how heated the moment, he'd been able to pull away, be the hero. Years of hearing Reverend Henderson reminding him that his body was a temple, of his mother shyly asking if so-and-so was a *nice* girl, of his father threatening to cut him off if he ever got some sweet young thing pregnant.

But mostly because he wanted more. Because he wanted what his parents had—a true love affair, even if it came late in life. He could wait. There would always be another baseball game to play, another girl to woo, another war to fight.

Finally he could make out the shape of his trousers hanging on one of the changing tent's poles. He took them down and sat on a bench, pulling them on, first one leg, then the other.

Would it have been so wrong, Lord? Not kissing Lilly, but all those others. *Just what, exactly, was I saving myself for? To be some kind of monk? Bad enough I have to go through life looking like a circus freak; now I have to do it alone?*

Oh, wait. Not alone. With my mother.

He stood and pulled up his pants, right over his swimsuit, trying not to think about the sand scratching around all that fine, expensive linen. He swept his foot across the ground until he found his shoes, then slipped his bare, beach-gritty feet into them. His socks and underwear were somewhere in the darkness. Maybe the next person could use them. Or throw them away. He didn't care.

When he returned, he was pleased to see his mother looking much more comfortable—more curled than slumped. The blanket trailed onto the sand, and Lilly was lying on it—flat on her back, hands behind her head, eyes closed. Freud couldn't have staged it better himself.

He nudged her hip with the toe of his shoe. "Lilly? Up."

She opened one eye, stretched, and reached up. "A little help?"

Despite his misgivings, he grasped her forearm and, perhaps not as gently as he could have, hauled her to her feet. "Go get dressed and gather Mother's things. I'll meet you in the car."

"Yes sir." She offered up a sarcastic salute. "On the double."

She ran, and though he should have been tending to his mother, he watched. Lilly's legs were flashes of white ribbon in the moonlight, swift and strong, and once they'd carried her safely into the striped tent, he bent down to gather his mother in his arms.

"Let's go, Mama," he whispered, intending merely to help her stand. But her head lolled back and her mouth fell open. She was sleeping soundly, and he knew from experience that to wake her at this point might prove disorienting and frightening to the mind that was much frailer than her body. So he scooped her up and then, focusing his strength on his legs, stood.

Days ago, when he'd found the incapacitated Lilly on his lawn, he hadn't been capable of such a maneuver. She was, after all, nearly as tall as he—all arms and legs like a pretty, pale fawn—and they they'd struggled and tussled just to get her to stand.

But Betty Ruth Burnside was a tiny slip of a woman. Eighty-five pounds including the wet suit and blanket. He knew she was small, but he hadn't anticipated her weightlessness. It was enough to send him staggering back a surprised step.

The blanket trailed in the sand as he walked back to the car. Lilly emerged from the tent at just that moment, wearing the dress she'd worn earlier. It was obvious in the way it clung to her body that she'd slipped it on over her wet suit. Her arms were full of his mother's clothing, and her hair nearly stood out straight from her head. Her feet were still bare.

"Oh, isn't that the sweetest sight?" She dropped the bundle into the backseat.

"Could you get the door?"

She obliged, moving around to the driver's side.

"And the seat?"

She bent forward, her perfect figure clearly defined beneath her skirt, and then released the latch to fold the seat forward.

By the time Mother was comfortably settled, Lilly had taken her place in the passenger seat. He got behind the wheel, soon thankful for the roar of the engine to fill the silence. They drove home, the night sky punctuated by streetlights.

It was a familiar route. As a boy he could run the distance, he and Bill and whatever neighborhood boys they could round up for a day at the beach. Later they made the trip on bicycles, and in high school, in his father's old Model T.

But tonight was a first. A night among nights.

When they arrived home, he idled the car and hopped out to open the side gate. When he got back, Lilly had moved herself to the driver's seat.

"I'll put it in the garage," she said. "You take your mother inside."

"Have you ever parked a car in a garage before?"

"Don't you know about girls like me? We're practically professional parkers."

He winced at the bitterness of her retort. "I apologize if I said anything…unkind."

Lilly looked like she was about to say something back when Eugenie came around from the back of the house.

"Well, what have we here?" Her tone was not entirely approving.

"I must have dozed off." His mother's voice piped up from the backseat. "But we're home now?"

"Yes, Mother." He helped her from the car. "Go upstairs with Eugenie. She'll help you get ready for bed."

"Do not talk to me as if I were a child," she said once she was steady on her feet. "I am not a child."

But her tiny self with her bare, sand-crusted feet and lopsided bathing cap gave her a childlike appearance. As did her soft voice. And her confusion.

Eugenie took her arm and the two started to walk away when she stopped and stared at his mother's feet. "Why, Mrs. B! What in the world happened to your stockings and shoes?"

Mother bent at the waist, then stood straight again. "I have no idea." She turned to Cullen. "Darling? Where are my stockings and shoes?"

It wasn't a simple question. He could tell by the nervous knitting of her fingers that she was on the edge of being truly agitated.

"They're right here," Lilly said. She'd turned off the car's engine and stood now at his side, holding the bundled clothing. "All wrapped up, safe and sound."

"Well, that's fine, then." After that, his mother walked straight and strong under her own power, Eugenie steps behind with a protective arm at the ready.

Once they were out of earshot, Cullen whispered out of the side of his mouth, "Where are they, really?"

"On the beach, where we were sitting. I'm sorry, I didn't think—"

"It's all right. I'll send someone out in the morning." He wouldn't mention what he himself had left behind.

"And I guess now you can park your own car."

She would have stormed off, but he called out for her to stop. "I want to talk to you. Go around back and wait for me on the patio. Please."

He eased the roadster into the garage and, getting out, got his first good look at what a trip to the beach had done to it. Sand everywhere, the damp blanket left on the backseat, and a pretty pair of sandals. These he took, looping their straps over his fingers, and then he made his way to the backyard. Lilly seemed none too eager to talk, and he braced himself for the disappointment of finding her not there.

After just a few steps, he realized just how uncomfortable his bare, sandy feet were in his shoes, and he kicked them off, holding them mingled with her sandals as he rounded the corner.

No Lilly.

The patio was lit from the house lights shining through the row of windows. He walked straight to the table, deposited the shoes on one of the wrought-iron seats, and was headed for the french door when he heard her voice.

"Cullen?"

He turned.

"I'm out here in the garden."

He headed across the soft, short-cropped grass to find her moving in a strange shuffling step all along the border of his mother's prized flowers.

"I'm trying to get the sand out from between my toes. Don't you hate that feeling?"

"I suppose so." He joined her, making his steps a decisive repetitive square. Up four, over four, and again. It gave him a focus for his concentration. Not that he didn't know what he was going to say. He did. To the letter. But it was hard to think about all that talk out here with the scent of salt and flowers so heavy in the air. A few cranks of a Victrola and they'd be dancing.

And then, music. Soft strains coming from Lilly herself as she hummed.

"What's that song?" He'd never been one to put stock in popular tunes.

She stopped long enough to say, "Certainly you know it," then continued on, gliding through the grass, circling him like a singing faerie in a ring.

He tried to place it. "No..."

She giggled and stopped in her tracks. *"Dear little girl, they call you a vamp. A flapper with up-to-date ways..."* She paused, leaning forward, as if expecting him to pick up the lyric, and when he didn't, she struck a pose that reminded him of his harshest schoolteacher. *"You may shine brightly, but just like a lamp—you'll burn out one of these days..."*

Now it was familiar, and he couldn't bear to hear another word. "Oh yes," he said, hoping that would stop her. Instead she stooped to pick up a handful of the flowers that lay loose in the garden bed, victims of her inauspicious arrival. She held them in her hands like a bridal bouquet and advanced upon him, one slow step at a time.

"Then your old-fashioned sister will come into view, with a husband, and kiddies. But what about you?" She stood straight in front of him, her eyes raised and shining, her hair billowing around her like so much silken floss. "There, I thought you knew it. Join me in the chorus?"

"Lilly, please—"

She hummed another note to set the pitch and touched a single finger on his shoulder, which she then moved to trace the orbit she danced around him.

"You're the kind of a girl that men forget. Just a toy to enjoy for a while..."

When she came full circle, she stopped and brought the sad bouquet of flowers up to caress his face. "*For when men settle down they always get*— What is it?"

Her taunts were growing tiresome, and he felt no shame forcing the croaking nature of his voice. "By now you might have noticed that I do not sing."

"Then just tell me, Cullen Burnside." She brought her face closer, and he could almost taste the lemon ice. "When men settle down, they always get..."

"The old-fashioned girl." Lord, how he wanted her to be. "With an old-fashioned smile."

She bopped him on the nose with the flowers. "Very good!" Then, arms uplifted over her head, she backed away, her legs impossibly long as she moved on the tips of her toes. "*And you'll soon realize, you're not so wise, when the years bring you tears of regret. When they play 'Here Comes the Bride,' you'll stand outsiiiiiiiiiiiiiiide...*" She held the final note as she assumed a very dramatic pose, her body arched, the back of one hand pressed to her forehead, the other listless at her side, letting the flowers fall one by one.

"*Just a girl,*" he attempted, "*that men forget.*"

She lifted her hand and leveled him with a glare. "I knew you'd know that one. How about a duet? Maybe 'By the Light of the Silvery Moon'?"

"You made your point." He bowed in her direction, as if conceding a match. "What I said—what I implied—was hurtful. And I'm sorry. Will you forgive me?"

"As in, forgive and forget?"

He smiled, relieved at the humorous tone that hinted grace, and gestured toward the patio. "Let's sit awhile."

In response she dropped to the ground, cross-legged in the grass, and patted the space beside her.

"Very well." Cullen followed suit, trying not to think about getting grass stains on his good pants. He reached for one of the discarded flowers and held its stem between the fingers of his wounded hand. "Look, Lilly...." He glanced up, and the sight of her, bathed in silver with nothing but blooms in the background, threatened to take what little breath he had.

"Yes?"

"You have to know that you're hardly a forgettable girl."

"Oh, I don't know about that. I'm sure plenty of fellows out there have forgotten all about me."

"Well, I certainly won't. But my mother—"

"Your mother adores me." Steel defense in her words.

He pulled a petal from the flower, resisting the urge to reassure her with his touch. "She does. Now. But more likely than not, the day will come when she won't."

"She thinks I'm delightful."

"That may be. But, believe me, one of these days she won't know you. No telling when. Two weeks from now, or tonight. She might come downstairs for a glass of warm milk, see you through the kitchen window, and think a stranger is in our yard. Or you might ask her to pass the salt at supper, and by the time you ask for the pepper, she'll have no idea who you are. You might be in your room, in your bed sound asleep, and wake up to find her screaming in your doorway."

"I don't believe you."

"Believe me. It happens. And when it does, Mother becomes very frightened. And when Mother becomes frightened of you, I'll have to ask you to leave."

"And then what?"

"And then, she'll forget she ever knew you."

"But if she forgets one minute, she might remember the next."

He shook his head. "Doesn't work that way. People leave and they're gone. So understand, while you're a lovely distraction for the moment, you don't have a place here. You could leave tonight, and soon she'd never know you were ever here."

"Is that what you want? Do you want me to leave?"

He was so unused to being asked what he wanted, Cullen found himself without an immediate reply. Not that he believed for a minute his desire mattered. Still, it wasn't this poor girl's fault that she'd landed in a home ruled by the still-warm fist of his dead father and the effervescent thoughts of his senile mother. She needed guidance. And until he heard from his mother, that guidance would come from him.

"I could help you. Find a job or a place to live." It's what his father would do.

"I don't want to go." Her voice was muffled. She'd drawn her knees up, and her face was buried in the pleats of her skirt.

"You don't have to. Not now. But when the time comes, promise me you'll go. Quietly, straight out the door. You can send for your things."

"Ah yes. My *things*."

"And I'll do what I can for you," he said, clutching at the very idea of her. "You just can't be *here*."

"Because I might, someday, upset your mother."

"Yes."

"Tell me"—she took the flower from him and nibbled its stem—"do you ever worry that she might forget *you*?"

He gave a rueful laugh and pulled out a tuft of grass, letting the blades trickle out of his fingers. "Lilly, my dear, she forgot me long ago."

11

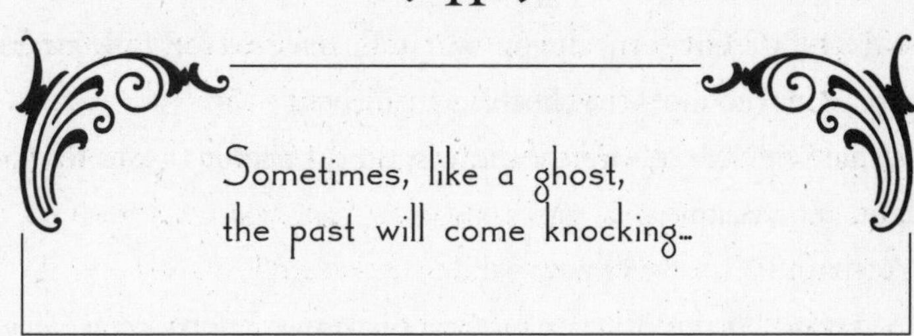

On Thursdays Betty Ruth played bridge, and it was a sacred occasion. Luncheon dishes were whisked away almost before the last bite was taken, and Eugenie shooed everybody away from the table and upstairs to rest up—as she put it—before the girls arrived.

"As for you," she said as Lilly headed upstairs, "you can stay down here and help us get ready."

"Yes m'am," Lilly said without hesitating. Anything to be indispensible.

Lilly's job was to smooth clean blue tablecloths on the card tables and fill little cut-glass bowls with an assortment of nuts and chocolates. For every two chocolates that made it into the bowl, one ended up as a snack for Lilly herself, and she sincerely hoped Eugenie wasn't planning to take an inventory at the end of the hour.

She placed two crisp decks of cards and a pretty little pad of paper at each table. She was spinning a pencil in a pencil sharpener to make the perfect point when the doorbell rang. One forty-five, and no guests were due until two thirty. Eugenie had been quite clear about that. Still, Lilly twirled and twirled the wooden pencil against the blade, holding it over a wastebasket to catch the shavings.

"Miss Lilly!" Given the disapproval in Eugenie's voice, Lilly just knew the woman had counted the chocolates somehow.

"What is it?" She hoped she didn't sound as nervous as she felt.

"You got a visitor."

"A what?" Who even knew—?

"*Meee-yow.* If this place isn't the cat's pajamas, I don't know what is." The voice echoed from the entryway, mere seconds before Dina Charlaine rounded the corner into the parlor. Her hair was a shining black helmet, and the neckline of her dress dipped low enough to accentuate the rib-thinness of her body. Strand upon strand of black and green beads hung from her neck to her waist, and they clattered with each step Dina took.

She gave Eugenie a dismissive pat on the shoulder. "Thanks for letting me in."

"I didn't let you in." Eugenie shrugged off Dina's touch. "I merely opened the door."

"Same difference where I come from," Dina said.

"Thank you, Eugenie." Lilly shot her a pleading look. "I think I'm just about done in here."

Eugenie said nothing, only looked around sternly and stomped away.

The moment the two were alone, Dina took a narrow case out of her little fringed handbag, produced a cigarette, and placed it between her lips. "Get her." She lit the cigarette and tossed the snuffed-out match in the wastebasket with the pencil shavings.

"What are you doing here?"

"Been worried sick about you. All of us have. Had visions of you rotting away in some dark alley. But this"—she walked in a wide, slow circle—"zee-wow, Lil. You've got yourself the Taj Mahal."

"I don't have anything."

Dina winked. Her lashes, thick with mascara, looked like they might leave crumbs on her cheek. "Not yet you don't."

"Not yet you don't what?"

Lilly turned to see Cullen standing in the doorway, his hands in his trouser pockets. The sight of him surprised her, not only because she wasn't expecting him, but because she realized she'd been missing him all day.

"Cullen. This is my friend Dina." As she looked between the two of them, she couldn't tell who was more disturbed by the other's appearance.

Cullen gestured for Lilly to come closer. "We'd prefer not to have cigarette smoke in the house. You'll have to take it outside."

Lilly held up her empty hand. "But I'm not—"

"By *it,* I mean *her.* Before Mother gets up."

"You don't think Betty Ruth will find her delightful?"

"She might. Her friends won't. I haven't decided what we're going to do about you yet come bridge time."

Lilly turned just in time to see the long ash of Dina's cigarette fall to the carpet.

"Come on." She grabbed her friend's bony elbow. "Let's go outside. Seems some people are parlor friends and some people are porch friends. Guess where you land?"

She began to steer for the front door, but a subtle shake of Cullen's head redirected her to the back, where she hoped to be on the porch before the next ash fell.

"Attagirl!" At least Dina had the sense to wait until they were safely on the patio before speaking. "Haven't you found yourself quite the daddy?"

"Don't be a dumb Dora. It's not like that."

"Hey." She held up her hand, sending a series of bangles clattering down her forearm. "No judgment here. The face is a shame, but with this kind of dough, I could learn to keep my eyes shut. What's the scenery from the neck down?"

"For crying out loud, drop it already. How'd you find me, anyway?"

"Aren't you going to offer me a drink?"

"The best I can do is offer you a seat."

Dina arched a brow. "I'll take it." She pulled out a chair from the table. "Aw, isn't this a sweet scene?"

Lilly looked to see her shoes and Cullen's mingled and dotted with sand. She pulled out another seat, offered it to Dina, and perched herself opposite the table. "Now, spill."

"Well, like I said, we was all worried about you when you disappeared from that party and—say, why am I on the hot seat? You're the one who tagged along for food and hooch and ended up at the Ritz. Why don't you tell me what's what?"

"Not a great story," Lilly said, her chin on her hand. "Some fella was getting fresh, trying to make me his personal petting partner, and I just needed some air."

"Which one? The cutie with the red hair?"

"No, some old guy."

"Why didn't you just go outside?"

"Tried that. He followed me." Even talking about it now brought back the creepy-crawly feeling on her skin. No amount of alcohol could alleviate it then, and none of the intervening pleasantness could erase it now. "So I told him, *'Listen, lover, go on inside and fetch me a drink.'* And when he left, I snuck out the side gate."

"How'd you get here?"

"I'm not sure. I mean, it's not far from the party—"

"Just around the corner."

"And I was here earlier, with the Dalliance Cosmetics hoopla. I guess my brain remembered and my body followed."

Dina knit her pencil-thin brows and took a victorious drag on her cigarette. "Freud would say your subconscious saw this as a place of safety and refuge. My last boyfriend was in college, and that boy knew his onions."

"Yeah, but my subconscious didn't know about the side gate. Instead, like a dumb Dora, I climbed the fence, fell over, twisted my ankle, and passed out."

Dina laughed. "You slay me! And they just found you?"

"Yes."

"And kept you? Like a dog or something?"

"Something like that," Lilly said, wondering how she ever thought this girl was a friend.

Dina exhaled a final puff of smoke and expertly flicked the butt across the patio, where it smoldered in the grass. Lilly would pick it up later.

"So then tell me, Lilly my love, besides the"—she tapped a red-painted finger to her cheek—"is everything else in working order?"

"Put a sock in it, smarty. It's his mother who's been taking care of me."

"His mother? He lives with his *mother*?"

"She's wonderful. You know, the whole time I've been here, she's never once asked me about where I came from. Nothing about where I was or what I was doing. It's like when she looks at you, she only sees what's good. I think she really cares about me, Dina. Like nobody's ever cared about me before."

"Oh, you're all wet. I care about ya, kid. Didn't I tell you? We was all worried sick, wondering if you'd been killed or kidnapped or, I don't know, worse."

"You couldn't have been too worried. I've been here for almost a week."

Dina had the good grace to look embarrassed. "Well, it was one full day before we knew you hadn't made it home." She counted off the days on tapered red nails. "Then a couple more. I was just too exhausted to even move. And then Rupert—that's the caterer who got us into the party—he got a new car so we all wanted to take you for a ride. And we went to that convent you was staying in, and the head sister herself said somebody in a spiffy suit came and cleaned out your room. So then we thought you was okay. But yesterday I went back and—"

"It's all right. Really. I like it here. Better than at Myrtle's."

"No kidding. But you be careful with the master of the estate."

"What do you mean?"

Dina took out another cigarette and drummed it on the tabletop. "Think about it. Even if he is Mr. Moneybags, he's not going to be a sheik with the ladies with that face. He finds a pretty girl like you, someone he can take home to mother, well then, it's all over."

"What's all over?"

"Life." She lit the cigarette. "Freedom. Pretty soon you're one of them, some rich old Mrs. Grundy playing bridge on a Thursday afternoon. You become our mothers."

"Not my mother." Lilly gave in, finally, and reached across the table for a smoke. "My mother does not play bridge on Thursday afternoons." She leaned forward and touched the tip to the flame Dina held out for her. Such a familiar feeling, the weight of it on her lips. Some girls liked those long holders, but Lilly always preferred the touch of tobacco on her tongue.

"And just what would Mother say if she could see you now?" Dina asked, taking a long drag.

Lilly puffed herself up, forming her hands into fists in front of her, prepared for battle. "My mother would say, 'Look at you, you worthless piece of trash. Lightin' up them smokes like a common tramp.'"

"Mine too." Dina sounded bored. "But only after a two-hour lecture on how our sisters fought to get us the vote, blah, blah, blah. And what about this new sweet little mother you've found?"

Lilly watched the white paper slowly turn to ash. "I don't know. She might say something like"—she pitched her voice higher, softer—"'Oh, darling. Is that what all the young people are doing today? What a shame, a shame indeed.'"

Dina laughed at the performance.

"Or," Lilly continued, "she might not even notice at all. Or she might light one up herself. With her, there's just no telling."

She brought the cigarette up to her lips and inhaled, filling her lungs with smoke, tasting it at the back of her tongue, down her throat, and was just on the verge of exhaling when Dina asked, "And what about Mr. Mister?"

Lilly nearly choked. In fact, if it weren't for her years of practice, she might have. As the last of the smoke coated her throat, she thought of Cullen. His voice. The poison that he'd breathed in, the toll it took. Smoke poured through her lips in a narrow, almost pretty stream, but it left a taste more bitter than ever before. She put the cigarette to her lips again, intending to inhale, *wanting* to inhale, but ultimately taking it away, focusing on the ribbon twisting up from its tip.

"He wouldn't like it."

"Of course. Listen, Lil, don't let them turn you into something you're not."

"And what exactly do you think I am?"

"You are a modern woman. You let them take this away"—she held up the cigarette—"they may as well put you right back in a corset and hoop skirt. This is the twentieth century. You have power, just as much as any man. All those grandmas want to talk about the vote. That's nothing but a load of applesauce. Being a woman today means you can have all the smokes, booze, and sex you want—just like men have had forever."

By now Dina was languid in her seat, seemingly propped up only by the one bony elbow on the table. She concluded her speech with a slow, satisfied drag on her cigarette, her cheeks caving in with the effort.

"That's the problem," Lilly said. "Doesn't seem fair that men seem to be enjoying this more than we are."

"Who's not enjoying it, baby?"

"Me, sometimes. Look, Dina, wouldn't it be nice to meet a guy and go on a date that doesn't end up in some backseat wrestling match?"

"Sure, but I want any boyfriend of mine to know that if we're gonna wrestle, it'll be an even match. You gonna smoke that or stare at it?"

Lilly took a quick puff, then ground the ashes under the tabletop. "Funny—take a few days off, and you kind of lose the taste for it."

"I oughta make you give me a nickel."

"Good luck squeezing one of those out of me."

"Tell you what. I'd rather have my friend back. What do you say we go to the movies? There's a new Charlie Chaplin playing the matinee. I'll spot you a ticket. And a bag of peanuts."

"I don't know…"

"What, you some kind of prisoner? You have to ask permission to go to the pictures?"

"No." How could she explain that it wasn't the idea of leaving that she questioned, but the idea of coming back. Specifically, would she be able to? So much of her days here seemed unreal, like the dreams that come with peaceful sleep. Maybe it would disappear if she walked away. Cullen said Betty Ruth might forget about her while sitting at the breakfast table with her. Wasn't it more likely that Lilly would be forgotten if she walked away for a couple of hours?

Then again, Betty Ruth was sleeping. And when she woke up, she'd have a grand parlor full of women and cards and chocolate to keep her entertained. And Cullen? Well, she wouldn't ask. Not because he might say no but because she didn't have to. A man who won't kiss a girl doesn't have the right to tell her what to do.

"Give me ten minutes to get myself together." Lilly jumped up. She still held the crushed cigarette in her hand. With all the nonchalance she could muster, she flicked it into the grass to join the others.

"Let me come with you. I'd love to get a look at your room."

Lilly made a mental run through the house, trying to think of some route to her room that wouldn't pass Cullen's office, the parlor, dining hall, kitchen, or Betty Ruth.

"Why don't you wait outside? Go around to the front porch and I'll join you there."

"Oh sure, sure," Dina said, but her voice held as much humor as hurt. "Make me out to be the old milk bottles."

"That reminds me," Lilly said with a wicked giggle. "The old bridge ladies will be coming any minute. Wait for me by the side gate."

Once she saw Dina safely around the corner, Lilly ran inside and upstairs. These past days, she'd spent fewer minutes looking in a mirror than any time she could remember. And it showed. Her face glowed with the sheen of Indian summer heat. Where her hair wasn't plastered to her forehead, it bushed out like a golden pyramid. Her lips were pale pink—just a shade darker than her skin—and the few hours spent wandering the garden threatened to bring a golden bronze to her bare shoulders.

"Like I just fell off a farm."

She ran across the hall to the bathroom and splashed water on her face. Then, back in her room, she powdered it to pale perfection, lined her eyes, and rouged her lips. She dug through her drawers and found a pale gray silk scarf that she wrapped around the top of her head and knotted just below her left ear, carefully tufting curling strands below it.

Luckily, she had a short-sleeved jersey dress with a wide chevron stripe of pale yellow and silver, perfect to match the scarf. Unfortunately, the sandals she preferred sat on a chair, nestled next to Cullen's, so she made do with the closed-toe ankle strap.

Finally, she chose one long strand of pearlescent beads and a thick yellow bracelet before taking a long look at herself. Up and down, head to toe.

"Too much," she said, and slipped the bracelet off her wrist.

12

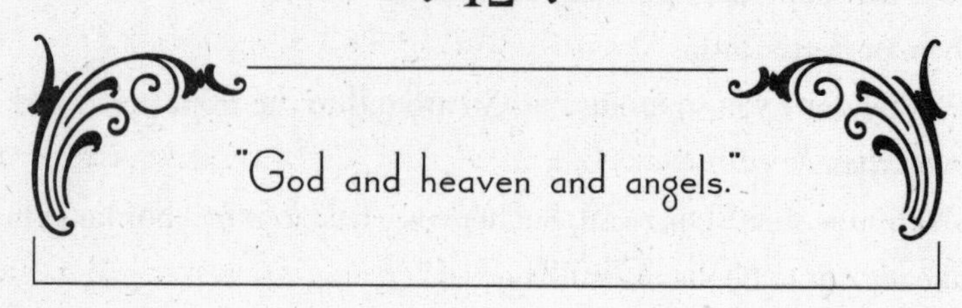

"God and heaven and angels."

He was sitting on the front porch when she got home. "Where have you been?"

"What's the matter, daddy? Past my curfew?"

It was, indeed, nearly evening. Not dark but shadowed. Her mind was too fuzzy to know the precise time.

"You're drunk."

"No I'm not."

He stood as she attempted to climb the stairs. "I can smell it on you."

"What you smell is what spilled." When Dina was holding the flask and laughing at the Little Tramp on the screen.

He caught her arm, just below her sleeve, and held her there, bringing his face close. "It's on your breath."

"A sip." And if it had been any good at all, he wouldn't smell a thing. The cheapest stuff always had the strongest odor. "At least a sip at a time. Those roasted peanuts can make a girl mighty thirsty." This struck her as quite hilarious, and she didn't stop laughing until she felt his grip tighten on her arm. My, he was strong.

"You can't go inside."

"Why? Have I worn out my welcome already? Did you send one of your lackeys out to drop my *things* on Mrs. Myrtle's porch?" It took several attempts to successfully pronounce "Mrs. Myrtle's porch."

"You can't go inside because Mother's been looking for you."

"She's been looking for me? I'd better go right in—"

Cullen practically hauled her off her feet. "I do not want her to see you in this condition. She spent all afternoon looking for you, asking for you, calling all over the house. She told all her friends about you, the magical flapper girl that fell from the sky. You should have seen their faces."

"Did they think she was crazy?"

His grip loosened a bit, and one corner of his mouth almost smiled. "A bit."

"Like I'm something imaginary? Like a faerie or an angel?"

"You're no angel." He stepped away. "Besides, angels are real."

"Of course." She concentrated very hard on keeping her footing on the narrow step with nothing to hang on to but him, and he kept moving away. "God and heaven and angels. Mama taught me all about that. All about it."

Cullen laughed.

"What's so funny?"

"You sounded just like Mother."

Lilly wanted to laugh too, but the whiskey caught in her throat and turned itself to tears. "I—I love—I love your mother." She buried her face in her hands and let the tears flow. Not on her scarf—that was silk—but down her face and between her fingers. She thought she heard his voice over her sobs, but it wasn't until a strong arm draped around her shoulders, drawing her close to a solid, strong chest, that she truly felt like he was there. With her. For her. She wrapped her hands around his waist and buried her face in his shirt.

This is when she should have felt the other arm wrap around her, drawing her closer, and when it didn't she looked up.

And, oh.

From this angle, this side, so close, he was perfect. Handsome, even. Dina said she should close her eyes, but Dina was wrong. She needed to keep them wide open, to just look at him close. Look at the tiny, patchy, soft whiskers and the mole she'd never noticed. At first he gazed over her head, but even when he angled his face to look at her, when she saw close-up every matted fold, it didn't matter. He'd never believe her, but it didn't matter. And even this close, she tried to wedge herself a little closer, the way men like. That's when he pushed her away.

"Mother's outside in the garden. Go upstairs. I'll send Eugenie up with some coffee."

"Not Eugenie." She wiped her face with the back of her hand and winced at the sight of the smeared black kohl. She hoped his shirt could be laundered. "She hates me."

"She doesn't—fine. I'll bring it myself."

Lilly left him there as she fumbled with the door. It was the first time she'd opened it herself, and the latch was a little tricky, requiring this finger here and that thumb there. Suddenly he was behind her, his hand pushing hers away and opening the door for her.

"Thank you."

"Go to your room."

She obeyed, not looking back again. Her steps were measured as she made her way through the house; her hand held the banister in a death grip as she climbed the stairs. Left at the top and straight to her room.

"Your room," he'd said.

First, though, she went to the bathroom, not fully prepared for what she would confront in the mirror. Powder and tears created a streaky paste, and the scarf had slipped to such an angle that she looked like a half-drowned pirate. Or maybe a drowned one. She splashed her face with cold water, washing it as best she could, and scooped handful after handful into her mouth, gargling and spitting over and over, wishing for a lemon ice.

Across the hall, the late afternoon had made the room almost unbearably warm. Somebody—Eugenie, begrudgingly—had opened her window and plugged in an electric fan, but still the air was close and sticky. She pulled her scarf from her head and raked her fingers through her hair, welcoming the breeze across her scalp.

She slid the yellow-and-silver jersey dress over her head and dropped it to the floor, and while she longed to run across the hall in her camisole and tap pants, she knew better. Cullen was coming with coffee.

She sat on the edge of the bed, kicked off her shoes, and fell flat on her back. The cotton coverlet felt cool against her skin, and she fanned her arms and legs out, like she used to do when she was a little girl making angels in the snow.

"You're no angel. Angels are real."

She brought her arms and legs in close to her, but the coverlet stayed in motion. Or the bed did. Or the room or the ceiling. She closed her eyes to block out the spinning, then dropped an arm over them to lock the darkness in.

God and heaven and angels.

God and heaven and angels.

God and heaven and angels.

She knew about God and heaven and angels. The day she bobbed her hair, Mama said an angel fell from heaven with every strand. And the first time she'd rolled her stockings, Mama sent her to her knees, kneeling on rice, praying for forgiveness until her blood seeped to the floor. And the first time she'd been caught necking in a car, brought home by the red-faced policeman who had the misfortune of patrolling on prom night, Mama slapped her with the back of her hand, saying, "There'll be no room for sluts in heaven." Lilly missed three days of school waiting for the bruising to fade.

God and heaven and angels.

The room was hot and it was moving.

Mazy's collar jingled right outside her door. It stopped, and then the unmistakable sound of the dog sliding against the wood, lying down.

Lilly took her arm down and looked at the clock. Nearly six. Just an hour before dinner. A loyal dog guarded her door, and Cullen was coming with coffee.

And Betty Ruth remembered her.

She closed her eyes. This time, the room—and everything—stopped.

When she opened them again, it was dark. Truly dark, but not perfectly so. Pale moonlight streamed through the window, intersecting with a thin ribbon of light from the hallway beyond her open door. She was still lying on top of her bedding, but she was now covered with a thin cotton sheet, anchored by Mazy at her feet.

"You're awake."

Startled, she clutched the sheet to her and turned to see him, perfect in shadowed profile.

"What—?" She tried to talk, but her mouth felt full of Mazy's paw. She swallowed, smacked her lips, and was about to try again when she noticed he held out a glass of water. Struggling to remain covered, she sat up, took it, and drank the coolness down. "What time is it?"

"Late."

"Past supper?"

"Past everything."

"Oh." She drank some more, wondering, as she did every time she woke up in this condition, why she was so stupid.

"What did you tell Betty Ruth?"

"That you went out to a movie with a friend and came home drunk."

"You didn't."

"I did."

"What did she say?"

He laughed. "She wanted to know what movie."

"Oh." Lilly found that funny too, but she dared not laugh.

He took the empty glass. "Tell me why I should let you stay."

"Maybe you shouldn't." Her voice was thick again, but the glass was empty. He took it away.

"God help me, I shouldn't. But you were gone for one afternoon, and she couldn't stop talking about you. Drove me crazy—Lilly this, Lilly that."

Lilly smiled.

"I'm her son, her only son, her only *child,* and she's surprised every time I walk into a room. Asks me, 'Are you still living here?' and 'When are you going back to college?' She knows I played baseball, but she doesn't know I went to war. She knows Father's dead, but she doesn't know I run the business. If I'm reading a magazine, she tells me to do my homework. When my wounds were healing, I couldn't talk to her about the pain, because she didn't see them. But you—she knows what you were wearing two days ago."

"Gray dress with a sailor collar."

"And a red tie."

"Yes."

"And even though I tell her you disappeared with a loose-looking flapper friend and came back staggering drunk only to pass out on your bed, she just wants to know what movie you saw."

"*The Gold Rush.* Charlie Chaplin."

"Stop it." Until now he'd been talking into the darkness, not looking anywhere near her way, but now he slammed down the empty glass on the nightstand, and her mattress shifted under his weight as he placed his fists on the edge and leaned in. "She may think you're adorable, but I don't. And it might mean she'll drive me crazy until the day she dies or I kill her, but this will not happen again. Do you understand?"

She nodded, speechless, then remembered the darkness. "Yes."

"I mean it. If you go out again and get yourself in this state, don't come home."

"I won't."

Without another word, he stood, took the glass, and whistled for the dog, but Mazy dug in deeper, and the ribbon of light from the hallway disappeared with him.

13

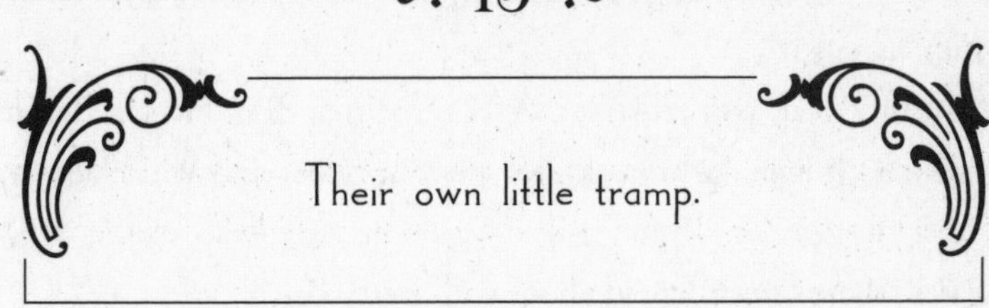

Their own little tramp.

Judging by the vision that greeted him the next morning at the breakfast table, Cullen never would have guessed that Lilly had passed out in a drunken stupor hours before. Her hair, still damp, waved softly around her face. Her skin glowed with something pink, her eyes bright, her smile wide, and something like a song under every word. As she passed by on the way to her place—or what had lately become her place—he caught a whiff of something floral. Not the airy sweetness of his mother's perfume, but darker. Like a garden after a hot summer rain.

"My Cullen tells me you went to the moving picture show yesterday," Mother said when they were all settled.

"I did, indeed." Lilly's eyes locked on to his, and he suspected what she might ask about next. Cullen speared his scrambled eggs, determined not to participate.

"And what did you see, dear?"

"The new Charlie Chaplin. *The Gold Rush.*"

"Oh, I have seen him a time or two. He is amusing, isn't he? Was it funny?"

"Yes," Lilly said thoughtfully, "and sad too. I've always thought the Little Tramp was more tragic than funny. He's always poor, and alone, and lonely."

"But, my dear, you mustn't dwell on the maudlin. How is that to go through life? It'll make you old before your time, and what lady wants that?"

"Well, there's nothing old about you, Betty Ruth."

"Then tell us about the movie. You'd like to know, wouldn't you, Cullen? Of course he would."

Nothing about the conversation made Cullen feel like he had anything to contribute. He didn't care about motion pictures—particularly those with the ridiculous Chaplin attached. But not even Lilly's prattling could spoil his mood this morning as he read the paper. His Pirates won yesterday, tying up the Series.

She described a tilting rickety cabin and an imaginary feast of a shoe. By the time he'd finished reading about the final decisive play, he noticed a silence built up behind the newspaper, a silence interspersed with very childlike giggles coming from his mother. He turned the page, giving it a little snap, refusing to participate in whatever shenanigans were happening on the other side.

"Oh, Lilly, really..." And then pure sparkling laughter.

He let drop a corner of the paper and, shocked at what he saw, closed it, folded it, and set it beside his plate.

Lilly had the small biscuit basket plopped upside down on her head, and a smear of blackberry jam dotted her upper lip. Two of the family's good silver forks were jammed into two peeled hard-boiled eggs, and they were dancing. It was like nothing he'd ever seen before. Right before his eyes, the cutlery and eggs became legs and feet, and the girl did something with the twist in her wrist to bring rhythm and grace to their movement. She began to hum a rambling, jazzy tune, her tongue clicking a beat and her fingers moving the illusion in a series of little kicks across the plate.

"Just what are you doing?"

"It's a scene from the film." Mother held her hand against the strand of pearls draped below her collar. "Oh, isn't she funny? Isn't she a hoot?"

"I'm surprised she can recall the scene in such detail." Suddenly his own breakfast seemed dull and unappetizing, but he stabbed a forkful anyway. "In fact, I'm surprised she can remember much of anything at all."

At that, the dancing eggs grew still—somehow gracefully so—and Lilly pursed her lips to the side, sending the blackberry mustache to an odd angle. Slowly, with great exaggeration, she looked over her left shoulder, then her right, then back at him and raised her shoulders as if asking, *Who? Me?* before wiggling her eyebrows and walking the eggs right off the edge of the table.

Mother clapped her hands and declared Lilly's show the most entertaining thing she'd ever seen. Lilly took the basket off her head and shook the crumbs out of her hair.

"You should see the picture." She used her napkin to wipe the jam from her lip, getting all but one tiny bit. It took all his strength not to reach across the table and dab it away. Instead it disappeared with a flick of her tongue.

"Oh, I don't go to the moving pictures. I wouldn't even know how to buy the ticket."

"You should take your mother to the movies," Lilly said. "Let her see what's happening out in the world."

"In the world where houses spin and eggs dance?" He picked up his paper and opened it. "No thank you."

The next thing he knew the tines of a fork appeared at the top of the page, and the entire paper crumpled beneath it.

"It was bread."

"What was bread?"

"In the movie. He made bread dance. And it was like magic."

"See there?" He pushed away the fork, then cleared the paper out from underneath the fork's grip and snapped it full again. "You've managed to bring the magic right to us. We are forever in your debt."

What the remainder of the meal lacked in levity, it made up for in amiability. Mother and Lilly chatted back and forth about, well, whatever women talked about when they didn't have to include a man in the conversation. And they didn't have to include Cullen, as he was quite content to read his paper, sip his coffee, and drop bits of sausage and toast to Mazy. On the occasions when he was drawn in, Cullen kept his contribution short. Five words or less. Partly because he truly was trying to focus on the sports stories, but also because he enjoyed Lilly's face—a mixture of frustration and amusement.

He found himself lingering at the table far longer than usual. In fact, he couldn't remember the last morning when he'd allowed Eugenie to pour him a third cup of coffee, or when he picked the last pieces of cold bacon off the platter. It wasn't until Eugenie came to clear the dishes that he folded his paper for the final time and set it on the table.

"My goodness, look at the time." Betty Ruth patted her lips with her napkin. "Cullen, darling, you need to get running or you'll be late."

"I've nothing to be late for," Cullen said, the pleasantness of the breakfast vanishing quickly.

"Oh, yes you do. Now go upstairs and get your books."

Which was worse? The fact that the man he was had no real place at this table, or the pitying look in Lilly's eyes?

"Betty Ruth." She offered a comforting hand across the table. "Cullen's not in school. He's a grown man."

"Almost thirty," he said.

"Like I said, a grown man."

This time she stressed the word *grown,* an obvious euphemism for *old,* though she sent him a smile as she said it.

"Oh, that's nonsense." Mother's voice was light, but Cullen recognized the first hint of panic in her eyes. "I think I know my own son."

"Of course you do, Mother."

"No, Betty Ruth. Listen to me."

"Lilly—"

She raised a hand to cut him off. "He is your son, but he's not a little boy. He hasn't been for a long time now."

Mother wrung her napkin. "Cullen, what is she saying?"

"Nothing, Mother. She's just—"

"He's running your husband's business."

"He's not allowed to go into his father's office."

"Enough." Cullen stood, but Lilly ignored him.

"It's important that you know your son—"

He strode to the end of the table, intending to grab Lilly's arm and yank her away from the table. At that moment, Mother stood too, and her calm presence exuded far more authority than his aggression ever could.

"I know my son, young lady. I know him. Far better than you ever could. Do you understand that?"

"But—" Lilly was shrinking in her chair, almost moving him to pity. Almost.

He moved behind Lilly and came up beside his mother. "Come along." He reached one arm out, gingerly letting his hand touch her shoulder, and waited. Sometimes she'd allow such an embrace, but other times, as if startled by his sudden growth, she'd jump away, frightened.

"Come along where?" She sounded skeptical but not startled.

"It's a beautiful morning. Nice and cool. Would you like to take Mazy for a walk?"

"Won't you be late?"

He looked at Lilly and silently told her to shut up. She folded her arms and pouted. "I can't walk with you. But we'll get Eugenie."

"What about the dishes?"

"They can wait. They'll be here when she gets back."

Which was more than he could say about Miss Lilly Margolis.

He whistled for Mazy and escorted Mother to the front parlor while he gathered the leash and tracked down Eugenie. When all were safely dispatched, he returned to the breakfast room, where Lilly perused the newspaper, dangling half a piece of toast over her coffee.

She looked up. "You know what we should have sometime? Doughnuts. Nothing's better than a doughnut dunked in coffee. There's a great little bakery—"

"Go get your shoes on."

"Oh, I didn't mean right now—"

"We're not going for doughnuts. We are going to my office."

"Your—"

"It's time you find a meaningful way to fill your time besides snooping through my house, drinking with your friends, and psychoanalyzing my mother."

"But—"

"Stop talking." His head felt like he'd been the one drinking all night. "Go upstairs and put on some shoes. We leave in ten minutes."

14

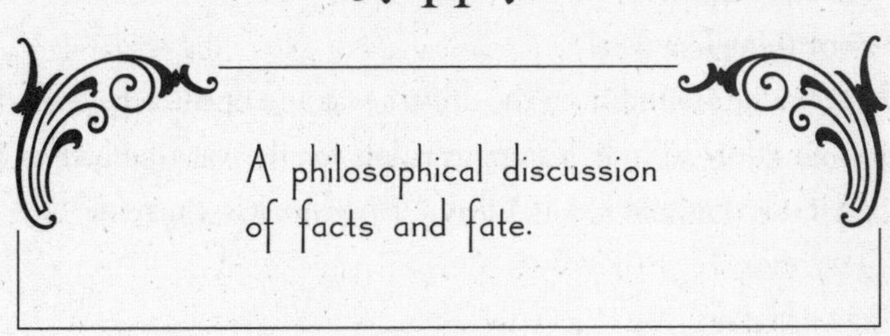

A philosophical discussion of facts and fate.

When Lilly came down the front steps twenty minutes later, Cullen wished he'd kept their destination a mystery. She wore a plain black skirt that fell to the middle of her shins and a long-sleeved plain white blouse buttoned to her throat. Her hair was slicked with something and pulled back from her face with such severity her eyes became like buttons ready to pop.

Her face was free of makeup, which he admittedly preferred, but the clothes and the hair seemed to have taken their toll even there, as all the animation and light disappeared under such severity. Heavy black shoes clomped down the steps, and the odd familiarity of the image hit him.

She was Hilda Meyers, twenty years ago.

At the bottom step, she gave a little turn. "I wanted to look a little more appropriate for the office."

"I see that."

"Do you approve?"

"I'm in shock."

"Fair enough." She looked at the car just pulling up the drive. "No snazzy ragtop?"

"Not for business."

"Just for pleasure?"

"Something like that."

Miles came around from the driver's seat and opened the back door, making no effort to hide his appreciation for the view he had as Lilly climbed inside. He held it for Cullen. "Where to, Mr. Burnside?"

"The office."

"On a Friday?"

Cullen rarely emphasized his position as employer to his staff, but he now gave Miles a look that settled any question about authority. Although as he climbed into the backseat, he did wish convention would allow him to ride in the front.

"I feel very official. I've never been driven by a chauffeur before."

She was sitting a little too close, but to nudge her was to touch her, so he refrained. "Don't get used to it." It came out harsher than he intended, but he made no point of apologizing. "Miles is our family's driver, not my employees'."

"So, you're giving me a job?"

"We'll see. You have secretarial training?"

"Two weeks' worth."

"Can you type?"

"Not really."

"Take dictation?"

"Not at all."

"Can you file? If you know your alphabet you can file."

As they rounded the first corner, he saw Mother and Eugenie headed home. Eugenie wore her usual blank, dutiful expression, but Mother looked peaceful. Happy.

"Would you like me to stop, sir?" Miles asked over his shoulder.

"No," Cullen said, though he did offer a wave through the window, which his mother returned. She might spend the morning questioning

Lilly's whereabouts, but this time it would be Eugenie who would bear the brunt. Poor woman.

They rode in silence, Lilly nervously drumming her fingers on her knees and Cullen holding himself tight so as not to brush against her. For a while, Miles had been whistling a popular tune, and Lilly had actually joined in, humming along until Cullen cleared his throat, and both stopped midnote.

"Traffic's heavy on Palafox, Mr. Burnside. Pretty tied up."

Cullen craned his neck to look out the window. Dozens of automobiles, just like this one, jockeyed for position on the crowded street. Only half a block remained between them and their destination.

"We can walk the rest of the way."

"You sure?"

"Of course."

Miles eased the car over to the curb and then moved to open Cullen's door.

"I've got it," Cullen said, eager to get away from this particular confinement. He held the door for Lilly, averting his eyes when a bare leg snaked out from the modest skirt.

"What time should I come for you, Mr. Burnside?" Miles's head popped up from over the roof.

"Noon." That would get him home for lunch. He spoke to Lilly, "Although your day might last a little longer."

"You're the boss."

The sidewalk was as busy as the street, but they eased through the crowd easily, partly because the oncoming pedestrians took one look at him and glanced away quickly, moving out of his path. Somehow, having Lilly by his side made him forget just how much he hated walking in the daylight.

"Which one is yours?"

He pointed to his building.

"Nice. You own it? The whole building?"

"Yes."

"And what else?"

"Are you hoping to start your employment as a property manager?"

"Just curious."

"I own what I own." His father had indoctrinated him long ago to talk business only with investors, clients, or colleagues. He would be appalled if Cullen strolled down the street with this woman, especially *this* woman, pointing to every third building claiming this one and that one as belonging to Burnside Enterprises. "That's not exactly true. *I* don't own any of it. Just a majority of the stock."

"Don't talk business with me. Goes straight over my head."

"I'm sure you're very bright. Mother says you like to read."

"I do. Too bad you can't get paid for that."

"Maybe you could."

"How?"

"Just wait."

They were at the front door of the Burnside Building, and today he'd be walking across the lobby. He held open the ornate, heavy door, allowing Lilly and several others to pass through. By the time he got inside, he found himself scanning the crowd looking for her. In fact, his eyes passed right over her twice without recognition.

It wasn't just the hair and the clothes, but something about seeing her in the midst of all these rushing, busy, preoccupied people made her disappear. She looked diminished, somehow. And lost, so much so that he was tempted to take her hand. He settled, however, for a small touch somewhere near her elbow and gestured toward the elevator.

"But it's a lovely staircase." She looked back as they walked.

"And when you know where you're going, you can take it."

Mr. Toretta waited by the elevator, his eyes wide at Cullen and Lilly's arrival.

"Why, Moon—er, Mr. Burnside! What is it, Wednesday already? Did I take me a long nap or what? Gotta remind the wife to set the alarm."

"Good morning, Mr. Toretta. Allow me to introduce Miss Lilly Margolis."

"Pleased to meet you." He held out his hand and Lilly took it. "I've known Moon here since he was a kid. He and my son was best friends."

"Really? And what was Mr. Burnside like as a little boy?"

"He was a good kid. Great kid. Heckuva ball player, pardon my language."

Lilly leaned in close. "If I come back later, will you tell me the truth?"

"Ooh-hoo, Moon." Mr. Toretta gave him a playful slug on the arm before opening the door. "You gotta watch this one, don't ya?"

"Perhaps you're the one who needs to watch her. I'm thinking of giving her your job."

"Pretty girl like this, and the gents'll be packed in the elevator like sardines." He closed the gate, pulled the handle, and the elevator jerked into motion. Lilly lost her footing and briefly fell against Cullen, steadying herself with a hand on his shoulder.

"How 'bout them Pirates, Moon? You still thinkin' they'll take the whole Series?"

"Of course."

"I dunno. Washington won it last year, didn't they?"

"New Series, new champions."

"Ah, this guy. Always the optimist. Always looking for that bright side."

"Statistics don't lie."

"Stats don't mean nothin' without the heart. Ain't that right, miss?"

Lilly looked surprised. "I suppose so."

"You see there? Facts and fate—facts don't mean nothin'. You wanna know who's gonna win a game? You gotta get your nose out of the paper and get your hinder—pardon my language, miss—get yourself into the game. Take a whiff of the field and listen to the crowd. Feel that heart. Then you know who's gonna go all the way. You remember what it's like to be in the park, don't you, Moon?"

"I do."

"You ever been to a ball game, miss?"

"Lots," she said, and it was the single most interesting word she'd said all day.

"Then you know. Nothin' like it. Fourth floor."

Never before had he been so unprepared for the end of an elevator ride, and when Mr. Toretta slid open the gate, Cullen stepped into the hallway reluctantly.

When they were alone in the hallway, she asked if he was still friends with Mr. Toretta's son.

"Tony died in the war." He concentrated on the lettering across the frosted glass.

"Oh, I'm so sorry. Wait a minute." She covered his hand with hers before he could open the door. "When we're in there, should I call you Mr. Burnside?"

"It doesn't matter. Once you're working, you won't see me much."

The same surprise that Mr. Toretta had expressed was multiplied tenfold once Cullen walked into his office. The clattering of typewriter keys went uninterrupted, although eyebrows danced up and down. Whether the secretaries' curiosity was aroused by his unscheduled appearance or by Lilly he couldn't say, but within seconds Hilda Meyers was striding down the aisle between the desks, looking her usual unflappable self.

"Good morning, Mr. Burnside."

"Good morning, Miss Meyers. May I present Miss Lilly Margolis?"

At first Hilda acknowledged Lilly's presence, taking no more account of her than she would some trifling pest. But then her granite-hard gaze wavered from Lilly to him and back before she said, "Ah yes. Miss Margolis. What a pleasure to meet you." Then to Cullen, "I did get that letter sent off the other day." She turned and began walking toward his office. As usual, he followed, gesturing for Lilly to do the same. "In fact," Hilda continued, talking as she looked straight ahead, "I sent it by telegram once we knew we'd found the correct recipient."

"You what?" He stopped, and Lilly ran right into him. "My office is just around that corner," he said. "Name's on the door. Wait for me there."

When Hilda and he were alone, or alone as they could be in the middle of the typing pool, he leaned close. "I didn't tell you to send a telegram."

"I—I'm sorry, Mr. Burnside." Perhaps she was flappable after all. "When you dictated the message, it seemed quite urgent. And I have the text, you said you wanted"—she looked to see if Lilly had turned the corner—"'*the matter*' resolved as quickly as possible. Have you had a response?"

"You are my secretary, Miss Meyers. This is a private affair."

"Of course, Mr. Burnside."

"Now phone up to the reading room and tell them a Miss Margolis will be up shortly to begin a term of employment there."

"Then she *is* to stay, sir. Oh—forgive me. Private matter. Yes sir."

"Better yet, go up there and tell them to see that she has a space prepared to start today."

He walked in to find Lilly sitting on top of his desk.

"If you don't mind..." He made his way around to his chair.

"Not at all." She hopped off and then sat in one of the leather chairs facing him. "Nice place here. Lots of light."

"The higher up in the company, the more windows."

"Why don't you spend more time here instead of at home?"

"Listen." He held a hand to his ear.

"I don't hear anything."

"Shhh..." It always took a moment for the silence to really settle, but then, always, there it was, the incessant ratting and tatting of typewriters.

Sometimes, if he closed his eyes, he could imagine himself back in his tent or in the trenches, listening to the gunfire. Incessant. Every shot a bullet, every bullet a body. Once he'd dozed off at his desk and spent the first few minutes of waking too terrified to leave his desk.

"Just the typewriters."

"They bother me."

She shrugged. "So, what's this job?"

"In our reading room."

"You pay people to read?"

"Our company has interests and holdings in other companies all over the country. We like to remain abreast of what's happening. So we have a staff that reads all the regional newspapers—every major publication in the United States—looking for stories related to our business interests. You will be assigned several publications, and you will read through them—every word—every day. And if you find something we need to know about, you'll clip it, put it in an envelope, and give it to your supervisor."

Lilly contorted her body into an exaggerated yawn. "I'm sorry. Could you start again? I fell asleep just listening to that."

"I admit it's not as glamorous as selling lotions door to door."

"Oh, there's no comparison. But really, Moon—can I call you Moon?"

"Can I stop you?"

She leaned her elbows on the desk. "Do you want to?"

Why did he have to have such an efficient secretary?

Three loud raps sounded on his door, which could mean only one thing. Before he could respond, it flew open and the expansive form of Bill Owens filled the frame.

"Burnsie!" His eyes zeroed in on Lilly. "And I shall never doubt the office gossip again. Although the girls in the typing pool said you were on the ugly side, but that's women for you. Tearing each other apart."

"Come in," Cullen said, feeling as useless as the command.

"Try and stop me." In a flash he'd taken Lilly's hand. "You must be the lovely Lilly." He planted a kiss on the back of her wrist, nearly sending Cullen out of his seat.

"Do I know you?" She indulged his brutish friend, though Cullen was sure she wanted to tug her hand away, and he was three seconds shy of helping her do just that.

"This is another childhood friend of mine, Bill Owens. I believe you attended a social function at his home the other night."

"Oh." And now she did pull her hand away, and Cullen couldn't help smiling as she shook her hand, as if to dislodge his kiss. "I believe you were the host of honor."

Bill hooked his thumbs in his suspenders. "I might spend most of my days in the offices of my favorite client, but not even thirty years old and I'm full partner in one of the biggest law firms in the state."

"It's your daddy's firm, isn't it?" Lilly slumped in her chair, looking unimpressed.

"Maybe"—he placed one foot on the chair next to Lilly and leaned forward, looming over her like a panther ready to pounce—"but I'm my own man."

"Actually," Cullen said, "a great deal of you belongs to Julia. Your wife."

"I met her at the party," Lilly said. "Charming woman."

Cullen said nothing. None of the three of them believed that.

"Well, I must apologize," Bill said, "for being a dreadful host. I'm afraid I didn't have a chance to meet you and thank you for attending my little soiree."

"That's all right. I was really more of a crasher."

"Well, a doll like you can crash my place any time she wants. But I guess you're the king of that, right, Burnsie?"

"Lay off, Bill."

He flashed a smile—thick-lipped with big square teeth—and wedged his bulk into the chair next to Lilly. "So tell me. What's a sweet thing like her doing in this place?"

"Burnsie's giving me a job." She uncrossed and recrossed her legs. "Can I call you *Burnsie*?"

"No."

"A job?" Bill sounded thrilled. "Don't tell me you're finally getting rid of that old apple Meyers."

"He wants me to work in the reading room."

"What are you, nuts? You can't take a girl like this and stuff her in some kind of dungeon—"

"It's on the fifth floor."

"Attic, then. Couple of years, and her eyes'll be crossed, her back all bent. She'll go in looking like Clara Bow and come out Lon Chaney."

She laughed, clapping her hands and lifting her feet in a little kick. "You're a scream. Tell me, do you need a secretary? I've got two weeks of school."

"What do you say, boss? If we're puttin' her on the payroll, why not let her be someplace where she'll be more appreciated for her very special talents?"

"Oh yes, Moonsie." She spoke the nickname like a cat dripping in cream. "Please let me work for Mr. Owens. I need all the exercise I'll get when he's chasing me down the hall."

"You heard the lady," Cullen said. "Now, go."

Bill looked incredulous. "Just like that?" He turned to Lilly. "Sweetie, please. You going to let him kick me out like that?"

"Sorry. Whatever Moonsie says goes."

Bill reached right over, grasped Lilly's shoulders in his massive hands, and pulled her close, planting a loud kiss right on her cheek. "Then you do what he says. He's one of the best guys I know."

Before Bill could leave the room, Cullen called out, "By the way, anybody suing us?"

"Not this week."

"Good job."

There was a vacuumlike silence after he left, soon enough filled in by the sound of the typewriters.

"He's a goof."

"He's a good lawyer and a good friend."

"Just what everybody needs."

"So about the job?"

She shook her head slowly, and he found himself missing the unruly curls that normally fell across her cheek. "It's not for me, Moonsie."

"You haven't even tried it on for size."

"Why the change of heart? I asked you about working here earlier and you wouldn't hear of it. If it's about this morning, I'm sorry. I'll keep my mouth shut from now on, I promise."

"If anything, this morning should have made you realize how fragile Mother is. I want to be sure that you're taken care of—that you have somewhere to go when it's time for you to...go."

"So I'm to live in the reading room?"

"The job pays well."

"How well?"

He thought, calculating as quickly as he could. "Fifteen a week. That should be more than enough for you to rent a nice room and have a good amount of pocket money."

"And glasses?"

"If necessary." Part of him hated Bill Owens. "Just give it a week. Two, tops. It's not so bad. We own properties in California. I could make sure you get all the Hollywood papers."

Something changed. "Really?"

"Plus we own a couple of theaters in New York, so it's good to know what shows are doing well..."

"Now that could be interesting."

Interesting, indeed. Never mind that he was grossly misrepresenting the reading-room job, that he'd never in his life taken seriously any of the New York theaters. The chances that any of their California holdings would be mentioned in an entertainment newspaper were next to none, seeing that they were nowhere near Hollywood, but he'd see to it that the company started taking subscriptions tomorrow. First, he'd have to find out the names of such papers. That would be Hilda Meyers's responsibility. She was so efficient, after all.

Another knock sounded at the door, this one smaller. "Yes?" he called out, but so much talking—all morning, in fact—and his voice was becoming paper thin.

Lilly echoed him, though, and the door opened to allow a boy in. He was about twelve years old, his hair an unruly mass of curls.

"Western Union—gee whiz, mister. What happened to your face?"

Lilly looked shocked and hurt, but this wasn't the first time Cullen had confronted the brute honesty of children. In some ways it was easier to handle than the overly polite conversation with somebody desperately trying not to look at his scars.

"War."

"Krauts get you with the mustard gas?"

"Yes, but they didn't kill me."

The boy offered a salute, which Cullen returned before reaching out for the telegram. He opened his top desk drawer, fished a quarter out of a little jar, and handed it to the boy.

"Gee thanks!" He offered a grin and tore out of the office.

In his wake, Cullen took the telegram out of its envelope, and when he saw the origin, all the warm, pleasing thoughts of the previous moments vanished.

Miresburgh, Pennsylvania. Lilly's mother. And it didn't take long to read its content. Three words:

Send her home.

"What is it?" She stood and, before he knew it, actually had the corner of the paper pinched between her fingers.

"It's nothing." He moved it out of her reach as nonchalantly as possible. "Just business."

"Well, I'm an employee now, right? I'm a reader, so let me read."

"This isn't for you—"

But apparently Lilly didn't realize that the playfulness, the easy, almost flirtatious time was over, because she was once again on top of the desk, all arms about him, reaching and grasping.

"Come on, Moonsie. What corporate secrets could I possibly spill?"

"I'm telling you, it's just—"

"Got it." Her voice was breathless with triumph, and in any other circumstance he might be offering her playful congratulations or indulging in an exaggerated sulk. As it was, he simply stood, hands in his pockets, waiting.

"This is from..." And her eyes took it in. Not that there was much to see. An office of origin, a date stamp, and three words. "Send her home."

They sounded worse when she said them.

She crawled down from the desk looking wounded. "You wrote to my mother?"

"I was worried."

"My *mother*? How *dare* you? Do you have any idea what this *means*?"

"I wanted her to know you were safe." Partly true.

She looked like she had so much more to say. Volumes and volumes of accusations and protest. Instead she crumpled the paper and threw it on the desk.

And then she walked away.

15

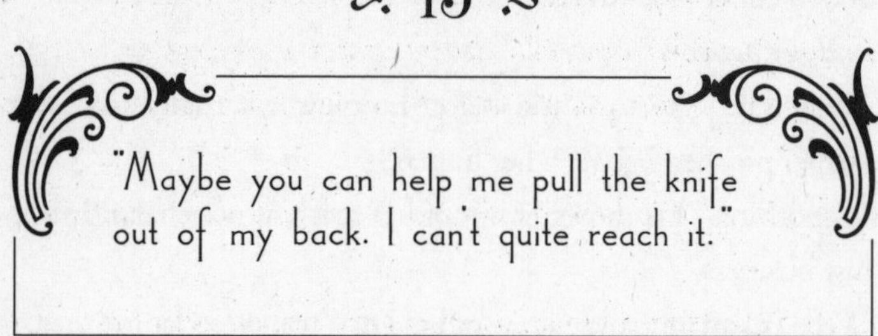

Lilly ran straight out of his office and up through the sea of typists. The clattering of their keyboards had a new sinister dimension with the whispers and titters, but she wouldn't stop to confront them. She headed straight for the door with the words *Burnside Enterprises* reading backward through the glass. She was almost there when she plowed into a massive barrel of a chest. She bounced back, held steady by the beefy hands of Bill Owens.

"Slow down there, sweetheart. You got some sort of spark in your socks?"

"If Mr. Burnside comes looking for me, tell him I—tell him I'm in the ladies' room."

"Burnsie? He try something fresh with you?"

"Just tell him." She wrenched herself out of his grip—a feat in which she'd become somewhat of an expert—and flew through the door. The ladies' powder room was to the left, according to the sign, the stairs to the right, and the elevator straight ahead. She headed for the stairs.

The wide marble steps made an echoing clump under her shoes. She'd be downstairs and out of this building before Cullen knew she'd gone. But where to go was another question. Once in the lobby, she tore across the floor, artfully dodging shoulders and suits, heading for the side entrance, not realizing that this would take her straight to the elevator.

The door slid open and she was face to face with Cullen. "Get away from me."

"Lilly, please." He looked over her head and all around. "Let me explain."

Mr. Toretta wedged himself between the two of them. "Hey, is there a problem here?"

"No," Cullen said.

"I wasn't talkin' to you, Moon." He turned to Lilly. "Everything all right, miss?"

"No." She spun around. "Maybe you can help me pull the knife out of my back. I can't quite reach it."

"I think you're being a little dramatic—"

"Don't touch me! And don't follow me."

A small crowd of onlookers had gathered by this time, and she burst through them all. She reached the side door and threw it open, knocking a delivery boy with a stack of boxes nearly off his feet. The coolness of the morning was long gone, but still her face burned hotter than the heat coming from the fledgling afternoon sun.

She closed her eyes and took two deep breaths. Three, trying to remember how she'd gotten here. Some parts of the city were still unfamiliar, and she'd been much too preoccupied with the proximity of Cullen in the backseat to pay much attention to the route.

Not that she knew where to go. She'd obviously overstayed her welcome with the Burnsides. Cullen had contacted her mother two days ago. Perhaps her first painless step should have been right out the door. But he had allowed her to stay. Arranged for her things to be brought from Myrtle's. Offered her a job.

Send her home.

But for those three words, Lilly might have been able to start up a real life here. She'd teased about the reading job, but it didn't sound so bad. Not too exciting, but fifteen clams a week would buy a lot of shoes. Might even be able to set aside a little, buy her own car. Or a little house. Someplace where she could have friends over and dance, where she'd make the rules and kick everyone out by midnight to cut down on some of the shenanigans that get to happening when a party goes on too long.

But now that Mama knew...

There wouldn't be any more telegrams; those were an expense Ella Margolis wouldn't suffer. But there would be letters, pages upon pages of anger-fueled rambling. One Bible verse after another—all of which promised Lilly a life in hell. Diatribes of warnings and accusations and threats.

The last envelope she'd actually opened was over a year ago, when she'd been sharing a house with three other girls in Atlanta. In a fit of drunken sentimentality, she'd lent her sloppy signature to a Christmas card, forgetting the implications of a return address. What came back was a fat packet of paper, her mother's strident penmanship listing every harlot in Scripture, with a page each on how Lilly was just like them. She spent nearly a month reading those pages over and over until one of the girls took them and burned the whole batch.

Then she'd packed up her bag and ended up here. After such a long silence, she feared Mama might just pack up a bag and come fetch her.

Still on the street, Lilly looked up the side of the building. She could have had a life here. Could have spent countless safe, happy hours reading entertainment newspapers and magazines. Sure, it was a job created by Cullen out of some sense of guilt. She knew what it felt like, what it sounded like, when she was being bought. But men had offered her much less for much more.

She shouldn't have teased him. If she hadn't, she might be up there right now on the fifth floor, following the sour-faced Miss Meyers around, seeing the room where the girls ate their lunch and hung their coats in the winter. She might never have known about the telegram. Never known the extent to which she wasn't wanted. Never known that her mother—

Surely this was the only address Mama had. Whatever he may have said, Cullen wouldn't give some strange woman his home address. He valued his privacy too much. It would serve him right to walk into his office one day and find Ella Margolis storming through, like a wave let loose from a storm, blowing from room to room, pounding on doors in a relentless search for her daughter. Let him try to soothe her. Let him try to speak rationally to the woman. He knew his Scripture; he knew Lilly. Maybe, just maybe, he would say something good.

"Miss?" She had the feeling the man had been calling to her for a while, but this was the first she'd clearly heard him. She looked over her shoulder. Miles, the chauffeur, stood, hat in hand, beside the car.

"Are you and Mr. Burnside ready to go back home?"

For now, it seemed like an answer. She took the five or six steps over to the car and waited for him to open the door.

"Just me." She folded herself into the backseat. "Mr. Burnside said he'd call for you later."

If Miles had any doubt, he quickly masked it, and the next thing she knew, Lilly was headed back to the Burnside house. She didn't pay any attention to the route this time either.

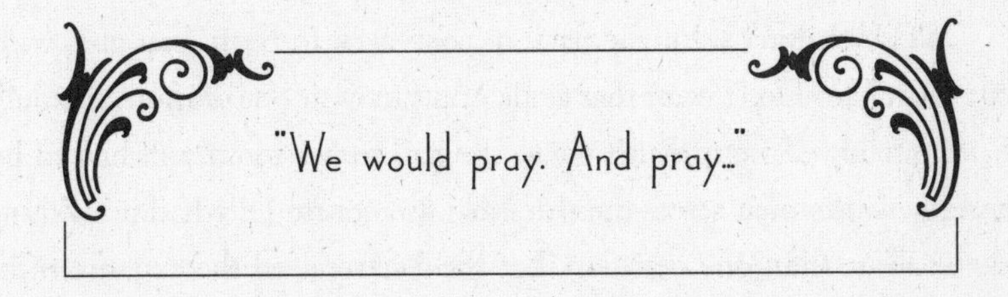

Lilly went straight into the bathroom, stood at the sink, and stared in the mirror. What had looked so sleek and professional an hour ago now made her feel naked and exposed. She loosed the tiny knot at the nape of her neck. The tap turned on full and warm, she bent to bury her head under its surging water, using her fingers to loosen and rinse the pomade out of her hair. Once satisfied, she rubbed it with a towel until it was just damp and went to her room. She kicked the heavy shoes against the wall and dropped the white blouse with its now-damp shoulders to the floor, along with the stifling skirt. She found a soft cotton sleeveless dress and folded a handkerchief into a headband, which she slipped over her damp hair.

In the middle of Lilly's mental debate about whether to put on rouge and powder, Betty Ruth's soft knock sounded at her door.

"I thought I heard you come in," Betty Ruth said once Lilly opened the door. "I thought you'd gone to school with my son, which is odd, because I believe you're a bit too old to be going to school, aren't you?"

There was no way to answer the question without in some way being complicit in Betty Ruth's misconception or adding to her confusion, so Lilly opted to ignore it. Instead she took note of Betty Ruth's wide-brimmed straw hat and dainty green canvas gloves.

"You look like you're ready to do some gardening."

"That's why I came looking for you. Just bushels and bushels of strawberries along the back wall. Would you like to come help me?"

The corners of Lilly's mouth watered. "I love strawberries."

"Then we'll have dishes of them with cream for lunch. Get your hat."

"I don't have one. Not a sun hat, anyway."

"Well, we don't want the back of your neck to burn, you girls with your short hair. Don't want that at all. You can wear one of mine. Come!"

She followed Betty Ruth down the hall to her room and had to be expressly summoned across the threshold. Of course Lilly had peeked inside on more than one occasion, but she'd never seen the expanse of it. This was no mere bedroom; this was a suite. There was a full sitting area with a fireplace and two comfortable stuffed chairs. A tall four-poster was covered with a thick brown quilt and mounds of pillows. The carpet was lush under her bare feet, and the smell of roses filled the air, but lightly so.

The windows were open, and lace curtains fluttered, occasionally whispering against the wall.

"This is a beautiful room."

Betty Ruth opened the door to a closet that spanned the length of a wall. "Oh, I do so love this room. Haven't changed a bit of it since, well, since we moved the baby's bed out."

"Baby Cullen?" She couldn't imagine such a thing.

"Yes, he was—is—our only child. Our only one."

As Betty Ruth rummaged, Lilly took a turn around the room. Pretty trinkets covered nearly every surface; a well-worn Bible, its pages swollen with use, was the only item completely void of delicate fragility.

"My mother has this same book." Lilly ran her finger along the gold-stamped title. "I mean, it looks just like it. She reads it every day."

Betty Ruth walked out of the closet, holding a wide-brimmed green hat of woven straw. "Sounds like a good woman."

"Lots of people think so."

"And do you have a Bible, my dear?"

Lilly shook her head. "I did, but I left it...somewhere."

"My goodness, no straw hat. No Bible. How will you ever survive in the South? When Davis and I married and moved here, those were the first two things his mother gave me. The hat is long gone, long gone, but that is the very Bible she gave me on our wedding day."

"And do you read it every day?"

Betty Ruth walked over and sank into one of the soft stuffed chairs. Nothing in Lilly's childhood home was nearly that soft. "Every morning, every night. Just as the Lord leads me. When Davis was alive, he'd sit right across. Right there." She leaned across and patted the empty cushion. Lilly could well imagine the man she'd seen in so many photographs sitting there, getting a loving pat on his knee. "We'd read together sometimes, sometimes not. But we'd pray. I do remember when Cullen went away, we'd sit here of an evening and pray. And pray. He was... We would pray.

And pray, because he was—now where was he? We would pray..."

Lilly sensed Betty Ruth's agitation. She'd never before been alone with the woman during one of her spells, and without Cullen there to reassure his mother, she had no idea what to say or do. She slipped into the opposite chair and reached for Betty Ruth's hand.

"It's all right, Mrs. Burnside. Cullen's just fine. He's—"

"Get out of that chair!" Betty Ruth stood, dropping the straw hat to the floor, and then she lunged for Lilly. "That is Davis's chair. He sits there and we pray. Every evening, together, we pray—"

She'd grabbed the front of Lilly's dress. Lilly covered Betty Ruth's hands with her own, wedging her thumb within those tight little fists, releasing their grip. Soon the woman was flush against her, arms wrapped tight around her waist. Betty Ruth's hat fell from her head; Lilly stroked her back, soothing, saying nothing.

"I still pray for him, you know." Her voice was soft against Lilly's heart.

"Of course you do."

"A mother always prays for her children, no matter how old they get. And I pray for him, because I know something is wrong. Something isn't right, so I pray..."

"That's good. Cullen's lucky."

Betty Ruth relaxed in Lilly's arms, and when she thought it was safe to do so, Lilly backed away, stooped to pick up the green hat, and handed Betty Ruth's to her.

"This is lovely."

"It's far too large for me. You may have it."

Lilly placed it on her head and walked over to the mirror above the white lacquered dresser. The wide brim extended nearly to her shoulders, and a yellow calico ribbon was stitched along the crown. When she saw her reflection, she looked headless. Faceless, actually, as everything above her neck disappeared into the hat's shadow. "It's perfect."

"Well, then, let's go to the garden."

16

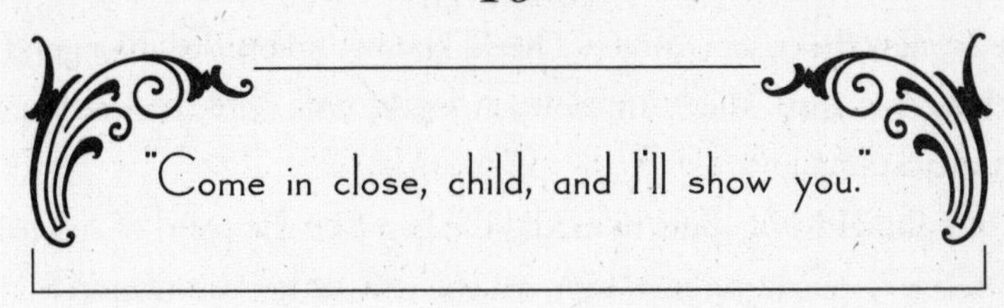

The strawberry plants grew from a planter box that ran the length of the yard's back wall. Bright red berries peeped from between lush green leaves, almost hidden. At least, this was the first time Lilly had taken notice of them.

"I didn't think strawberries grew this late."

Betty Ruth held a finger to her lips. "Shhh. They're not supposed to. But I employ a fabulous gardener. What's the use having this much money if you can't have strawberries in October?" She gave Lilly a small basket to loop over her wrist. "I'm afraid I don't have gloves for you."

"That's all right. I've never picked strawberries before, so I'd rather know what it feels like."

"Never picked a strawberry?"

"Never picked anything."

"Well, I never thought I'd see the day. Come in close, child, and I'll show you."

Lilly crouched down at eye level with Betty Ruth, ready to follow instruction.

"First of all, you have to be so careful in how you handle the berries. So very careful. They may look hearty, but they bruise easy. You might not be able to tell it now, and you can just grab them and pull them and toss them in the basket. And they might look just fine, just fine. But when it's time to enjoy them, you can see. They'll be soft and bruised. Not good for anything but jam. They can fool you, make you think they're tougher than they are."

She showed Lilly how to cradle the berry in the palm of her hand, then reach to pinch the stem between the nails of her thumb and middle finger. Lilly obeyed, feeling the crispness as her thumb pierced the thin green skin.

"But you don't tug on it. Don't tug. That pinch lets it know what's coming. Gives the stem a chance to loosen up and let go. Ripping's too hard, but this gives it time to think. Little by little, each twist, it remembers and remembers, but it starts to realize it can't hold on to that fruit forever. It's got a bigger purpose, but it decides when it's time to"—the stem snapped—"let go."

The strawberry, now loose, rolled in Lilly's palm, and she was about to drop it in her basket when Lilly stopped her.

"Oh no. Now you have to go to the next one and lift this little one up. Let them touch each other."

"Why?"

"Oh, it's such a frightening thing, being ripped from your stem, wouldn't you think? How comforting it must be to know you're not alone. That you have another little berry friend waiting to share a new life with you, don't you think?"

"Yes." Lilly's throat burned as she twisted the second stem, feeling the soft touch between the two berries in her hand.

"I suppose most people think I'm silly, talking this nonsense about a bunch of strawberries."

"I don't think you're silly at all." The second stem broke, and the berries rolled toward each other.

"Now, you'll do the third one just the same, until your hand is so full you can't hold any more."

"All right." She noticed Betty Ruth had yet to pick any berries of her own. Instead she stood right beside her, moving her little body like a shadow, reaching almost to where Lilly reached, touching almost what she touched.

"It seems to me that God tells us all kinds of little stories in His creation, all kinds of little stories."

"I could listen to you tell them to me all day." Lilly was on her fourth berry. "I don't think I can hold any more."

Betty Ruth inspected and nodded. "Now you can put them gently in the basket. Set your fingers down in it and let them roll off. See? If you dropped them one at a time, they'd have one shock after another. Drop! Drop! Plop! Plop! But this is one gentle roll, and they cushion each other. And then you start again."

They worked together. Occasionally Lilly asked if a berry looked ready to be picked, but for the most part, the only sound was the faint rustling of the leaves and Betty Ruth's humming.

"I know that song," Lilly said after a while. "We used to sing it in church."

"I come to the garden alone," Betty Ruth sang, inviting Lilly to join.

"Oh, I don't remember the words."

"That's a shame." She went back to humming.

"No, please." Lilly rolled a handful of strawberries into her basket. "I'd love to hear it."

And so down the row they went, Betty Ruth's sweet voice singing the story of a woman in a garden, alone. By the time she sang the familiar chorus a third time, she nudged Lilly with her shoulder, as if she wouldn't continue until the girl joined her. Giggling, the two women exaggerated the first two notes, stringing them out like a wheezing organ.

"Aaaaaaaaaaaannnnnd He walks with me, and He talks with me,
And He tells me I am His own;
And the joy we share as we tarry there,
None other has ever known."

Betty Ruth clapped her gloved hands. "You have a lovely voice. Just lovely. My goodness, another talent discovered."

"Can I tell you a secret?"

"Of course." They were picking side by side again.

"I never knew that song was about God. I mean, I knew because we sang it in church. But I used to imagine it was just a love story. I used to think, that's what I want. Just a man to walk and talk with me." And for a few days, she thought she'd found it.

"But, my dear, it *is* a love story. The way God loves us, it's the greatest of all love stories."

Lilly pushed away the leaves. "I've never felt that way."

"Never felt that God loves you?"

How grateful Lilly was to have the wide green brim to hide her face. "I've never felt like anybody loved me. I never knew my father, and I think Mama always blamed me for running him off. He didn't want no baby." She said the last two words in her mother's thin, clipped tone. "And when she talked about God, well, it's nothing like what you have to say. She just said that God wants me to have long hair and long skirts and to be good. But I...I don't know how to be good. Not good enough. Never good enough."

She ripped the strawberry from its stem, sending the whole plant trembling. "Oh, I'm sorry," she said, not knowing if she spoke to Betty Ruth or the berry itself.

"There, there, dear," Betty Ruth said. "I like to believe God has better things to worry about than the latest fashions, though I do wonder what will become of my Cullen when he grows up. Goodness! What will the girls be wearing then?"

Lilly couldn't help it; she laughed into the back of her hand.

"But your mother was right about one thing. God does want us to be good, and don't you dare tell me you don't know how. Don't know how? Why, that's ridiculous."

"I try—"

"Nonsense. And how can you not know that God loves you? Look around."

"I've never had anything like this before."

"Look in your basket. What do you see?"

"Strawberries."

"Now, take one out. Go ahead, the biggest, reddest, juiciest one you can find."

Lilly rolled them to and fro, but really, there was one she had in mind. She found it near the bottom and pulled it out.

"Now, eat it."

"But they're for lunch."

"They're my strawberries; they're for when I say. Eat it."

Lilly licked her lips, then popped the whole berry in her mouth, sinking her teeth just at the base of its little green collar. Her mouth filled with the sweet juice, overfilled, spilling out at the corners. Worried for her dress, she brought her hand up, catching what she could with the back of her wrist, wiping her forearm across her chin. She chewed and swallowed and tasted the residue off her skin.

"How was that?"

"Yummy."

"So how could you ever eat another strawberry and not know that God loves you? I want you to think about that every time you eat a strawberry. Do you hear me?"

Lilly moved the brim of her hat away with a salute. "Yes m'am."

They resumed their picking, and even continued singing, with Betty Ruth prompting Lilly along on the verses. Try as she might, Lilly could not capture the sense of peace the song brought to Betty Ruth. No doubt the same trick in her brain that allowed her to ignore the ugliness of life also made real beauty elusive. For Betty Ruth, God was here, in this garden. She probably talked out loud to Him, probably heard Him too, speaking to her, just like the song said. Loud and clear.

But not Lilly. She sang to please Betty Ruth. She sang because concentrating on the lyrics kept her from thinking about her mother's telegram. Maybe if Mama had a garden… Most of all, Lilly sang so she could forget the last time she sang in this garden. In the moonlight, with Cullen. The song that used to be just a silly tune, something that she and her friends would sing in a rousing, booze-driven performance, accompanied by a well-worn recording.

Just a girl that men forget. That's what she'd been a week ago. And happily so. But something changed when… She giggled.

Betty Ruth stopped midverse. "Your laugh is beautiful, my dear. Just as lovely as the music."

"I was just thinking. This song is like how I met you, when I came to the garden. Alone."

Betty Ruth gave a trill of a laugh. "That's when you met my son. As I recall, you met me the day before."

"You remember?"

"Of course I do, don't be silly."

"And do you think you'd remember me if I…if I went away?"

"You, my child, are written on my heart. As it beats, I shall love you."

The basket grew heavy on Lilly's arm, and she made an effort not to drop it as her body withstood the wave of Betty Ruth's words. "You love me?"

"Darling, who wouldn't love you?"

Even though the woman barely came to Lilly's shoulder, she wanted to go to the shade of the red-tipped maple and crawl into her lap. The proclamation had a far less dramatic effect on Betty Ruth, who was now back singing to the strawberries, but Lilly remained still.

She was loved, loved by this woman who barely knew her.

She couldn't leave this. She couldn't go home. Mama's command didn't come from love; it came from something darker, and Lilly could ignore it, forever. Or at least as long as Cullen would allow.

"There, I think that's enough, don't you?"

Both small baskets were nearly filled with the bright ripe berries, and the sun was beginning to feel more than warm on Lilly's back. "I think so."

"Good. I told Eugenia to set up some iced mint tea in the front parlor. I think I'll read in there until lunchtime. You may join me if you wish."

Lilly lifted the brim of her hat to look at Betty Ruth before answering. "All right." Something had changed in just the last few moments. The lilt was gone from her voice, giving her words an almost authoritative tone they'd never had before.

"Here, give me your basket." She held out her gloved hand. "I'll take it in for you. Eugenia doesn't like strangers in her kitchen."

Stranger? Lilly felt a lump in her throat ten times the size of a strawberry.

Oh, God, she thought, being that He must be in the garden, *it's beginning. Just like Cullen said.*

She handed over her basket, not wanting to risk upsetting Betty Ruth with the news that Lilly had often been in Eugenia's kitchen, though truthfully, the woman had never welcomed her presence. Once inside, Betty Ruth peeled off to the left, and Lilly went upstairs to hang her green straw hat on the hat rack behind her door and wash her hands in the bathroom sink. Then she returned to her room to gather the latest edition of *Cosmopolitan* and take the ribbon from her hair, using her fingers to both coax and tame the curls.

When she walked back out into the hallway, the sight of Cullen waiting startled her, and she nearly dropped her magazine.

"Sorry," he said, his voice dry. "I have that effect on people."

"You just scared me is all. I wasn't expecting you."

"I guess I'm grateful Miles thought to come back for me."

"He's a good man. You're surrounded by good people just waiting to do your bidding. Fetch my clothes, send your telegrams..."

She attempted to walk past him in the hall, but he blocked her.

"Let me explain."

"Let me get by." Lilly won, perhaps because he was too much of a gentleman to push back when she thrust her shoulder into his withered arm. But he did follow, his voice trailing behind her every step.

"I was worried about you. Young girl, all alone, living in some boardinghouse. And then, to hear that Bill Owens talk about you—girls like you—"

She spun around in the middle of a step. "What's that supposed to mean?"

"What he said you were, or what he—"

She was on her way again, heading straight for the front parlor.

"I thought, somewhere, this girl has to have a mother who cares about her."

"You were wrong."

Two electric fans crossed their breezes from opposite corners of the parlor, and a pitcher of iced tea and two glasses sat on a silver tray on top of the coffee table in the center of the room. There was a silent beat before he spoke, and Lilly knew he was catching his breath. Much as she would have liked to storm over him with her argument, she allowed that moment of peace and stood still, letting the fan blow cool against her skin.

"I admit," he said, then breathed, "I was wrong not to tell you. To go behind your back. But I'm not wrong about the fact that she cares about you."

"My mother hates me."

"Mothers don't hate their children."

"Mine does."

"Maybe if you talked to her. You could telephone, long distance. Just call her."

"No."

"Or write to her? Just let her know that you're safe. She's probably worried."

"I don't care if she is."

"She's your mother. She loves you."

"No!" Lilly threw her magazine to the sofa, where its pages splayed before falling to the floor. She strode across the room to where Cullen had stopped in the doorway. "My mother hates me. She hates everything about me. *Your* mother loves me."

"She does now—"

"Well, that's enough for me. One week, and I'm happier than I ever remember being in my entire life. You grew up with this. You have a lifetime of memories and joy and...and, *her.* Don't be so selfish! Let me have what I can. I believe you, I know it won't last forever, but—"

"What do you mean you '*know*'?"

She stopped short and rocked back on her heels. "What do I mean?"

"You said you know it won't last. What's happened?"

Lilly cringed under his scrutiny. "I—nothing. We were picking strawberries in the garden—"

"Where is she now? Where's Mother?"

"In the kitchen, I think."

"Wait here."

She stood, rooted in place. How pathetic she must seem. Like those girls, the ones *like her,* who threw themselves at men. Only here she was, face to face with a rich eligible bachelor, throwing herself at his mother. But she'd traveled enough roads to know that another man—rich, bachelor, or otherwise—was around the next bend. Love like Betty Ruth offered, that was—

Suddenly a scream pierced her thoughts.

"Betty Ruth?" Lilly called the name over and over as she ran through the entry hall, back to the breakfast room, and over to the kitchen. At first the screams were just short bursts of panic and terror, but as Lilly got closer, they took on language.

"Who are you?"

And then a pause.

"Where did you—?"

And another. The words weren't clear, but the soft rasp of Cullen's voice was unmistakable, even at this distance.

"Oh, God! Oh, God! What happened? What happened to my son? Oh, God! My boy!"

Lilly rounded the corner into the kitchen, nearly slipping as her foot hit one of the dozens of strawberries rolling all over the floor. Eugenie stood frozen at the sink, paring knife in hand, and Betty Ruth was backed up to the icebox, her face buried in her juice-stained hands. Cullen's back was to her, but Lilly knew well enough how to interpret the stoop in his posture, the hanging of his head, and the arm, twisted and useless, at his side.

"You." Eugenie gestured vaguely with the knife. "You just get yourself out of here. Caused enough trouble I'd say."

"It's not Lilly's fault," Cullen said.

At the mention of the name, Betty Ruth's eyes peeked out from between her fingers. "Who are you?"

Lilly took another step and tried to keep her voice from shaking. "It's me, Betty Ruth. Lilly."

Betty Ruth looked at her, then at Cullen, and fell to the floor.

17

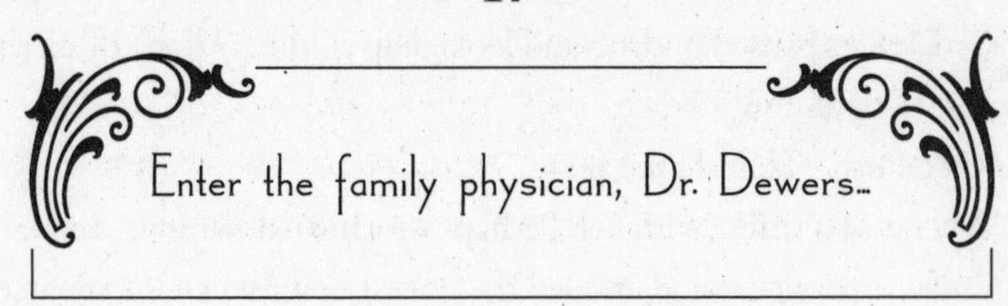

Enter the family physician, Dr. Dewers...

Cullen paced the hall outside of his mother's room for the entire hour, measuring prayers with his steps. He relived the moment over and over: his mother's face, the terror of seeing for the first time the man he had become. And for the first time, he felt ashamed. That was new.

He knew well the searing pain of the burns, the fight that came with every breath, the fear that welled up with every step he took out of the house, the apology that he swallowed every time a frightened child was pulled to its mother's side. But she'd looked at Cullen with both fear and accusation, like he'd been hiding a secret in plain sight.

Now he faced Dr. Dewers, a small man who seemed incapable of carrying on a conversation without simultaneously cleaning his spectacles. He pulled a handkerchief from his vest pocket and began a ritualistic rubbing of the lenses.

Cullen could not wait for the glasses to be thoroughly clean. "How is she?"

"Resting peacefully. I gave her a mild sedative."

"Her heart?"

"Stable."

"Thank you, God." Cullen's heart swelled with more gratitude than he could speak out loud. "Can I go in and see her?"

Dr. Dewers paused midrub and looked up at him. "I don't think that's a good idea right now."

"Of course." That shame again.

"My nurse is sitting with her. Perhaps we can go downstairs and talk?"

Cullen gave a curt nod and led the doctor downstairs, unprepared to find Lilly sitting on the bottom step. She was obviously lost in her own thoughts, as he had to clear his throat to get her attention before she jumped up.

"How is she?"

"Stable," Cullen said, unwilling to share anything more than the doctor's single-word reply. He turned to Dr. Dewers. "We can talk in my fa—my office."

"Are you sure?" Lilly seemed determined to place herself in his path. "I helped Eugenie make up a tray of sandwiches. You haven't had lunch yet, so you must be starving."

Dr. Dewers rocked back on his tiny heels, taking in the entire vision of Lilly, who, despite the bedraggled ribbon hanging from her hair and the dot of sunburn on her shoulders, still managed to make a fetching picture.

"I could use some lunch."

"Fine," Cullen said. "Lilly, you can bring the tray into my office."

Dr. Dewers's eyebrows shot up above the rim of his spectacles. "So you are Lilly?"

"Why, yes." The girl's face lit up. "Did she ask about me?"

"She mentioned you, yes." Dr. Dewers took off his glasses and held them out, inspecting for spots. "You know, Cullen, I think it might be important to include this young lady in our conversation. With your permission, of course."

"Would you like to be included in our conversation?" Cullen's tone held no invitation.

"Oh yes!" She hopped up and down, as if she'd been invited to a birthday party rather than a discussion of his mother's collapse, but Dr. Dewers seemed charmed.

He folded his glasses and placed them in his front shirt pocket, offering his arm to Lilly, escort her to the kitchen, where a tray piled high with triangular sandwiches sat in the middle of the table, along with the pitcher of iced tea from earlier. Never mind that it might be upsetting to Cullen to come back into the same room where his mother had fainted dead away just a short time ago.

Lilly looked at her little lunchtime spread with pride and directed Dr. Dewers to sit.

As he looked down to pull out his chair, he said, "Goodness. Is that a cut on your foot?"

Lilly lifted it. "No, just strawberry juice." Her chin quivered and she looked away.

Cullen took the chair opposite the doctor, leaving Lilly to sit at the head of the table. She went about filling plates and pouring tea while Dr. Dewers invited Cullen to tell him exactly what happened.

"I walked into the kitchen. Mother and Eugenie—she's our housekeeper and cook—were at the sink."

"Cleaning strawberries," Lilly interjected. "Betty Ruth didn't want me to—"

Cullen held up a hand. "I'd been having a conversation with Miss Margolis, and she said something that made me feel concerned about Mother's health. So I came in here to check on her, and the moment she saw me..." He looked away, concentrating on the curtains above the sink.

"She screamed." The girl probably thought she was being helpful, but she shrank away when Cullen glared at her. "Well, she did."

"It was more than a scream." Cullen got up from the table and walked over to the icebox and leaned against it. "She was in shock. Complete and utter shock. And, something else."

Suddenly hungry, he grabbed a sandwich and ate it as he strode around the kitchen. "It was like when I was little, and I'd be outside playing with my friends, and something would happen. I'd fall and skin my knee, tear my pants, and when I ran to her, she'd be this mix of anger and surprise. And if I was really hurt, this guilt. As if she'd caused it or had failed to protect me in some way."

"Mm-hmm." Dr. Dewers chewed thoughtfully.

"Can you imagine, I'm perfectly fine, walk out that door, and then walk back in looking like this?"

"I was waiting for this to happen," Dr. Dewers said. "I knew it was only a matter of time."

"Doctor, what's wrong with her?" Lilly tapped her hair ribbon. "In here?"

"I am not a psychiatrist, but I have studied a little on Mrs. Burnside's behalf. It's a selective senility. She allows her mind only to process so much information at a time. Picking and choosing, if you will, what she wants to know. Suppressing the rest. But it is interesting that this would come on so suddenly. Have there been any changes in the house? Anything stressful?"

Cullen leaned against the icebox and pointed his last bite of sandwich at Lilly. "Her."

"Interesting." He took his glasses out of his pocket and began cleaning them with his napkin. "And you..."

"I..."

"Mother has grown quite fond of Lilly."

"She loves me."

"And how is it you have come to be in this house?"

Cullen continued walking his slow circle around the table as Lilly explained everything that had happened from the time she knocked on the door selling cheap cosmetics to the moment she stepped on the strawberry on the floor. She failed to give any details about the party with Bill

Owens but spent excruciating detail on her midmorning conversation in the garden.

"And she, Betty Ruth, just sounded different."

"Different, how?"

"Less lost."

"Interesting."

"Yes, Doctor, it's interesting. Now what do we do for Mother?"

"For her heart, keep her resting comfortably. I'll be by in the morning, but she is not to get out of bed for any reason until I say, understood?"

"Absolutely," Cullen said.

"Posi-lutely." Lilly looked pleased at the doctor's smile.

"And, Cullen," he said, "I know this might sound harsh, but I don't think it's a good idea for you to visit her just yet. We don't want to take the risk of another shock. Even if she says she remembers, she might not."

"For how long?"

"That I don't know. In the meantime, we have the lovely Lilly here. I'd like her to spend as much time as she can with her, and I'll consult with you tomorrow."

"All righty!" Lilly sat up a little taller in her chair, making Cullen want to knock the legs out from underneath her.

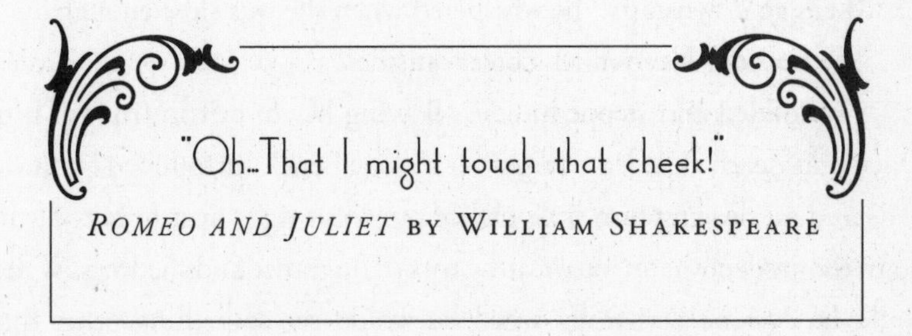

Later, Cullen found himself once again outside Mother's room, only this time he wasn't praying. He stood just outside the open door, watching. Lilly sat at the bedside, never taking her eyes off the tiny woman, even though the sleeping Betty Ruth did nothing to deserve such attention.

How had a stranger managed to earn such a respected place? How was it that in just a few short days, Lilly Margolis—whoever she was—earned the right to sit bedside vigil, while Cullen—the only son and heir—got booted to the hall?

He must have made a sound, because Lilly looked up and offered him a smile warmer than the lamplight. She lifted her hand and beckoned silently, but he shook his head. She beckoned more forcefully, then folded her hands together and touched them to her face, indicating that Mother was in a deep sleep.

"Oh, that I were a glove upon that hand." He shook his head again to clear his thoughts. Here his mother lay, sedated from shock, and he was quoting *Romeo and Juliet.* Instead he crooked his finger toward Lilly, summoning her to him. When she didn't respond, he repeated the same sleeping gesture, then pointed to the very capable nurse who sat in the corner reading a magazine and looking like she disapproved of the silent conversation happening in her patient's room.

After a last lingering look at Betty Ruth, Lilly tiptoed across the room—unnecessary, seeing that her feet were, as always, bare.

"Let's go downstairs," he whispered when she was close enough.

"Or outside? It's so much cooler outside."

He nodded and stepped aside, allowing her to exit in front of him. Once outside, she headed straight for a stone bench surrounded by flower beds and sat, leaving him little choice but to sit right next to her. At this hour, the garden was an intoxicating mix of fragrance and shadows. Where could he ever be with Lilly when he would see something other than beauty around her? Even his office, with its stark colors and sour faces, had taken its first step toward being a place of splendor the minute she walked through the door.

Then her hand was on his knee. "It wasn't your fault."

He shifted away. "I know that."

"Isn't it better, even a little bit, that she can see you for who you really are?"

"Do you think this is who I really am?"

She didn't answer, and he didn't blame her. It wasn't a fair question. How would she know?

"How long has she been this way? Forgetful, I mean?"

"*Forgetful.* That's a good word for it. I guess always, a little bit, but my father always kept her so sheltered. If they went anywhere, he was always right at her side, whispering in her ear, reminding her of who people were and how they were acquainted."

"And now you take care of her?"

"Mother's world is small. She doesn't like to go out, so we don't go out."

"Her life doesn't have to be yours, you know."

He looked at her and smiled. "I don't like to go out much either."

His ear picked up the song of a cicada from somewhere in the yard, and its volume grew with the silence between them.

"I love that sound." Lilly drew her knees up and hugged them to her. "Have you ever noticed, it never seems to just *start*? At some point you realize—"

"—they've been singing all along." He wasn't quite in sync with her, but trailing by a word or so, enough to bring them both to soft, self-conscious laughter.

"I've never actually seen one."

"Really?"

"What can I say? In some ways my life was sheltered."

"They molt, you know. And you'll find their shells stuck on a wall or a rock. It looks like a perfect hollow mold. When we were kids, Tony and

Bill and I used to go around collecting them. All summer, filling an old cigar box with cicada shells."

Lilly wrinkled her nose. "What did you do with them?"

"You name it. We put them in girls' hair, dropped them into kids' lunch buckets. You saw those little dishes of candy Mother set out for bridge? We'd hide one or two in there. Got the licking of my life from my father, but it was worth it. And Tony, he had this older sister, Marie. Ah, she was beautiful. Thick black curly hair all the way down to"—he reached behind to touch the small of his back.

"Just like you men like it."

"Everything about that girl was beautiful. Anyway, one day, Tony drops a cicada shell in her soup."

"No!"

He chuckled. "Oh yes. And she has a spoonful when she sees it. She screams and jerks her arm like this, and when she does, hot soup goes flying into her eye. And she goes screaming, 'I'm blind! I'm blind!' and Tony's scared to death, thinking he blinded his sister, so he jumps out the window to hide and ends up breaking his arm."

By the time Cullen finished the story, laughter had stolen half of his breath.

"He deserved it," Lilly said, laughing too.

"And then Bill gets a hold of him and says, 'Tony, if you ruined that girl's face, I'll break your other arm.'"

They laughed some more, and for a moment, Cullen felt like the same boy he'd been all those years ago. And Lilly, rumpled and barefoot with her legs curled beneath her, looked like any other grubby kid. On second thought, though, when she turned her head and looked straight at him, she wasn't a kid at all. Young, yes, younger than him, but a woman. And a beautiful one at that, even with the sadness behind her smile.

"Tony's the elevator operator's son?"

"Yes."

"I'm sorry." She reached for his left hand and held it, refusing to let go even as he instinctively tried to jerk it away.

"He was a great guy."

"Did you serve together?"

"No. He went in early. First to sign up, I'd wager. I was too busy playing baseball to care about a war."

"What changed your mind?"

Cullen shifted his weight on the stone bench, dislodging her grip on his hand. "When I was in high school, all I ever thought about was baseball. I played every day, on Saturdays, Sundays after church. Told my father all I wanted to do with my life was play in the major league."

"You were good, Moonsie." She leaned her body and nudged his shoulder. "He must have been proud."

"Oh no. He thought it was disgraceful. Impractical. Irresponsible for the son of a self-made businessman like himself to throw a successful future away on some silly game. But I went to college—"

"Where?"

"Yale." As Father insisted.

"Let me guess, you played for them too."

"I was on the team, second nine."

"Second nine?"

"That means I only got to play if one of the top nine players couldn't. I found out that a high school star doesn't shine much on a college team."

"But you made it to the majors."

"Like you said, my father knew some important people. He pulled strings, and suddenly I was playing for Pittsburgh. I wasn't ready, and deep down, I think he knew it. It was awful—I stunk up that field like you wouldn't believe. Things people said. They found out my old nickname and started calling me Blue Moon."

"That has a nice ring to it." She puckered her lips. "Blue Moon."

"They called me that because that's how often I got a hit. As in, 'Once in a blue moon.'"

She covered her pretty puckered lips, but not in time to stop the laugh that bubbled out. "Oh, I'm sorry. It's not funny. But—well, it is."

"I went back to my hotel room after the last game of my rookie season—my *only* season—and my father was waiting for me. He had two tickets home and an office door with my name on it. He said, 'You had your shot, Moon. Now it's time to come home.'"

"But you didn't."

"I left right then and signed up for the army. I never saw him again."

To his horror, he felt the sting of tears in his eyes. He looked up, noticing the sky had turned purple with night. This darkness, like the cicada's song, seemed without beginning. Like he had always lived this moment, sitting in the garden with Lilly Margolis, spilling his secrets as he never had before. She, to his relief, said nothing. No words of sympathy, no questions. Just her, silent as the stone on which they sat, her skin awash in the last of the light. Her eyes mirroring his in unshed sadness.

"After I got...hurt," he said when he felt he could safely continue, "I went to a hospital in Arizona to finish my recovery. He got on a train to come see me. Mother didn't. She's always been terrified of trains. He got sick—too sick to continue. Hopped on a train to come home, and didn't make it. That's when Mother had her first spell with her heart; she was in bed for two months. It was a year before I was well enough to come home, and when I did, Mother was, well, the way she is now."

"Forgetful?"

"She'd always been a little forgetful, but when I came home, the mother I knew was gone."

"And you had to pick up where your father left off."

"I was lucky to have something to come home to. Lots of guys didn't."

"But it's not what you want?"

"I try not to think about it in terms of what I want. You do that and you'll go crazy. Look at Mother. She wants me to be her little boy. She simply chooses the reality she wants and lives in it."

"I think that's sweet."

"I think it's nuts." It was the first time he'd spoken such a thing out loud, and the confession lifted a burden he never knew he carried. "Did you hear that?" He raised his face and spoke to the emerging stars. "My mother is crazy."

Lilly swatted him on the arm. "Stop. She's..."

"Don't say 'forgetful.'"

"No, she's forgiving. She'll forgive you, you know, for going to war instead of coming home. And for getting hurt. You frightened her is all. But wait. She'll accept you for who you are, and then she'll forget all about it."

Now it was his turn to lean over and nudge her shoulder. "How did a perfume-selling flapper get to be so wise?"

"Because I have a mother who doesn't forgive. Or forget."

Grateful for the cover of night to hide him, Cullen's face flushed with shame thinking of the letter dictated to Hilda Meyers. *"Your daughter has found her way to our door. We have her well-being in mind and fear that she has fallen in with some unsavory practices. For your sake as well as her own..."*

That girl facedown on the lawn, the girl stumbling up the stairs, the eyes rimmed with kohl and the ruby red lips, the short skirts and brazen ways—all of it nothing but the empty shell of this woman.

"You need—"

"No." If the night had brought new warmth and understanding between them, it disappeared with the vehemence of her protest.

"I'm not saying you need to go home to stay, but trust me, you don't want to live with the regrets I have."

"You have no idea how she hurt me."

"So you won't forgive her either?"

"I'm tired." She stood and stretched, and when she did, her blouse raised, revealing a triangle of perfect white, skin at her waist. He should have looked away, but he claimed the darkness and his position behind her to excuse his stare.

The cicadas chose that moment to end their song, or perhaps they had five minutes ago. At any rate, a new silence dropped between them like a hammer. His mind echoed with confession, both the revelations of his past and the unrealized desire of this moment. She was not the same girl who had spun and danced and sung the other night. She was not a girl to be forgotten; she was a girl who needed to be forgiven. Whatever he thought—whatever he'd held against her—he let it go, and she became something entirely new in his eyes.

"Lilly—"

Before either could say another word, the void left by the cicada's song filled with a new sound—faint and high, and almost as shrill. His mother was highly displeased about something and making it known at the top of her lungs, her protests wafting through the open windows down into the garden.

"We should go check on her."

"You go," he said. "I'll be right up."

She pointed to the window that belonged to her room. "If she asks for you, I'll poke my head out the window."

"I'll be waiting."

He was praying the moment she took her first step away.

Lord, what have I done?

18

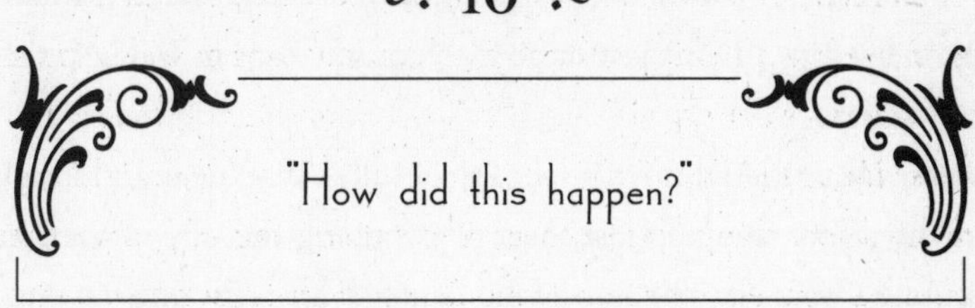

"How did this happen?"

The house had turned dark, and no one bothered with any of the lights. Still, expertly, Lilly maneuvered around the furniture, up the stairs, and to the place where soft light beckoned in the dark hallway. Betty Ruth's words were muffled through the closed door, but their intent was clear. She wasn't happy, and nothing spoken in the intermittent silences had any effect.

Lilly knocked as she opened the door, peeking her head around the corner.

Betty Ruth stood in the middle of the room, her face raised in defiance to the nurse whose figure rivaled the mass of Davis Burnside's beloved overstuffed chair.

"And I said for you to get back into bed!" The nurse spoke with such force that the little cap pinned to her hair looked ready to take flight.

"And I said I'm fine and I want to go downstairs and talk to my son."

"And Dr. Dewers said you were to stay put."

Lilly opened the door wider, waiting for Betty Ruth to notice her presence. Notice, first, and then remember. She didn't have to wait long. Before her next retort, Betty Ruth glanced over and closed her mouth. There followed a beat of two seconds, three, where none of the women spoke, until finally Betty Ruth, looking completely exasperated, planted her hands on her hips. "Don't just stand there, dear. Come in and help me talk to this woman."

Such a fear lifted right from the top of Lilly's shoulders, and she glided across the room, stopping just short of swooping the tiny woman in her arms. Actually, it was the nurse who stopped her with one outstretched meaty arm.

"Now, you leave her be. She needs to get back in bed."

"And I told you I'm fine."

"Why don't you come sit instead?" Lilly took her hand and looked at the nurse. "Would that be all right?"

"As long as she's off her feet."

"Thank you, Nurse—" The nurse stared, either not understanding that Lilly was looking for a name, or unwilling to give it. "Why don't you go downstairs for a bit? Have you had supper?"

"Just a bite."

"Well, go on down to the kitchen and see what you can find."

Nobody listening in would have the least doubt that Lilly was the mistress of the house, and even she was taken aback by her confidence. Something about being near Betty Ruth gave her a sense of peace or power—or both. Lilly helped her ease into her favorite chair, and then, remembering the mistake of earlier in the day, sat on the floor at Betty Ruth's feet. In an instant, from nowhere, Mazy arrived, bells jingling.

"Get down!" Lilly lifted the dog's front legs that were planted in Betty Ruth's lap.

"Oh, she's fine." She scratched Mazy's head and behind her ears. "I don't know why you all think I've gone dying."

"We're worried," Lilly said. The three looked like a set of half-opened nesting dolls, Mazy's head now in her lap, and Lilly's hand resting on Betty Ruth's. "Don't you remember?"

Betty Ruth's face went from anger to something profoundly sad. "I was afraid—he just frightened me so."

"Would you like to see him?"

"Oh, please, bring him to me. Bring him here."

"Just a minute." Lilly jumped up and ran to her own room, across to where the curtains billowed in the breeze.

Cullen looked so quiet and contemplative there in the garden, and the words of the hymn Betty Ruth and she sang earlier came to her mind. Was he praying at that moment? She was hesitant to interrupt. Still, if he was praying, it was about his mother, so she leaned as far out as she dared.

"Moonsie!" It came out as something between a hoot and a howl, a sound that pleased her so much she attempted again, only louder. "Moonsie!" He looked up, more startled than she would have imagined. "Your mother wants to see you!"

By now she knew that he hardly had the voice to carry a reply, so she didn't wait for one. She did, however, finally take the ribbon that seemed to have long outserved its purpose out of her hair and run her fingers through the curls. Her dress was still rumpled and her feet were dirty, but she didn't want to leave Betty Ruth alone any longer than necessary. Still, she ended up crossing the top of the stairs the same moment he came up the last step, and the two stopped just short of colliding on the landing.

"How is she?" His whisper disappeared into the darkness, or so it seemed because she stood so close. She looked up, trying to make out his features in the shadows.

"She's…feisty. And, sad."

"But lucid?"

"I think so."

He started to walk away, then stopped. "This is so hard. Why don't I want to go in there?"

Lilly didn't have an answer—not that he was really asking her anyway. Without a thought, she moved in front of him and, before he could protest or push her away, wrapped her arms around his waist and laid her head on his shoulder.

"You'll be fine," she said, waiting for that moment when his arms would come around her, and after a moment they did, though never quite reaching past her shoulders.

"Thank you." He stepped back but not away.

Even in the dimness of this light, Lilly could see the pain in his eyes. She felt the reluctance in his body and wished more than anything she could fix this for him. If she could, she'd crawl inside his broken, tattered flesh and take on this moment. She knew the blunt pain of rejection; she could weather disapproval and disgust. More than that, though, she knew he'd face no such thing with Betty Ruth. He was walking in with a fear Lilly couldn't imagine, and one she couldn't take away. Yet she felt compelled to try.

Before her own fears could overtake her, she rose on her toes and planted a soft kiss on Cullen's cheek. "For luck."

And while the two were caught in the surprise of the moment, she put her hands to his face, turned it, and gave another, more lingering kiss to the other side. She could feel his sharp breath, and it made her want to weep.

"Now go talk to your mother." She whispered so close, her bottom lip grazed his skin.

"Come with me?"

She rocked back on her heels. "Of course."

She trailed behind him, though this would be a moment best shared by the two of them alone. Cullen stood in the doorway and said, "Mother?" with such hesitancy that her own heart ached. Betty Ruth was hidden behind the breadth of his shoulders, but her voice was calm and clear.

"Cullen, darling..." And he was at her feet, his head held against her as her bare fingers combed through his hair. "Now, sit back and let me look at you."

He sat down in his father's chair, and she did not protest.

"How did this happen?" she asked. "I don't recall—some days are lost, you know. Was it something to do with the car?"

Lilly could tell by his delay that he was considering telling her just that. Silently she pled with him, *Tell her the truth.*

As if he heard, he looked up. "Come in here, Lilly."

"Actually, I'm beat. I think I might go rest for a while myself, if that's all right with you."

Something between fear and disappointment crossed his face, but no matter. This was a reunion between mother and son—one long in the making, even if they'd seen each other just that morning. Try as she might, Lilly had no place in it. Betty Ruth might love her, but she was not a daughter, even less a sister to Cullen. In fact, she was growing less and less sure what she was to Cullen. No longer a blatant nuisance, but not quite a guest. There'd been a moment out in the garden, then this other at the top of the stairs and, thinking back, quite a few where the animosity between them seemed more like a mask than anything else.

Turning the corner, she heard his voice. "You remember, don't you, that I played baseball."

"Yes, of course."

"Well, after my last game..." And he launched into the story she'd heard in the garden. Of seeing his father for the last time. But he shared more. The pain he felt knowing his father didn't believe in him. The fear of coming into a business that he little understood, and most of all the resentment at having no choice in the matter. How he needed one thing in his life to be free from the orchestrations of Davis Burnside.

So we're not so different after all. Lilly leaned against the wall and slid until she was sitting on the floor, listening to every word.

"So you joined the army?" Betty Ruth's voice was as stable as Lilly ever remembered.

"The next day."

"And you fought in that awful war."

"I don't want to tell you about that."

"Oh, but you must."

"I've never talked to anybody about any of it."

"Is it very painful to talk about?"

"It's ugly, Mother. Everything about it. And I don't want to fill your head with such horrible things."

"They're only words, dear. Words don't last, but for a little while, let me share them."

And so he began. Innocuous stories at first, the camaraderie of men becoming soldiers. The understandable fear of the unknown, the long journey across the sea. But then, endless marching, punishing cold. Rain and mud and frozen ground. Hunger and wet socks.

Lilly listened to it all and, for the first time ever, thought Betty Ruth was wrong. These weren't just words. Her own feet ached and her stomach twisted with the details. He shared stories with his mother the way a little boy might, and Betty Ruth listened with an occasional, "Oh, my!" as if these were mere school-yard adventures. But Lilly knew the tale was about to turn dark, and when Cullen said, "Then, one day..." she braced herself against the wall, not knowing if she was prepared to hear the details of that one day. She'd almost grown accustomed to the scars; the unimaginable pain that they covered seemed unreal. She didn't want to think about it because she didn't like the thought of him suffering.

I've blocked it out, just like she did.

But it wouldn't stay blocked forever.

"The Germans—wasn't enough to shoot at us with bullets. You don't know how often I wish I'd just been shot."

"Don't you say that, Cullen Burnside."

Yes. Don't.

"This gas. Mustard gas, they call it. It hits you and it burns. Like you're on fire inside and out. You feel it, and the first thing you want to do is run, like you can get away. But that's the worst thing you can do because then it spreads. So when it hit me, I just stood still, burning. Feeling it down my throat and in my chest. Closed my eyes so I wouldn't go blind. Couldn't call out. Couldn't move."

"Oh, darling."

"Know how I got through it? I pretended I was in a game, standing with a lead off third, waiting for the hit."

"How did I not know?"

"I didn't write. I knew the army would inform you—or Father—and I didn't know how I would face you. They set up a hospital in Arizona for all of us who got burned, an old tuberculosis clinic, and when I got there, that's when I wrote."

"I don't remember." Her voice was losing its strength.

"Maybe Father didn't tell you. Wanted to spare you until we knew just how bad it was."

"No, he must have. Because I remember sitting in these very chairs, praying..."

Lilly rested her head against the wall and closed her eyes, better able to home in on the voices that grew fainter as the conversation went on. In fact, after a time, she felt not so much like one eavesdropping on a conversation as one listening to a confession. She heard more tender words exchanged between mother and child during that hour than she and her mother had spoken to each other in her lifetime. And what was the difference? Both Lilly and Cullen had rebelled, run away, fought against the restraints their families tried to impose. How, then, could it get to this point?

She couldn't listen anymore. The day weighed heavy on her, and she wondered if she had the strength to stand and walk to her room. But for the fresh raw skin on the tops of her knees, she would crawl straight into her bed. Then again, if anything sounded better than sleep, it was a nice long bath—tepid, given the warmth of the evening. The thought of it drove her to her feet, and within minutes, the sound of the water filling the tub soothed her.

She used the little silver spoon to add Dalliance bath salts, and once the tub was halfway full, she climbed over the edge and sank into the water until it reached her chin. She dipped her lips to blow bubbles.

"Moonsie." She spoke the name into the water, entertained both by the echo of her voice against the walls of the tub and the way it sounded within the bubbling. "Moonsie."

She giggled, enjoying the release of such a simple pleasure.

"Moonsie."

And then a knock at the door, with that distinctive voice on the other side.

"Lilly? Are you all right?"

Water sloshed as she gripped the side of the tub, pressing herself against it lest he open the door. She couldn't remember if she'd locked it or not. "Don't come in here!"

"I thought I heard—"

"It's nothing! I'm sorry—just, go."

When there had been silence on the other side of the door for at least five minutes, Lilly rose and reached for the clean white towel. She rubbed it over her damp hair and along her body, then wrapped herself in her blue kimono robe before gathering her soiled clothes from the floor and venturing out into the hall. Two steps to her room, but before she reached it, Cullen called to her once more.

Lilly clutched her laundry closer to her as he approached. "How is she?"

"She's better. Tired."

"And you?"

"The same. And grateful too. Thank you."

"I didn't do anything."

"I think you did. Something happened, started happening the day you showed up. And now, look at us."

"Us?"

"Mother and I," he said quickly. A little too quickly, maybe, and she had more than the bath to blame for the warmth she felt within.

"Can I see her?"

"She's tired. The nurse is sitting up with her; another one will be here to relieve her in about an hour. The doctor will be back in the morning."

"Well then, if you don't need me, I think I'm ready to hit the old hay. Not much of a flapper, am I? Bed by nine. Not the same girl I was last week."

"No." Speaking, by now, appeared to cause him pain, yet he seemed determined to hold her here. "You kissed me earlier."

She'd almost forgotten—almost, and now she could think of nothing else. The silence between them drew her, as much as the promise of warm, clean water did, and she had to force herself not to lean in when she said, "Yes?"

"Please, don't do that again."

19

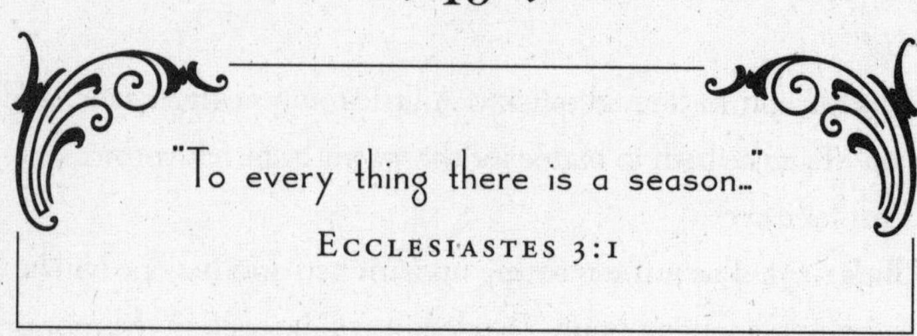

"To every thing there is a season..."

ECCLESIASTES 3:1

The next morning Lilly helped prepare Betty Ruth's breakfast tray, though Eugenie made it perfectly clear the houseguest was neither competent nor welcome.

"A fine day when I can't fix a meal alone in my own kitchen," she muttered, eyeing the pancakes on the griddle.

"It's not your kitchen." Lilly picked a fifth perfect strawberry from the bowl and snipped its green tip.

"More'n it is yours."

Lilly chose to ignore the slight. "And cream." She tapped her fingers together and looked around the kitchen.

"Haven't had a chance to bring it in yet."

Through the pantry was a door leading to a small porch meant for deliveries and packages. Lilly went there and opened it to find a small carrier filled with four bottles of milk, along with two smaller ones of heavy cream. She brought these in, remembering what a treat it had been as a child to rise early enough to get to the milk when it was still icy cold from the truck. Their own icebox never could get it to that tooth-aching cold she loved. If her mother was asleep, she'd take a swig straight out of the bottle, then add a little water to bring the level back to the top. Never mind that the rest of the milk was watered down and weak; she'd already had the best.

She smiled, thinking about that early rebellion, twisted the lid off one of the bottles, and lifted it for a satisfying swig.

"Are you insane?"

The last few drops drizzled down her chin, and Lilly wiped it with the back of her hand. Cullen stood, surrounded by groceries, holding a box of Cream of Wheat in his hand. The man on the box had a wide, welcoming smile. Cullen did not.

"It tastes best this way. Don't tell me you've never drunk milk straight from the bottle."

"Mother would kill me. And Eugenie will kill you."

"Eugenie doesn't have to know." She held out the bottle. "Come on, you know you want to."

Cullen frowned. "I'm not ten years old."

"No, but one drink, and you'll feel like you are. Don't be such a drab."

"Are you daring me?"

"Are you afraid of an old woman in a gray dress?"

He took the bottle and lifted it to his mouth, keeping one eye on the pantry door as he took a deep gulp. Just as he finished, Lilly gave him a little shove, causing him to jerk the bottle away and dribble milk down his chin and onto his clean shirt.

"Why would you do that?" But he seemed more amused than angry.

"Evidence. In case you decide to turn me in."

He wiped his chin with his sleeve and handed the bottle back. "Put this straight into the icebox, then put a glass in the sink."

Lilly nodded approvingly. "Very clever. I could learn a few tricks from you."

She started to sweep past him when he caught her arm. "I came looking for you. Mother wants to see you this morning. She has"—he had trouble controlling his expression—"something, well, *important* to share with you."

With his touch and those words, the playfulness of the moment vanished, bringing back all that happened yesterday. The argument, the shared confidences, the betrayal, the kiss. For a moment, the kiss dominated; then she moved on.

"I'll take her breakfast tray up."

"Eugenie won't like that."

She smiled up at him. "Then you can stay here and keep Eugenie company while you explain your new mustache."

He followed her back into the kitchen, where Eugenie was pouring coffee into a little silver pot. She looked up the minute they walked out of the pantry and set the pot down with a clatter.

"Just what have you two been up to?"

Immediately Lilly lifted her hand to her mouth and, to her amusement, saw Cullen doing the same. Both muttered, "Nothing" simultaneously and, in response to the rising suspicion in Eugenie's glare, both laughed.

"Whatever it is," she said, with a hint of the closest thing to a smile Lilly had yet to see, "I don't want none of it goin' on in my kitchen. Or my pantry."

"Yes m'am." Lilly adopted a posture of proper chastisement.

Cullen said nothing, but he took the milk carrier from her and, one by one, set the bottles in the icebox, leaving out the cream at Eugenie's instruction.

"Just this for me today." He set the box of oatmeal on the counter. "And maybe stir in some of those strawberries. I have a meeting at nine."

Eugenie grumbled something about how much easier her life would be if everybody would eat the same thing at the same time as she put a silver dome over Betty Ruth's stack of pancakes.

"I'll make up a double batch." She lifted the box. "And you can have what he don't finish."

"Sounds perfect." Lilly forced a smile, sensing that Betty Ruth's illness made her own presence that much less welcome in Eugenie's eyes. Lilly lifted the tray—gaining a new respect for the woman's strength—and went upstairs.

Betty Ruth's door was closed but not latched, and it took only a nudge of Lilly's knee to open it.

Her eyes lit up. "Oh, my dear. This is a treat. A treat, indeed."

"Nobody knows better than I do how wonderful it is to have breakfast in bed." Lilly set the tray on the foot of the mattress, where the covers were smooth and undisturbed. "Coffee?"

"Please, yes."

Lilly poured the steaming black drink into the china cup and added three sugars and cream, just the way she'd seen Cullen do. For good measure, she blew across its surface to give it one more bit of cooling.

"And there's fresh strawberries in cream. And pancakes."

"Oh, I'm not as hungry as all that. Not hungry at all, but you can leave it on the tray. I might try a bite later. But first"—she took the cup and saucer from Lilly—"I need to tell you the most exciting thing. Move that tray over to the table, then come sit."

Lilly obeyed and perched on the end of the bed, careful not to move the mattress lest Betty Ruth slosh her coffee.

"What is it?"

Betty Ruth took a sip, declared the coffee deliciously perfect, and sipped again. "Now, you might want to dismiss this as the ranting of an old woman, but last night, after Cullen and I talked—we had the nicest, longest talk, you know—I opened my Bible and—dear, fetch my Bible, would you?"

Lilly got up and brought the Bible back from its place on the little table between the chairs. She started to hand it to Betty Ruth, but the woman's hands were occupied with coffee.

"No, dear, you look at it for me. Ecclesiastes."

Lilly's thumb fanned across the pages. It had been a long time since she'd held a Bible, let alone read one. The name of the book was familiar, but that was all. She forced a brave smile, said "All right," then began flipping, watching the words at the top fly by. If Betty Ruth sensed her awkward discomfort, she made no attempt to ease it. Rather, she sipped her coffee, looking over the edge of her cup with twinkling eyes.

Something with an E. "Ephesians?"

"Ecclesiastes. Look toward the center, after Psalms and Proverbs."

"Oh, that's right." Given direction, she found it easily. "Now what?"

"Third chapter. And read it, dear. Out loud, please, so I can enjoy it too."

Lilly turned the page and began to read: "'To every thing there is a season, and a time to every purpose under the heaven: a time to be born, and a time to die; a time to plant, and a time to pluck up that which is planted; a time to kill, and a time to heal; a time to break down, and a time to build up—'" She looked up, not sure how far Betty Ruth wanted her to read.

"Go on, dear, finish the chapter."

It went on. A time to weep, to laugh, to mourn, to dance. To embrace and refrain from embracing. Silence and speech. Love and hate, war and peace. In short, everything she had lived during her week in this home. Her tongue reveled in the poetry of it, even as some of the language was confusing. The moment each verse was read aloud, Lilly wanted to go back and read it again, pondering its meaning.

How had she lived her entire life with Mama and Mama's Bible and never heard any of this? Or maybe she had, but the beauty of it got lost in the strident voice of Ella Margolis.

She got to the final verse in the chapter and looked up from the page. "I'm not sure I understand."

"Start again."

Lilly refocused and began, anticipating the rhythm of the language this time, enjoying it, when Betty Ruth interrupted her at verse fifteen.

"Read that verse again."

"That which hath been is now; and that which is to be hath already been; and God requireth that which is past." She looked up again, wary of the eager anticipation in Betty Ruth's eyes.

"Do you see?"

Lilly shook her head. "No."

"I've read those verses countless times. Over and over. But last night, it was all brand-new. So many things were brand-new and hurtful. Do you know what it felt like to see my baby boy?"

"I can imagine." But she couldn't, not really.

"It's all about time. People think that life happens in a sequence, but it doesn't. Not at all. Things happen when God reveals them. And it's different for each person. My Cullen wasn't hurt before yesterday. You didn't exist before you came to my door, but then I've loved you forever. Haven't you ever felt it? That you're living a moment for the first time? Something you know you should have lived before?"

Lilly's mind raced with Betty Ruth's words. So this is what it must be like to live inside her mind, with the past and the present meshing together moment to moment.

Betty Ruth continued. "We live what God wants when He wants us to. He withholds joy for a time, then lavishes it all around. He shelters us from pain until He knows we'll live through it."

"Or maybe He takes us through it early so we can get it out of the way."

Betty Ruth snapped her little fingers. "Exactly! The point is, what matters is this moment. How precious, precious time is. The past had to happen, and we cannot stop the future. Why, then, should we live with a spirit of fear and regret?"

"Betty Ruth, do you remember anything about what Cullen told you?"

She smiled weakly and handed her coffee to Lilly, who set it on the nightstand. "Bits and pieces. Some of it I'll treasure, but I'm afraid I'll let the rest of it go."

"You can decide what you'll forget?"

"That is how God has chosen to care for me, I suppose. It's how He heals me."

"I envy you. I wish I could have just come to this house and forgotten about everything I've done. Everything that's happened to me. I guess that's been your gift to me. You…you seem like you love me, no matter what. Without question."

Betty Ruth reached out and patted her leg. "Don't lose sight of where that kind of love comes from. That is how Jesus Himself loves you. When you are His child, and you open your heart to accept that He has forgiven you, He sees you through eyes of love, and He restores you back to that place of perfection. Pure perfection."

Lilly looked down at the tiny hand on her knee and covered it with her own. "That's what Mama always said. That I needed to beg Jesus to forgive me. That I could never be a child of God with so much darkness in my soul."

"Land sakes, child. There's no begging to be done. Forgiveness is for the asking, but most of all, for the accepting. Sin wounds us, but Jesus heals us. We're clean in His eyes. The scars are in ours."

Unless He hides them. And how she wished He would hide hers away.

"Now—" Betty Ruth turned her hand palm up and gave Lilly's fingers a squeeze—"let me tell you about the vision the Lord gave me."

"Please do." Lilly's heart wrapped around the seed of hope that had been planted.

"I said, 'Lord, take back this time and set it straight.' And when I closed my eyes, I saw this scene so clearly." She closed her eyes now, both shutting Lilly out and begging her to follow. "I saw my boy—not a boy but a man, so tall and proud—standing at home plate, in the middle of an enormous stadium, the crowd cheering."

Betty Ruth drew her hand away and, right there in bed, assumed a batter's stance. "I could see his face, so handsome. And nothing..." She touched her cheek, and her face twisted in pain. "No hint of his pain. He was healed." She opened her eyes. "Do you understand? Healed completely."

"That's a beautiful thought." Lilly proceeded cautiously, as Betty Ruth's voice had begun that dangerous fading trail that often signaled a break with the moment at hand. "You must be remembering a time when—"

"I've never seen him play. Not since high school. I do not travel by train, never have. And his father, well, baseball was not a priority for him."

"But you could imagine—"

"This was not a feat of my imagination." Her curls quivered with the protest. "This was a vision sent from God. From God Himself. And He showed me, if my boy could just go back to that time, *that* is his time to heal."

"But we can't go back in time."

"The past is now. We can go back and be there now."

"I don't understand."

"Don't you see? He has to go back. He has to play again. Just once, and he will be healed. Completely." Betty Ruth's eyes were focused and clear, her voice steady, no hint of distance in her demeanor. This was not the woman who roamed the hallways looking for her nine-year-old son, nor was it the woman who believed he was still a major league player. She knew. Everything. And however long that knowledge would last, Lilly had no idea.

Lilly remembered last night, Cullen looking to the night sky and proclaiming his mother to be insane. This was not insanity, not to Betty Ruth, at least, so Lilly chose her words carefully.

"He was burned. He has healed as much as he's ever going to be."

"No. God showed Cullen to me. Not a bit of it."

"But remember, you've been looking at him for years, and you didn't see—"

"I have seen him now! And I will—oh, I knew you wouldn't understand."

Lilly took a deep breath. "I understand. I do. But how can such a thing happen?"

Betty Ruth brightened and winked. "Don't you worry about that. The Lord gives us visions and the legs to chase them down. Now, I do think I'll be able to eat a bite or two." She sat up straighter and patted her lap.

Lilly gathered the tray and lowered its legs. "Have you told Cullen about this yet?"

"Oh yes."

"Really?" Lilly thought back to their interaction in the pantry. "He didn't say anything to me."

"That's because he thinks I'm nuts." She speared a strawberry and popped it in her mouth, declaring it delicious. "That's why I told you."

"What can I do?"

She speared another and pointed with it. "Convince him. Crazy things sound better when they're coming from the mouth of a pretty girl."

∴ 20 ∾

Seeking spiritual guidance, our hero turns to Reverend Thomas Henderson, longtime family minister.

The cavernous quiet of the empty chapel never failed to strike a reverent chord in Cullen, and as he removed his hat and dark glasses, he felt his very breath become slower, his heart calm. Although alone, he still gravitated to his family's place and sat, resting his elbows on the back of the pew in front of him and his forehead on his folded hands.

Heavenly Father, I don't know what to do. You know Mother's heart, and You know mine. And I suppose You know Lilly's too. He smiled. *Of course You do. I wish I did. I wonder if she has—could ever have—a heart for You. And then, for me. Because then—*

Cullen shook his head, clearing his thoughts. He'd come to pray about his mother, her health, and the implausible tale she'd put forth this morning, and here he was, consumed with thoughts about Lilly.

Forgive me, Lord. But she tends to take over. And it was true. Wherever they were, the space got smaller. The beach, the garden, the pantry. The backseat of his car. The elevator.

He opened his eyes and looked at the icon of Christ the Good Shepherd above the altar at the front of the chapel and felt another twinge of conscience. Not since Anna Sherwood sat directly in front of him with her hair pulled up off the back of her neck had he felt so guilty about the state of his mind in church.

"Good morning, Cullen," Reverend Henderson's voice boomed. "I thought we were going to meet in my office."

Cullen stood to shake the reverend's hand, which was as soft as the fringe of hair that stretched from one small ear to another. "I was a little early."

"So you thought you'd talk to the boss first?"

Cullen laughed politely. "I suppose so."

"Well, I just got kicked out. Martha insists now is the only time she has to dust and straighten. Volunteers, you know. Can't tell them what to do."

"I suppose not." Cullen matched his tone to the reverend's good-natured one, though he couldn't imagine anybody in his own employ making such a demand.

"We can talk in here if you like."

"Or"—Cullen glanced up at the icon—"maybe we could walk outside?"

"I'll see if Martha will allow me to get my hat, and I'll meet you on the front steps."

The church sat in the middle of a crisp green lawn kept mowed to the point of velvet. The two men walked along its edges, both with their hands loose in their pockets.

"Missed you at church last Sunday," Reverend Henderson said. Though he was close to twenty years Cullen's senior, his statement carried no hint of condescension.

"We had an unexpected guest." Sunday was Lilly's second day of convalescence, and while he had no contact with her himself, he wasn't about to leave Mother alone in the house with this stranger.

"Ah yes. The flapper."

Cullen stopped, as did Reverend Henderson. The two were matched in height, with the reverend the slimmer of the two.

"How do you know?"

"Both my wife and daughter are in the same gardening club as Julia Owens. It would seem there were some aspects of her husband's celebration she chose not to keep secret from the pastor's wife."

"I guess it is perfect fodder for gossip."

"Best I've heard in years."

They began walking again, comfortably silent for a while.

"You know, Reverend, it's not—"

"What the ladies think it is?"

"She's a troubled girl, and Mother took her in."

"And what do you think of this troubled girl?"

"I didn't come here to talk about her. It's Mother."

This time Reverend Henderson brought them to a halt. "Is Betty Ruth all right?"

"As much as she ever is. Maybe we should sit down, after all."

They headed for a spot on the side lawn where two benches faced each other under the spreading shade of an oak tree that had been planted at the consecration ceremony. How many Bible stories had he listened to in the shade of that tree? A parade of middle-aged women flashed across his mind, all of them with loving, soft faces, picking out the squirming hand of the first child who could recite the week's memory verse. Right now there was only one passage of Scripture in his mind—the third chapter of Ecclesiastes. And it haunted him.

Once they were seated on the benches, facing each other, Cullen began his tale. Everything from the moment Lilly landed facedown in their yard, until yesterday when he'd come home to find her in their parlor—though of course he left out the description of her beauty in the moonlight at the beach and her tantalizing dance in the garden.

"I thought this was about your mother," Reverend Henderson prompted.

"It is. Mother loves her. I simply cannot understand it."

"Can't you?"

Now he was grateful he'd opted to wear his glasses in the shade. "No. And you can understand my frustration. You know how Mother is, how her mind—"

"Yes."

"But this girl, she *transcends* that somehow."

"She must be remarkable. I hope to meet her someday. Now, about your mother."

"Yesterday I came home, and she and Lilly—sorry—Mother was in the kitchen..." He steeled himself but found the telling of the scene from the night before much easier with the reverend than he had with Dr. Dewers.

"Do you see, then, how this is a cause for praise? A healing has taken place, deep in your mother's mind. God is the Great Physician."

"Which is what I thought as I went to bed last night. And then this morning, when I went to check on her—"

"She'd relapsed?"

"No. In fact, it might have been better if she had."

The reverend's brow wrinkled. "Then?"

"She has it in her mind"—Cullen touched his temple—"*firmly* in her mind, that I can be healed too."

"I don't understand."

"I'm not sure if you will once I've explained it to you. It seems she had a vision."

"A vision?"

"A vision." Somehow, this was more embarrassing than last Easter when she insisted that he be allowed to participate in the Easter-egg hunt.

"Last night after I left her, she took her Bible and began reading in the book of Ecclesiastes."

"Ah, searching for wisdom, perhaps?"

"Perhaps." Cullen shifted his weight on the uncomfortable wooden bench slats. "And she fixated on this verse." He quoted it—as he had all morning.

Reverend Henderson nodded but offered no commentary.

"She says she had a vision where she saw me at home plate, and that if I could just play baseball one more time, I'd be healed."

"That's right, you played for Pittsburgh. Congratulations, they're one and one in the Series."

"Did you not hear what I said, Reverend?"

"I heard you."

Cullen took off his glasses and leaned forward. "She thinks that one at bat in a major-league stadium is going to take all of this away."

"And what do you think?"

"I think she's nuts."

Reverend Henderson laughed. "So you wouldn't have been lending your tools to Noah, eh?"

Cullen put his glasses back on and stared up through the leaves. "It's not nearly the same thing."

"I suppose not, but I've known your mother for more than twenty years. I know the woman of God she was before this unfortunate condition stole her mind, and I can't imagine that His presence is any the less for it. Sometimes our logic does more to hamper His voice than anything else."

"'*Healed,*' she said."

"I know what she said. Now, what are you going to do?"

"Oh, that's easy." Cullen leaned back and stretched his arm across the back of the bench. "I'm going to march up to the plate during the first inning of the World Series and say, 'Step aside, Carey. I'm going to take this one so my scars will disappear. That's what my mother told me to do.'"

"You wouldn't be the first to respond to God's directive with sarcasm."

Cullen shook his head. "I can't believe you're taking this seriously."

Reverend Henderson held up a calming hand. "I'm saying it doesn't deserve to be mocked. Who are we to question what God has spoken to one of His children?"

"You don't understand. She really wants me to go."

"I'm sure she does."

"How do I tell her that this is impossible?"

"Is it?"

Cullen stood, raking his fingers through his hair. This conversation was proving to be every bit as frustrating as the one he'd had earlier that morning.

"Can't you see," the reverend continued, "the timing involved here? Your team—"

"Former team."

"—former team is playing in the World Series at the same time the scales fall from your mother's eyes? It seems like divine providence to me."

Cullen scrutinized the clergyman's face, trying to gauge the sincerity behind the collar. The slight smile could be taken as reassurance, but there was an element of indulgent humor there too.

"What do I tell her?"

"Tell her you'll go."

"But I don't believe *any* of this."

"I'm not asking you to believe, Cullen. I'm asking you to act. This is a matter of your mother's faith, not yours."

He collapsed back onto the bench. "Unbelievable."

"Perhaps, but God can work through our disbelief. Look, you've asked my advice and I've given it to you. What you do from this place is up to you."

The Mercedes pulled up and parked in front of the church. Miles, early as usual. Cullen didn't know if it meant intrusion or escape. "I suppose there's a chance I could go home and she won't even remember any of this. She could forget everything."

"But will you? How often do you think about playing baseball?"

He looked to the car. Definitely escape. Still, the white collar of his family friend welcomed confession. "Every day."

"Betty Ruth knows this. A mother knows her son's heart. What could it hurt to indulge her?"

He wanted to say that the depth of that hurt was unfathomable, almost as great as the depth of his disbelief, but there were some parts of his heart he refused to share.

Cullen forced a smile, stood, and held out his hand. "Thank you for meeting with me. You realize this means we won't be at church on Sunday."

"You'll be in our prayers." The reverend looked past Cullen to the car. "Not in the roadster?"

"Not today. Miles thinks this is more dignified."

"I must agree. Can I pray with you before you leave?"

Cullen nodded and bowed his head while listening to Reverend Henderson ask for wisdom on his behalf. When he finished, the older man clapped him on the shoulder. "You'll keep me informed?"

"I will. Thank you." As Cullen walked away, he heard his name called again and turned back.

"Maybe next time we can talk about that girl?"

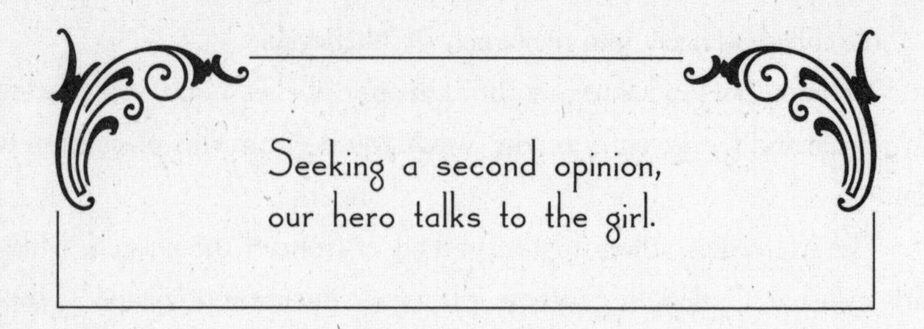

Seeking a second opinion, our hero talks to the girl.

Lilly sat on the front porch, elbows on her knees, face in her hands, looking like one of the neighborhood kids waiting for her friends to come join her for a game of hopscotch.

"Take the car to the garage, Miles, and then I won't need you for the rest of the day."

"Yes sir, Mr. Burnside."

She looked up as he got out of the car but made no attempt to stand. She did, however, scoot to the left, making room for him to sit next to her, which he did.

"Did she tell you?"

"Yes."

"And what do you think?" Somehow, he was anticipating her response more than he had the family's pastor.

"I think she's the wisest woman I've ever met."

He couldn't help laughing, though he kept it to a respectable chuckle.

"It's as much for her as it is for you, you know," Lilly said. "She's missed so much of your life. She just wants to get some of that time back."

"You can't get time back."

"Maybe not, but there's no harm in chasing it a little. At least take her to a game."

"And how do I get her there? She won't take a train. She hated them even before Father died, and since then, she won't even hear of it."

"I looked in the paper. Today's only game three. There's time. We could drive."

He twisted his neck as far as he could to look at her. *"We?"*

She looked straight out into the street. "Forbes Field? Pittsburgh. Right by my hometown." She turned to him then, her eyes huge and brimmed with tears. "I think I'm ready to go home."

The air balled up in Cullen's lungs and his hands into fists. Somehow, in the midst of Mother's revelation, this possibility had slipped his mind. He blinked madly behind his shades and fought to find the perfect response, but he could only come up with, "Why the change of heart?"

"Betty Ruth says that people can change. And, I think I have. Who knows? Maybe Mama can too. And maybe if she meets your mother…"

Her voice trailed off as Miles came from the side of the house. Cullen stood and reached into his pocket, pulling out a few folded bills. "Miles?"

He tipped his cap to Lilly. "Mornin', miss. Yes sir?"

"If you don't mind, would you run an errand to the petrol station? I need a map."

He looked puzzled. "Florida map?"

"Road atlas. Eastern coast. We're going on a little trip."

21

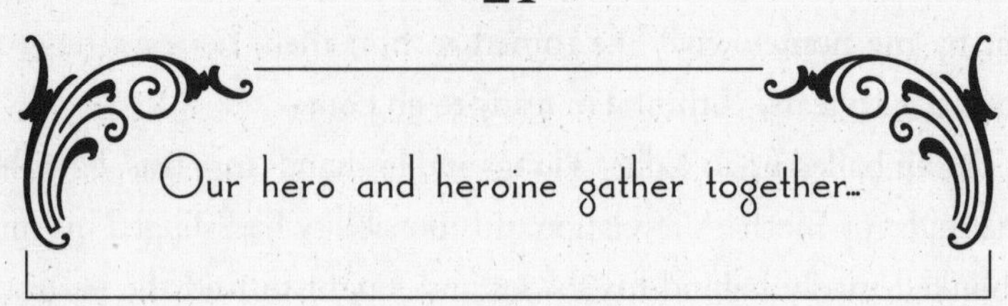

Lilly couldn't sleep. Usually the comfortable canine weight of Mazy snoozing on the foot of her bed was enough to wipe out the lingering worries of the day, but not tonight. In fact, Mazy put forth a little growling noise with every toss and turn and once stood and stretched, as if threatening to kick Lilly out of the bed.

The house was quiet, save for the occasional groaning of the dog and the ticking of her bedside clock. She reached for it and brought it close to her face, groaning. Eleven o'clock. Too early for anybody to be asleep—early-morning departure time or not.

Resolved, she swept off the covers and climbed out of bed. Her kimono robe was packed away, but there was a light afghan draped across the wing-backed chair. She wrapped it around her shoulders and stepped out into the hall.

Mazy yawned, at first seemingly uninterested, but soon the bells on her collar echoed in the empty house. The two of them crept through the halls, down the stairs, and into the kitchen, where Mazy's nails clicked straight across the room to the back door to be let outside.

That done, Lilly went to the icebox and retrieved a bottle of milk.

Rather than take a sip from the bottle, however, she took it over to the stove, set it down on the counter, and searched in the cabinet below for a small saucepan. Admittedly, the searching would have been easier had she turned on a light. Just as she thought this, the light *did* come on, scaring her to death and sending her flat on her bottom, with a terrific clanging of pots and pans.

"You'd make a terrible thief," Cullen said, his hand still on the switch. He wore pajamas and a navy blue robe cinched with a belt.

"And you'd make a horrible cop." Lilly grasped a suitable pan and stood, forgetting to clutch the afghan until it was too late, leaving it puddled at her feet. She could have bent right away to retrieve it, but watching Cullen try so hard not to notice proved far too amusing. "I could be halfway down the block by now with this very valuable saucepan."

"Then I might have to whip out my gun and shoot you. That's what the Keystone Kops do."

"So you *do* go to the pictures every now and then." She lit the stove and poured milk into the saucepan. "Couldn't sleep. This is supposed to help."

"Always works for me." He crossed over to the breadbox, opened it, and took out a cloth-covered plate. "I asked Eugenie to make these for the morning, but I don't think it'll hurt to break in now."

He took off the cloth, revealing a perfect pyramid of golden doughnuts.

"Oh, my..." Lilly took one off the top of the stack and set it on the stove. Cullen took the next before he rearranged the remaining pastries to resemble their original shape, only smaller.

"Shhh..." He held a finger to his lips. "She's staying the night and her room's just down the utility hall."

"Shhh..." Lilly mimicked the gesture before sticking her finger in the milk to test it. Still cold.

Cullen brought down two glasses and set them on the table before pulling out a chair. "You'll want to keep stirring that, or else it'll scorch."

"I think I can manage." Her nightgown fell to her knees, but it was a thin white cotton, making her feel every bit as naked in front of him as if she were. With an attempt at nonchalance, she stooped to pick up the afghan from the floor and wrap it around her, holding it closed with one hand, stirring with the other.

"Here." Cullen stood and walked to the stove. "I'm afraid you're going to set yourself on fire." He handed Lilly her doughnut, which she took with her to the table.

For a while there was no sound but the occasional scraping of the spoon. After testing it with his finger, Cullen brought the saucepan to the table and, without spilling a single drop, filled the two glasses.

"Good work," Lilly said, drawing the glass to her.

"I worked as a waiter at a few fashionable restaurants when I was in college."

"Daddy didn't give you enough allowance?"

"Wasn't about the money." He ripped the doughnut in half and dunked it into his milk. "It was about the pretty girls who came in with *their* daddies."

"I see. Make them fall in love with the poor waiter, then spring it on them that you're the heir apparent."

"Something like that." He dangled the doughnut over the side of the glass until the milk stopped dripping before popping it in his mouth and chewing thoughtfully. "You ever care about any of that?"

"Money?" She pinched off a bite and nibbled from it. The cake was flaky and sweet. Perfect. "Oh, sure. What girl doesn't? All those dinners and drinks and dresses aren't going to buy themselves, you know."

"But you don't worry about your reputation? What men might think? Or"—he stared into his milk—"expect?"

"You men expect too much whether you're footing the bill or not."

"Not all of us."

"That's not what my mama taught me. Guess I worked a little too hard trying to prove her wrong."

"You know," he said, unable to meet her eye, "if you like, I could meet her. Maybe vouch for your character."

His small, self-conscious laugh made her question the sincerity of his offer, but she was absolutely certain as to how she would respond. There were poisons in this world, and his very flesh bore the scars of one of the worst. But there was no poison as dangerous as the disapproval of Ella Margolis.

Right there, resting in the safety of the Burnsides' kitchen table, Lilly felt a cocoonlike protectiveness toward Cullen. He may have known war, but he'd never seen hate up close and personal, and she'd never take the chance of being the one to introduce him to it.

"She doesn't like surprises."

"I understand." He spoke a little too quickly for that to be true.

"No, it's not—it has nothing to do with—"

"It's fine. I can't imagine any mother being thrilled to have me walk through the door with her daughter."

Milk and doughnut twisted in her stomach, fighting as bravely as he seemed to be. "I guess I don't see the point. It's not as if we're—"

"Of course not—"

"And if you can manage to live a life without meeting my mother, well, that's one favor you'll owe me."

"Put it on my tab."

They both laughed, as warm and genuine as the fresh pastries.

"So," he said when they were quiet again. "Since Mrs. Margolis doesn't like surprises, should we send her a telegram before we leave? Or telephone her?"

"First"—Lilly disintegrated a crumb between her thumb and finger—"she isn't *Mrs.* anybody. I've never had a father. Second, we don't have a telephone, and third, no."

"But you said—"

"I won't be a surprise, Moonsie. She said to send me home and I'm going home. It's the first time she's ever wanted me back."

22

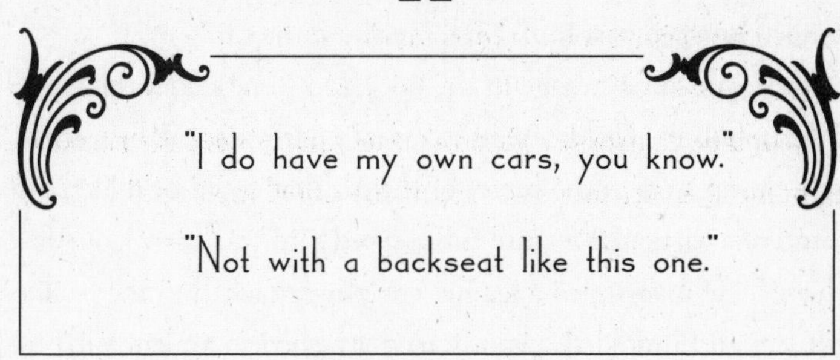

Bill Owens arrived at promptly six o'clock the next morning with his 1923 Peerless. "There's an easier way to get yourself to Pittsburgh." Bill handed Cullen the keys. "Great little invention, almost as modern as the automobile. It's called a train. With your boys down two to one now, you might want to opt for speed."

Cullen closed the door behind him as he went out to inspect the car. "Mother won't ride in a train, you know that."

"Since when does Betty Ruth like baseball?"

"She's taken a sudden interest." The last thing he wanted to do was share Mother's prophecy and vision with Bill Owens. He might be a regular at Christ Church on Sunday mornings, but he remained a far cry from what Cullen would call a man after God's heart.

"You're taking the girl with you?" His eyebrows jumped with the question.

"I'm taking her home."

Bill gave a long, low whistle. "Now, that's a shame. I think she might have been good for you."

Cullen brushed past him. "Tell me about the car."

"You've got some storage in the boot and some under the seats." Bill lifted the upholstered leather seats to reveal a narrow trunk beneath. There were two jump seats in the center of the car that could be folded into the floor, and one particular feature Bill assured him was every lady's favorite. "See here?" He unsnapped a leather covering attached to the back of the driver's seat and unfolded a windscreen attached to an extended folding arm. "This way the backseat passengers can get a break from the wind when the top's down."

"But it won't work with the jump seat up, will it? They'll have to sit three across."

"*Three*? Ah, don't tell me. You're taking one of Miss Lilly's little party friends too?"

"I am taking my mother and her maid."

Bill closed the car door and leaned against it, his thick arms crossed. "Burnsie, Burnsie, Burnsie. You have an opportunity to escort a willing young woman halfway across the country, not to mention a chance to watch your old team play in the World Series, and you're taking not only your mother, but her *maid*?"

"And Miles, our driver," Cullen said, enjoying his friend's frustration.

"You sure that gas didn't burn your brain too? Flip you back into the last century? Forget this baby." He slapped the car's hood, his wedding ring making a distinctive *click*. "If you can wait just a minute, the company owns a few cotton plantations. Let me get you an old wagon and a couple of mules. Think how pretty Miss Lilly would look in a sunbonnet."

"Last night," Cullen said once Bill had settled down, "when I told you

I was planning a little road trip and I needed to borrow your Peerless, what did you think? I do have my own cars, you know."

"Not with a backseat like this one. Let me tell you, I take the wife out driving in this car, find a little country road…but you? You've got more chaperones than the senior prom at St. John's."

Cullen laughed, both because he was amused at his friend's outburst and because he was relieved that he hadn't shared the entirety of the reason behind the journey he was about to take. He held out his hand—his burned one, a gesture he offered only on the rarest occasions. "Listen, friend, I appreciate your optimism, if nothing else."

Bill shook Cullen's hand, but his face and tone turned serious. "No, *you* listen. I think you think you're not good enough for this girl. You're getting rid of her because you're scared."

"Well, maybe that's a nice turn of events." Cullen postured, attempting to emulate Bill's light, comedic tone. "Usually the girls see this and they're scared of me."

"Horse feathers. I'll bet you haven't let a dozen girls see you since you got back. Now, I'm not saying you need to do anything…unreasonable. But let yourself have a little fun."

Cullen didn't want to think about Bill's idea of fun, let alone what he would deem unreasonable. Instead he reached into his pocket and pulled out a key. "This is to the side garage door. If you find yourself in need of another car while we're gone, you're welcome to any one of mine."

"So that's it?" Bill stared at Cullen, who stared right back, calling on all his strength not to flinch. "Keep it." He pushed Cullen's hand away. "I've still got the Ford. When will you be back?"

"Can't say." And that was an honest answer.

"Well, give me a ring when you are. Good luck to you." He turned and started down the sidewalk.

"Do you need a ride home?" Bill's house was at least two blocks away.

"Nah," he said over his shoulder. "If that girl can walk it, so can I."

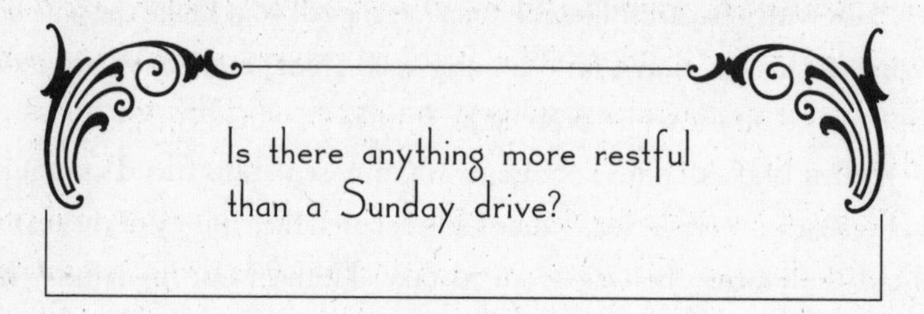
Is there anything more restful than a Sunday drive?

It began well enough as the five of them gathered outside the car while Cullen led them in prayer for a safe journey. He'd asked God to give them clear roads, fine weather, and a well-running engine for the duration of their trip. He neglected, however, to petition for cool heads, logical thought, and a spirit of cooperation. Before Miles even turned the key in the ignition, there'd been an argument over who should sit where.

"It's unbecoming for the master of the house to sit up front with the driver," Eugenie said, though Cullen suspected she merely wanted to have a front-seat view. After all, it wasn't every day a woman in her position was offered such an opportunity.

"I will not sit on that middle seat," Betty Ruth said. "It looks like it'll spring right up and throw me over the edge."

"Sir, if we don't get a move on, we'll still be in Florida by lunchtime." Miles had been given the responsibilities of driver, navigator, and time-keeper, just as he'd always been, only on a grander scale.

Only Lilly remained quiet, waiting for direction.

"Why don't you get in the backseat with Mother? Eugenie, you can ride up front, and I'll take the jump. Everybody happy?" If they weren't, nobody said so, and just as the sun popped up at the end of their street, the tires took their first turn.

They weren't even twenty miles down the road and Cullen was ready to turn back. They'd already changed the seating arrangement twice.

First after the incident involving Mother's hat in which the long pins that anchored her old-fashioned wide-brimmed hat to her head proved useless against the specific wind created by an automobile traveling over forty miles an hour. The hat flew off her head not two miles outside of town, and the tire tracks of other motorists rendered it ruined by the time they turned back to retrieve it.

Ruined too was the highly complicated hairstyle his mother had perfected over the years. Great strands were pulled from their anchors, valiant hairpins still clinging to the ends. She looked like a banshee, albeit a harmless one, with cheeks already turning pink in the sunlight. At the first stop—the attempted rescue of the hat—he offered to put the top up on the car.

"Really, Mother, you can't go on like this for three days."

"If it was good enough for the pioneers, it's good enough for me." Her little chin was set in determination as she sat patiently waiting for Lilly to twist her mass of hair into a single long rope.

The task would have fallen to Eugenie had she not been charged with the rescue of the hat. She herself was decked out in a driving coat and canvas hat with a chin strap tied under one ear. Fifteen years ago, she could have been one of the girls in the old automobile advertisements.

"The pioneers had horses. Not horsepower." It was an old joke, one of his father's. Perhaps it was funnier ten years ago.

"Actually," Lilly said, "most pioneers used oxen when they could. Much stronger and sturdier than horses." She licked her palm and smoothed Mother's hair, anchoring it with pins at her temple. "There, that should hold."

"I look like I ought to be on my way to bed." Mother patted her hair. Looking at her like this, completely devoid of the artifice of her normal fashion, Cullen was struck by how aged she looked. The simple style, as it exposed every root, showed his mother to have much more gray hair than he ever knew. Indeed, she looked like a woman who should be wearing a little lace cap and glasses, waiting for the Big Bad Wolf to come devour her.

"You know," Lilly said, "there's one way to keep your hair under control." She smiled mischievously and ran her fingers through her short, curly locks. They'd been protected by the bell-shaped hat she wore and looked none the worse for the drive so far.

Mother looked shocked. "You're not suggesting that I cut my hair? Like yours?"

"Think how modern you'd look." Lilly smiled. "You'd be the envy of all the women in your bridge club. Why, I bet they're just waiting for someone to be brave enough to—"

"Mother is not about to bob her hair."

"Cullen's right, dear. Hair is a woman's crowning glory."

"Not that yours doesn't look nice," Cullen rushed in, before Lilly's feelings could be hurt. "It's just not something a mother should do."

"I might be a mother someday." Lilly dropped her hairbrush into her handbag and snapped it shut. "Will I have to grow my hair long then?"

Cullen tried to imagine Lilly holding a child and found it surprisingly easy. "If you're finished now, let's get back in the car. I'll sit back with you and we can put up the windscreen."

Which brought about the second change in seating, wherein Mother wedged herself between Cullen and Lilly—the three of them behind the accordion-style windshield that folded out from the front seat.

"Well, this is lovely," Mother said.

The glass and the open car afforded them an unobstructed view of the passing countryside while the wind was kept out save for the occasional strong gust that made its way around the shield. This protection even made it possible for some conversation. Before, with the open car, Cullen's shouts were carried off on the breeze. But now, he and Mother and Lilly could talk for hour after endless hour, something of which the two women took full advantage.

They talked about the trees, flowers, clouds, and sky—Mother extolling the greatness of God's creation.

"I had a boyfriend who was an evolutionist," Lilly said. Cullen listened more intently. "He was an atheist too, I suppose. He was the saddest person I've ever known."

Mother clucked her tongue. "Such a shame, that is. Such a shame."

Cullen leaned forward and talked across his mother. "Is that why he's no longer your boyfriend? Because he didn't believe in God?"

Lilly leaned forward too. "I didn't think about it at the time. He was just a sad sack. All day, every day, moping about how this is all there is and this is all we're ever going to have. No hope. I've always been the person to think a better life is just around the corner." She stood, bracing herself with one hand on top of the windshield, the other clamped down on her bell-shaped hat. Braced against the wind, she looked like a brave figure carved into the helm of an ancient vessel.

"Look!" she shouted, and both Miles and Eugenie turned around in their seats. Eugenie sent a disapproving glare, and Miles temporarily lost his grip on the wheel. The entire automobile lurched as he regained control, causing Lilly to nearly topple as she leaned over the edge of the car. Still, she never lost her smile. "The road looks straight right now, from here, from what we can see. But you know it's not. You saw it on the map."

He did think about the atlas with its pale blue cover illustrated with a bird's-eye view of a lone car driving across a bridge over a stream cutting through tree-dotted mountains. Inside, Miles's meticulous notations and a curving red wax line mapped out their journey. Neither image hinted that such an undertaking could be anything less than ideal and simple.

While he appreciated the philosophical turn of the conversation, he worried for Lilly's safety and was grateful when Mother clutched at the fabric around the girl's bottom and tugged her back into the seat.

"You'll get yourself killed," Betty Ruth said, chastising. "Absolutely killed."

"Anyway," Lilly continued, not skipping a beat, "how sad would it be to look at this little stretch of road and think, 'This is all there is?' I'd go crazy. I have to believe there are better things ahead."

Mother patted Lilly's leg. "And there are, my dear. There are. I can't wait to see the healing God is going to do."

"Here, here." Lilly raised an imaginary glass.

"So you do hope to find better things on the road ahead?" Cullen asked.

"I have to, Moonsie. If I didn't, I wouldn't go."

He cut off the conversation there, before Mother could question the specifics of exactly where Lilly was going. Besides, he was tired after a nearly sleepless night, and thankfully the two women had no problem finding endless things to talk about that didn't involve his input. They talked about fashion, specifically hemlines. They debated something called Coco Chanel. He closed his eyes and lived through three Lillian Gish movies as they were reconstructed—down to the last detail—by Lilly.

After a time, he stretched his legs into the cavernous opening in the middle of the car and felt himself dozing. For a while there was nothing but the roar of the car's engine, the wind, and his mother's familiar voice explaining how preserves and jelly and jam were indeed quite different from each other. The last thought he had before going to sleep was that he too had always had such confusion. And then, rumbling, humming, gusting silence.

He woke up to find his mother dozing contentedly against him, and his arm stretched out across the back of the seat. More than that, he was touching Lilly's shoulder. Not with his whole hand, of course, but the two untwisted, unscarred fingers had found their way to a perfect patch of warm, sun-kissed skin. Her dress was sleeveless, and so his fingers had actually made their way under the fabric, and the silk beneath them felt suspiciously like some kind of strap. In fact, he knew exactly what kind, because he'd seen her that night she came home from the picture show, when she'd passed out on her bed, uncovered. Here, halfway between waking and sleep, he remembered that image. Perhaps he'd been visiting it in his dream.

Obviously he should remove his hand, but the days he had with this woman were fast dwindling, and after this he'd see to it that the opportunities to touch her would disappear with them. His head lolling in her direction, he peeked, thankful for his sunglasses for more reasons than simply the protection they offered from the nearly noon sun.

She was sleeping too, her head resting against the back of the seat, her face turned toward him. Would he never tire of seeing this sight?

While the ride had not been exactly smooth, the car hit a particularly rough patch of road, causing Lilly's head to bounce against the seat. Cullen immediately began to withdraw his touch, but before he could, Lilly's hand came up, covering his, holding it there. Her palm was somehow cool, and the contrast between it and the warmth of her shoulder was as refreshing and welcome to his spirit as a cold drink would be to his parched throat.

Her eyes remained closed, though he caught the slight twitch of her lashes against her cheek. Lips once parted in sleep now came together, twisting into a small, slight smile. Then a squeeze of her fingers, and she released him.

It might not be the backseat experience Bill Owens envisioned, but it would be all Cullen had. He and Lilly, bathed in sunlight, cocooned in wind, all the way to Alabama.

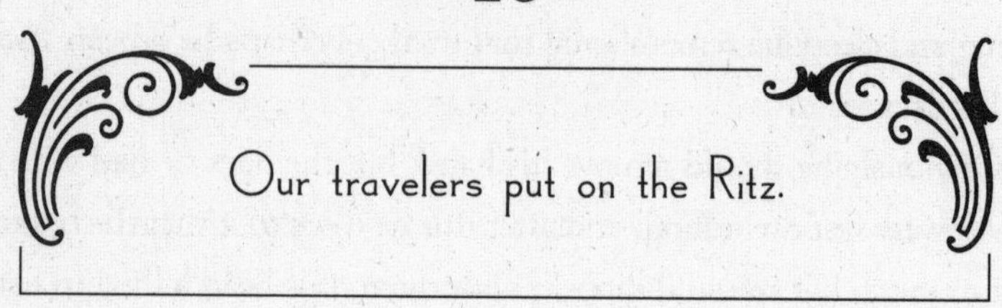

23

Our travelers put on the Ritz.

Although no one was likely to say so out loud, Lilly knew: if it weren't for the unbridled enthusiasm of Betty Ruth, the entire traveling party would abandon Bill Owens's Peerless and pile into the next train bound for Pensacola. But throughout the day Betty Ruth continued to declare that she'd never before felt so much a part of God's great creation. Who would dare take such a thing away? Yet for the last few hours, at least, when darkness turned the wind to chill, they'd driven with the car's canvas top up.

As they approached the outskirts of Birmingham, Alabama, Cullen moved to the front passenger seat so he could help Miles navigate to the hotel where they would spend the night. Lilly suspected his reason for the change was partly due to not wanting to share a backseat with her in the dark, but she made no teasing claim.

He might think he was hiding behind his dark glasses, but she knew enough of men to be able to read more than their eyes. The way his touch sought her when he was deep in sleep—and she knew he was asleep, as he would never attempt such boldness otherwise—spoke volumes about his attraction. If he ever gave himself a chance, he might even love her a little bit.

"It should be just ahead. On the right. I came here once with Father for some kind of railroad convention, but that was years ago." Cullen was leaning out his window, and Lilly wished they could put the top down again while they cruised through the city's busy streets. She loved the adventure of a new town.

"Are you sure we're in the right city, dear?" Betty Ruth asked, wringing her hands. "They've all started to blend together. All the same..."

"There it is!"

Lilly leaned across Betty Ruth to look out and up—twelve stories up, to be exact—at the regal facade of the Tutwiler Hotel.

"Jeepers, creepers," she muttered. "That's like some kind of city or something."

"Oh my." Betty Ruth patted her hair. "And I look such a mess."

"That's a lot of floors to mop," Eugenie said. It was one of the few times she'd spoken since lunch, and everybody laughed.

Miles pulled the car alongside the front entrance; immediately a dark man in a long coat came to open the doors.

"Good evenin' and welcome to the Tutwiler Hotel. May I get your bags?"

"Please." Cullen handed the man a bill from a folded pile he had taken from his pocket.

Yet another man in a similar long coat stood at the entrance to the revolving door—a contraption that at once befuddled and delighted Betty Ruth. She and Lilly stood on the sidewalk, Betty Ruth watching the door's openings go by, and by, and by, like a little girl waiting to jump in a twirling rope.

"And when you find yourself on the other side," Lilly instructed, "you just step out. See? Watch Cullen."

Cullen walked in, then out, raising his hands victoriously on the other side.

"Now, watch Eugenie."

"I'll wait out here," Eugenie said before adding something about wanting just a tad more fresh air before going inside.

"Then watch me." Lilly stepped into the next rotating section, then out into the lobby, where she looked out at Betty Ruth. "Come on!" she beckoned, but Betty Ruth did not budge. Lilly cupped her hands around her mouth and shouted, "I'll catch you!" She pantomimed her promise, though she had no real idea what it would take to catch a full-grown woman on her way out of a revolving door.

Emboldened, Betty Ruth stepped in. At that point, Lilly was glad to have made the promise to catch her, because the older woman kept her eyes closed with every step—and from the look of it, she was holding her breath too.

The second Betty Ruth came within reach, Lilly reached for her hand and pulled her from the turning door. "There, see? That wasn't so bad."

"What the world is coming to, I don't know. I just don't know." But Betty Ruth was fairly beaming with pride in her accomplishment.

That left the two of them to encourage Eugenie, who had finally removed her tan riding coat and hat, looking relatively dust free and coiffed, considering. Unlike Betty Ruth's timid steps, Eugenie took a running jump into the rotating door and two or three stumbling steps on the other side.

"Like to know how you'd lock that against a stranger," she said, eyeing it suspiciously.

Now that they were all inside, Lilly could take a long, appreciative look at the lobby.

Magnificent. White marble floors interrupted with ornate rugs; smatterings of sofas and chairs in conversational clusters. The mezzanine ran along three walls, palm fronds and ferns spilling over its columns. The far wall was dominated by a dark mahogany counter that ran its length, and there Cullen stood, conducting business with the well-dressed clerk behind the desk. Lilly led the ragtag group of women to stand behind him.

The man behind the desk was taller than Cullen but twice as slender. His thin hair was slicked across his head—side to side—revealing great stripes of scalp. "You reserved the four-bedroom suite?"

"Yes," Cullen said. "I telephoned yesterday."

"I see." No doubt he did, given how he looked down his nose at the entire company. Lilly wanted to smack him, but Cullen spoke up for them instead.

"You'll have to forgive our appearance. We've decided to take on a bit of adventure. A road trip of sorts."

"We are going to the World Series," Betty Ruth said. Her long, graying hair fought to free itself from the twisted braid that fell to her hips. Eugenie loomed over her more like a guardian than a maid, and Lilly could only imagine what a dusty, wrinkled mess she herself was.

"I see," the clerk repeated, but this time the phrase held a touch of disapproval. "Baseball fans. How...nice."

"Oh, it's not for the game," Betty Ruth piped up, and before anybody could stop her—"we're going to see the healing of my son. God showed me in a vision—"

"That's enough, Mother." Cullen's slightest touch to her hand brought Betty Ruth to silence. He turned back to the clerk. "We've had an especially long day."

"I see." He was holding the key now, though he looked like he'd just as soon swallow it as hand it over. "Do you have luggage?"

Just then the porter from the sidewalk and Miles arrived, each carrying bags.

The clerk curled a long finger, beckoning Cullen to lean in and listen across the desk. Lilly followed suit.

"You do realize," the clerk said, "that we won't be able to let your boy stay in the room."

"My boy?"

Lilly's face burned as hot as it did driving in the sun. She dared not turn around.

"Whatever you want to call him. With the bags. He can't stay here."

"I've paid for the rooms," Cullen said. "Technically they are mine for the night."

"Now, sir, you know that's not how it works." The clerk stood straight and raised his voice, addressing the man who helped Miles with the luggage. "Benny? Surely there's a place close by where Mr. Burnside's, er, *driver* can get a room for the night?"

Benny's well-worn face took on a knowing look. "Yes sir. I can surely find him a place."

"And it's good and clean?"

Lilly eyed them both. They'd played out this conversation before.

"Oh yes sir. And reasonable too. Dollar a night. Throw in another six bits for supper and breakfast in the mornin'."

"Does that sound all right to you, Miles?"

"Oh, yes sir, Mr. Burnside. That sounds just fine."

"Very well." Cullen reached back into his pocket, but Miles held up his hand.

"No sir. I'll pay for my own room."

Cullen continued, undaunted. "I was going to give you money to fill up the car, if you don't mind. And be here at eight tomorrow morning? Eight thirty?"

"Yes sir."

A young man came with a cart for their luggage, and Lilly noticed Miles hadn't brought his own bag in. Of course he'd known better. He and Benny loaded the bags they were carrying onto the cart. Cullen gave a single bill to Benny, and the bellboy took the bags around to the service elevator.

The guest elevator was as plush as any room Lilly had ever seen. Carpet on the floor, dark wood paneling along the lower half of the walls, ornate velvet wallpaper along the top. The operator greeted them warmly and seemed prepared to abandon any further conversation, except for the fact that Cullen asked if he knew the score from that day's game.

"Senators took it, sir. Four, zip."

"I see," Cullen said.

Lilly understood the pain on his face. That gave them three wins. If they won tomorrow, the Series would be over, and all of this would be for naught. And they wouldn't know until the day was well under way.

After that, Betty Ruth filled the quiet void, remarking each time the ornate arrow passed another floor that she'd never been above a third floor in her life. "In my very life," she insisted, to which Cullen said, of course she had, she simply didn't remember, and the argument ensued until the operator, sounding relieved, announced, "Tenth floor!"

The bellboy was in the process of unlocking the door as they walked out of the elevator, so a set of shining white double doors stood open and ready to welcome the ragged travelers. The lobby was majestic, the elevator plush, but nothing could have prepared Lilly for the unabashed luxury of the Tutwiler Hotel's four-bedroom suite. The main room looked like something out of a movie—white couches and potted palms, gilt-edged tables and thick carpet, a rolling bar stocked with crystal decanters and glassware, an enormous silver bowl overflowing with fresh fruit, vases of cut flowers on every possible surface.

Out of the corner of her eye, Lilly saw Cullen give the bellboy a bill, which he eagerly accepted before bowing out of the room. It never occurred to her until this moment how much money the Burnside family must have. Their home was lovely, to be sure, and she'd had plenty of opportunity to watch Cullen act the part of a business mogul. But this? They would be in this place for one night. Not much more than twelve hours, really. And already he'd given away more money in tips than most people she knew earned in a week.

Maybe it was just hunger, or the result of a day spent in the backseat of a bumpy car, but her stomach knotted and turned. If she had so misjudged his wealth, he had probably misjudged her poverty. In his mind, she might be going back to some quaint, square, small yellow house with a picket fence and a rosebush by the front door. If he only knew.

"Mother"—he picked up Betty Ruth's bag—"you'll take the master bedroom over here to the left. And I can take the room next to you. It doesn't have its own bath, so I'll share yours if that's all right."

"I'd rather have Eugenie," Betty Ruth said. "I simply must wash my hair, and it's such a tangled mess. I'll need her to pull out the knots. And I have my clothes that need to be pressed..."

Her voice trailed as she walked toward the room, Eugenie in her wake carrying their bags. To his credit, Cullen tried to take them from her, but she shrugged him off and followed her mistress.

It was the first they'd been alone since the night before with the doughnuts and milk, the very thought of which reminded Lilly of how very hungry she felt. Her stomach gurgled loudly to confirm. Loud enough, in fact, to attract Cullen's attention.

"I'm starving." She eyed the bowl of fruit. "Is that real? Or wax?"

"Let's see." He picked a grape and popped it in his mouth. "Definitely wax."

"Good enough for me." She selected a pear and followed suit, sinking into the white couch.

"I'll order up some supper for us." He crossed to the back of the room where an ornate desk sat in a corner and picked up the shiny white telephone. "Something simple, don't you think? Ham and cheese omelets?"

"That sounds fine." A bit of pear juice trickled past her wrist, and she licked it.

He spoke the order into the phone, adding a dozen biscuits and coffee, and replaced the receiver. After that, he didn't seem to know quite what to do.

"Come sit." Lilly scooted to the far side of the sofa, patting the cushion next to her.

"I've been sitting all day." He slid aside the white gauzy drapes revealing an enormous, clear plate-glass window with a view overlooking the city below.

"Let me see." She took a final bite of fruit and left the core on the table and then joined Cullen, who stood, his hands in his pockets, looking down at the lights. "It's beautiful."

He looked up, and their eyes met in the reflection of the glass. "Yes."

"This whole room," she said, forcing lightness to her voice, "it's the bee's knees. Thank you."

"My father was here for the grand opening a little over ten years ago. Not much has changed."

"Well, I've never been any place like it in my life." She turned her attention to the view below. "I wonder where Miles is."

"I hated that. I should have known better."

"Miles did."

"Yes, he did."

"I'll bet that Benny has a place. Maybe even his own. You're not the first guest here with a Negro driver. He's probably got some nice setup somewhere, and dollars to doughnuts that desk clerk has a stake in it."

"Well, how do you know so much about the dark underworld?"

She smiled at the admiration in his tone. "I've known a few Negroes in my time. Don't tell me you've never been to a jazz club?" Their eyes met again. "Of course you haven't." She leaned her forehead against the cool glass and her palms too, knowing full well they'd make a smudge that some woman who would never be allowed to be a guest here would have to clean.

"You should go sometime. It's amazing. The music"—she hummed a few bars, turning her voice into some kind of sultry brass—"there's nothing like it. It's like magic, only not fairy-tale magic. It's darker, and real. The doors close behind you, and you're like the rabbit in the hat. That's what a guy told me once. My boyfriend and I, we were the only white people in the place, and he said with my skin, I looked like that magic rabbit inside a black hat."

For all she knew, Cullen wasn't even listening. He offered no comment, but what was there to say? He was the man who peeled dollar bills off of thick rolls to tip the black man who carried his bags, and she was the girl who would dance with that same black man in a jazz club later that night.

"If it wasn't so late," she said, speaking to the dark city on the other side of the glass, "I'd take you to one right now. But you just ordered omelets and coffee from room service."

"Let me carry your bag to your room," he said, as if he hadn't been listening after all. "You might like to freshen up before the food gets here."

"I might, indeed."

She'd been right about leaving a smudge on the glass, and she wished she had a sleeve so that she could try to wipe it away. Perhaps later. Right now, she stopped briefly at the table to pick up her pear's core and then followed Cullen as he carried her suitcase to her room.

She was almost afraid to look, thinking that what might be behind that bedroom door would be beautiful enough to make her cry. And it nearly was. A large four-poster bed made of the same dark mahogany wood she'd seen throughout the hotel was covered with a thick white quilt that looked like a covering made from stitched clouds. There was a marble-topped sink, as well as a long, low chest of drawers with a glass-domed lamp at either end and a vase of fresh flowers in the center.

"My room is next door." Cullen set her suitcase on the stand at the end of the bed. "Our rooms share the bathroom, but you can lock the door."

Lilly simply nodded, unable to speak.

"Is everything all right?"

"I...I can't wait to go to sleep."

"I'll let you know when supper's here."

She did lock the door separating his bedroom from the bathroom, not because she felt there was any danger that he would barge in, but because she knew he wanted her to. Then she drew her first bath with water that flowed from a gold-plated faucet and added a generous helping of Dalliance bath salts, quite possibly a first for the tub as well.

Sinking down into the water, grateful to wash the dust of the road off her skin, she heard the sound of water running on the other side of the wall. He, too, must be washing up at the sink in his room. The thought of it made her uncomfortable, having him just outside the door, and she moved in the water very slowly, cautiously, not wanting to create any undue splashing noises that might attract his attention.

The square of soap provided in the porcelain dish at the edge of the tub was pure white and had a slight scent of gardenias. She lathered it against the plush white washcloth and, satisfied with the thick foam, ran it along her warm, wet skin, erasing every mile and every speck of dust. The water around her, already clouded from the bath salt, took on a grayish hue, and while the luxurious surroundings may have invited a lingering soak, she had no desire to slosh around in her own dirt.

Promising to rise early and treat herself to a longer bath in the morning, Lilly rose out of the water and reached for a towel. Slowly, without making a single sound, she slid the little post, thereby unlocking the door leading to Cullen's room, and then ran into hers, closing the other bathroom door behind her.

Though clean, her skin still felt dry and windburned from the drive, so she opened her remaining jar of Lilies in Moonlight body crème—the very one that introduced her to this family—and slathered a generous amount on her arms, working the lotion into her elbows and over her shoulders, inhaling the sweet scent as she held her bathed arms out, admiring their soft sheen. She sat on the edge of the bed and applied the crème to her legs and feet too. Just as she was closing the jar, she heard a knock and the words "Room service!" muffled through two closed doors.

Quickly she dropped the towel and put on her blue kimono robe, tying it tight as she prepared to receive the delivery. Apparently Cullen had the same idea because they opened their doors simultaneously and stepped out—he in his pajamas and bathrobe too.

"I'll take care of this," he said, only briefly acknowledging her appearance. "You go get Mother."

The carpet was the softest surface Lilly's feet had ever walked across. Plusher than velvet, it cushioned every step as she made her way to Betty Ruth's door.

She knocked. "Betty Ruth? Eugenie? Food's here." No answer, so she knocked again, and after knocking a third time, she pushed the door open just enough to poke her head through. "Betty Ruth?"

But it was Eugenie who answered with an unintelligible scream.

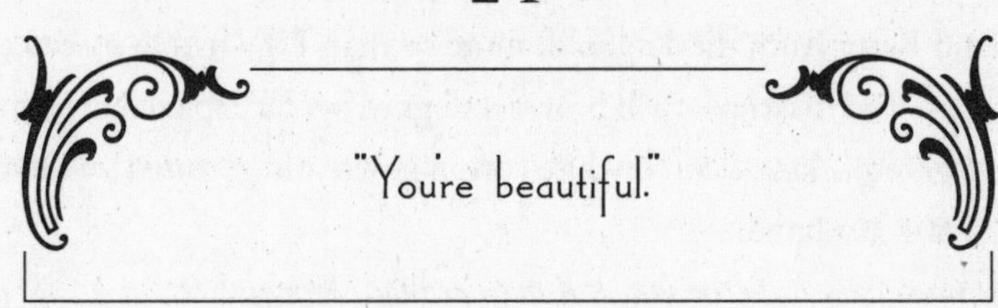

24

"Youre beautiful."

The room was empty, though Betty Ruth's suitcase sat spilled open at the foot of the bed. Leaning in, Lilly picked up the sound of voices—Betty Ruth's and Eugenie's. Neither sounded happy. They were in the bathroom, and as Lilly crept closer, their words became clear, yet she remained confused.

"You know there's not much I wouldn't do for you, Mrs. B, but I've got to draw the line somewhere."

"Then I'll do it myself. I swear I will!"

If the escalation of their volume wasn't enough to make Lilly break into a run, the clattering *thud* that followed definitely spurred her on. She walked in to find Eugenie and Betty Ruth locked in battle, Betty Ruth holding a straight razor in one hand while Eugenie seemed bent on taking it away.

"Ladies!"

Her shout caught their attention, and they stopped midstruggle.

"Well, thank the Lord you're here." Eugenie dropped her grip. "Maybe you can talk some sense into this old woman."

"You see? You see?" Betty Ruth approached Lilly with an attitude that could only be described as imploring. "That's why I want her to do it. I'm not brave enough, not brave enough at all. And I don't want to just get older and older and older."

And Betty Ruth did look old, more so than Lilly had ever seen. Her hair was a wild disarray of ash brown and gray, her face splotched from the sun. She wore a long-sleeved white cotton gown and gestured wildly with the razor in her hand.

It must have been the sun. It drove her mad. Suicidal.

She couldn't let Cullen find his mother in this state. She jerked her head, indicating that Eugenie should leave, and made her voice as calm and soothing as possible.

"Betty Ruth, you know you're not old. Why, you're one of the most vibrant, interesting women I know."

"But look at me!"

A mirror ran the length of the bathroom above the marble countertop. Lilly came up beside her and carefully put one arm around her shoulders, ready to snatch the razor at the first chance. "You're beautiful."

"I look like somebody's crazy old grandmother. Oh, how I'd love to be a grandmother."

Lilly ignored her own pang of sadness, wondering if Betty Ruth would ever have that chance. "See? You have so much to look forward to. So much to live for."

"Oh, for the love of Pete," Eugenia said from outside the door. "She doesn't want to kill herself."

"Kill myself?" The razor clattered to the marble. "Who says I want to kill myself?"

"I thought—"

Betty Ruth burst into soft rippling laughter. "I want—oh, my..." She couldn't go on speaking, so Eugenie invited herself back into the bathroom.

"She wants—" Then Eugenie started laughing, something Lilly never thought she would see, and the sight of it caused her to join in, even though she had no idea what they were so amused about.

"Oh." Betty Ruth wiped the tears from her eyes. "I wanted to—"

"She wants to bob her hair," Eugenie said, her feet planted as firmly as her frown. "And it ain't going to happen on my watch."

"Then don't watch." Lilly turned to Betty Ruth. "You want to cut your hair? Why?"

"Oh, it'll sound silly to a modern young thing like you."

Lilly stooped and took the woman by her shoulders. "Tell me."

Her bright eyes filled with tears. "I've seen so much of the world today. So much. And I feel like such an old-fashioned old woman."

"Class is what you have," Eugenie said. "With the crowning glory the good Lord gave you."

"I think you would look beautiful. Even more so," Lilly added before Eugenie could speak. To prove it, she gathered all of Betty Ruth's hair in her hands and held it, letting it fold just below the woman's chin, giving her a preview of the style. "And think, no more brushing and pinning. All that weight gone in the summer."

"Can you do it for me, Lilly? Have you cut anybody's hair before?"

Lilly smiled. "Dozens. Half of the girls in my class, to tell you the truth. But we can't use that." She pointed at the razor. "Where did you get that, anyway?"

"It was in the room," Betty Ruth said. "Isn't this the most wonderful place? Just wonderful. Like a little home in the sky."

Lilly agreed and remembered a writing desk in the main room. "Wait here."

Eugenie tried to block her exit, but Lilly simply edged her way between the woman and the door frame, then made a beeline for the desk in the main room. There was a table set with a half-dozen domed dishes, but Cullen was nowhere to be found. Moving quickly and silently, she went to the desk, rolled up the top, and found a full assortment of supplies—a pad of writing paper, several pens, and a pair of scissors. These in hand, she went back to Betty Ruth's room, moving with all the stealth of a silent-movie villain.

"We haven't much time." She made her way past Eugenie, who hadn't abandoned her post. "Our supper will be here any minute."

She pulled out the little bench tucked under the counter and had Betty Ruth stand on it, bringing the nape of the woman's neck level with Lilly's eye line. Once again, she gathered the woman's hair into three sections and gave it a quick, tight plait, securing both the top and bottom of the braid with a piece of ribbon.

"Last chance." She stood in front of Betty Ruth, scissors in hand.

"Don't do it," Eugenie wailed, her hands over her eyes, as if about to witness a butchering.

"I'm ready." Betty Ruth looked quite the martyr.

"Dear Lord," Lilly said under her breath. "Don't let me mess this up."

There followed the distinctive sound of steel against hair, and with a few tortured cuts, the thick gray-speckled braid was loose in Lilly's hand. At that moment, the final slice, all three women squealed, each for her own reason.

"Oh, let me see, let me see, let me see." Betty Ruth took Lilly's arm and stepped down from the bench, taking the braided rope as soon as her small feet hit the floor. "Well, look at that."

"It's a lifetime," Lilly said. "And now you're getting a new start."

"Whatever shall I do with it?" Betty Ruth held the braid aloft, swinging it like a pendulum.

"I left my hair on a barber shop floor. Never looked back. But you might want to keep a few strands, at least."

"And what use would that be?" She dropped it into the waste bin. "I can't think of a thing more useless."

Eugenie wagged her finger. "I'm going to go tell Mr. Cullen, and I think he'll have a few words to say to you two."

"Tell him we'll be out in five minutes." Lilly felt as invigorated as if it were her transformation taking place.

She took one of the towels and draped it across Betty Ruth's shoulders, then wet a comb under the faucet and ran it through the newly shortened hair. It was all soft and gray, and Lilly circled around creating an even edge across the back and shorter bangs over her twinkling eyes. After every discerning look, she took off another little bit, and another, finally bringing it to where her hair hit at the same spot where her garnet drop earrings dangled.

Satisfied, she took another towel and rubbed it over the shorn hair, loosening all the remaining little bits and pieces, bringing it closer from damp to dry.

"Look at those curls! I haven't seen such curls since I was a child."

It was true. The new style looked like a gathering of spring storm clouds framing Betty Ruth's face.

"You look ten years younger." Lilly had always been impressed with the smoothness of Betty Ruth's skin, and that dewiness combined with this new style made her look like a star.

"Whatever is my son going to say?" She fluffed her hair with her jeweled fingers while Lilly held out a floral silk dressing gown.

"He's going to say you look beautiful."

The two women emerged to find him standing at the window. When Lilly called his name, he turned around, looked at his mother, then at her.

"What's happened here?"

A shadow flitted across Betty Ruth's face as she patted her curls. "You aren't angry are you, darling?"

"How do you feel?"

"Twenty years younger, and alive."

"How could I be angry with that?"

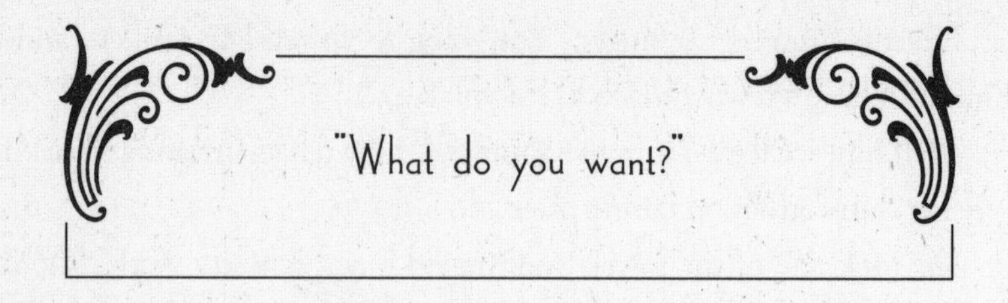

"What do you want?"

Later, after the dirty dishes had been rolled out the door, Betty Ruth proclaimed she'd never been so tired in her entire life and took herself off to bed. "I cannot wait to feel my head hit that pillow. Simply cannot wait."

"You'll feel it all right," Eugenie said, following just steps behind.

Lilly worked her fingers like an imaginary pair of scissors. Her action was not menacing, but Eugenie took it as a threat and stepped up her pace, almost overtaking Betty Ruth in the process.

"So, tell me what you really think, Cullen," Lilly said the moment the two were alone.

"I think one of these days she's going to wake up and wonder where her hair is. And she's going to be frightened, and I'm not going to know what to say."

"She's the same woman. It's like putting on a new dress."

"She hasn't bought a new dress in years."

"Then we'll do that tomorrow."

"Ah yes. Tomorrow."

Drawn by the starlight and the city, Lilly opened the glass door leading to the balcony and stepped outside. She could hear automobiles and music on the breeze, but it was another sense entirely that announced Cullen's presence.

"Sorry to hear your team lost."

"You know what that means, don't you? They lose again tomorrow, and it's all over. No more game to crash."

"I know."

"My instinct says to stay here, wait and see if there's any reason to go on. But I don't even feel like I have that choice. From the moment Mother opened her mouth, it's like I was thrown into this against my will. Like something's pulling me. Drawing me."

Lilly affected a dramatic pose and deepened her voice. "Drawn to the loadstone rock."

He laughed. "The what?"

"The loadstone rock. It's when sailors—"

He held up a hand. "I know what it is. How do you know about such a thing?"

She turned her back to the balcony and leaned against the railing. "Do you think I lost my brains when I cut my hair?"

"I'm sorry. I didn't mean—"

"When I was in high school, my senior recitation was from *A Tale of Two Cities,* the passage where the guy is going back to France to make good his family name. Everybody else got up in front of the class and recited their pieces, but not me."

"Chickened out?"

"No, meanie. I made an actual boat out of glue and newspapers, like this"—she demonstrated an imaginary boat wrapping around her waist. "Held it up with suspenders." She moved now to the end of the patio, gathered herself as if holding an invisible oar, and took the first of several sweeping steps.

"'For the love of Heaven, of justice, of generosity, of the honour of your noble name!' was the poor prisoner's cry with which he strengthened his sinking heart, as he left all that was dear on earth behind him, and floated away for the Loadstone Rock."

Cullen applauded as Lilly took a deep bow. "And so we add acting to your list of talents."

"It does seem endless, doesn't it?"

He became serious. "Can I ask you a question?"

"Not if it's about that book. I only read the part I memorized."

"It's not about the book. It's about you." He reached out, touching her chin, then tilting her head to meet his eyes. "What do you want?"

She froze. His tone was light, but the question felt like a million-pound weight dropped between them. Nobody had ever asked her that before, at least not anybody who ever really wanted to hear the answer. Still, she pushed through. "Just to be happy."

"And what does that mean for you?"

She stepped away from his touch and turned back to the city. "The same as it does for everybody, I guess. To have a home and a family. Love, and all that stuff they write the songs about. The big happy ending at the end of the show."

He was next to her. Right next to her. "I hope you find it."

Those words built an ocean between them.

25

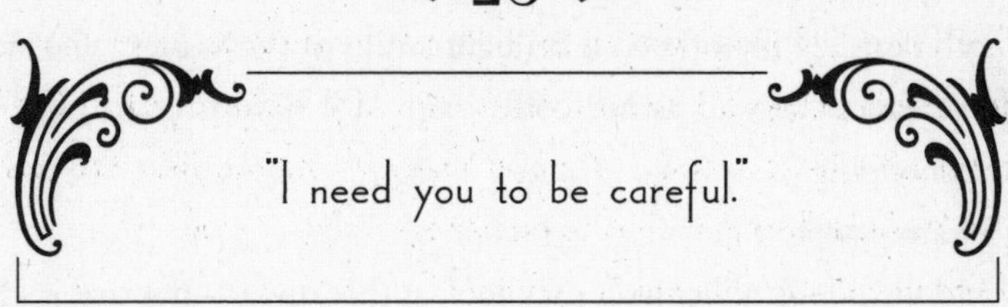

"I need you to be careful."

They breakfasted in the hotel's restaurant, a decision Cullen regretted the moment they walked past the reservation desk. Of the group, Lilly alone looked like she belonged with the other patrons. She led the party, not giving a glance to the left or the right. Mother followed behind. Even with his limited interest in women's fashion, he knew her dress was three times as expensive as Lilly's, but it was one she'd been wearing since he was in high school.

He'd lay money down that no other woman in the dining room wore a dress for more than a season. Maybe it was the modern style of Mother's hair that made her dress look so matronly and dowdy. Still, she looked like a fresh-faced flapper next to Eugenie, who lacked only an apron to complete the uniform of a loyal housemaid.

As Lilly and Mother and Eugenie progressed from table to table, the guests' reactions followed a particular pattern. An admiring gaze, turning to a quizzical expression, to mild disapproval. Then when they saw Cullen, they looked away.

With only Lilly to shine, their party was given a table so close to the kitchen he felt he had to dodge the swinging door.

"I've asked the kitchen to prepare a lunch for us," Cullen said, "so we'll be leaving a bit later than I'd anticipated."

"Fabulous!" Lilly offered a brilliant smile to the waiter, who nearly filled her saucer as well as her coffee cup. "I'll have time to take your mother shopping."

"No, you won't."

"Moonsie, look at her hair, then look at that dress—not that it's not a lovely dress, Betty Ruth."

"This old thing?" She waved it off dismissively.

"At the very least she needs a new hat, or the sun is going to burn her face right off."

A cannonball dropped into the middle of the table couldn't have brought a more stunned reaction. Eugenia shot her a withering look, and Lilly herself looked like she wished she could crawl under the table. Her hands flew to her mouth, and he could clearly see red-tinged cheeks between her fingers. Only Mother remained nonplussed, stirring cream into her coffee.

"I'm so—I didn't think—" Lilly stammered.

"One hour," he said, hoping to assuage her embarrassment. "I'll ask the concierge to recommend some shops that are open this early in the morning."

"Thank you," Lilly said, and he knew her gratitude extended beyond the hour's worth of shopping.

Once they'd given their order—eggs Benedict all around, except for Eugenie's request for oatmeal—Cullen got up from the table and bid Lilly to follow him into the lobby. He offered the concierge a generous tip in exchange for the names and addresses of boutiques that could accommodate his mother and Lilly within the hour. But before returning to the table, he pulled her aside near an arrangement of potted palms.

"I need you to be careful."

"Just tell me your budget and I'll make sure we don't go over."

"Money is not the problem."

She looked around and then back at him. "Obviously."

"Remember, this could be a disaster when this little spell is over and she looks in a mirror and sees that all of her hair is gone."

"You don't know that's going to happen."

"And you don't know that it won't. You don't know her as well as I do. Let me assure you, my scenario is much more likely. Just don't change her completely."

"She's still your mother. She's always loved you, no matter who she thought you were. I don't think either of you are likely to forget that."

He peeled off one hundred dollars and pressed it in her palm. "And don't you forget we have limited space in the car."

They were, of course, late. He paced the sidewalk in front of the car, the only thing left to load being their two bodies. Miles, having arrived thirty minutes before, sat patiently behind the wheel, and Eugenie far less so in the jumper seat. And he waited. But more than merely waiting, he was anticipating Lilly's arrival. *Looking* for her. It seemed he spent a lot of time looking for her. In fact, nearly every time she went away.

He stopped his pacing and stared at the corner. The sidewalk teemed with people, but his eyes invented her appearance. He remembered her dress, knew her face, tensed his hand to return her cheery greeting. Any second now she would appear in the empty spaces between the people. When she did, he was quite glad to have been so familiar with her, because he would not have recognized his mother at all.

"Don't leave without us!" She grabbed Mother's hand and led them in a soft trotting run.

For a moment she could have been holding the hand of her sister. Last night he'd been reluctant to join in the string of compliments claiming that Mother looked ten years younger, but at this moment, he had to agree. Her dress had the same cut and silhouette as Lilly's, though with longer sleeves and a more conservative hemline. Her new hat appeared to be made from some sort of cotton with a wide brim that ran the circumference of the crown. To his amusement, Lilly wore an identical style. Apparently he'd bought her a gift as well.

She touched a hand to the brim. "I hope you don't mind. Betty Ruth insisted."

"I did. I did, indeed."

"Not at all. You both look lovely. Now, get in the car."

Eugenie had her customary sour expression as Lilly and Mother clambered past her on their way to the backseat, and she held it until Lilly dropped a small round box in her lap.

"We got one for you too, 'Genie. Nothing improves the mood like a new hat."

"My mood is just fine, thank you." Still, there was a hint of a smile as she plucked at the string holding the lid.

Cullen took the seat beside Miles, led them all in a prayer for a safe journey that day, and then they were off. Cullen wanted to ask where he had spent the night, if indeed the place had been clean and reputable, but this didn't feel like the right time. In fact, Miles had barely looked him in the eye since he arrived with the car, and the two men hadn't exchanged more than a dozen words all morning.

As they reached the outskirts of the city, the toll of poverty was clearly evident. It became more and more difficult to remember the luxury of the Tutwiler Hotel when faced with the dilapidated shacks and narrow dirt roads of Birmingham's poor. Of course he knew the poor existed in every city, his own no exception, but he'd crafted a life that kept them largely out of sight. Right now, though, he was hardly out of theirs.

Many of these roads had not been updated to allow for automobile travel, and their narrowness and ruts required Miles to drive at a frustratingly slow pace. The car crept along, dozens of dark eyes in dark faces staring after it. Why would anybody feel shame in being poor? At this moment, his wealth felt like an almost suffocating embarrassment.

Nobody spoke until they were once again surrounded by open country, when Cullen asked Miles if he thought they would be able to make up their lost time on the road ahead.

"Yes sir." And nothing more.

He turned to Eugenie. "Any problems getting our lunch packed?"

"No sir."

Back in the third seat, Lilly and Mother were hunkered down, their new hats inches away from each other, giggling over a secret.

Gradually Miles picked up speed, and the cool of the morning took on the chill of wind. Cullen turned in his seat and inquired if anyone wished to have the top put up.

No one did.

And so they rumbled on, mostly silent, through open country and small towns, passing small hand-lettered signs offering direction and mileage. Some towns they entered and left without seeing another soul, and Mother would say, "Imagine living here. How lonely." Cullen wanted to contradict her, knowing it was possible to be lonely in a city of any size, but the prospect of carrying on a philosophical conversation across the great divide of the Peerless did not appeal to him.

They stopped for lunch right over the Tennessee border in a shady grove off the main road. Miles and Eugenie spread the gray plaid blanket, still studded with dirt and grass from Alabama. Lilly carried the picnic hamper that contained Tutwiler's thirty-dollar lunch. At that price, he half expected solid gold sandwiches.

He wasn't far off the mark.

The meal—prepared for five—consisted of two loaves of sourdough bread wrapped in crisp, clean linen, and something like a large cigar box, also lined with linen, contained a variety of sliced meats and another held cheese. There was fruit in a brown paper sack and cookies in a small round tin emblazoned with a picture of the hotel's lobby on the lid.

The real prize, the one most likely responsible for the inflated price, was a porcelain bowl with gold-leaf edging, packed to the top with potato salad and covered with waxed paper. Similarly styled plates were strapped to the hamper's lid, each with the Tutwiler Hotel etched in gold at the center. To complete the offering, there were two bottles of wine and a stack of waxed paper cups.

"Well, what have we here?" Lilly took one bottle from him. "The illustrious Tutwiler in violation of Prohibition?" She studied the label and frowned. "Never mind. Just grape juice."

"All the better." He gave her a knowing look and took the bottle away. "Look and see if they included a corkscrew."

They had, and once the food and plates were spread out on the blanket, they gathered, each at a corner, prepared to eat, when Cullen realized Miles had returned to the car.

"Miles," he called, and when the man didn't answer, he got up and walked over to him. "Come join us."

"I'm fine, sir." He held up a small brown bag. "Got my own dinner here."

Guilt tore through his mind as Cullen remembered—Miles hadn't eaten with them the previous day either. He thought nothing of it at the time, thinking the guy simply wanted a break from the noisy chatter, but in light of last night, his drawing apart took on a malicious meaning. And Cullen had allowed it. Worse, he'd ignored it. He might have been powerless to allow Miles to sleep in one of the Tutwiler Hotel beds, but there were no such restrictions at this picnic.

"There's plenty," Cullen insisted, fighting the shame he felt. "More than enough. And I'd be honored."

"Well, then, who am I not to honor a man?"

Miles dropped the bag onto the floor of the car and went with Cullen to join the others. By then, Eugenie had sliced the bread and assembled the sandwiches, loading each plate to capacity. Cullen bowed his head to speak a blessing over the meal.

"Heavenly Father, we thank You for Your provision in this meal and the safe travel You have granted. And for the fellowship we share. And, Lord, forgive me—" The words lodged in his throat. Not that he didn't know exactly what he sought forgiveness for, but in that instant he measured the blow to Miles's pride should he voice his repentance. The woods rang silence around them, echoing his request. He knew he couldn't—he *shouldn't*—leave the thought so unspoken, and as he sought the proper words, another voice joined his prayer.

"Forgive us all, Lord Jesus." It was Miles, his voice deep and resonant. "Forgive us for we all have sinned and fallen short of Your glory. Help us seek always to live a better life in the pattern of Your righteousness. May we love one another as You have loved us. May we help one another as You would have us do. And may we forgive one another as You have forgiven us. Without exception, and complete. Amen."

"Amen." Cullen's ears were so full of Miles's prayer he had no idea if any of the others agreed as heartily, but it didn't matter. In those moments, through Jesus Himself, he and Miles had struck new ground, and Cullen promised himself never to forget.

The silence that had pervaded the car disappeared with the meal, and they ate and talked with great abandon. Here Cullen learned that Lilly's hunch had been correct, and Miles had indeed spent the night at the porter's house.

"Best dollar I ever did spend. No offense to this cookin' here, which is mighty fine, but that man's wife made a pork roast and greens like I've never had before. Then I spent the night playin' cards—won back my lodgin' money, so my wife don't need to know."

They laughed and ate, each of them complaining that they'd done too much of the latter. For Cullen, at least, the return to the road seemed an almost unwelcome necessity. He would have loved to stretch out right there under a tree and take a well-deserved nap, but they'd already lost a great deal of time that morning.

He tipped his paper cup and drank the last of the juice. "All right, everybody. Let's clear out and go. As it is we're not getting to Knoxville until late tonight."

In preparation to get back on the road, Miles excused himself to walk deeper in the woods, and Mother and Eugenie did the same, going in the opposite direction. Lilly gathered the dirty plates, stacking and wrapping them in the same linen towels that once wrapped the bread.

Cullen joined her in helping with the cleanup. He lifted a nearly empty bottle of grape juice. "Want the last of this?"

She took it, held the bottle to her lips, and took one great swallow. "Thank you."

He couldn't help smiling at her manners, all the while imagining what his mother would have thought. Not Mother today, or even of this past week, but the mother he'd grown up with. The one who'd ensured they were always fully staffed with servants. The Betty Ruth Burnside of his youth would never sit down to a meal with her maid, no matter the color. And with a black man of any class? Unlikely.

Lilly interrupted his thoughts. "Why isn't Eugenie black?"

"Excuse me?"

"I don't mean her herself, of course. I'm just curious as to why you have a black driver and a white maid."

"My father hired Miles twenty years ago after buying his first automobile. He liked the prestige of owning one but had no idea how to operate it. He told everybody that Miles was his mechanic, but secretly, at night or outside of town, Miles gave him driving lessons. Funny, once Father learned how, it suddenly became more impressive to have somebody else drive for him."

"So does that explain Eugenie too? More impressive to have a white maid?"

"You might find this hard to believe, but we don't base all of our decisions on race. We had maids of every shape and size and color growing up. Eugenie has been with us for over a year, the longest in quite some time."

"Oh, I can't see Betty Ruth as such a taskmaster."

They'd put away all the remaining food and dishes, closed the hamper, and set it to the side. Cullen picked the blanket up by the corners and gave it a shake, sending dirt and leaves and crumbs into a disconnected cloud between them.

"It's not that. It's Mother. Her forgetfulness. One day a woman would be bringing in the wash, and Mother would just start screaming, 'Who is this woman!'" He flailed his arms and shrilled his voice in imitation. "I'd try to convince them to stay, but..."

"She's doing so much better now." Lilly picked up the opposite corners of the blanket and walked toward him.

"Now, yes." Their fingers touched as he took the scratchy material from her. It was almost like dancing. Then she walked away to repeat the step.

"Strange, even as your mother went in and out of memories, Eugenie remained a constant."

"It's because she doesn't look like anything."

"What?" Again, their fingers touched. He would fold the rest alone.

"Or maybe she looks like everyone. Think about it. Her hair, her face, her clothes—all pretty much the same color. Her eyes even blend in, and her mouth. Look at her sometime and squint, like this." Lilly lifted her chin and looked at his hooded, quivering lids. "She'll turn into a blur."

"I'll have to remember that."

He took the blanket to the car and laid it across the luggage in the boot. When he turned around, Lilly had followed him, carrying the basket to be put on the floor in the middle section.

"One other thing." She dropped her voice to a whisper and glanced over her shoulder before continuing. "Are you planning for us to stay in another fancy hotel tonight?"

He pictured Knoxville's St. Oliver. "Yes."

"I think I have a better idea."

26

Knockabout Campsite, Knoxville, Tennessee.

"A place where the weary road warrior can receive water, fuel, light, shelter, and towels."

Auto Trails Atlas of the United States

"The turn should be coming up soon. Just past the petrol station." Lilly was on her knees in the front passenger seat, leaning over the side of the car door.

She felt Cullen grab a handful of skirt—close to a handful of something else too.

"You're going to get yourself killed."

"Not if you can manage not to drive into the side of a tree." But she sat down all the same. It was not quite dusk, but the coming darkness made it difficult to clearly see the road.

"Is there a sign?"

"I don't know, Moonsie. Last time I was here I was coming from the other direction."

"There should be a sign. They should have a sign."

"We could stop at the station and ask directions, just to be sure."

"No. If you say the turn's ahead, it's ahead. We'll find it."

Miles leaned forward, popping his head over the back of the seat. "You all sure you don't want me to drive?"

"Not now." Cullen spoke over his shoulder. "We're almost there. I think—"

"There's the sign!" Lilly couldn't have felt more triumphant if she'd discovered the New World. "Knockabout Campsite. Turn here."

The turn was sharp enough to knock Lilly off balance and send her slamming into Cullen's shoulder. If she didn't know better, she'd swear he'd done it on purpose. As it was, he'd turned onto a narrow road, carved through trees so dense it felt as though they'd entered an evergreen tunnel.

"Good heavens!" Betty Ruth called from the backseat. "What kind of establishment are you taking us to?"

Lilly turned around. "Remember? We talked about it. We're going to a campsite. You'll love it."

"If we're not cut down by savages."

"Well, I can't guarantee anything." But she wasn't really worried. After all, she'd been to plenty of these places.

The road twisted and switched and narrowed. Cullen turned on the headlights and slowed the car to a creeping pace. "This can't be right."

"Hold on." She peered forward. "All of a sudden, this is just going to open up into a clearing and—"

It did. One more turn, and the road widened enough to branch out in two directions, with a small log cabin right in the middle.

"Now, stop here," Lilly said, and as she did, a tall, gangly red-headed man came out of the cabin. He wore a pair of faded denim overalls over a sleeveless undershirt. As he stood in the flood of the headlights, he lifted one hand to shield his eyes and the other to take the stubby pipe out of his mouth.

The moment Cullen brought the car to a full stop, Lilly threw the door open and ran.

"Rusty!"

Just before the headlights went out, she saw the recognition in his eyes.

"Lilly-bird!"

She ran to him and leaped into his arms, which felt long enough to wrap around her twice. He smelled of tobacco and sweat, with a little bit of corn whiskey mixed in for good measure.

"Whoo-hoo! Girly, I never did think I'd see you in these here woods again." He stood back and held her at arm's length. "Where'd you take yourself off to?"

"Been down to Florida."

"And what about that man you was with?" He clamped the pipe in his teeth and looked out toward the car. "That him in the car? You marry him?"

She shook her head. "No…and, no."

"Well, praise the Lord for that. He never was no good. What was his name?"

"Doesn't matter. Look, do you have any cabins? We'll need two. Just for tonight."

By now Cullen was at her elbow. "I had no idea you were acquainted with the proprietor."

It was the first time her past and present truly collided, a moment she'd been worried about since suggesting they stay at a campsite. She wrung her hands, nervous about the introduction. "I wasn't sure if he would still be here. People tend to come and go."

"And such is the life of a nomad. Rusty Tatters." He wiped his right hand on his pant leg before extending it.

Lilly cringed, knowing he was reaching for Cullen's injured hand and that he preferred to shake with his left. But he extended his right hand too, and maybe it was her imagination, but he seemed to go up on his toes a bit with each pump.

"Cullen Burnside. Pleased to meet you."

Rusty broke off the handshake and took the pipe out of his mouth. "France?"

"Excuse me?"

"You get hurt in France?"

"Ah. No, Germany."

"Well then." Rusty took a step back, turned his head, and spat into the dirt. "And that'll be the end of my politics talkin'. Now. You and my Lilly-bird need a cabin, do ya?"

"No!" They both shouted at the same time and with such fervor that Rusty took another step back.

"Hey, hey, now. You don't got to convince me. I may not approve of the way the world's turnin', but I'm not the soul to stop it."

"Mr. Burnside is simply taking me home."

"Back to your mama?" The concern in Rusty's eyes made Lilly want to cry.

"Yes. And he is going to the World Series."

"Well, I'll be fishin' in a mud hole. And you comin' to my little place here." He held his hand over his heart. "What an honor indeed."

"So we need at least two cabins." Cullen's scowl was something she hadn't seen before. "Three, if possible." He turned to Lilly. "So you and Mother won't have to share."

Rusty craned to look into the ever-darkening distance. "You got your mama with you? Well, I guess my Lilly-bird's in good hands after all."

"And her maid and our driver." Cullen reached into his pocket, ready to pull out the roll of money, as if that would impress Rusty. Lilly almost told him to put it away.

"Don't you be givin' me no money." Rusty took a first long step to the car. "Let me just meet ever'body."

Momentarily alone, Cullen looked at her, asking a million questions.

"I lived here for about a month. Worked here, actually. Doing laundry and things."

"Why didn't you tell me?"

"Because I didn't know what you'd think. Or if you'd let us come here."

"Why wouldn't I?"

"You don't seem happy now."

"I don't like surprises." He touched a finger to the end of her nose. "Remember that."

By the time the two made it back to the car, Rusty had worked his charm on all of them. His elbows firmly planted on top of the door, he leaned in and delivered a punch line to a joke funny enough to make Eugenie laugh.

Cullen waited until the laughter died down before saying, "The rooms?"

"You sure are a busy britches, aren't ya? Well, you're lucky because it just so happens I have plenty of vacancies tonight. Slow night, middle of the week and all. I can give you five even, so's nobody has to share." He turned his back to Eugenie and Betty Ruth and leaned forward to whisper in Lilly's ear. "Lessin' they want to."

"They don't," she whispered back.

"Just four, I think," Cullen broke in. "Mother, do you want to share with Eugenie? I think that might be for the best."

"Oh, of course, dear. Of course. Whatever you think is best."

Rusty clapped his paddle-shaped hands. "Well then. That's done. But first up, I'm bettin' you all haven't had no supper yet tonight. That right?"

"Not yet," Lilly said. They'd finished the last of the fruit twenty miles ago. "You have anything good cooking up here?"

"Nope. Not a bite. But if you're interested, there's a Baptist church not two miles up the road. They're havin' one hootin' of a tent meetin' goin' on and a potluck supper to boot. My Ginny—you know she's the spiritual one—she's taken a big ol' mashed-potato casserole. Nothin' like the cookin' of good Christian women seekin' the spirit of the Lord. If you'll let me hitch a ride with you all in this fancy boat here, I'll give you direction."

"I don't think that's quite what we—"

"A tent revival!" Betty Ruth's enthusiasm overtook Cullen's reluctance. "Oh, I haven't been to one of those since I was a girl. And how I loved them! Simply loved them."

"The lady has spoken," Rusty said with a grand gesture. "Now, one last thing." He turned to Miles. "You are more'n welcome to sleep in one of my beds. I never did know a bed yet that could tell whether the person atop it was a white man or a darkie, and I don't believe the good Lord sees a difference neither. But I can't speak for all the people gathered under that tent yonder. We all tend to have our own churches 'round these parts. You understand?"

"I understand," Miles said. No defiance and no shame. "I still have some of my dinner left from earlier today. I'll be fine."

Lilly thought of that brown paper bag, dropped to the car floor. She'd stepped on it a half dozen times. She turned to Rusty. "He's got to come with us."

Miles protested. "Don't you worry about it, Miss Margolis."

Lilly went on. "He's just as hungry as we are, and just as Christian. More, even."

Rusty puckered his lips around his pipe and looked up at the now-night sky for a moment. "Well, I reckon there's always a time for a first." He pointed at Miles with his pipe. "You stick right next to me and Ginny then, and we won't have no trouble."

He gave Lilly a list of numbers—the cabins they'd be occupying—and excused himself. "Looks like I'm gonna be stayin' for the service after all. Best get a shirt on and a nickel for the plate."

Under Lilly's direction, Cullen drove the car along the path circling to the right of Rusty's cabin. He leaned over and, speaking from the side of his mouth, asked, "Who's Ginny?"

"His wife."

"He's married?"

Lilly looked at him, pleased to see the smile that hinted at relief. "Don't tell me you were jealous of Rusty Tatters."

"I was curious, the way he picked you up and all."

Her heart warmed when she realized the cabins he'd given them. The best he had. She reached out and stilled Cullen's arm as he moved to turn off the car's ignition. "There was a time when Rusty and Ginny were like family to me. He was like a brother."

"A big brother."

"Yes, like that."

Quickly, under the pressure of empty stomachs and a waiting guide, they piled out of the car and into their respective cabins. None had its own bathroom, but the four were just steps away from the common toilet and shower area kept meticulously clean by Ginny Tatters herself. Miles and Cullen each had his own cabin on one side; Lilly walked Betty Ruth and Eugenie to the door of theirs. The key hung on a hook by the door—guests would keep it in their possession for the duration of their stay. A lamp and matches sat on a small table in the center; she found them by memory and plunged the room into light.

"Oh, isn't it dear! I feel just like a little pioneer girl. An absolute pioneer." Betty Ruth's smile rivaled the lamplight. Eugenie's shoulders slumped with the weight of the bags.

There were two small beds against opposite walls, and the wall directly across from the door had a sink and stove with a single burner and a cabinet above stocked with one saucepan, one frying pan, four plates, bowls, cups, and cutlery. There was also a table in the center surrounded by four chairs, and that was it. The beds looked warm and inviting with their colorful quilts, and for just a moment Lilly nearly forgot her hunger, knowing the same scene awaited her next door.

"So it will do?" Lilly asked, feeling responsible and shy. "It's not nearly as fancy as where we stayed last night."

"That's for sure," Eugenie said, looking around.

"It's perfectly perfect." Betty Ruth sat on the edge of the nearest bed. "I don't wonder if I'm not too tired after this day to go to a church meeting." She took off her hat and ran her fingers through her hair, bringing it to a perfect frame around her face. "I do remember them from my youth, but..." The rest of her thought disappeared behind a tremendous yawn, which brought Eugenie to do the same.

"Let me just cook something for you here, Mrs. B." Eugenie turned to Lilly and dropped her voice to a whisper. "She looks so tired. I think it would be too much."

Lilly agreed. The tiny woman drooped on the bed, like weights were attached to her shoulders.

Lilly went to her knees. "Betty Ruth? Would you rather have a simple supper here?" She looked up at Eugenie. "Rusty keeps cans of Campbell's soup in his cabin, for guests who don't have anything to eat." He sold them for a dime each, but Cullen wouldn't mind.

"That sounds heavenly." Betty Ruth sounded like she might not have the strength for soup. "But you should go."

"Oh, I don't know." Suddenly fatigue was about to win over hunger. "Soup sounds pretty good to me right now too."

"It could be that the Lord has a word for you tonight, my dear. Go and eat and listen. And think what fun it will be telling me all about it tomorrow."

"All right, if you say so." Besides the fond memories of Ginny's mashed-potato casserole, there would be the chance to see Ginny herself.

"And if there is any cobbler, perhaps you could bring back a dish for me? Baptist women always make the best cobbler."

Lilly hugged the fragile woman, careful not to break her. "I will. I promise—even if I have to sneak it out in my pocket."

She stood, told Eugenie she'd be back with the soup, and stepped outside. A few other guests were milling about, and Rusty had a few tall gas lamps bringing some light into the clearing. Rusty himself was across the way talking with Cullen and Miles. She didn't know if their conversation was dangerous or risqué, but there came an obvious protective silence at her approach. She explained the women's preference to stay back.

"You know," Miles said, "I think I might hang back too. Be easier all around."

"Well, here I was thinking we was goin' to be off on an adventure. How about you, Lilly-bird? You wantin' to stay here too?" He turned to Cullen. "I was plannin' to walk up there anyway. On my way when you all pulled up."

"Oh no," Lilly said. "I do want to see Ginny. And I've been charged with bringing cobbler back for his mother."

"And I wouldn't dream of letting you bear that responsibility alone." Cullen took an almost imperceptible step closer to her.

Rusty clapped his hands. "That's settled then. You come on with me, brother Miles, and I'll get you and the ladies the finest supper the Campbell's soup company can make. Might even throw in a few crackers if'n I got 'em fresh."

Cullen remained close as they watched Rusty and Miles walk away.

"Lilly-bird?" he said playfully, nudging Lilly with his shoulder.

"Hey." She nudged back. "Only Rusty can call me that."

"It suits you."

"Why? Because I'm a birdbrain?"

"No, because sometimes"—he turned to her—"like right now, you have such a dancing fear in your eyes. You look like you could fly away at any moment. I might turn around and you'd be gone."

She felt like a bird right then, or at least like one was batting its wings against her ribs, sending feathers throughout her body. Like the cat clamping it between her teeth, she smiled.

"Don't worry, Moonsie. I'll be around as long as I have a perch in your gilded cage."

27

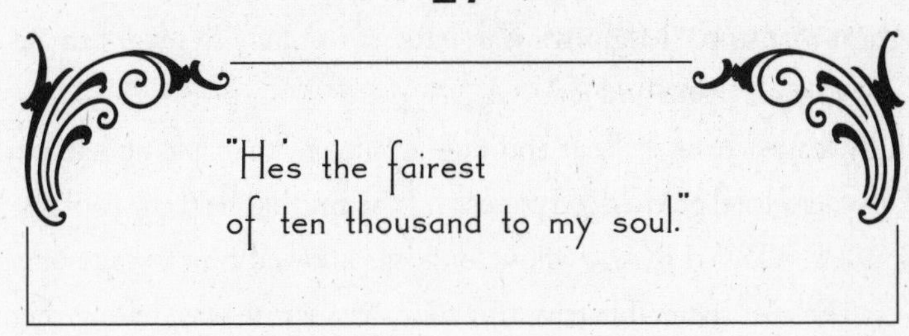

"He's the fairest
of ten thousand to my soul."

They rode three in the front seat, Lilly squished between Cullen and Rusty, who had taken time to put on a shirt and toss his pipe. He and Cullen talked across her, all about engines and pistons and other such things that held no interest for her. The night was quite chilly, giving her license to sit as close to Cullen as possible, her arm warm in its constant contact with his. Still, no thought was given to closing the car—not with the cool scent of forest or the fact that Rusty might not be able to sit up straight if they did.

"Now, you're goin' to want to take this turn real slow. It's a bit tight."

Cullen did, but not so slow that Lilly wasn't slammed against him.

"I'm so glad you're here, Rusty," she said, righting herself. "It can be so difficult to find your way around here. You know, no signs."

She returned Cullen's withering glare.

They would have to be driving blind not to find the revival tent once they rounded the final bend in the road. Electric lights were strung from posts surrounding an enormous blue-and-white-striped tent. Automobiles of every make and model were parked without any care given to organization, their drivers and passengers milling about.

Rusty slapped his thigh. "Whoo-hoo! Got more'n we had last two nights combined. Let's go." He leaped out of the car before Cullen had brought it to a stop. "Might want to park 'er out here so's you can get out after. Grab your plates and let's go!"

Lilly leaned over the seat and dug around in their picnic hamper for the Tutwiler Hotel gold-edged plates and the tin that held the cookies. She and Cullen followed Rusty, whose long legs allowed him to take one step to every three of theirs. He gave directions the entire way, telling them to fill up their plates and not be shy. This meal was set up for those who didn't have a meal of their own.

"That explains the crowd," Lilly said, trotting.

Long tables ran the length of the tent wall, and a solid line of men and women shuffled past. Children ran in and out, snatching food straight from the serving trays, despite the chastisement of a dozen mothers.

"Hop in anywhere," Rusty told them. "No rules here. I'll go find Ginny."

Cullen insisted they go to what seemed to be the end of the line—he on one side of the table, she on the other. They filled their plates with fried chicken, baked beans, carrot salad, and sausage. When she couldn't decide, Lilly told Cullen to get biscuits while she got corn bread.

"Then we'll share."

It wasn't long before every bit of the Tutwiler engraving was buried under piles of Christian cooking. When they came to the end, they set down their plates so Cullen could hold the tin as Lilly spooned it full of cobbler. As she replaced the lid, she heard a familiar voice call her name.

"Ginny!" She dropped the tin on the table and opened herself to receive the soft hug that only a woman with Ginny's particular figure could give: the sensation of being wrapped up in warm ginger-scented pillows.

"Girl! Rusty told me our Lilly-bird was passin' through. You missed out on my mashed-tater casserole, though. It went first thing."

"It doesn't matter. It's just so good to see you." She stepped back. "Ginny, this is my…friend. Cullen Burnside."

"Rusty told me about you too, sir. God bless you."

Cullen was in the process of holding his hand out when he was engulfed in the same warm, fluffy embrace from which Lilly had just been released. He was granted a little swing-around, and he looked at Lilly imploringly over Ginny's broad, soft shoulder.

"Well, now," Ginny said, having set Cullen to right. "You both got here late, but I see you found plenty left."

"It all looks wonderful," Lilly said. "And I hope nobody will mind that we're taking some dessert home for the rest of our little party."

"Not'all. Bigger problem's gonna be findin' a seat. Been full up since an hour ago. I swear this man could preach the legion back to heaven."

"I'm sure we'll be able to squeeze in." Truthfully, though, it didn't matter. She did not share the same fond memories of tent revivals that Betty Ruth did.

"Tell you what." Ginny pointed a round, wobbly arm. "You see that truck right there? Backed right up to the tent?"

"The black one with the wood-slat bed?"

"The very one. It's our'n—got me a good spot, bein' the first one here. Why don't you take yer food and have a seat up in it? Dare say you'll be able to hear the singin' if nothin' else. And he has one of them squawk boxes to make hisself louder. Should be able to hear ever' word."

"Speaking of which…" Cullen tried to give Ginny a collection of folded bills, which she refused with a soft hand.

"Now, yer not to pay for the meal."

"It's for the collection. I assume they'll pass a bag."

"Well, then." She deposited the money between her ample bosom and once again pulled Cullen into an embrace. "If yer not the sweetest thing."

Lilly watched, offering no help. Upon his release, Cullen picked up both plates of food, extending them in front of him like a shield.

"And if'n you check under the seat, there's a few bottles of Dr Pepper. Rusty keeps 'em hid, 'cause they got so much sugar, but I'm on to him."

Lilly hugged her again, this time offering a kiss on the woman's wide, soft cheek. "Thank you, Ginny. You don't know how good it is to see you again."

"You too, Lilly-bird. Me'n Rusty say a prayer when ya cross our minds. Now, go get to eatin' 'fore you fall over."

Lilly and Cullen picked their way through the dispersing crowd. When they came to the pickup, Cullen set the plates on the bed, grasped her waist, and lifted her to the bed. He went to the cab and came back with not only two bottles of Dr Pepper but a thick red sweater he'd found on the seat.

"I thought you might be chilly."

"Thank you." The sweater had been knit to Ginny's proportions. Lilly giggled as she pulled her arms through the sleeves. "Let me know if you get cold too. I think we could both fit in here."

"She seems like a wonderful lady. Very friendly."

"So you noticed?"

Cullen climbed up beside her and they sat on a pile of feed sacks, quietly eating. *Quiet* meaning they spoke little, but the eating itself was anything but. Neither had remembered to bring any sort of fork or spoon, and rather than venture back in search of one, they used fingers, corn bread, and biscuits to somehow transfer the food from the plates to their often-laughing mouths.

"I feel like a cave man." Lilly picked up peas one by one.

"A cave man eating from gold-rimmed plates?"

"Fine, a rich cave man."

The edge of the truck bed served as a bottle opener for the Dr Pepper, and an evening spent under a truck seat on an early autumn evening gave it the perfect chill. Lilly downed two big gulps and felt an enormous burp building.

"Oh, excuse me!"

"Such a lady." Then he burped too.

The first notes from a piano sounded just as they finished eating. Feed sacks became napkins as they wiped their fingers, forearms, elbows, mouths, chins, and cheeks.

"So, Miss Margolis, shall we go find a seat in the meeting?"

"I think I'm peachy right here, thanks."

"You sure?"

"Absatively."

"Who could argue with that?"

They sat opposite each other, each leaning against a tire well. Both had their legs extended, her right knee less than an inch from his left one. She pulled the sweater tighter around her and snuggled down. Stomach full, breeze cool, end of a long day—she could have fallen asleep right at that moment. The strains of music formed into a song, and the crowd gathered inside began singing about having a friend in Jesus, then continued with "Rock of Ages" and "Jesus Is the Sweetest Name I Know." Lilly remembered most of the hymns, and when a phrase or verse came to her, she sang, softly, mostly into the generous folds of the red sweater.

An unfamiliar sense of comfort came, a warmth that had little to do with the yards and yards of red wool wrapped around her. The words of those old songs brought back a feeling she hadn't had since she was a very little girl.

"You really do have a lovely voice."

"Girls chorale. Ninth and tenth grades."

"What happened after that?"

"I'm not quite sure."

She wished he hadn't said anything, hadn't interrupted her thoughts, because now whatever memories were coming back to her scattered again in light of what happened after tenth grade. A boy. That's what happened. A boy and a brief struggle in the backseat of a Buick. After that, sweet songs about nightingales on the wing lost their beauty. These songs did too.

Then the jaunty introduction to a familiar hymn rang out.

"Do you know that song?"

He cocked his head to listen, then a slight smile. "Well, how about that?"

"My mother named me after that song. It was her favorite. She would sing it over and over all day long." She listened, tapping her toe against his leg, waiting for a new measure. *"Though all the world forsake me, and Satan tempts me sore, through Jesus I shall safely reach the goal."*

She directed him to join her in the chorus and, to her delight, he did. *"He's the Lily of the Valley, the bright and Morning Star, he's the fairest of ten thousand to my soul."* Cullen even offered up the echoing, *"To my soul"* at the end of the line.

As the congregation lit into the third verse, her memory of the words were lost. When Cullen moved to speak, she held up a hand. "Wait...my favorite line's coming up." She listened with her ear turned toward the tent. "There! I love that line, '*A wall of fire about me, I've nothing now to fear.*' Sometimes when Mama sang that, I could just see her standing in the middle of a wall of fire."

"I don't think that's exactly what the song intends."

"You're probably right. Have you ever seen a lily of the valley?"

"The flower? No."

"I did. I told you, Mama always sang that song, and I used to feel so happy because I thought it meant she named me after Jesus. I told her that one day. I was little. Eight or nine. Some of the kids were teasing me because I didn't have a father, and I said I did too have a Father in heaven. I said God was my father, and I was named after His Son, Jesus, because we were both lilies. Then they called me a blasphemer, and I didn't know what that meant, so I ran home and told Mama."

"And what did she say?"

"She slapped me. Said no one but the Son of God could bear that name."

"That's awful." The words sounded like they were caught in the scars of his throat.

"So then I went to the library to look up *lily of the valley* in the encyclopedia."

Cullen burst out in a laugh. "I didn't know you were such a little intellectual."

"There's a lot about me you don't know! So I looked it up, and there was a picture of this beautiful flower. It hangs off these enormous green leaves, like teardrops. And I read that the legend of the lily of the valley is that it came from Eve's tears after she sinned. My mother didn't name me after a Savior; she named me after a sin."

"Lilly—"

She dissolved in tears, and in an instant he was beside her, his arms wrapped around her, though she could feel nothing of him through the layers of Ginny's sweater. She wept and wept as he held her. He made soft *shushing* noises into her hair and pulled her a little closer with every sob.

After a while, when her breath was even with his, she spoke, comforted by how her words echoed against him.

"My Sunday school teacher used to tell us that we had to give our hearts to Jesus. Or that we had to ask Him to come live in our hearts. And I felt too ashamed. I tried once. When I was sixteen. I remember getting on my knees in my room and begging Jesus to forgive me. I hated my mother, you see. Hated her. And I asked Him to come and live in my heart and help me love her, because I thought, maybe then, she would love me. But it was too late."

"It's never too late." He held her close, his hand stroking her arm.

Even through the bulk of the sweater she knew. This was why. This—how she made men feel, what she made men do—this was why her mother hated her.

Lilly pulled away, moved to where no part of her touched any part of him, though his hand lingered. "By then I'd already cut my hair. I was smoking, drinking when I could." She looked at the pattern on the feed sack. "Had boyfriends. Mama said I was a lost cause."

"My father said the same thing about me, you know. Those exact same words. 'Lost cause.' But he soon found it in his heart to forgive me. It was the only letter he wrote me, and I never had the chance to write back. I walked away from him, turned my back on everything he wanted for me, and yet he forgave me."

"You went off to defend your country in a war."

"I was running away. Angry that my first year in the majors went so badly, and too stubborn to go back home."

"Even so, I didn't do anything half so noble."

"But nothing that can't be forgiven. And maybe not by your mother. You'll know that soon enough. But she and Jesus aren't the same. There's nothing He can't forgive. Both Father and I knew that we had to ask forgiveness of Christ first before we could reconcile with each other. And I never got the chance to really make up with him. Not face to face. And that's something I'll always regret. You have a chance."

"I'm terrified of that chance."

"Then do the easy one first. Go to the Lord."

She laughed, wiping a tear on the voluminous sleeve. "I don't know why we should bother listening to him." She pointed at the tent, now emitting the strident southern diction of an evangelist. "Sounds like I already got my sermon."

"What do you want to do?"

She thought about it, listening. Only a few minutes into the sermon, and already the preacher shouted the glories of salvation. He threatened hell with the same passion Mama did, and the convicting accusation behind his words made Lilly cringe.

"I want to go home. I mean, to Rusty's. To my cabin."

"I think that's a great idea." He jumped down from the truck, and she put her hands on his shoulders and allowed him to lift her down. Once she was there, however, neither let go, until the preacher inside let forth the fiery details of hell. And while she now knew, for certain sure, that the forgiveness of Jesus would never send her there, she didn't want to hear about it. Not under this sky; not in his arms.

28

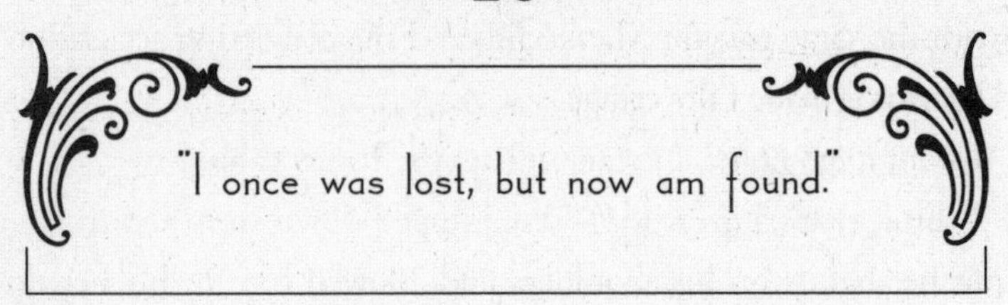

"I once was lost, but now am found."

The bed was nothing more than a wooden platform with a thin mattress on top. The pillow stuffed with dense feathers, the quilt obviously made from old pieced-together clothing. No insulation with the wood-slat walls and a window that wouldn't quite close all the way meant a cabin full of cool night air, not to mention the constant song of crickets and owls and who knew what else skittering about.

But Cullen had slept. Heavier than he had since before the war. Deep, dark, and dreamless. He might have done so until noon if it hadn't been for a gentle hand on his shoulder. In one move, his feet hit the floor and his eyes opened, heart entangled with the first waking breath, his right hand useful again to grasp at the one so near his throat.

"It's me, Mr. Burnside. It's just me, Miles."

His vision cleared and his mind caught up with racing reflexes. "Of course. Good morning."

"That it is, sir. Beautiful day, but nice to see you takin' advantage of a night's rest."

"Yes." His heart slowed to a pace befitting a new day. Thin gray light seeped around the cabin's cheerful calico curtains. "Is it late? It seems late."

"Just a bit past seven. But I know you want to get on the road early."

Cullen ran his fingers through his hair, stood, and stretched, taking in the deepest breath he dared, not wanting to dissolve into a fit of coughing.

"It's a good shower they got here." Miles opened a trunk at the foot of the bed and produced a faded blue, worn towel and washcloth. "Got a soap hanging in a mesh bag—wisest thing I've ever seen. Good smellin' too." He lifted his forearm to his nose and took a long whiff. "I asked that Mr. Rusty what kind it be, and he says it's Lifebuoy. Gonna tell the wife back home from now on, it's nothin' but Lifebuoy soap for me."

"Well, you know what they say..." Cullen rummaged through his bag for a clean pair of pants and shirt.

"What's that, sir?"

"The Phillies use Lifebuoy, and they still stink."

Miles matched his laughter. "Oh, I heard that, sir. I heard that. You sure you want to wear your pj's out to the shower? It's a short walk, but no tellin' if the ladies will be about."

He took the towel from Miles, draped it over the clothing on his right arm and clutched clean underwear, socks, and shoes in his left hand. Using the ,toe of his shoe, he pulled the curtain aside to see if the coast was clear.

"I think I'll make it. If I run."

And run he did. The air was cool and moist, the sun full of promise. And what was this lightness in his step? His bare feet carried him over hard-packed ground, and he didn't begrudge a step. He was *carrying* his shoes, for Pete's sake. And a good pair of slippers left in his bag. If Mother could see this, she surely wouldn't recognize him.

Neat hand-lettered signs directed him to the men's shower. He rounded an open doorway to find a long row of wooden stalls, each cordoned off with a blue oilcloth curtain. After hanging his towel on the hook between stalls, he stepped off the clean, polished wood floor and onto the cold tile. The shower head hung straight down from the ceiling, and there was one knob on the wall. One knob could mean only one thing. He held his breath, bracing himself for the first icy blast.

Twisting and turning, he felt rivulets run down his face. He worked the Lifebuoy soap into a lather with the tattered rag and ran it over and under his arms, his chest, lifting one leg and then the other. The bottom of his feet. The bottom of his feet again. The scent of the red soap met the heat of his skin, cooled by the water. Every inch of him felt alive and clean—a certain fire beneath the chill. This was a shower to be taken on a day meant for living.

Rinsed of every trace of soap, he turned the water off and reached his hand around for the towel, first sinking his face into the scratchy cotton. It was worn almost as thin as his shirt but smelled of good clean detergent. He rubbed it over his hair before retracing the trail of his shower: arms, chest, legs, feet. But slower now, thinking, *These are the arms that held her.* His chest. *She laid her head right here.*

Something had happened last night. He'd been willing to think he loved her before—and what man wouldn't? But last night had been consuming. If she could have known as he held her how her tears fueled him. Made him want to hide her away, wrap her up like that sweater had and keep her protected from any harm.

He spread the towel on the ground to walk the step between the shower and the bench. Quickly, feeling exposed, he dressed, sitting down to pull on socks and shoes. Four narrow mirrors hung, interspersed, along the wall, and he stood in front of one, straightening his collar. The glass was little more than polished tin, making his features so indistinct he could hardly tell where skin turned to scar.

Outside the distinctive clang of a cowbell sounded, and the unforgettable voice of Ginny Tatters announced breakfast awaitin'. Cullen dropped the towel and washcloth in the canvas bag provided and grabbed his pajamas. The sun was higher now, beaming right into his eyes as he stepped out of the entrance. The combination of eyes full of sunshine and a mind full of Lilly proved dangerous, because he didn't even see her in front of him until their bodies collided.

"Oh—" They spoke apologies over each other and laughed and tried again until, resigned, each apparently chose not to lay blame.

"Beautiful morning," he said.

"It is." She nodded.

"Nice, cold shower."

"Yours too?"

And he realized they'd been showering at the same time. Here she was, wearing that blue silk robe with the golden Chinese dragons. With its long bell-shaped sleeves and knee length, it covered more of her body than most of her dresses. But underneath he knew…right now, he knew she wore nothing else. After one quick look down to make sure she wasn't walking in the dirt with clean feet, he forced his eyes to look at the ratty pink towel wrapped around her head.

"You heard the call to breakfast?"

"Yes. I need just ten minutes to get dressed. Honest. Your mother and Eugenie are already there."

She inclined her head and he turned to see Mother holding court at a long redwood table. Her attendants, Ginny and Rusty Tatters. Eugenie too, though she looked nowhere near as enthralled.

"I think she's telling them about you." Lilly pointed right into his clean shirt.

"What makes you think so?"

"Look at her face."

A few minutes later, when he came out of his cabin after dropping his pajamas in his bag, she was still talking, and as he approached, he walked up into what was now a familiar story.

"It was a vision I had. An absolute vision. I could see him standing at—there you are, dear. What is it called where you hit the ball?"

"Home plate, Mother."

"Yes. And the Lord showed me. If Cullen could go back one more time, he would be healed."

"Praise the Lord." Ginny pulled a handkerchief from the front of her dress and wiped her eyes.

"We packed up and got in the car the very next day. The very next day."

"Now that's faith right there," Rusty said. "And the good Lord rewarded it, because you know your boys won that game yesterday."

"Did they?" He'd completely forgotten to ask. "Well, some would call it folly." Cullen planted a kiss on top of Mother's head as a morning greeting.

"It's faith pure'n simple, an' don't you let nobody tell you different. Not even yourself. People who ain't got no faith"—he turned and spat over his shoulder—"that's all I got to say about them."

Ginny slapped his massive arm. "Oh, you stop with that. Can't go judgin' another's faith. Now, if we're all here 'cept our Lilly-bird, let me go get our breakfast. Miss Eugenie, if'n you don't mind givin' me a hand?"

"Not at all." In fact, she looked relieved to have something to do.

"And I'll go see what our Miss Lilly is up to." Mother stood, and Rusty did too, in a gesture quite formal for such a rural setting. But Mother looked like a woman befitting such an attention. Even this early, in these conditions, she looked no different from the way she did any morning back in their home. Save for the hair, of course, but even that took on an elegance not every woman could manage.

He watched her walk away, feeling troubled, struck by her hesitancy. She'd corrected her direction twice and now took an unusually long pause between each step. He was about to call out to her, offer to escort her to Lilly's door, when he felt a shadow pass over him. Rusty standing—looming—over him, a thick red-knuckled fist less than an inch from his nose. To be more accurate, there was a pointing finger too, but Cullen focused on the fist.

"I gots somethin' to say to you, mister hero."

Cullen gazed up, ignoring the pinched feeling in his shoulder. Rusty's head blocked out the sun; its light shone through the wild shock of red hair, though, creating a menacing halo. Cullen forced himself to keep his breathing even and his feet planted firmly, denying himself permission to either run away or charge headlong into the massive chest. His ears rang so with the rush of his own blood, he questioned whether he would be able to hear what Rusty had to say at all, but he told him, "Say it."

"Our Lilly-bird is a special girl."

"I know."

"Oh, I don't think you do. Fancy-pants car and servants, always flashin' some wad of money."

"Simply to pay—"

"I'll tell you what you can pay. Now, we pert'near took care of the girl for most a summer when she was here with some slick bit o' trash, looked just like you 'cept without the noble wounds of war. An' she spent enough nights cryin' 'bout how he treated her. So I'm tellin' you this. I ever find out you made that girl cry, I'm gonna pop you like a chigger. You understandin'?"

"Perfectly," Cullen said, and Rusty dropped his fist. "But let me reassure you, I have no intentions of...of anything. I am only here at the whim of my mother."

"That's another thing. That woman is a saint, you hear me? A saint. How many you know gettin' visions straight from God? Don't ever let me hear of you disparagin' her faith. You do, an' I'll—"

"Pop me like a chigger?"

Rusty broke into a slow smile, revealing the extent of his tobacco-stained, sparse teeth. "You're a quick study, brother."

Breakfast consisted of an enormous bowl of fluffy scrambled eggs, sausage links cooked on a grill stationed between the tables, a cast-iron skillet of gravy—so heavy Rusty himself carried it—and dozens of biscuits. One by one, guests emerged from their cabins. Three families in all—sleepy mothers had barefoot children by the hand, and fathers brought up the rear, herding the older ones with orders barked through cigarettes. There were a handful of single men too, who obviously chose to forego the amenity of even a cold shower.

"Good morning again." Lilly stood at Cullen's elbow, her hair damp, her skin clean. "Smells wonderful, doesn't it?"

He sniffed. "I think you have different soap in your shower than we do."

"Silly. I meant breakfast. Venison sausage, I think."

No reply could ease his embarrassment, so he chose not to offer one. Then he felt her hand in his, and he looked down to see her pressing two quarters into his palm.

"What's this?"

"They charge a dime for breakfast. I know Rusty doesn't want to take our money because of me, so when you get to him, just drop it in the jar real fast so he can't stop you. I couldn't stand for the rest of these people to see us getting away with a free meal."

That's when Cullen took another look at the gathering crowd. Mothers dropped their children's hands and turned to counting heads, then calculating. A family of seven, another of four. One mother drawing her daughters close, telling them they could share a plate since they were little. Another whispered conversation about what the price would be for just a biscuit. He'd never known a single day in his life when his mother had to make such a choice.

He did his own quick calculation. Twenty-seven people, maybe. Twenty-eight counting the baby. Rounding up, he took three bills from his pocket—a five and two singles, folding them so the single was on the outside. Rusty was now at the grill, using a long fork to move the sausages to a platter. Careful not to startle him, Cullen came around his side and showed him the money.

"Breakfast is on me this morning. Everybody's."

"I told you I don't want yer money."

"It's not mine. It belongs to God, and I'm giving it to you." He placed the money in the front pocket of Rusty's overalls, clapped the man on the back, and went back to bask in Lilly's approving gaze.

"That was very generous of you."

"It's the least I could give, with the accommodations and food. Are you hungry?"

She clutched her stomach. "I think I'm still full from last night."

He nodded. "I'll think of it as the most expensive cup of coffee I've ever had. Want some?"

Together they walked over to the large steel tureen that sat on a table surrounded by two dozen white cups. He worked the spigot to fill two cups, and they went to the table farthest from the breakfast line and sat. Lilly blew across the top of her coffee, then set the cup on the table, tapping her fingernails on its side.

"Do you think we'll make Miresburgh tonight?"

"Not sure. It'll be late if we do." He craned his neck looking for Miles and saw him at the edge of the campground with two other men admiring the Peerless. "Are you sure you don't want to call your mother? Does Rusty have a telephone?"

"Yes, he does, and no, I don't. Might lose my nerve."

Cullen reached across the table and covered her hand with his. "You'll be fine."

She turned her fingers within his, looking at them as if together they created some new, strange creature. She was staring, brows furrowed, when she said, "Thank you for last night. For listening."

"You—" He drew his hand away, ostensibly to drink his coffee. For the first time he was grateful to have a hand too twisted to hold a cup. Her touch was distracting, made him want to drag her to the Peerless and drive straight back home before anybody noticed they were missing. Once he'd swallowed a good, hot sip, he continued. "You've become quite special to me, Lilly."

"Do you know what I did last night? I prayed. That's why I didn't talk all the way home, I was talking to God."

"I thought you might be." Because he had been too. Praying that God would give him the strength not to let her offer herself to his embrace. Not while he had an entire cabin at his disposal.

"Strange thing, though. All the drive home. I was asking God what I should say."

"To your mother?"

She giggled. "To *Him.* I haven't prayed in so long. The words, you know..."

"I know." He watched the tip of her lip test the coffee. She made a tiny slurping sound and put the cup down.

"I feel like I can face her now, mostly because of you—your family, I mean. Your mother."

"Ah. Of course."

She looked shy for just a moment. "I mean, I see how you are with her. How patient, no matter what's coming out of her mouth. You forgive her."

"There's nothing to forgive. She can't help the way she is. She's sick."

"That's just it. I'm wondering if my mother isn't sick too. Not like Betty Ruth, but in her own way. And I realized last night—the strangest thing. Almost the way Betty Ruth describes her vision—I got this feeling. Like a voice but not really, and I knew."

He didn't need to ask; he knew it too. The moment they collided outside of the shower, the second he saw her face in the light of this new day. The girl who stared into her coffee, running her finger around the edge of the cup, this wasn't the same girl he'd found face first in his backyard. Or the one slurring her speech and staggering up the steps. Or even the one who had wept, brokenhearted, in his arms last night. Still, he prompted, "Knew what?"

"Since I can remember, all Mama ever saw was my sin. She couldn't see me or hear me. And I thought, maybe she was trying to tell me that God feels the same way. So last night I knew I needed a clean slate. I prayed and I asked Him to forgive me." She looked up. "And He did. I know He did, and now, somehow, it doesn't matter what she says. I don't need her approval anymore. I don't need her forgiveness."

A spark of hope ignited within him, something he couldn't have imagined before this morning. "So, you're not going home after all? You don't want to see her?"

"No, I have to see her. *I* have to forgive *her.*"

Before he could suggest that she could express such forgiveness nicely in a letter, Eugenie set a plate of food in front of each of them and a third next to Cullen.

"Oh, them Tatters have me working so hard I feel more like hired help than a guest." Her beaming smile—as beaming as Eugenie ever achieved, anyway—betrayed her contentment at being so employed. "Will one of you go get Mrs. Burnside and tell her breakfast is ready?"

"I will." Lilly swung her legs over the bench. "Is she in your cabin? I haven't seen her since before I showered."

The niggling sick feeling Cullen had watching his mother walk away wormed itself back to the front of his mind. "She didn't come see you?"

"No, why?"

"She must have gone to her cabin." *Please, God, let her be in her cabin.* "I'll go see."

He tried to keep his nerves steady as he scanned the crowd. Maybe there weren't a lot of people, but she was a small woman. Once Lilly, right behind him, said, "That one, number twelve," he made a beeline for the little wooden structure—completely identical to all the others, save for the number on the sign beside the door.

He knocked. "Mother?" He opened the door without waiting for a reply. Empty, save for her and Eugenie's neatly packed luggage at the foot of the bed.

"She's not in mine either," Lilly said, back, breathless from a sprint.

"We'll have to check them all."

By now both Eugenie and Miles had joined them, and they went to the four corners of the campsite. Twenty cabins in all, most unoccupied, none with Betty Ruth.

Oh, God. This is my fault. I knew she wasn't up for this. I knew it was a bad idea, that this nonsense of hers would pass—

"Any sign of her?" Rusty Tatters, alerted no doubt by Lilly, had abandoned his grill to meet Cullen at the final cabin. The two men stood just steps away from dense forest.

"None."

"I'll get the guests organized. Circle around and walk straight out. Don't worry; this happens with kids all the time. Can't get far 'fore she'll hit a road or farm or somethin'."

He fought to maintain control, to accept Rusty's offer as a gesture of genuine concern. "She's not a kid. She won't even know she's lost."

"Well, don't you worry. I seen about a thousan' people stayin' here over the years, and ain't lost a'one yet." Rusty left him, calling for everyone's attention.

Lord, where would she be? Where would You lead her? Because she listens to You. He let out a bitter laugh. *We wouldn't be here if she didn't listen to You. Call to her, Lord. Bring her back into the camp. Touch her mind, turn her steps.*

Engrossed in prayer, he made his way back to the center of the camp where one of the younger children had been given the job of ringing the cowbell. It was a little boy—probably about five or six—and he stood on one of the tables between plates of half-eaten food, looking quite pleased with his task. By the time Cullen got there, Rusty had organized everybody into teams of two or three, and they walked into the surrounding woods.

Soon the trees echoed with the sound, "Betty Ruth! Betty Ruuuuuth!" like the call of so many owls. Cullen, being unassigned, stood in the deserted campsite with the cowbell-ringing boy, thinking. And praying.

Don't let her be frightened. So many strangers, and she won't know how they know her name. And she hates to be treated like a child, but she is, Lord. She's Your child. Calm her fears.

He didn't want to acknowledge his own. Not until he had to.

Across the site Lilly emerged from the women's shower area, shaking her head. "Have you checked the men's?"

"I doubt she'd go in there. She can still read."

"Still..."

"Why don't you? Just in case..."

He paced the length of the building until Lilly came out. She ran straight into his arms, and he welcomed her, drawing her close and feeling stronger for the feel of her.

"I feel so useless," she said, her voice muffled against him.

"Don't." Her hair felt like silk against his lips, and he turned his face away. "She hasn't been gone long. She can't have gone far." But the voices in the woods were growing more and more faint.

She stepped out of his embrace. "Has she ever done this before?"

"Yes." She'd wander into a room and not know why she went there. Every once in a while she ended up at a neighbor's house. Or in the garden. "But that's back home. More familiar. Here..."

He looked around. There was nothing here of home. The air was too cool, the woods too thick, the sun almost powerless against both. The only link to home—besides Cullen and Eugenie and Miles—was the car. And it wasn't even their own. Why couldn't they have brought the Mercedes? Why had he insisted on borrowing Bill Owens's Peerless? Even though

Mother had declared more than once that she loved it. Wanted to buy her own once they got back. Declared it—

His eyes wandered to where the car was parked at the edge of the campsite. At first he almost didn't recognize it; Miles had been demonstrating all the conversion possibilities and had left the ragtop up. Maybe as an effort to avoid driving in the morning chill. He'd been meticulous about keeping the car clean, hosing the road dust off at every petrol station, so why would the windows be so dirty? Wait, not dirty. Fogged. In the back.

"Stay here." He didn't want to get Lilly's hopes up, nor his own, for that matter.

Lord, let me be right. If I am, please give me the right words to say.

He approached the car and peered inside, seeing nothing at first, as it was parked in the shade of the surrounding trees. He had only to open the front door and look into the backseat to have everything he felt for this woman collide within him.

She sat with her straw handbag primly resting on her lap, her face a serene mask bathed in silent tears.

"Mother?"

Her head turned slowly, as if her mind were traveling a great distance to find him. When she did, there was no change in her expression, only a glimmer of recognition.

"Cullen, dear. I simply didn't know where else to go."

He'd never seen her like this, so lost and small. "You did the right thing."

"Could you ask Miles to drive me home now? I'd like to go home."

"Of course. I'll send Lilly to go find him."

"Who?"

He should have been prepared. In one way or another he'd been preparing for this moment the minute he picked Lilly up from the lawn. First, impatiently, as if waiting for an annoyance to lose its novelty, and later—since that night at the beach if he were to be honest with himself—with dread. His own feelings had never determined what place Lilly would have in his life. Until Lilly, he hadn't any feelings to consider. Not until this moment did he realize his own heart had been in his mother's hands. The same hands that trembled now as she touched the soft cloud of hair around her ears. That, at least, she didn't question.

He allowed a momentary bit of hope that she simply hadn't heard him and repeated the name.

"I don't know anyone named Lilly." Her voice was as thin as the fog on the window.

"My mistake."

He could hear Lilly's footsteps on the hard-packed dirt, running up no doubt to share in the joy of finding the lost one. Ducking his head under the canvas top, he stood, ready to be an obstacle between them.

"Is she in there?" Lilly attempted a dodge around him. "Betty Ruth?"

"Don't." The softest touch on her arm stopped her.

"What's wrong?"

"She won't—she doesn't know you."

"That's because she hasn't seen me."

There would be no stopping her now as she shouldered past him and poked her head inside the car. "Betty Ruth?"

And from within the darkness, his mother's small voice. "Yes?" The same response she'd give to a stranger on the street, or a salesman asking directions, or this unfamiliar, beautiful woman in the front seat of her car. "Can I help you with something, dear?"

"It's me, Lilly."

"I...I don't know you."

All of this coming from the closed shadows of the car. He didn't need to see Lilly's face to know the pain it showed, and his mother's look of sad bewilderment would haunt him always.

"Betty Ruth! I'm Lilly! You—you *love* me!"

A small jeweled hand slammed against the backseat window, rapping frantically while his mother called, "Cullen! Cullen!"

He wrapped his arm around Lilly's waist, easing her out of the car, though she fought him, elbows flailing, feet refusing to stay on the ground. All the while Mother screamed his name and Lilly screamed Mother's. It was enough to draw the attention of the little boy who'd been given charge to sound the cowbell, and Cullen released his grip on Lilly long enough to send the boy a signal.

"We found her!"

Though his voice hardly carried across the screaming of the women and the distance of the campsite, somehow the boy got the message, and within the first clangs of the clapper, all those sent to seek emerged from the surrounding trees.

Miles came out from not a hundred feet away, and upon observing the flailing Lilly and the shouts still coming from the car, he took off his cap and scratched his head. "Thank you, Lord, and give us mercy."

Cullen jerked his body, hauling Lilly momentarily off her feet, and whispered, "Hush, now" in her ear. She collapsed against him, lolling her head back until he felt her skin—porcelain and perfect—against the scarred ruins of his.

Suddenly Miles looked concerned. "Is Mrs. Burnside all right?"

"Yes." Cullen inched away from Lilly until it was clear she could stand on her own. "But you might want to ask Tatters if he'll let you take a Thermos of coffee."

"Why's that, sir?"

"Because you're in for a long drive. Mother wants to go home."

29

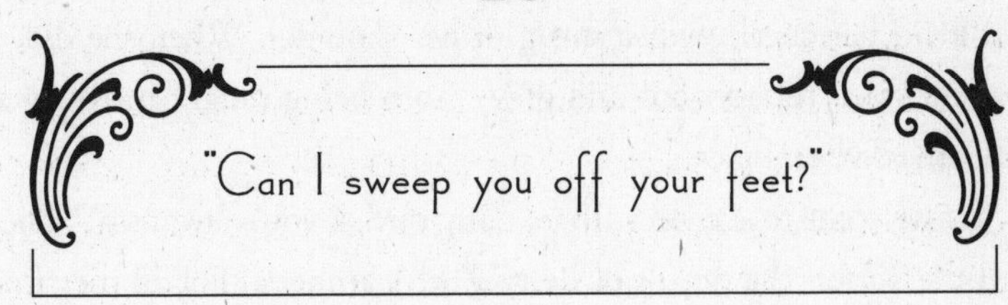

"Can I sweep you off your feet?"

For the first time since leaving Pensacola, Lilly found herself in the front passenger seat with Miles behind the wheel. Betty Ruth hadn't said a word to her since their less-than-illustrious reunion. The fact that she'd been allowed in the car at all was largely due to Eugenie's powers of persuasion. There they were, bags loaded, Betty Ruth settled in the back-seat with her new hat—with which she seemed completely familiar—pulled down to her eyes and Eugenie sitting staunchly beside her.

"I do not see why we have to let that girl in the car. I simply do not see it."

"Now, Mrs. B., leave the girl alone. We're giving her a ride, that's all. To the train station. She's our responsibility for a little while longer. Then she'll be gone."

Lilly had been standing behind the car throughout the conversation, hearing every word, and Eugenie must have known, because later, when Lilly climbed in beside Miles, she gave her a look of such smug satisfaction Lilly wanted to crawl back and smack her.

Someday she'd know why that woman hated her. Then again, she wouldn't. Because after today it wouldn't matter.

So it was that she'd been banished to the front seat. The wind in her face helped to hold her tears at bay. Still, occasionally one escaped and she wiped it off her cheek with a shrug of her shoulder. When she did, she could still smell the tobacco and gravy from being caught in Rusty and Ginny's massive embrace.

"Yer welcome to stay on with us, Lilly-bird, if you're awantin'." They'd spared the Tatters the details of Betty Ruth's amnesia. For all they knew, Lilly was simply going home.

With concise directions given by Rusty, Miles drove up to the Knoxville railroad station without trouble. The white walls of the station stood out against a bright blue sky; the enormous round clock set into a gabled tower gave the time as just before ten o'clock, and the walkway leading from the road to the station doors bustled with midmorning travelers.

"Now," Cullen said, looking deflated in the middle jump seat, "if you all will wait here, I'll take Lilly in to get her ticket, then we'll be on our way." He tapped Miles on the shoulder. "Why don't you come in with me, and we can look at a map. With this late a start, we'll never make Birmingham tonight."

"Birmingham!" Betty Ruth made the city's name sound profane. "I don't want to go to Birmingham. I want to go home. Take me home!"

Lilly winced in her seat, not daring to turn around.

Cullen laughed; it wasn't a pleasant sound. "Do you have any idea why we're here, Mother? What am I saying? Of course you don't."

"Stop it," Lilly whispered, staring straight ahead.

"You have no idea what we've gone through because of you and your crazy—"

"Stop it!" She turned, angling herself to keep Betty Ruth out of her line of vision but facing Cullen head-on. "Don't speak to your mother that way. I don't need you to take care of anything."

She threw open the door, climbed out, and grabbed her suitcase from the center of the car. "Thank you for bringing me this far." Holding back tears, she slammed the door and rushed to join the crowd of would-be travelers. Seconds later, she heard Cullen calling her name, and then his fingers wrapped around her elbow. She stopped, the weight of her suitcase threatening to pull off her arm.

"Where do you think you're going?"

"Home. You know that."

"I'm taking you to the ticket counter."

"I'll be fine."

"You don't have any money."

"Do you think this is the first time I've ever gone to a train station without a dime? I know how to take care of myself. You need to go take care of your mother." And now she really did need to go, because whatever tears she'd been able to hold at bay now pooled in the back of her throat, making her feel like her head was about to snap and fall off.

"Lilly, I—" By now her tears had obviously become an impediment, and she allowed him to lead her over to one of the arches lining the suspended walkway. "I didn't want this to end. I mean, I didn't want to send you off this way."

"You tried to warn me. I just wish Betty Ruth could have known how much she—I wish she could have seen me, changed. I wish she could have known that my heart...that I prayed."

"Come back. Come tell her."

"I don't want to make things worse. Think about how frightened she must be right now. Confused. Go."

"I have to get your ticket. I owe you that much."

"No."

"You're being unreasonable."

"And you're being cruel. I can learn to live with the fact that Betty Ruth has forgotten me. She can't help it. But if you buy me that ticket and put me on a train, it's like you're sending me away. *You*. And I can't bear the thought that you don't want me. So don't do that to me, Cullen. Just let me disappear; I'm good at that."

"Not anymore. Not with me. You're always going to be..." His words trailed off, and she could tell he wanted to kiss her.

And she wanted to kiss him too, maybe more than any other man she'd ever kissed. But if she did, she'd never get on a train to go home. Or any train to go anywhere. She'd never reconcile with her mother, never heal that wound left gaping and oozing with hate.

Most of all, if she kissed him, she'd lose this delicious feeling of *wanting* to kiss him. And then, for the rest of her life, she'd remember what it felt like to be loved—and to *love.* How well she knew the emptiness of the end of love; this was new. This would carry her home.

"Good-bye, Cullen."

He released his grip, and she knew she could walk away.

She ignored the lines at the ticket counter and headed straight for the ladies' room. The wall was lined with mirrors, with a wide wooden shelf running the length beneath them. She set her suitcase on the ground and opened her handbag, finding her rouge and kohl pencil and powder. She hummed as she worked, re-creating the face that had served her so well for so long.

I'm sure You don't approve, God. But it's the last time. I promise. I'm going home, just like You told me. Home to Mama.

She lined her eyes and painted her lips. Squatting down to her open suitcase, she dug around to find a much cuter hat—a blue felt cloche that picked up the stripe in her dress—and her camel-colored patent-leather ankle-strap high-heeled shoes.

Satisfied, she closed her suitcase and lifted it with a new resolve. Head up, chin out. Big smile.

The majority of the travelers standing at the ticket windows appeared to be families, not a good bet for winning a free ticket. As she surveyed the room looking for an eligible candidate, another sign caught her eye: Restaurant Downstairs, First Level.

"There's a start." Perhaps some of her lightheadedness came not only from leaving the Burnsides but from hunger as well. She took the wide marble staircase to the first level, half of which was dedicated to a slew of small tables and chairs. A few were empty; none occupied by a single man. She was beginning to think her best bet might just be with a ticket agent himself. Resigned, she turned and her suitcase bumped into something. Not a great collision, but enough to jolt her arm.

"Sorry," she said absently, and that might have been the end of it if the recipient of her blow hadn't said, "No problem, sweetie," in just that way.

She stopped, keeping one foot stationary while the other twisted on point, until she was looking at him over one dropped shoulder.

"I hope I didn't hurt your leg." She gave her bag a little lift. "It's kind of heavy."

"Not at all." His voice was deep and smooth, the kind that made a girl feel like she was being wrapped up in honey. He'd been talking into one of the telephones along the wall. Now, without taking his eyes off Lilly, he said, "I'll get back to you in a while," and placed the earpiece in its cradle.

He might have been somebody's father; he was certainly old enough to be. Tall and, for the most part, lean with the hint of a paunch poking out from beneath a well-worn tweed jacket. His hair had gone to gray at the temples, a salt mixture on top. He might be old enough to be a father, but he looked at her with the eyes of a man half his age.

"Something I can do for you, miss? Carry your bag? Buy you a cup of coffee? Sweep you off your feet?"

Her smile snapped into place. "I'm a big, strong girl who likes her feet on the ground, but a cuppa joe sounds pretty good right now."

"Well then." Hat in hand, he gestured toward the dining room, and as she passed him, he swooped down and took the suitcase right out of her hand. "Wouldn't be a gentleman if I let you lug this all over."

"And that's what you are, huh? A gentleman?"

"Through and through."

She continued to walk in front of him, giving him enough of a sway-show to keep him interested, but not so much that he'd go overboard. They came to a small two-top and she sat, elbows propped on the table, eyes looking up under furiously batting lashes.

He stashed the suitcase behind him and joined her, assuming an identical position. "So, kid. You here by your lonesome?"

"Am now. Just got dropped off by a, shall we say, disinterested party."

"Who in his right mind wouldn't be interested in you?"

"You'd be surprised."

A rumpled middle-aged man with a small notepad stopped at their table. "What can I get you?"

The man held up two fingers—"Coffee"—never taking his eyes off Lilly.

"And a ham sandwich." Lilly stared straight back.

The man's eyebrows lifted, then settled back, knowing. "Anything else? Side of potato salad, perhaps? Caviar?"

"Just the sandwich, thanks. And coffee."

Her companion looked at the waiter who, if nothing else, looked slightly less weary. "You heard the lady."

"Thanks," Lilly said. "You're a peach."

"I buy you lunch, you can at least tell me your name."

She reached her hand across the table. "Lilly. Lilly Margolis."

"David Voyant. Call me Dave."

"If I ever call you, I will."

"So, Lilly—if I may call you Lilly—may I be so bold as to ask where you're headed off to today?"

It occurred to her then that she could go anywhere. Name a city, and off she'd go. Always before there'd been a man she'd been following. Now she was bound by another promise, albeit one she'd given to herself alone. Mama didn't know she was coming, Cullen had no say in the matter, and to Betty Ruth, she was lost.

"Well, I hope it's not Pittsburgh."

"What—?"

The waiter returned with two cups of coffee, sloshed into the saucers, and a sandwich made with thick white bread. She allowed this distraction to give her time to formulate her question.

"Why would you think I was going to Pittsburgh?"

"Because everybody wants to go to Pittsburgh. Little something called the World Series of baseball. Ever heard of it?"

"What if I were? Well, Miresburgh, anyway. Pitts is the closest station."

"Well then, I hope you enjoy the beauty of Knoxville. Because the last train left thirty minutes ago. I missed it myself, something for which my editor is none too pleased."

"You're a writer?"

"Yep. You got a story?"

"Oh, daddy, you have no idea." She sank her teeth into the sandwich, just then embracing her hunger. She'd barely swallowed by the time she took the next. And the next. When she looked up, he was smiling.

"So what's the story?"

"It's not so much."

"Try me. I'm not going to make it to my interview anyway. Gotta have something to phone in."

"What kind of stories do you write?"

"Sports, mainly."

"Bunch of who scored what and big-time winner stuff?"

"Something like that, but I try to find the human-interest angle. Story-behind-the-story type of deal."

"What if there isn't a story behind the story?"

He winked. "Trust me. There always is."

She finished her sandwich, down to the last bit of crust, and drained her coffee. "That hit the spot. Thank you."

"You are most welcome. Now, you say you're headed to Miresburgh?"

"I was. I am. I guess tomorrow."

"What's there?"

She stared at the grounds in the bottom of her cup. "Home to Mama."

"Where does that put you tonight?"

The sandwich and coffee churned in her stomach like the past and present colliding. Before last night she would have had an easy answer—flippant and flirtatious, enough to keep him interested for the rest of the day. Long enough at least for dinner, maybe a movie, or if she was lucky, a cute piece of jewelry. But that instinct was gone. Plus, he seemed sincere—too nice for those old tricks. It was a tricky thing messing with these older guys. Young men—they understood. A little dancing, a little drinking on the sly, a few hours at a Chinese noodle bar, and maybe a little bit of necking at the door. All fun, no harm. But these older guys, they took to girls like a hound dog to a pork chop.

Now this one, he looked harmless enough. Nice face, easy smile. Still, a girl couldn't be too careful. "Look, mister. Thank you for the sandwich and coffee. Really. That was a kindness, but I'm not that kind of girl."

"Well, that's a good thing, because that kind of girl can get herself into a heap of trouble. Like getting dumped at a train station for starters. I just wanted to make sure you have someplace to spend the night. No funny stuff."

Her mind went to the Tatters. She should have stayed there. Not that she couldn't walk, after changing shoes, of course. Or ask this guy for a ride. Better yet, ask him for a nickel.

"I have someone I can call."

Without her having to say another word, he dug into his pocket and dropped a handful of coins on the table. "I'm a big tipper." He nodded toward the phone. "Go ahead. I'll watch your bags."

She extracted a nickel and tapped it on the table, thinking. She had to call, and why shouldn't she? The Tatters would give her a place to stay, let her work to earn a little money. Until she could pay her own way home. There was one other choice, though. The one Cullen had given her before they even left Florida. *"Call her,"* he'd said. And she hadn't because she wasn't prepared. Didn't know what to say. In that matter, little had changed. She rode all those miles, imagining the moment when she'd walk through her old front door. Like a scene from a movie, she saw herself in a shaky black-and-white scene, standing on her porch, suitcase at her side. But every time, once the door opened, the screen went blank.

Perhaps that was because she wasn't meant to go home at all.

With the side of her hand, she swooped the pile of coins from the table, leaving a dime for the waiter, and made her way to the bay of telephone booths along the far wall.

God, I don't know what You want me to do anymore. So, I'm trying this. I'm counting on You to tell me what to say.

At the first available phone, she walked into the booth and folded the door shut, then lifted the earpiece and deposited the nickel.

"Number please?" The operator sounded efficient.

"Long distance. Miresburgh, Pennsylvania."

"Deposit ten cents, please."

Lilly dropped a dime into the coin slot.

"One moment, please."

The phone line crackled in her ear as she waited. As far as she knew, Mama still didn't have a phone, but the Bylers across the street did. If Lilly lost her nerve, she could leave a message with them. Leaning her forehead against the smooth polished wood of the phone booth, she summoned the courage to speak those first words. So lost in the void of static and imagined conversation that the knocking on the phone booth's window startled her, and the poor operator who next asked, "Number, please?" got only a short, shrill shriek in reply.

Lilly spun around, dropping the earpiece completely and sending it clattering against the wall.

"Cullen?"

He opened the door, then picked up and handed her the earpiece. Lilly stammered, "Th-thank you, good-bye," before hanging it in its slot.

"Who were you calling?"

"Why are you here?"

He repeated his question.

"I thought I might call Mama after all."

"Oh." She couldn't tell if the syllable was fueled by compassion or curiosity. Perhaps a mixture of both.

"Where's Betty Ruth? And the others?"

He looked at the clock on the wall. "Probably pulling out of the station just about now."

For a moment it seemed there was a crackling static under his words. "What? How?"

"After you left, I went back and told her everything. All about who you are and why you were here—why *we* were here. Your mother, her vision, all of it."

"And what did she say?"

"Nothing. It was the most frightening thing. She said nothing at all, only that she wanted to go home. She remembers home. So I checked, and there was a train leaving within the hour. I said, 'Mother, get on that train and you can be home for a late supper with Mazy.'"

"And she was fine with that?"

"Once I took her on board and showed her what a private car looked like. I have a feeling she and Eugenie will sleep most of the way, but I bought a deck of cards from the porter just in case."

"And you? Why didn't you go?"

"I couldn't very well leave Bill Owens's car sitting at the Knoxville train station, now could I?"

"Miles?"

"I put him on the train too."

"So, why are you here?"

"I'm going to take you home."

Her heart took hold of the possibility of this moment. Which home did he mean? A million questions, only one answer, and in the end nothing was asked or answered, because the man who paid for her sandwich, coffee, and phone arrived and stood ready to wedge himself between her and Cullen.

"Everything all right here?"

Cullen stepped back, sizing him up, then gave Lilly a quizzical look. "Friend of yours?"

"Momentarily."

He, too, took inventory of Cullen, and having done so offered his left hand to shake. Lilly loved him just a little bit for that.

"David Voyant." He left off the "friends call me Dave."

Cullen's eyes lit up. "Dave Voyant? The journalist?"

"Depends. You a fan?"

"I've been reading your articles for years. Cullen Burnside."

Now it was Dave's turn to light up with recognition, but rather than a spark, a meandering light moved across his brow. "Burnside...Burnside... Blue Moon Burnside?"

Cullen looked down at his shuffling feet. "Unfortunately, yes. In another time."

"Why, Miss Lilly, I had no idea you were rubbing elbows with such royalty."

"Neither did I."

But Cullen's reaction made her want to move closer to him, link her arm in his, and hold him up straight.

"Pittsburgh Pirates, 1916. Set a record for never getting a single hit on his home field. A record, by the way, that still stands."

The look of chagrin on Cullen's face made her suddenly protective of him. "People know this?"

"People who care about such things," Cullen said.

"And thank God people do, otherwise I'd be out of a job."

Her mind traveled back to his room, a shelf full of magazines, lined up in perfect reverence; this man's words could be in any one of them. And here Cullen had to face him. This couldn't be any worse than facing her mother.

"I'll be happy to sacrifice the title."

"Looks like you sacrificed plenty already. For something a heck of a lot more important than baseball. And if you know me, you know I don't think there's much out there more important than baseball."

The men shared a laugh, and Lilly pinched herself to make sure she hadn't disappeared.

Dave put his hands in his pockets and rocked back on his heels. "So, are you the disinterested party?"

Cullen looked at Lilly. "I don't know. Am I?"

"Careful. He's looking for a story. Be nice, or I might just tell him one."

"I've got time," Dave said. "Won't make today's game at any rate."

"Interested in a road trip?"

Lilly had been twisting her head back and forth during the exchange, and Cullen's question brought the final snap around. "Aren't you headed the other way?"

"I said I'd take you home, and that's what I intend to do." He turned to Dave. "We're heading that direction. It'll take a bit longer than a train ride, but you're welcome to join us. There'll be one more game tomorrow."

"Tempting," Dave said, but Lilly wasn't sure she believed him. "But why don't you all go on ahead. I'll find me a nice hidey-hole for tonight and get the first train in the morning. Might even spend the night here."

"In the station?" Lilly had spent her fair share of nights in a train station. Never voluntarily. She turned to Dave. "You said you're always looking for a story."

"And you said there wasn't one."

"And you said there always is."

Dave tugged his chin, thinking. "You know, sometimes the bigger story isn't the game, but getting to it." He turned to Cullen. "I'm in."

30

Sing in me, Muse, and through me tell
the story of that man skilled in all ways
of contending, the wanderer, harried for
years on end, after he plundered the
stronghold on the proud height of Troy.

OPENING LINES OF HOMER'S *THE ODYSSEY*

Dave Voyant was a man full of stories, and in love enough with his voice to tell them. Mile after mile he talked, sometimes sending Cullen into such fits of laughter they nearly ran off the road. He told of his big break into sports journalism, covering the story of a spectator who got conked in the head by a fly ball.

"Guy was in a coma for three days, and I was the only one with the story. Had an inside scoop."

"What was her name?" Lilly asked. She sat between them in the front seat. A bit crowded, but nobody complained.

"A gentleman never tells," Dave said, hat over his heart. He'd spotted Babe Ruth's talent when he was pitching at St. Mary's Industrial School for Boys, convinced Eddie Cicotte to come clean about the 1919 scandal, and was single-handedly responsible for the career of Duke Dennison.

"Any bozo can type up a bunch of scores and statistics. It takes an artist to get the story behind them."

And he wanted to write Cullen's. For even as they traded driving duties, they traded tales, and Cullen found himself again relating his past. The father who disapproved of a baseball career but got him a choice spot anyway. The humiliation of going from a high school star to a major league joke. Walking away from it all to go to war.

But he wouldn't talk about the war. Not in front of Lilly. He tried searching his mind for any kind of beauty to share. Any bit worthy of being put into her mind and found nothing.

The distance and the day flew by with the words, and it was late afternoon when both the car and the conversation came to a spluttering halt twenty miles outside of Roanoke.

"This is my fault," Cullen said as the three worked together to push the car off the main road. Neither Lilly nor Dave disagreed. "It's what happens when you depend on a driver. Miles always takes care of these things."

"Do you remember the last petrol station?" Lilly asked.

"At least five miles back," Dave said. "Might be one closer up ahead, though. You a gambling man?"

"No," Cullen said. The idea that he would survive even a five-mile walk was gamble enough.

"You can stay here, Moonsie. Dave and I can go."

Dave pulled on his jacket. "Somebody needs to stay with the car. And I don't want to be slowed down by those shoes of yours, Lilly, my love. As fabulous as they are. So if I can leave you two lovebirds without a chaperone, I'll be back after a while."

He wasn't twenty paces away when Lilly said, "I like that guy."

"He's a brilliant writer."

"I could be a brilliant writer."

"Lilly, put your mind to it, and I think you could be anything you want."

"Ah, thanks, Moonsie. It's the nicest thing anybody's said to me all day."

The quiet settled in around them. Cullen stretched out across the front seat, Lilly the back, and aside from the occasional inquiry about the time, neither spoke. He'd never imagined one could enjoy silence with a woman.

It had been just over an hour when a blue pickup truck pulled up in front of the Peerless, and Dave hopped out of the cab. He grabbed a metal can with a long spout from the flatbed in one hand and held up a cardboard case of Coca-Cola in the other.

"Enjoy life." He handed a bottle to Lilly, Cullen, and the driver of the truck, a tall, lanky man with skin so dark it glistened almost blue. Dave introduced him as Johnny.

"Much obliged." Johnny drained the bottle with three enormous gulps followed by a healthy belch, then took the gas can from Dave and proceeded to fill the car.

Cullen drank his too, not enjoying the beverage as much as the others; the fizz wasn't pleasant to his throat. But Lilly sat atop the car taking sweet, satisfying sips, beaming after each one. Behind her the trees were taking on the tinge of their fall colors, and the setting sun framed her in golden light. The picture was one worthy of a magazine ad, and he enjoyed the drink a little more.

"That'll do you for now." Johnny slapped the car's hood. "And you just remember what I told you. 'Bout fo' miles up, red fence markin' the path. Tell 'em Johnny D sent you, and they fix you up right."

"I will, indeed." Dave shook his hand.

Cullen, too, reached for Johnny's hand, holding a folded bill. "For your trouble."

"Hear now, mistuh. Wasn't a trouble. You was in my path, is all. But

I reckon I can put it in the plate at church on Sunday." Johnny tucked the bill into the front pocket of his coveralls and headed for his truck, calling over his shoulder, "You remember what I tol' you!"

The tires of the truck spun in the loose gravel, and the final gun of the engine took it to the road, just as the empty Coca-Cola bottle flew out the window.

Lilly winced at the sound of the broken glass. "He coulda got a penny for that bottle."

Cullen finished his drink and tossed the bottle into the backseat. "What's four miles up?"

"Well, I have two bits of news for you. First, I used the phone at the station and called in. Congratulations, your boys won today, and the Series is all tied up. Tomorrow decides it all."

Cullen let out the closest thing to a *whoop!* he could manage. "What could be better than that?"

"We have been invited to a barbecue."

"Is that so?"

"Oh, yeah." Dave lost his deep, cultured baritone in favor of a deep southern tone. "Place called Lickey's. Pulled pork, baked beans, collard greens, and sweet tea. Mmm, mmm."

"Sounds fabulous!" Lilly dropped down into the backseat. "Let's go."

"I don't know," Cullen said. "We've lost so much time already."

"We're driving all night anyway," Dave said. "What's another hour or so?"

Lilly leaned over the seat, her face inches from his. "Come on, Moonsie. You're not afraid to add a little color and spice to your life, are you?"

"Of course not." Cullen pulled the car onto the road. "But I am glad that Mother's somewhere on a train."

He slowed the car considerably after three miles, and Dave hung over the edge of the door keeping an eye out for the red fence marker. After two false sightings, they passed it, and as Cullen turned the car around, he realized why and stopped the car at the turn.

"Headlight's out."

"You're kidding." Dave hopped out and walked to the front. The grim expression on his face confirmed the theory. "Broken."

That explained the sound of broken glass when Johnny's truck pulled out. Not a bottle hitting the ground, but a rock hitting his headlight.

"So where does that put us?" Lilly asked.

"Puts us here for the night if we can find someplace close," Cullen said as Dave got back in. "It's not safe to drive like this—not when I don't know the roads."

"You know," Dave said, "if I knew I was hitching a ride with Odysseus, I would have waited for the train."

"Relax," Cullen said. "We'll be on the road at first light, get you to a station, and you'll be at Forbes Field by game time."

The turn at the red fence marked the beginning of a twisting path cut through trees, and more than once Cullen wondered if this wasn't some sort of scheme to get a rich white man's car off the beaten path. He'd never admit such doubts to his fellow dupes, but he did pray with each turn: *Lord, forgive my doubt in the kindness of strangers and keep us safe.*

Soon enough his fears were allayed by the scent of pork and the sound of music. The final turn brought them into a clearing where a shack straddled a stream. Light poured from its windows as well as from lanterns dangling from the trees.

"Oh, man!" Lilly was bouncing in her seat. "You, Moonsie, are in for the night of your life."

He pulled his car in with the gathering of others—most of them looking like they'd been brought there to die. Before long a welcoming party—a group of six men of varying sizes and shades of black—emerged from a gathering on the other side of the stream. Dave went out to meet them as envoy.

"Good evening, gentlemen. A man named Johnny D said we might be able to get some supper here."

"Did he, now?" Their spokesperson looked like a wall of dark brick, arms straining beneath the sleeves of his shirt. "An' how do you know Johnny?"

"Helped us out a while back. He told us right how to get here." Dave looked around. "That's his truck."

Cullen decided this wasn't the place to mention that the man had also broken his headlight.

"Well, I'm guessin' a friend of Johnny's is a friend of our'n." The Brick Wall's change of heart probably had as much to do with Lilly's long-legged emergence from the car as much as the offstage endorsement of Johnny. "I'm Will Lickey and behind me is my empire. Y'all are welcome."

"We'd like to pay, of course," Cullen said, holding his voice steady.

"Ooo-wee, look at you. God bless you, son. That happen in the war?"

"Yes," Cullen said, oddly at ease with the confrontation.

"Had two brothers go over there. One came back without his legs, and the other didn't come back at all. You thank God every day you're livin'. Unnerstan'?"

"I do."

"Now, it don't seem right takin' money from y'all for the pleasure of feedin' ya, but I 'spose I can add it to the plate at church." He held out his hand, the palm light in the darkness, and Cullen peeled off a few bills, having no idea of their value.

They followed the men down into the base of the shallow valley and into the shack, where the lamplight made impressive shadows on the walls. A four-piece band was in full swing—an upright bass, a guitar, a single snare drum, and a saxophone. The music was without lyrics, sounding like it was born from the shadows cast on the wall—dark and erratic. Men and women danced on a dedicated floor, their bodies in full motion, connected sporadically at the hand, the waist, the cheek.

Cullen felt Lilly's hand take his.

"Dance with me, Moonsie?"

"I don't think so. I—"

Before he could finish, she'd moved on.

"Davey? Dance?"

"Sure, sugar. But how about we eat first?"

They walked straight through to a door on the opposite side and emerged to find a gathering of about thirty men and women. Their ages ranged anywhere from eighteen to eighty, and their skin a spectrum of copper, cocoa, and ebony. When they all seemed to turn at once, he was glad for Lickey's escort.

"These here's friends of Johnny's. Feed 'em right."

A young woman came forth with three glass jars. "I'm Arlene. Follow me."

"Yes, m'am," Dave said, and Cullen understood his enthusiasm. She was young—probably Lilly's age—and her sepia skin reflected the lamplight. Hers was a body of curves, and walking behind her gave the impression of following a pendulum covered in lavender silk. She brought them around the back of the shack where, on a shelf built right into the side, two barrels sat. One big, the other bigger.

Arlene handed each one a jar and pointed to the first barrel. "This here's sweet tea. This other one"—the smaller of the two—"is Lickey's *special* sweet tea. Folks here like to mix 'em."

"Thank you." Cullen took his glass and tried to keep his expression neutral as Lilly filled her jar.

She held up her hand as if taking a pledge. "Don't worry about me. I've learned my lesson. New leaf turned and all that."

"Well, I'm carrying around the same old leaves I ever have," Dave said before holding his glass under the spigot of the special barrel, filling it a third of the way up before finishing it off from the second. He took one sip and then a staggering step, letting out a sound somewhere between a wolf and hound.

"I tol' you it was special," Arlene said, her hand on her generous hip.

"And you did not lie."

"Now you all go inside and find a seat. If there aren't none, kick someone out. Tell 'em Arlene said so, and I'll bring you your food."

Cullen hoped it wouldn't come to that. After all, they'd lost their brick escort. But inside, the band had abandoned their instruments, and most of the patrons had stepped out. They managed to find a table, and one of the men he remembered from the greeting party scrounged up three chairs. Minutes later, Arlene arrived with three bundles of newspaper. To his surprise, she set each bundle down and unrolled it to reveal supper: a generous pile of pulled pork, two slices of white bread, a spoonful of something yellow, beans, and greens.

"That's my mama's creamed corn." She leaned over the table and spoke straight into Dave's ear. "Makes some men cry."

He didn't know about crying, but Cullen's mouth was definitely beginning to water, and it seemed only one thing was missing. "Where can I get a fork?"

Arlene leaned farther across the table. "That what your bread is for." To demonstrate, she pulled off a corner, ran it through the corn on Dave's paper, and placed a bit of pork on top—all of which she popped into her mouth. She chewed with the same rhythm as her swaying walk, then swallowed. "Get it?"

"Got it."

"You just let me know if you want more."

Although they were the objects of understandable stares, they were largely left alone as they ate, a fact Cullen appreciated as all of his senses were wrapped up in the food in front of him. None of it tasted like anything he'd ever had before, and as he ran his bread along the paper, wiping up the last of the creamed corn, he asked Lilly if she thought there was any way he could convince Eugenie to cook and serve like this.

"Now, that I'd like to see." And though the comment was light-hearted, there was an underlying sadness to it too. "Be sure to send me a picture postcard of her face when you ask her."

"Who's Eugenie?" Dave was on his third serving.

"Our maid—I mean, his maid. His mother's maid."

Dave chewed, swallowed, and took another sip of his special tea. It was the second serving of that. "Okay, folks, it's time."

Cullen felt uneasy. "Time for what?"

"For you two to spill. How did we get here? What's the story?"

"Oh, it's a doozie," Lilly said. "You sure you're up for it?"

"Oh yeah."

She turned to Cullen. "Mind if I tell him?"

"That depends. It'll be off the record?"

"Brother, I couldn't write it down if I wanted to at this point."

His words had an almost pleasant slur, making Cullen think that maybe Dave wouldn't even remember them in the morning. "Go ahead." Cullen sat back and listened to the past days unfold through Lilly's eyes. Her hand fluttered and her inflection adjusted itself to the characters—four in all, including Eugenie, whom she always represented with a dour expression and hunched shoulders. She left nothing out—not her inauspicious arrival, the beach, his mother, or the vision.

Dave's fingers moved with an invisible pencil.

"*Healed*? That's what she said?" And Lilly confirmed it, pantomiming an underline on the table. "And what do you think of that, Moon?"

Dave had been calling him by the familiar moniker all day, and as long as he dropped the "Blue," Cullen was almost flattered.

"Doesn't matter what I think. She's forgotten all about it, so I can too. I guess we'll never know."

Lilly slapped the table. "What do you mean *'we'll never know'*?"

"I mean, under no circumstances am I going to walk onto that field. You know I've only gone along with this to humor her. Now I'm off the hook. I took a gamble, and I won."

"C'mon," Dave said, cajoling. He pointed to the phone on the wall. "One call to McKechnie, he's a pal of mine. I once wrote a heartwarming piece about his third baseman without revealing the fact that the guy had five different girlfriends in four different cities. He owes me a favor."

"No. I started my baseball career with some guy who owed a favor to my father. I'm not visiting that again."

"But Betty Ruth—what if it comes back to her someday? And she asks you?"

"I'll tell her we went, and it didn't work."

"But that will be a lie."

"I lie to her every day when she's in her spells."

"This seems so much worse," Lilly said. "This is a lie about God. You can't do that. You can't just say God didn't do something when you haven't even given Him a chance."

The band resumed their place on the makeshift stage, and the saxophone let out a long, wailing note. Instantly the floor was packed with people, and this seemed like the last place anyone would talk about the wonders of God.

Dave had been chewing thoughtfully, eyes tracking them like a spectator at a tennis match. At Lilly's statement he reached for his notebook. "I might just use that..."

"This is not a story," Cullen insisted.

"But if it was, and Davey here wrote it, you'd have something to show Betty Ruth, in case she remembered again." They now had to shout over the music.

Dave held up his hands as if projecting a headline. "*Maligned Rookie Vet Seeks Second Shot.* That has a ring to it."

"I'm not seeking a second shot."

"What are you seeking then, Moon?"

"I'm not seeking anything."

"Oh, brother. I don't think that's true."

Arlene sashayed by at that moment, proving irresistible to Dave, and the two joined the crowd on the floor. Gray hair and paunch aside, he moved as well as any other man out there, and soon he was sharing his prowess with three women.

"I could never do that."

"Sure you could, Moonsie. It's just a matter of moving. Come on."

She took his hand, and there he was, someplace as foreign as if she'd taken him to Mars. The air was thick with smoke, as most of the dancers had a cigarette hanging from their lips, and between that, the heat of the bodies pressed all around, and the feel of Lilly against him, he fought for every breath.

"Like this." She took his hand and bent her body to his. "Like you're bowing or something." He complied. "Now move with me."

He tried, closing his eyes and listening to the unfamiliar music. She whispered a little "Da-da, da, da" in his ear, an attempt to reinforce the rhythm, but they were doomed. He was moving on borrowed feet at best, and he could feel nothing but the sensation of his scarred cheek pressed against her perfect, smooth one.

"This is silly." As he spoke, his flesh moved against hers.

"Just give it a try, Moonsie. For me."

So he redoubled his efforts. After all, when would he have this chance again to hold her this close? In fact, he doubled that too, pulling her body closer to his, until more of him touched more of her. On the stage, the guitar player sang a story about a woman who did him wrong, and he tried to concentrate on the lyrics so he could ignore the thoughts going through his mind.

But as the music went on, more bodies came to the floor, pressing him closer and closer to Lilly. The music turned slow, sensual. Dave had narrowed his attention to Arlene, who was pressed against him like a circus act. Nobody would care—nobody would know—that he and Lilly weren't doing anything close to dancing. They simply moved, not even room for smoke between them.

He put his lips to her ear. "This has to stop."

She turned to him, her lips as close as their bodies. "Let's go outside."

Somehow, they made their way through the crowd and outside, where the night air had grown cold. A welcome feeling to his overheated body. They touched only in the fact that she held his hand, but within a moment she was pressed up against the side of the shack, pinned there by a body he seemed no longer able to control. Her hands were around his neck, drawing him close.

"No, Lilly."

"Just give it a try, Moonsie. For me."

"You don't want this."

"How do you know what I want?"

He closed his eyes, summoning the same strength he'd needed when he stood stock-still in a cloud of burning gas. He wouldn't be responsible for undoing the work that God had done in her life. In her heart. "I don't want this. Not here. Not with you."

She smiled. "I don't believe you."

"You don't have to. Let's go to the car."

From the snatches of conversation he heard, every person they passed had their own idea of where he and Lilly were headed, and his face flushed with their implications. If he heard them, doubtless Lilly did too, though she seemed to take it in stride.

"Backseat," he ordered, and once she was in, he shut the door.

She rolled down the window and poked her head out. "What's your plan, Stan?"

"We'll wait here, until Dave comes to his senses. Then we'll take our chances on the road."

"Well, get inside the car. I promise I won't bite. I just thought you might want to kiss me a little is all."

"Well, I don't." At least not a little. "Get some rest. It's going to be a long night."

He got on top of the car's hood and fixed his eyes on the shack. He could go back and pull Dave away, but his protective instinct prevented him from leaving Lilly alone in the car. So he waited, lying back on the hood, staring at the stars. Bits and pieces of conversation floated around him, the voices as warm and full as the food in his stomach. Every now and then he heard laughter and, always, music.

This would be a perfect time to pray, if he could shut everything else out. He tried, choosing a single star and picturing God behind it, watching him.

I resisted, Lord. Again. But it's not getting easier. I don't know what You want from us. From me. But I won't let us get that close again.

It may have been his imagination, but he could have sworn the star winked at him. Twinkled, he supposed, the way stars do. His mother used to say, *"Oh, that's just a winking sin,"* whenever he'd committed a minor transgression. *"Sometimes God just watches with one eye."*

So Cullen winked back. After all, they had one more day together.

31

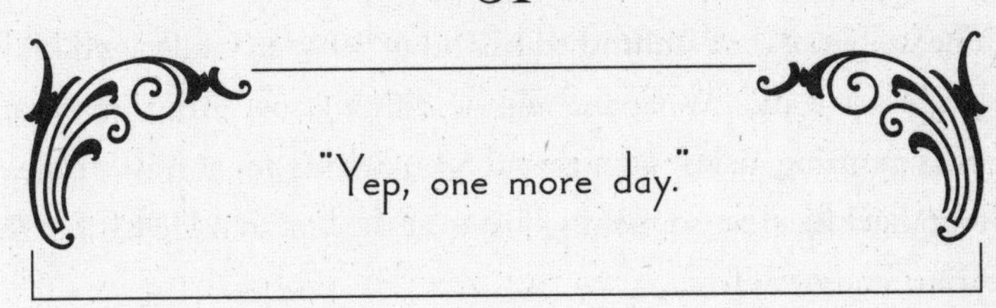

As it turned out, they didn't leave that night, nor did they leave at first light. In fact, it wasn't until nearly dawn when Dave Voyant came stumbling to the car, rousing Cullen from sleep when he fell in beside him. And, as was usual when Cullen was roused unexpectedly, he came up with a violent rush, grabbing Dave's shirt collar and throwing him back outside the car.

"Hey, hey!" The fallen man rose, dusting the seat of his pants.

"Sorry," Cullen said, catching his breath. "I'm a light sleeper." He looked around. "Where have you been?"

"In the arms of the lovely Arlene. And before you deliver a Sunday school lesson, we just danced."

"All night?"

"With a girl like Arlene you can dance all night. Oh, if I was twenty years younger."

"Try thirty."

"She kept calling me her little silver fox. Can you beat that?"

"Get in. It's going to be a long day."

And it was. The lively, easy banter of yesterday seemed to have been left behind at Lickey's. Dave alternately held his head in his hands, then over the edge of the car, then within an ice pouch he procured at the same petrol stop where Cullen had the headlight repaired.

The weight of their unfinished kiss hung between Cullen and Lilly—at least he felt it did. What she felt, he didn't know. After muttering a sleepy "G'morning, fellas" after they'd been driving for at least a mile, her eyes remained fixed on something just over the horizon. He left her there in peace.

They'd been too early to catch a train in Roanoke, and Dave had declared he was in no condition yet to take one, so they continued up to Arlington, taking a gamble that there'd be one left to get him to the game on time. It was midmorning—ten o'clock—and they piled out of the car, each of them looking every bit like they'd spent an illicit night at an off-road shimmy-shack in West Virginia. They undoubtedly carried with them the odors of the night—pork and sweat, special sweet tea, and a night spent sleeping in, and on, a car. The passengers at the Arlington station made their disdain known and made a wide path for the newcomers as they approached the row of phone booths just inside the main doors.

Cullen dug in his pockets and found a handful of coins, depositing them one by one at the operator's instructions until he was rewarded with the sound of Eugenie's voice on the other end of the line.

"How's Mother?"

"How do you think she is? She's a mess."

"Tell her I'll be home soon."

"She'll want to hear more than that."

"Tell her I'll be back today. And tomorrow, tell her the same thing. Sooner or later it will be true."

He'd brought his barracks bag in with him and went now into the men's washroom to clean up. A splash of water, a run over his teeth with his toothbrush, a comb of the hair, and a clean shirt. Not like the bracing shower at the Tatters', but it would have to do. He was buttoning his shirt when he looked in the mirror and saw Dave coming up beside him.

Dave turned on the faucet and bent to splash water on his face, which he dried with Cullen's discarded shirt. "So"—Dave dropped it back in the open barracks bag—"do you believe in miracles?"

"Always."

"We missed the last train to Pittsburgh by ten minutes."

"That's your miracle?"

He waited for an answer while Dave swished water in his mouth and spat in the sink. "So I called my editor to tell him he could go ahead and fire me because I've fallen in love with a girl named Arlene and plan to spend the rest of my life running Lickey's special sweet tea, and he says it's not a problem, because they've postponed the game."

"Again?"

"Rain checks all around."

"So that means—"

"I'm sticking with you. Yep, one more day."

They stopped at a market to buy food for the road. Apples, peanuts, crackers. Bottles of Coca-Cola and candy bars Cullen never even knew existed. Dave told stories and Lilly told jokes, and Cullen soaked it all in. Life was going to be so quiet when he got home.

The first patter of rain came with the full-on chill of night, and when they pulled over to raise the roof of the car, Lilly declared she was exhausted and retired to the backseat to curl up under the picnic blanket.

She slept there now.

According to Dave Voyant's watch it was nearly midnight, which explained the dry ache behind Cullen's eyes.

"Do you want to pull over and let me take the wheel for a while?"

"I'm fine." He didn't want to risk waking Lilly. Besides, the rain was pounding, and a moving car was far less likely to get stuck in a muddy road. "We've got to be getting close. Would have been there two hours ago if not for this rain."

"What's her story anyway?"

"It's hers."

"Okay, we'll stick with the noble act. What's the story between the two of you?"

"Nothing beyond the fact that I am returning her to her mother."

"Lovers' quarrel?"

"No."

"But you love her, don't you?"

Cullen hazarded a look away from the road. "What makes you say that?"

"Thirty years of watching people. Learning about them. It's my job to size up a life and cram it into a thousand words. You two could fill a book."

"Perhaps she'll be more generous with details. Perhaps instead of taking you to Forbes Field, I'll drop you off with Lilly. The two of you can share a chat with her mother."

"Dropping her off, eh? If you ask me, I think you're making a mistake."

"But I didn't ask you. You're the reporter. That's your job."

"So indulge me. Nothing between you? Never was, never will be?"

As if Cullen could make that decision. He couldn't bring that wisp of sunlight into his dark world, couldn't risk the constant disruption of his mother's frail mind. Lilly had a life to mend at home, and, once mended, who knew if she would ever want to leave it again. She was on the brink of a new start, one that didn't include him. In fact, the worst thing he could do would be to stand in her way.

"No, no, and no." But only two of the three were true.

"You think Miresburgh will have a sign?"

Cullen peered into the rainy darkness. "At this point I don't think it'll make much difference if it does or not."

"Then maybe we need to wake the sleeping beauty. Wouldn't want to keep her any longer than we need to, right?" Dave leaned over the seat and cupped his hands around his mouth. "Lilly? Oh, Lilly! Wake up, darling. I think we're close to home."

A few minutes later her head was next to his. "Where are we?"

"Close," Cullen said, maintaining his grip on the wheel. "Hard to look for turnoffs in this rain, though." He gave her a rundown of all the landmarks he remembered since she went off to sleep. "Any idea where we are?"

"I'd have a better one if I could see. This is brutal."

"That's why I say, give me the city!" Dave said. "Lights everywhere, and there's no place you need to be that you can't walk to."

No reply but the *thump, thump* of the windshield wipers.

"Will this road take us right into town? Or will there be a turnoff?"

She hesitated a bit too long. "Right into town. Just stay on it, right into the town square."

From that point, every turning of the tires felt like a countdown, and he used the excuse of the weather to further slow his speed. He could just tell her. There was still time. How much, he didn't know, but what good would it do to go through life with another regret? How simple to say, "I love you, Lilly." What's the worst that could happen? She'd leave? She was leaving anyway. She'd stay? Forget her own mother and go back to Pensacola to live with him and his mother?

No, the worst that could happen was a combination of the two. First she'd stay, then she'd leave. He'd listened to enough of her stories to know how they started—*"I used to have a boyfriend who..."*—and he didn't need to hear the ending to know it. He'd learned to live with Lilly; he'd learn to live without her. It wouldn't be the first time he had to come back after being close to death.

"There it is." Her smooth white arm invaded the space between them. "Baylynn's Tire Yard. Now isn't that a lovely greeting?"

The headlights swept over the mountainous piles of black rubber made slick by the rain. At the foot of them, a sign welcoming the weary travelers to Miresburgh.

The next thing Cullen knew, Lilly was sliding over the seat, seemingly diving headfirst into the dashboard, before twisting, bending, and somehow landing squarely between Dave and him.

More and more hints of a township passed by. A petrol station, a row of houses. At some point he came to an intersecting street and found his headlights trained straight ahead on an ominous, looming structure. It had all manner of gables and towers and iron-barred dark windows.

"Beware all ye who enter here," Dave said.

"Miresburgh courthouse." Lilly shivered. "Turn right."

One shop window after another—florist, photography studio, bookstore.

"Keep going."

Library, school. High school, from the looks of it.

"Turn left."

A corner market and then houses. A few had lights still burning, bright squares centered in solid red brick. But most were dark, and as he drove farther, the houses got smaller. The streetlights ended, and the streets themselves were darker.

"Here."

Without question, he brought the car to an easy stop and set the parking brake.

"Turn off the lights, would you? People get curious."

Cullen pushed the knob into the dash. "This is your home?" He tried to keep his voice neutral, but it wasn't easy given the image before him. White clapboard, peeling paint. The single tree in the yard had created a blanket of leaves that, mixed with rain, gave the appearance of tar on the ground. Weeds sprouted up along the walkway, and the single step up to the front door appeared broken.

"Actually three houses down. But who knows what Mama would say if she saw me getting out of a car with two men. She might not let me in."

"I'm going to walk you to the door, at least."

"No. That's the worst thing you could do. I...I have to do this on my own." She turned toward Dave and offered her hand. "Thanks again for looking out for me. I knew you were a good egg when I saw you. Kind of fatherlike."

Dave pulled an imaginary knife out of his heart. "I don't think you could have said anything crueler."

Lilly laughed. "Okay, a real daddy, then. That better?"

"Much."

She leaned over to offer him a chaste kiss on his cheek, and Cullen steeled himself for the same. He opened his door and then stepped out into the rain, breathless at its initial cold onslaught. He dreaded every step she'd have to take in it. Her suitcase sat in the well between the seats, and he pulled it out, gauging its weight by imagining her shoulders bearing the burden.

By the time he closed the back door, she was at his side, rain pelting the blue cloche hat that was quickly losing its distinctive shape. A few drops found their way to her chin and clung there, like tears. Or maybe they were tears. The droplets on her cheeks appeared to be so, but he wouldn't know unless he touched them, tasted them for salt.

And he was determined not to do so. If he knew she was crying, he'd want to take her into his arms as he did the night of the revival. As he'd done again last night—was it only last night? How was it he made the mistake of letting her go? If he touched her again, he wouldn't make the same mistake.

"I'll take that." She reached for the suitcase handle and their hands touched. Already she was cold.

"Are you sure I can't walk you to the door?"

"Posi-lutely." Her smile couldn't shine through the rain.

"I'm not leaving, you know, until I see you safe inside."

She nodded. "Fair enough. And if Betty Ruth—if I ever come to her mind, if she ever remembers me, even for a minute, will you tell her—tell her that I love her? And tell her that you brought me home."

"I will." Never before had he been so grateful for the wounds that brought such hoarseness to his voice. He lifted his face to the rain.

"Good luck to you, Moonsie."

"And to you, Lilly."

"I have to do this."

"I know."

"I wish I didn't."

He couldn't answer that. He didn't trust himself. He leaned forward and placed a kiss on top of her hat. That would have to do.

He didn't get back into the car until she reached the walkway to what must be her home. Then from his place behind the wheel, he watched her, a vision obscured by the intermittent blanket of rain. Minutes later, a light came on behind one of the windows in the side of the house. Then another in the front window. Soon the front door opened, creating a wedge of amber. Try as he might, he could not see what was on the other side, though it opened wider and wider until Lilly eventually walked inside. Then she was gone, swallowed up.

Five minutes passed by. Then ten—just in case she'd change her mind. He looked for a silhouette in the window, waited for the door to open, but the scene did not change. She was gone. She knew he was here, but she wasn't coming back.

Thankfully, his normally loquacious traveling companion kept silent until Cullen grasped the door handle, preparing to open it.

"Whoa, buddy. What do you think—?"

The rest of his question was lost in the slamming of metal. Cullen sloshed his way around the front of the car to the passenger side, opened the door, and leaned forward. "Move over."

Dave complied, with just a slight complaint about the wet seat, and Cullen slid in.

"It's not too late, Moon. I can drive you up to that house as easy as I can drive you to Forbes Field."

"This is done." Cullen leaned his head against the back of the seat and closed his eyes, feeling the car change direction beneath him.

32

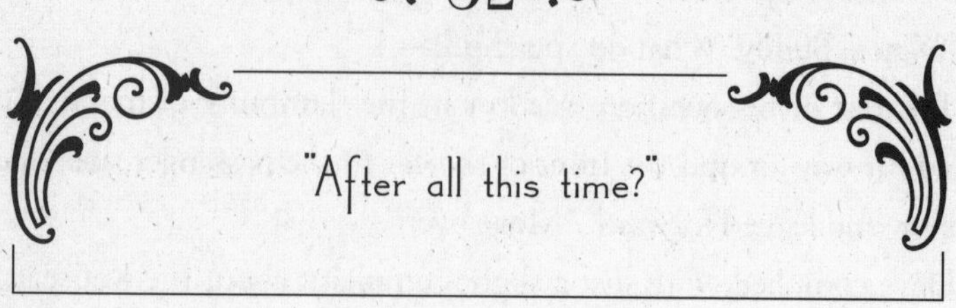

"After all this time?"

She looked the same. Exactly the same. Long white hair loose to her waist, dark brows knit together over button-brown eyes. Chalky white skin, pink lips set in a straight line. If she was surprised by Lilly's late-night arrival, she showed no sign. The door had been eased open cautiously, little by little, until all of the shabby room bathed in amber light framed the figure clutching a green shawl around her shoulders.

Lilly tightened her grip on the suitcase handle. "Hello, Mama."

"It's the middle of the night."

"I got here as quick as I could."

"You by yourself?"

"Of course."

"Well, come on in, then."

Mama took a few steps back to allow Lilly room to walk inside. The minute she did, the familiar scent of beeswax brought home the meticulousness of Mama's housekeeping, making Lilly immediately aware of just how much she was dripping on the carpet.

"You must be tired," Mama said, closing the door.

"Is that all you have to say to me, Mama? After all this time?"

Mama gathered her shawl tighter and headed for the kitchen. "You hungry? Go change out of those wet things before you catch your death, and I'll have a little something ready for you. I'll make you some oatmeal, just like you like it."

Before Lilly could answer, she found herself alone. Her arm ached with the weight of the suitcase, and she dared not set it down on the clean floor, let alone rest herself on any piece of furniture.

This is what You brought me back for, Lord? Oatmeal?

She wasn't sure what she'd been expecting. Certainly not a tear-filled embrace at the door; she couldn't remember the last time there'd been an embrace of any kind. She could blame the lateness of the hour; her mother's unease at having been roused from sleep; the pathetic, soggy, bedraggled sight she must be. But this?

Had she known, she would have waited until morning, somehow. Would have given Cullen one last chance to ask her to stay, to bring her back to *his* home. But one more night wouldn't have changed anything. She ached with his rejection at Lickey's. Her ears rang with the words he said when he thought she was sleeping.

"No, no, and no."

All those moments they shared—just what happens when a man gets around a pretty girl.

Their little house had no hallway—just two bedrooms right off the living room. Through the cracked door, she could see her mother's in the dim light of the bedside lamp. The door to her own room was closed, and she well imagined it had been since the day she left. With steps made heavy by more than the water in her shoes, Lilly walked to the door and grasped the handle, half expecting it to be locked. It wasn't, but it had swollen in the jamb, and she had to use her shoulder to finally push the door open.

It was like opening an old trunk. The very air felt solid, like it had been trapped and doubling like yeast all these years. She reached for the switch on the wall, only to find that the gas had been cut off to this room. If nothing else, her mother was a practical woman. Thrifty too, hence the three-word response in her telegram: *"Send her home."* But no light to beckon her.

She kept the door open a fraction and, once her eyes adjusted, found her surroundings hauntingly familiar. Her small bed was in the corner, with its familiar oval-shaped depression in the middle of the mattress. The four-drawer bureau with the lace runner across the top, and the calico curtains—one at the window, the other creating a closet door over a series of hooks on the wall. A full-length mirror in the corner where she'd stood for countless hours watching her body change, brushing the hair grown down to her waist, and then that afternoon when she first came home having left it all at the corner barbershop.

No smell of beeswax in here. In fact, she was a little grateful for the darkness that hid the dust.

She set her suitcase on the floor at the foot of her bed and knelt to open it, but the chill of her wet skin began to take its toll, and none of the light summer clothing within it appealed to her. Never mind that very little would meet the approval of her mother. Hands working by memory, she went to the bureau and opened the second drawer, feeling around until she found a pair of flannel pajama pants. Then down to the bottom drawer, where her fingers encountered the distinctive, soft texture of her oversized high-school sweater.

Her entire body turned to goose flesh as she dropped her wet clothing on the lid of her closed suitcase; her hands shook as she attempted to tie the drawstring on the pants. It seemed to her that she had to pull the string so much tighter to get them to fit around her waist; she never remembered her hip bones jutting out when she was younger. The sweater was pulled over her head, and she felt deliciously warm within it. She ran fingers through her damp hair and, opting to remain barefoot, headed for the kitchen.

The smell of cinnamon greeted her as she found Mama at the stove, stirring.

"I guess I am hungry."

Mama turned around. "Look at you. You could be fifteen years old again."

It was the closest her mother had ever come to warmth. She went to the table and folded herself into one of the chairs. "I feel like I am."

"You want me to put some coffee on?"

"No, thanks. It'll make me jittery."

The oatmeal was served in the same blue-speckled bowl she'd been eating out of since she was a child. The very first bite, hot and savory, brought back memories both good and bad. Good, like this, when Mama and she shared a moment in the quiet. And bad, like all those times it was all there was to eat, and it was thrust upon her in stony silence.

She swallowed. "Just like I remember."

"Have you completely forgotten how to ask a blessing for your food?"

That first bite turned to stone in her otherwise empty stomach. "I'm sorry, I just—"

But Mama's head was already bowed. "Father God, we thank Thee for Thy blessings and the simple food on this table. May it give nourishment and strength so we can be better servants for Thee. In the name of Jesus, amen."

"Amen." Oddly enough, the next bite wasn't nearly as good.

"You saw that your room's still waiting."

"I did see that, thank you. But there's no light."

"I'll get that fixed in the morning. I assume you'll be here in the morning."

"Yes, Mama."

"Needs a good cleaning too. If I'd known you was coming, I would've spruced it up a bit."

"You knew I was coming. Cullen—Mr. Burnside wrote to you. You said to send me home."

"Never heard nothing back. For all I known, you was dead in a ditch somewhere. All these years...I never know what to expect."

"Then I'd think you'd be a little happier to see me here."

"This is where you belong. How I feel won't change that."

Lilly dragged her spoon along the edge of the bowl. "How do you feel, Mama?"

"I don't know. Guess it depends on what brought you back."

"A millionaire brought me back. A millionaire who just might have loved me a little. He drove me here all the way from Florida."

Mama got up from the table and went to the hanging basket by the door where she kept important papers. After a little searching, she came back and set a folded telegram in front of Lilly.

"Read that. See how much he loved you."

Hand trembling, though she was now warmed both inside and out, Lilly unfolded the paper and pressed it flat on the table in front of her.

"*'It has come to my attention...'* This was before."

Mama's eyes turned into slits. "Before *what*?"

"Before he knew me. Before we'd ever really talked to each other."

"And after that, he was begging you to stay?"

"Not begging, no. But offering..." A job. A room somewhere.

"But he didn't put up a fight getting you here neither. Did he? I didn't think so."

Lilly balanced a glob of oatmeal on her spoon, turning it upside down to test its weight. How could she bring the spirit of Betty Ruth into this room? How could she ever begin to explain the woman's vision for her son? What at the time seemed a conviction of faith now seemed, well, silly. So silly, in fact, it surprised her that Cullen had gone along with it at all. Unless he saw it as an excuse. Appease his mother, go to the game, and drop her off in the process.

"There was more to it than just bringing me here. He had his reasons."

"I'm sure he did. No man ever does nothing unless he's gonna get some kind of benefit. Remember that. 'Course, no doubt in my mind you know more about men than I'd ever hope to. No thanks to God in that."

Lilly shoved her bowl away. "Honestly, Mama. Don't you have a single kind word for me?"

"That depends. Have you had a change of heart? Because I won't have anybody living in my house who doesn't have the love of Jesus. I'm a God-fearing woman in a Christian home. And for years"—she pounded a single thick, strong finger on the tabletop—"*years* I sat back and watched you live an abomination of morality under my roof. Never had such a sense of peace as the day you left."

"Mama, you don't mean that."

"I sure do. Didn't have to put up with the stench of liquor and cigarettes. Didn't have to sit up at night feeling the shame of what you was out doing with them boys. Didn't have to ask God to forgive me for bringing such a vessel of sin into this home."

"And you call that the love of Jesus?"

"I am keeping His commandments. For me and my household shall serve the Lord. You could not keep even one, to honor thy father and thy mother that thy days might be long upon the earth. You did not honor me."

"Did you ever think that was because you didn't love me? Certainly there's something in the Bible that tells parents to love their children."

"Of course I loved you."

"You never told me. You never *showed* me." She'd seen love, been loved by Betty Ruth, whether Betty Ruth remembered it or not. "I know what it feels like."

Mama sneered. "You just think you do. Men don't love girls like you, no matter what they say."

"Girls like you." The words were like a slap across the face—they stung—but she pressed on. "I'm not talking about men, Mama. I'm

talking about family. I lived—worked, really—at a campsite. One of those, oh, you don't know. But this couple, they took care of me. And this other family—they didn't care what type of girl I was."

The more she talked, the more she could see her mother's heart hardening. Her own pitch was getting higher, her words more frantic. This wasn't why she had come home. She closed her eyes—*Lord, give me the words here. Don't let me make this worse*—and then opened them again, feeling calmer.

"I want you to know, Mama, that I went to a church service two nights ago. A revival."

She snorted. "Could hardly get you to step foot into church when you was here."

Another deep breath, no need to mention that she'd never actually gone *into* the tent. "I want you to know, that night when I got home, I prayed. And you're right, I hadn't prayed in a long time. God showed me that I'd been wrong. I'd been *that kind of girl*."

Her mouth quavered, and she stopped for a moment to recover. "I remembered everything I've ever been taught about Jesus, about His blood washing away my sins. All the things you tried to teach me. I'm sorry, Mama, for the hurt and the worry and the pain I've caused you. I want you to know, I asked God to forgive me."

"And did He?"

The question chilled her heart. "You know He did, Mama."

"I mean, could you sense a change in your spirit? Did you feel clean?"

"I did." Yet, sharing that moment now somehow sullied it.

"But you couldn't keep clean, could you? Had to hop right back in that automobile with that man. Good girls don't ride in cars with men."

Lilly thought back to that last night—the dance floor with Cullen. Pressed up against him. Something that would have been harmless before, but now, seeing it through her mother's eyes... *Forgive me, Lord. Help me see Your grace in her eyes.*

"Mama, I'm trying to tell you that I came back to God. That I prayed and asked forgiveness for my sins—all those sins you've been telling me about. I realize now I was wrong. And He forgave me. Why can't you accept that?"

"Give me time. Let me see it in you—is that why you came back?"

"No, not really. Someday I'll tell you the whole story, but I saw just how people who truly love each other are able to forgive each other. And I *do* know my commandments, Mama, and I knew I couldn't honor you if I didn't forgive you. So...I do. I forgive you, Mama."

The rush she felt simply saying the words—like the breath of God taking her own away and rushing back with something sweeter. She felt almost giddy. "Do you hear that? I love you, and I forgive you."

Lilly moved her feet to the cold, hard floor, ready to leap up from her chair if Mama chose to do the same, but the woman sat, stonier than before.

"You forgive me?"

"I was never happy, Mama. Never. And I blamed you. But I think, maybe, you loved me the best you could, and it's not your fault if that wasn't enough. For whatever was lacking, well, I can forgive that." More and more she seemed to be talking to a wall, and if there were to be any crack at all, it would be this: "Do you think you could forgive me?"

"Do you even know what you're asking?" Mama swiped the bowl off the table and went to the sink, where she scraped it clean. "All those months of people pointing at me and talking. Then you come along, this beautiful baby girl, everybody thinking you're some kind of angel. You just had to prove them wrong, didn't you? Had to drag my name through the mud with your morals."

The damp hair on the back of Lilly's neck had nothing on the chill that ran beneath her skin. It formed a block of ice at the base of her skull and froze her into silence.

"He wasn't no millionaire, but he was good. And decent. And he might've married me if it weren't for you. Didn't want kids, and left me all alone. That's how I know." She scrubbed and scrubbed. "God will punish your sin. Don't matter how much you ask forgiveness. The consequences are going to follow you."

"Mama, it…it sounds like you want me to ask forgiveness for being *born.*"

She rested, at last. Her hands on the edge of the sink, her rounded shoulders slumped. "Not for being born, but for squandering the life I gave you. For making the same mistake I did."

"I've told you, I'm sorry for the worry I caused. And the pain."

She whirled around. "Promise me."

"What?"

"Get on your knees and promise me that you've repented."

"Mama—"

"I put up with it all I could when you was young and there wasn't a choice. But I don't have to take you back. Now, right here. Just like we done when you was little. On your knees and promise me that you repent your sin and you promise to go and sin no more."

Mama's eyes blazed with a terrifying mix of passion and vengeance. Lilly imagined her mother having this conversation countless times, with an invisible Lilly penitent at her feet. She felt invisible now—at least, everything about her that was good. Even she would admit that wasn't much, but her heart was pure. Her intentions, her motivations unselfish. The Lily of the Valley, the legend of Eve's tears.

"I won't get on my knees for you, Mama. God told me to forgive you, and I do. And to ask your forgiveness, which I did. What you choose to do from here is between you and Him."

Then she was fifteen again, getting up from the table and running to her room to slam the door. Only it wouldn't slam. She had to repeat the shoving process with her shoulder to get it to shut, but after she did, she turned the lock. The room was as dark as ever, and she stubbed her toe on her suitcase as she made her way to the window to open the curtain and let in what light she could. There wasn't much outside either. The rain had stopped, but the sky remained blanketed with clouds.

She fell back on the bed; even the squeak of the springs rang familiar and sad. She threw her arms above her head and stared up into the darkness. The bed sat up against the walls, and it was then that she noticed her mother hadn't left the room completely untouched after all. When she was home, these walls had been covered with pictures torn from fashion and movie magazines. Now, all that remained were the tacks, with shredded remains clinging to them from when they'd been ripped away.

God, I've been in some horrible places. You know, You've seen me there. And I guess I should thank You for bringing me out of them, but I can't thank You for bringing me here. I'm sorry. But I can't. I don't know what You wanted, why You told me to come here. But I'm here and now. You've got to get me out. I'll do it right this time. No sneaking off in the middle of the night. Especially on a night like this, but tomorrow, Lord. Or the next day, but soon. She's worse than I remember. She's—

A pounding on the door.

"Lilly Ann Margolis!"

She surrendered but did not move. "Yes, Mama."

"Don't you think you can come into my house and talk to me that way. Don't you think that for a minute!"

"I'm sorry, Mama."

"Open this door."

"Mama, I'm tired. I've been driving for four days. Can't we talk in the morning?"

Silence, long enough to make Lilly think Mama had walked away, and then the closing of the other bedroom door.

33

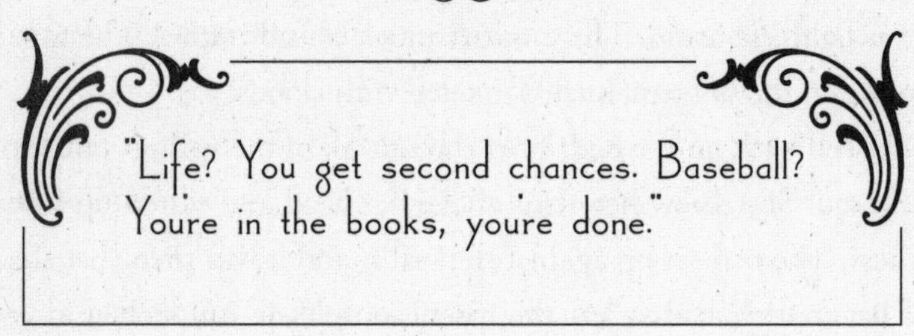

"Life? You get second chances. Baseball? Youre in the books, youre done."

Cullen woke up with two distinct pains. One in his neck, the other at the small of his back. Apparently he was too old to sleep in a car. At least for two nights in a row. Still, without sleep, he might never have survived the forty-mile drive away from the Margolis house. He opened his eyes to a windshield filled with the letters PAC—short for the Pittsburgh Athletic Company—and the distinctive red roof slashed through the gray sky. Forbes Field, just past dawn. Theirs was the only automobile in sight.

The sound that had awakened him resumed, a rapping on the window. He rolled it down and Dave Voyant handed through a small white cardboard box and a Thermos of coffee.

"Breakfast. Kolaches and coffee." He went around to the other side of the car and slid in behind the wheel.

"From Revek's?"

"You remember that place?"

"Every game-day morning. For luck."

"Maybe you should have stuck with pancakes."

"Very funny." Cullen found two plain white cups in the box and handed one over to Dave, who was unscrewing the Thermos lid.

"Guy charged me two bits for the cups and a three-dollar deposit on the Thermos. Highway robbery."

"World Series robbery more like it." The coffee hit him like a wild inside pitch. A particular chicory that took him back to the long counter lined with red stools.

Dave turned his head to look out the window. "Think they're going to get to play today?"

"Rainout yesterday. Stakes are high. I think my guys would play in a lake to cinch this thing."

"Might have to. Thanks again, by the way, for the ride. I'd still be sitting in the station."

Cullen nodded. "Glad to have the company."

"Does that mean you'll give me the story?"

"I told you, there's no story here."

"Think what it would mean to stand at that plate and get a hit. First one at home. That's a story."

"Exactly. It's a story. Not life. It's not going to change my standing in the record books, not going to get that season back."

"Not in the books, but in your head. In your heart. You can't tell me that hasn't been on your tail all these years."

"Look at me, Voyant. I've had bigger things to worry about."

"Even better. Wounded-warrior angle. People love that."

"You really are a vulture, aren't you?"

Dave shrugged. "I've been called worse."

The sun crept up but kept hidden behind a veil of clouds. Cullen bit into the kolache, savoring the spice of the sausage mixed with the sweet of the roll. "I should find a phone. Check up on Mother."

"I'll get us into the pressroom. Plenty in there."

"I appreciate it."

"Then, you tell me. You want your story in *Life*? *Saturday Evening Post*? *Sports Life*? You name it; I've got a byline coming to me in any of them."

"Fame holds no temptation for me."

"None?"

Cullen shook his head. "Nope."

"Then why are you here?"

"I wanted to appease my mother. And take Lilly home. And now, to bring you."

"And what about you? What have you got for yourself?"

"Last time I did something for myself, I came here to play ball and didn't get a single hit at home. That's what happened the last time I looked for any fame. I'm not cut out for it."

Dave popped the last bite of kolache in his mouth and spoke through it. "I'm a big believer in second chances. One hit, and that ugliness next to your name goes away."

"You're forgetting one thing. I might not get that hit."

"Three pitches, friend. And if you don't, what have you lost? Who'll know?"

"You. Me. The thirty thousand people in the stands. Subscribers to the *Saturday Evening Post*."

"No hit, I kill the story."

Not until this moment had his mother's vision held any interest to him. Before, it was little more than the ramblings of a feeble-minded woman. He knew his physical wounds were as healed as they were ever going to be. These were scars he would wear forever. His would always be a voice fueled by lungs that were just short of breath. The fact that he was alive at all spoke of God's mercy. Each day of his recovery, when he woke to find the pain lessened, he looked upon it as healing.

There would be no divine magic at the home plate at Forbes Field to restore his body. But that part of him marred by failure, that could be touched here. All at once, here in the shadow of this steel-and-concrete stadium, it made sense. Optimistic logic that Mother could never in a million years begin to grasp. *Maybe, just maybe...*

"McKechnie would never go for it."

"Leave him to me," Dave said. "All managers want good publicity for their team. Think about it. They came back from three-to-one. If they win today, they'll be the first team in history to beat that deficit. Why wouldn't he want another comeback story to tag along?"

"You know what you're going to say?"

Dave consulted his watch. "Press box opens at nine o'clock. I'll know by then. Now, if you'll excuse me." He got out of the car, moving from the front seat to the back, where he stretched himself as well as he could and pulled his hat over his eyes. "One more hour of sleep can't do any harm."

Unwilling to spend another hour in the car, Cullen poured himself a second cup of coffee and stepped out. The morning was too cold to be comfortable in shirt-sleeves, but that's all he had. The coffee helped somewhat, but he was still cold. And as uncomfortable as the external cold was, it didn't compare to the misery of breathing cold, damp air.

That's why the chemical-burn hospital was in the old tuberculosis hospital in Arizona. Hot, dry air—easier to breathe. This air hurt, each breath a little like drowning. It would be better once the sun was up, once the rainwater dried and the clouds dispersed. But for now he inhaled and exhaled with tiny spasms of pain, and the next breath seemed forever unattainable.

Coffee cup in one hand and the other in his pocket, he wandered away from the car and strolled down the sidewalk along one side of the stadium. Here was the vendors' entrance, and it was already a bustle of activity—cases and cases labeled Peanuts and Cracker Jack. A flatbed truck loaded with kegs of root beer backed through the gate, followed by another with crates of Coca-Cola.

When Cullen was younger, before Prohibition, Father used to take him to games, and it was the one time Cullen ever saw his father drink beer. One frosty, foam-spilling mug at the top of the fifth inning. Something to look forward to, savor, and recover from.

The businesses lining the street across from the stadium catered to the baseball crowd—diners where people would argue the merits of the players, bars where patrons would listen to the radio broadcast. There were barbers and newsstands and cigar shops, each advertising a special this week. The hotels started around the corner, the style and price of each in direct proportion to its distance from the stadium.

He and three other players had shared a house not four blocks from here, and this had been his world when he wasn't on the road. Even when his notoriety came into play, when he couldn't walk into the diner and order a short stack without incurring the wrath of erstwhile fans, he loved it here. Everything a little grimy, a little cheap. Miles away in every way from home.

He found himself in front of Revek's bakery and, admitting he had probably been heading there all along, walked in, sending the little bell on top of the door ringing at his arrival. Four of the stools were filled with men hunkered over their coffee. Their hats turned in perfect synchronicity as they looked to see who had just walked in.

"Morning," Cullen said to the group in general.

He got a few grunts in reply, but nothing that could be called a greeting. One of them, the man on the end, yelled, "Hey, Revek! Customer out here."

Revek emerged, the same short, balding man with the prominent nose, wiping his flour-dusted hands on his white apron the way he had every morning Cullen had ever been here.

"How can I—help you?" The question was interrupted by the look of surprise that came whenever anybody addressed him for the first time.

Embarrassment, followed by a mighty effort to appear not to have noticed the tangled scars covering half his face. None of the men at the counter had looked long enough to notice.

"I wanted to return your cup." He offered it over the counter, holding it in his good hand. "My friend was just in here, getting coffee and kolaches."

"Wit' the Thermos?"

"The very one. He mentioned paying a deposit, but I'd like to keep it. What do I owe?"

Cullen reached into his pocket, trying to ignore the fact that Mr. Revek seemed unsure about adding his cup to the vat of unwashed dishes behind him. He finally did, with an almost furtive movement, then held up his hand.

"Hey, nothin' now, right? You bring it back; I fill it up for a buck even."

"Fair enough."

Before Cullen could turn to leave, Revek said, "Hey, wait a minute, you. I know that face."

Once again the hats spun, bringing with them the heads of the men at the counter, and Cullen found himself the subject of scrutiny.

"Warn't you a player here? 'Bout eight, nine years back?"

"Yeah, yeah," said the man on the first stool. He wore a suit as rumpled as Cullen's, with a stained tie to boot. "Lemme look at the eyes." He held his kolache up and squinted. It would be just as easy and less humiliating to simply tell these men his name, but something in him needed them to guess. "Burn, Burns—"

The other three men joined in a chorus of, "Hey! Give the guy a break!" but the rumpled-suit man waved them off.

"Shut up, boys! I'm thinkin' here."

"Dat's it!" Revek slammed his hand on the counter. "Burnside."

Rumpled Suit snapped his fingers. "Blue Moon Burnside."

The other three men made no attempt to hide their disdain as they turned back to their coffee.

"Right?" Revek pushed. "Blue Moon never got a hit at home, right?"

"That's me," Cullen said, not sure whether he should feel offended or flattered.

"Hey, I apologize for the rudeness of my customers here, and it looks like you hads your share of trouble over there, but no one was exactly bawlin' when you left. Unnerstand?"

The four hats nodded in agreement, as the first man once again turned his back.

"Perfectly."

"And now, look. Today, it's gonna happen. Today, your team wins World Series. Am I right?"

"That's right," the men chorused. Two on the end clinked their coffee cups. Rumpled Suit snorted. "If them girls don't get too antsy about playin' in a little rain. What's it gonna hurt, a little rain?"

"Nah, not today." Revek took a clean cup from the pyramid and set it down on the fifth stool. He held the pot up as an invitation, and Cullen accepted, taking his place at the end of the line. "Nah. No rain today. Sun goes down tonight on a new champ'un. I predict, it happens." He made his way down the line, topping off everyone's cup. "Youse can take that to the bank."

"How can you be so sure?" Cullen asked. Revek's predictions were rarely accurate.

"Look. They's down three games, right? Three to one, and they fights their way back, tie it up. Can't walk away from that, right? Can't come up from nothin' and get so close and hand it over. Yesterday they gots a nice rainy day to think it over, right? So today, they nails it down."

All three men slammed their fists on the counter echoing, "Nail it."

"So, tell me. Guy like you comes back, what kinda seats they giving you? Behind first base, right? Or are they gonna let you in the bull pen?"

"Anywheres far from the batter's box is fine wit' me," said the guy next to Rumpled Suit.

Cullen laughed. "Not a forgiving bunch, are you?"

"That's life." Without asking, Revek set a doughnut warm with glaze in front of him. "Then again, no, that's baseball. Life? You get second chances. Baseball? You're in the books, you're done."

"Cooked," said the man at Cullen's elbow.

He said nothing, only took a bite of the doughnut and chewed—an unnecessary act, as the concoction nearly melted in his mouth. *Lilly would love this.* The food, the conversation. She'd have these men wrapped around her finger in a heartbeat. It was—almost—the first he'd thought about her that day.

"What if I told you fellows that I was here seeking a little redemption?"

"Ah, geez." Rumpled Suit slammed his coffee down, demonstrating how his tie might have come to be stained. "Save it for the old-timers' game, would ya?"

"Nah, they ain't gonna let him suit up," said the guy next to him. "Not with these stakes."

Revek roared over them. "Shaddup, ya lugheads! Lettum tell his piece."

"My mother had a vision. She told me if I came back here, had a turn at bat, God would heal me."

These people revered their mothers as much as they did the game. Two of the men and Revek quickly made the sign of the cross.

Rumpled Suit leaned forward, talking down the line. "Did God tell her you needs to get a hit? Or just stand there? 'Cuz I watched you that whole season, and you stand there pretty good."

"Or a foul ball," the man next to Cullen said. His accent made the two words rhyme. "That gonna do it?"

"How's about a pop fly?" The middle man whistled, spiraling his finger upward. "Straight up to heaven before the Big Man drops it in a glove."

"I'm sorry I said anything." Cullen kept his tone good-natured. In fact, hearing this impossible scenario bantered this way was almost a relief.

"Hey! Hey!" Revek pounded through the laughter. "Lookin' at them storm clouds out there, I don't wanna be anywheres near youse when Holy Father sends down the lightnin' for laughin' at the words of a godly vision." He crossed himself again before walking down to Cullen's stool and leaning over the counter. "Whad'ya think it's gonna prove now, gettin' a hit? You seem like a nice enough guy. You a nice guy?"

"I like to think so."

"You got your health, right? Such as it is?"

"Such as it is, yes."

"Gotta job?"

"Yes."

"House?"

"Yes."

"Girl?"

Cullen hesitated long enough to send the fellows into a raucous choral response.

"There it is," Revek said, summing up their response. "Always a woman, right? Listen, guy, you don't wanna put yourself through this for no girl. Your mother? Yes. Your kid? Maybe. One of them daredevil stunts gonna pay you five bucks? Sure. But a girl? That's nuts."

"It's not for a girl. It's for me."

"And what's it gonna get ya? The girl? Nah. Your season back? This ain't about baseball, buddy. Life has handed you somethin' bigger.

But"—he clapped his hands, releasing a puff of flour—"you do what you gotta do. Lemme know how it works out."

It wasn't exactly a statement of dismissal, but Cullen knew there was nothing left to say. Revek refused to be paid for either the doughnut or coffee, bringing heckles from the men who wanted their own free breakfast.

"The day youse play in the majors and fight a war, free coffee. Until then, gimme your nickels."

Cullen walked out. Was he doing this for Mother? for Lilly? for his legacy? for his soul or his mind? Or for God? All of them, he supposed, though his mother might never know, God didn't demand it, and Lilly might not care.

As for himself, perhaps the healing he'd come seeking had already occurred. And now, it was just a game.

34

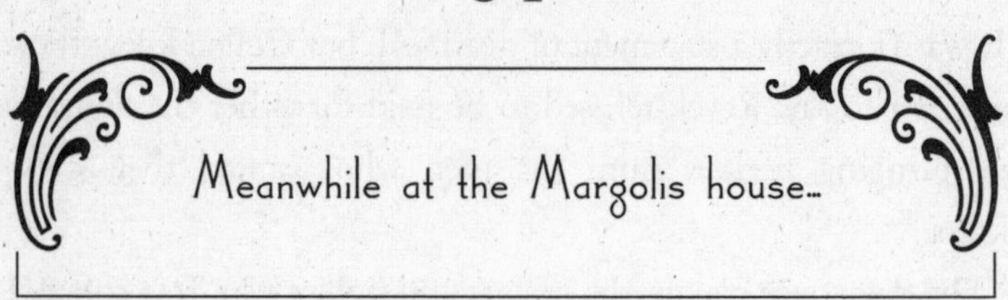

Meanwhile at the Margolis house...

Lilly had to open the door sometime. Ideally, when Mama stepped out to run an errand or go to work. But her job as a janitress for several buildings on the square meant she wouldn't leave until after six o'clock. That could mean a long, miserable day. For now, at least, Lilly had her familiar blanket pulled up to her nose, and not even the mustiness could mask its familiar scent.

Rain drizzled on the window, clouds kept the room in relative darkness, and she'd sneaked a trip out to the bathroom just before dawn. Outside the door, Mama was moving furniture, the daily dusting and sweeping that had awakened Lilly almost every morning of her life, underscored by hymns sung in a fierce soprano. As far as she could remember, it was the closest she knew of a lullaby, and this morning it served that purpose. She turned to face the bare gray wall, tracing her finger along the plaster.

A knock. "If you want breakfast, tell me now because I'm about to clean the kitchen."

Lilly pulled the blanket up over her ears. She was hungry, but she'd been hungrier. Nothing was worth facing that woman now.

Tell me when, Jesus. I'm here.

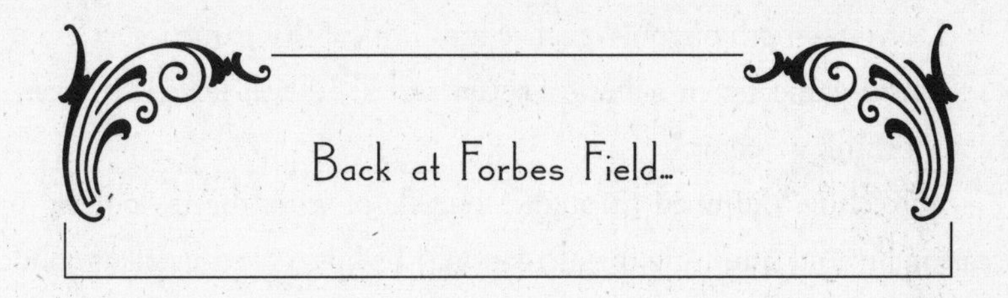

"Tell me again?" Bill "Deacon" McKechnie leaned forward in his chair. The three men were in the small office off the Pirates's locker room.

"Just one time up to bat." This was the third time Dave Voyant explained the scenario, and Cullen was beginning to think his old teammate, turned manager, had taken one too many balls to the head. "Not in the lineup. In between innings. Blue Moon Burnside, returning hero, gets a shot at getting a hit at home."

McKechnie's ribbon-thin lips flattened against each other. "Some kind of publicity stunt?"

"A story. Nothing more. Little four-inch story under the headline when you win the Series."

"I like the sound of that."

"Thought you would."

"How 'bout you, Burnside. What's in it for you?"

Cullen had been pacing the room, looking at pictures on the wall, noticing his wasn't among them. "That's another story."

McKechnie rubbed his hands together in his distinctive way, making one then the other into a palmed ball. "I'm lookin' at you now, Moon, and I gotta tell you, I know a little about what you—guys like you—went through. And I don't mean just the face, 'cause there's plenty of ugly mugs out there. But you sure you're up to it? Takes a bit to hit that ball. What with the problems you had even before..."

The man never could answer a question straight. "Say what you mean, Bill."

"Do you—both of you—realize how critical this game is?"

"Three-game tie in a best-of-seven series?" Dave licked his pencil point. "I think we get it."

McKechnie thumbed through a bundle of score sheets, looking up occasionally and squinting in calculation. His lips moved in silent counting, which he double-checked on thick chapped fingers before finally seeming to come to a conclusion. "Tell you what. We get us to the top of an inning, and there's a tie, we'll bring you on out. Voyant, you write up a little something for the guys in the booth."

"That's radio." Dave looked at Cullen. "You fine with that? Might mean a story before the hit."

Cullen thought about the conditions. "Might mean nothing at all."

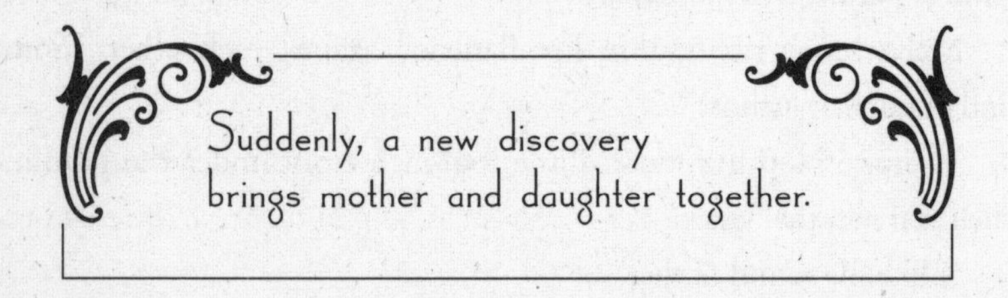

If anything, the room grew colder with the afternoon. The rain was continuing its relentless drizzle when Lilly awoke for the third time that day. She swung her feet over the edge of the bed and sat—head in hands—staring at the floor.

Jesus, this is it. Getting up. Going out. Please make it better than last night.

She stood, stretching out the ill effects of too many hours spent on a broken bed, and then took quick steps over to the bureau to get a pair of thick wool socks from the top drawer. When she sat on the edge of the bed to put them on, she heard the first strains of an unfamiliar noise.

The bedsprings creaked when she stood, just as they had when she sat, and the sound coming from the other side of the door seemed at first to have a high-pitched, metallic quality. Ear against the door, she turned the lock, then turned the knob, then heard the sound amplify as she poked her head around the corner.

Music. In her home.

Stepping carefully in those places where waxed floor was not covered by worn carpet, Lilly emerged from her room and, for the first time, noticed the small wooden box on the bookcase across the room.

A radio. In her mother's house. The Burnsides didn't even have a radio. Cullen explained once that the sound of voices and music coming from thin air might frighten Betty Ruth. She'd barely come to accept a Victrola. Mama sat in the straight-backed chair, her profile to Lilly as she came out of her room. The sound of the opening door had done nothing to draw her attention, and it wasn't until Lilly sat in the chair directly across that she gave any acknowledgment that she wasn't alone.

"'Bout time you got yourself out of bed. Lazy days make lazy ways."

Lilly chose to ignore the comment. It would be her first attempt at peace for the day. "You have a radio, Mama?"

Her mother got up and took hold of one of the round knobs, twisting it until the music faded. "Why shouldn't I?"

"It seems extravagant. For you, I mean."

"I work hard. I figure I can spend my money how I want, seeing as I'm all alone."

"You can, of course you can. I didn't mean—" But Mama apparently didn't care what Lilly meant because she was already twisting the volume knob again.

"At two o'clock every day there's a gospel group that sings. The Jobe Family Quintet. I like to listen."

"Is it all right if I listen with you?" Maybe, if they could just be quiet together...

"Ain't that jazz music you like so much?"

Lilly balled up her fists, squeezed, and relaxed her hands flat in her lap. "I like all kinds of music."

"Suit yourself."

Soon the little room was filled with the warbling music of a pipe organ playing a tune Lilly recalled from childhood. She leaned back in her chair, splaying her legs out in front of her and looking out the front picture window to the gray day outside, listening to the singers—a family, apparently, two men and three women—their voices melded in perfect harmony.

Marvelous grace of our loving Lord,
Grace that exceeds our sin and our guilt.

"You know what, Mama? I think—"

"Hush." She put a red, chapped finger to her lips. "After the song."

The family took turns, a different brother or sister singing each verse, but they came together on the chorus.

Grace, grace, God's grace,
Grace that will pardon and cleanse within;

Grace, grace, God's grace,
Grace that is greater than all our sin.

Their words made clear the picture of Jesus on the cross, His blood spilled. Herself, the sinner cleansed. How often had she heard "whiter than snow"? It seemed here, where she lived, snow was never white; it was always a dingy gray. Not much different from the sky outside.

She turned her face from the window and looked at the small cloth-covered speaker in the wooden box, wishing she could see their faces instead of the one across from her. Mama stared straight ahead, her eyes fixed and set on…nothing.

As the final note faded, and the radio broadcasted the sounds of shuffling paper and movement, Lilly tried again. "Do you know what I think, Ma? I think you and I are the lucky ones."

"Why's that?" Her voice was flat, distant.

"I think, maybe, if I hadn't been so wild, sinful, you know, I might not realize how good it feels to be forgiven."

Mama's head didn't move, but her eyes found Lilly's. "And what does that have to do with me?"

Lilly took a deep breath. "I wonder if part of the reason you're so angry with me all the time is because you see me making some of the same mistakes you did. With men."

"We aren't the same. I had one lover in my life, and God took him from me that I might sin no more. I was never a tramp."

The word died between them as the Jobe Family Quintet ushered in the first lyrics to "What a Friend We Have in Jesus."

Lilly closed her eyes.

I can't do it, Lord. I've been dying since I stepped foot in this house. She loves You in a different way. Sees You in a different way. Don't make me sacrifice for her sin.

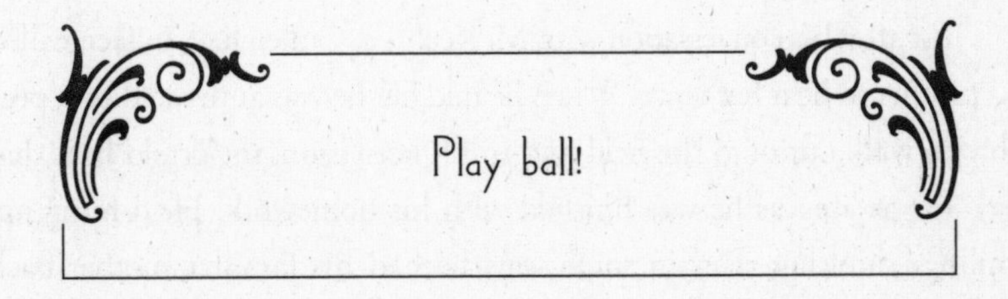

Cullen couldn't decide which was more exciting. The game being played on the field or the activity in the press box. All around him men barked into telephones—whenever the phones weren't ringing—and the constant rhythm of the ticker tape underscored everything. Next door, a man sat tall in his chair, microphone poised at his lips, speaking every detail of the vision in front of him.

"That's Graham McNamee," Dave said under his breath. "Doesn't know much about the game, but he turns the action on the field into a story."

And from the first pitch, Cullen knew there would be a story. The ground was still wet from the previous day's rain, and the effects were immediate. Players slid in the grass, sloshed through mud. There was, from the beginning, an insidious, intermittent sprinkling that seemed to dare another postponement. The people in the crowd hunkered under raincoats and umbrellas, using both to try to shield themselves from the wet bats that flew out of hitters' hands.

"You still thinking you want to go out there?" Dave asked between notes.

"I'm waiting. Tie at the top of an inning."

"That's your sign from God?"

"That's my sign from McKechnie."

Dave clucked his tongue. "Borderline blasphemy. What would your mother say?"

"No telling."

Just after his conversation with McKechnie, Cullen had, in fact, called his mother to hear her voice. When he told her he was at the stadium, possibly to walk out onto the field and fulfill her vision, she'd told him that was fine as long as he was finished with his homework. He'd hung up, smiling, thinking that, in some way, he had his familiar mother back again. His next thought was an overwhelming desire to share that moment with Lilly.

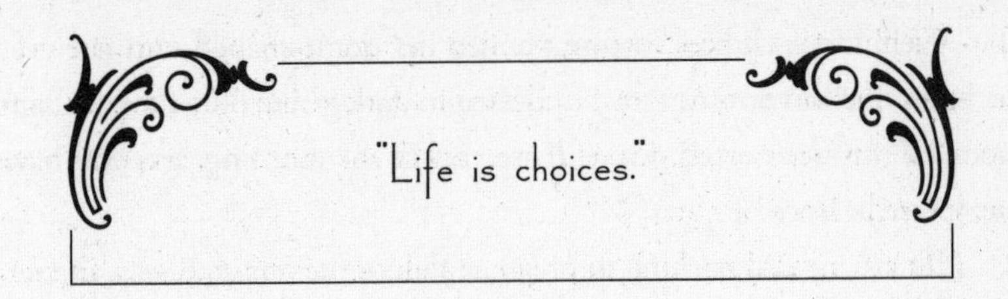

At three o'clock Mama was cinching the belt of her rain slicker and stepping into her galoshes. "Day like today, no telling what them people have tracked onto the floors."

"Isn't it a bit early?" Lilly never remembered her mother going in to work until after dinner.

"These two weeks them people been closing up shop early on account of that game. Going down to the bar to listen on the radio. Middle of the day. Can you imagine such a thing?"

"You could always invite them here. Serve up some lemonade."

"Don't get smart. There's leftover pot roast in the icebox. You look pale, need some meat."

"Thanks, Mama." Her body felt like lead poured out on the chair where she'd sat listening to the Jobe Family Quintet for two hours. The house had taken on the damp chill of rain, and she wished her mother was just as concerned with her warmth and would bring her a blanket. Lilly couldn't bring herself to get up.

"If it clears up tomorrow, you can go about seeing if you can find yourself a job. Can't sit around all day."

"You know, I had somebody offer me a job once to just sit around and read all day."

"Should've took it. You was always one for reading."

"But then I wouldn't be here." She hadn't even meant to say as much out loud, and it was too late to tone down the sarcasm in her voice.

"Well, life is choices." Mama pulled her dome-shaped rain hat over her head. She was now top-to-toe covered in dark green; only the pale half-moon of her face peered out. "I'll see you in the morning 'less you have someplace better to go."

Her leaving did nothing to breathe life into the house. It was, in fact, more tomblike than ever. Clean and cold, exactly as Lilly remembered. She'd gone from death, to hell, to life, and back again. Staring through the window, watching the figure of her mother disappearing down the street, she tried to recall one moment of joy. A single day of happiness within these walls. But when she closed her eyes, the sound of the rain became the lapping of waves, and her mouth puckered around the taste of lemon ice.

The final strains of the Jobe Family Quintet grew into the song of a congregation, somewhere off in the darkness, as she rested in the arms of a man who might have loved her. She felt the slick of dampness and dirt all along her skin, trapped beneath the sweater and the flannel, and remembered that morning at the Tatters' campsite, how very clean and fresh she felt. Like new snow, inside and out, and Cullen was the first one to see her as such.

"Life is choices." This was the worst one yet.

She went to the kitchen, found the cold pot roast, and wrapped up a portion in a slice of bread, washing it down with milk straight from the bottle. Cold but filling. She put on a pot of water for tea and, as it boiled, went into the bathroom to draw a hot bath. The next few minutes she spent running back and forth—checking the water on the stove, checking the water in the tub—all while water poured over the windows.

It was the first time she'd been alone—truly alone—in weeks.

After living with so much noise, the rattle of the car, the songlike quality of Betty Ruth, the silence here felt oppressive. Maybe that's why Mama bought the radio. When Lilly lived here they may have been constantly fighting, but at least that was noise. She set her tea to steeping, feeling a pang of sympathy for her mother.

Lord, I wish she knew. How could she have given so much time trying to teach me about You and know so little herself?

Leaving the tea, she went to take her bath but paused on the way to inspect the radio. Only twice in her wanderings had she ever had one under her roof, and then she'd been afraid to touch it, lest she do something wrong and break it. But now, she had the whole afternoon and evening looming silently before her. So, cautiously, she twisted the center knob, eliciting a soft *click,* and sounds came out. Music again. Soothing and danceable. She sang along on her way to the bathroom. *"Your silv'ry beams will bring love's dreams, we'll be cuddling' soon by the silv'ry moon."*

She continued her dancing step even though the radio's broadcast had become a crackling silence. Grateful to be warm at last, she sank into the hot water, until only her nose was above the surface, and sang, *"By the light, of the silvery moon."* She held the note for *moon* and blew bubbles that rippled over the surface of the water. *"I want to spooooon, to my Moonsie I'll crooooon love's tuuuune."*

This was the song she should have sung that night in the garden. In the moonlight. But she'd been too hurt, wounded because he didn't want her. Couldn't love her. But now, looking back...maybe he didn't kiss her because he wanted to. Didn't love her because he wanted to.

She stared at the spotless, shining rim running around the tub, trying to recall every moment they'd spent together. Every word, even those not spoken. Every touch, even those cut short. He'd wanted her, of course he did. What man didn't? And he was a man, wounds and scars and all. But he'd given her away. Given her up, like he had everything else.

But he did love me, didn't he, Lord? I need to think that somebody—somebody as good as him—could.

The crackling from the radio in the next room gave way to a deep baritone voice saying, "Good afternoon, ladies and gentlemen of the radio audience," as she held her breath and sank under the water.

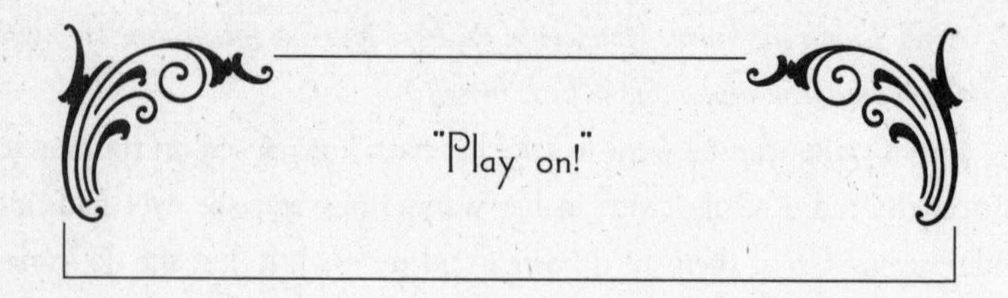

"Play on!"

Cullen had never seen anything like it. Players' uniforms blackened with mud, baselines smeared out of their boundaries. Sheets of sometimes sideways rain falling in the outfield; spectators watching from under—or behind—umbrellas. Word came up to the pressroom: neither side would call it. "Play on!" was the decision at the top and bottom of every inning. Cullen understood why. Too much at stake, and the chance that your opponent might be weaker than you.

God had seen him through enough trenches and battlefields soaked in rain, taken him through more mud than sand. Some of those fellows playing out there, he knew, had been soldiers, too. To them, this storm was nothing. They'd run through showers of bullets. But the younger guys—rookies like he'd been—had never held a bat on anything less than a sunny day. He almost felt sorry for them.

It seemed evident from the first, however, that the decision to persist despite the storm would be a foolish one. Washington took the lead early on and held to it for the first, second, and on and on through the seventh inning. His Pirates chopped away at the deficit, but it seemed for every run they scored, the Senators scored two.

"They could have walked away," he said when he had a chance to talk to Dave between innings. "Postpone and play tomorrow."

"They've given out two rain checks already. Win or lose, it's time to play."

The voice of Graham McNamee filled the room, and Lilly, bundled in silk pajamas and a tight-knit blanket, sat next to the radio, transfixed.

"And with that second run, we go into the eighth inning with a tied score, six all."

She'd clung to every word the man said since emerging from her bath, and now, with her hair nearly dry and her body clean, curled up and cozy, she felt like she'd seen every minute of the game. This wasn't some boyfriend's monologue of scores and statistics, but a story. Pirates and Senators battling on a stage, through wind and rain and even fog.

"What's this?" McNamee, who'd delivered every line of his commentary with fluid assurance, sounded truly confused. "There's some movement at home plate here while Senators's Walter Johnson warms. Highly unusual to have someone at the bat during warmup but"—a rustle of paper interrupted him. "This just handed to me. Apparently the man at bat is none other than Cullen Burnside. Pittsburgh fans remember him as Blue Moon Burnside, holding the inauspicious record of never getting a hit at home."

"Moonsie!" Lilly leaped from her perch and fell to her knees at the radio. She almost kissed the speaker.

"Given that history, might be a good thing fans can't clearly see who's on the field. Might dampen their spirits in a way the rain never could. But folks, today is a day of redemption. We're seeing the Pirates back from a three-one deficit; we've seen them battling up the scoreboard all day, and now this."

"You can do it, Moonsie. Lord, let him hit it."

"So, for the warmup at least, we have Blue Moon facing the Big Train..."

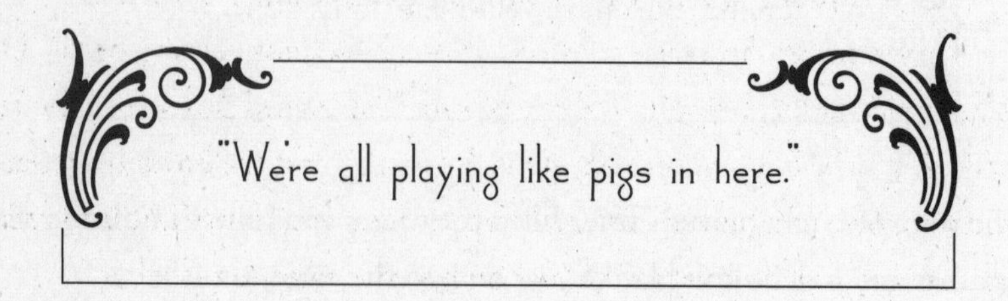

At first, Cullen saw nothing but fog. The seating around Forbes Field had created a bowl to hold the soupy stuff, and it snaked around the field in sheets and rose up in clumpy wisps. He could picture Johnson's pale, piercing eyes on the other side of it. He couldn't be facing a more humbling opponent.

He'd had ample opportunity to back out, starting at home when Mother first shared her vision, and every road stop in between. Even as he had stood at the entrance to the field, with both team managers, McKechnie and Bucky Harris, good-naturedly egging him on, he could have turned around. Walked away. But that would have been another unmet challenge. More unfinished business.

The roar of the crowd was muffled by rain, and they disappeared behind the curtain of mist distorting the stands. No other players were in the field, so in a way it seemed like cheating. A hit would be a hit. Not a pop fly dropped into a glove, not a home run, passing one baseman after another as the number changed on the board, not a foul tipped behind him. Hit or no hit. Three pitches.

So he stood, his good hand gripping the bat, the other supplying what support it could.

Just like that machine at home, isn't it, Lord?

He heard the first pitch when it hit the glove behind him. The umps were taking a coffee break, so there was no one to make the call, but he knew. Strike.

"So this your big comeback?" said the guy behind the mask.

Cullen forced his concentration. "Not so big. Not coming back." He focused on the hazy figure in front of him and braced himself at the release. With the ball not quite in sight, he swung, but the ground beneath him was close to a puddle, and the force of his swing caused him to twist and lose his footing until he was flat on his back within it.

"Hey, buddy. Careful there." The catcher threw back the ball, then extended an arm to help Cullen stand. "We're all playing like pigs in here. Gotta get used to it if you're gonna be in Pittsburgh."

"Don't think you'll be here much longer," Cullen said, and assumed his stance again. This would be it. He'd promised himself—three.

This is Mother's vision, Lord. Not mine. But I thank You for it anyway. If there's any way You could just keep me standing, I'll—

Swing. Now.

The contact between the bat and the ball shook him to his shoulder and rattled his teeth. Clean and centered, he felt it. It was the kind of hit that made you want to stand and watch, just to see the beauty and power of the trajectory, but you couldn't. You had to run, make first base at least. But today, no need. There was nobody to defend his hit, no reason to leave this place. God had sent sheets of rain and rivers of mud to keep him here, watching and watching, until the red-stitched orb disappeared into the fog.

And then it was gone.

He dropped the bat listlessly to his side, not prepared for what he felt. Not joy, not triumph—not any of the things that would make a good ending.

Vanity, vanity. Like the Scripture said.

"That it, buddy?"

"That's it."

Cullen walked off the field to find a beaming Dave Voyant, who stood with his ever-ready notebook and pencil. "And there's my story."

"Do me a favor?"

Dave scowled. "Depends."

"Leave Lilly out of it. At least until we know how it ends."

And the smile was back.

"No more rain checks?"

"Nope. Time to play."

35

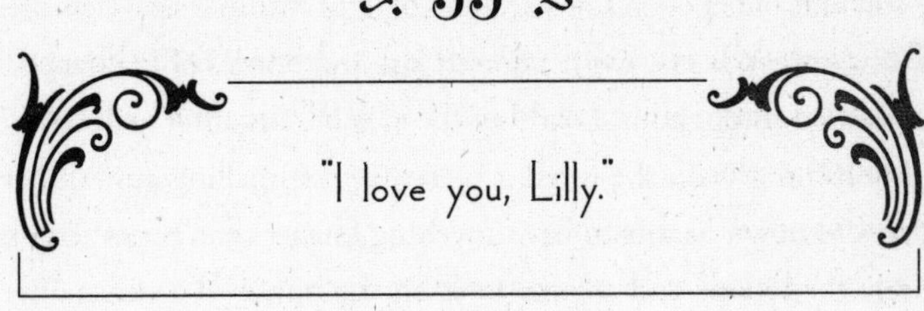

"I love you, Lilly."

By evening, the rain had stopped, which was a good thing because neighbors had poured out of their houses into the streets, dancing and cheering their victory. Lilly watched through the window, having danced her own steps inside.

Mama would have a fit at such a display, even if she didn't know that half of the people were fueled by drink that would put Lickey's special sweet tea bootleg whiskey to shame. Lilly'd had more than a taste of it herself; in fact, smacking her lips, she could almost taste it now. From her perch, she could name a dozen people outside, and no doubt if she stepped onto the front porch, somebody—Trina or Stacia or Mark—would find her, fold her into the party, and pass her a flask. That's why she stayed inside, watching. It all seemed as unreal to her as a movie. For all she belonged out there, she could be watching cowboys or Arabs or Keystone Kops.

She ran away once because the life outside this window wasn't enough. Now, having come back, it still wasn't.

But I can leave without running away, can't I, Lord? Surely there's a difference.

In her room, by the light of the emergency kerosene lamp, she stared at the contents of her open suitcase. Piles of light summer sleeveless dresses, shoes, underwear, hats—with assorted jars and bottles of Dalliance Cosmetics nestled throughout. Loathing the idea of relegating such fashion to mere hooks on a wall, she lifted a pretty, sweet-smelling jar. All her life she'd never known Mama to have anything fancier than Snowberry soap. Suddenly the lotions and creams took on the power of a peace offering, and Lilly gathered all she could to take to Mama's room.

The light revealed a space only slightly less spartan than what Lilly had returned to. A narrow, sunken bed with a stiff chenille spread, a small writing desk with a large Bible, a bureau with no mirror, and a faded round braided rug.

She went to the bureau, intending to leave the little collection of cosmetics there. The top was bare, save for the framed photograph. Lilly, eight years old. Not a speck of dust anywhere on the ornate frame; the glass shone. Her wide eyes stared out from a face framed by mounds and mounds of curls. Mama looked at this every day. Certainly she loved her—had loved her, as a child.

Why can't she see that I'm the same girl?

Lilly stacked the creams and lotions and went back to her room. There was a large, flat box under her bed. She pulled it out and lifted the lid, rummaging around until she found what she was looking for: her high-school yearbook, stuffed into this box to be forgotten along with everything else about this town.

Page thirty-six, her head angled to show off her newest short haircut. No nickname, just Lilly Margolis, and her heart leaped at the quote beneath it: *"Vanity of vanities; all is vanity."* Even then she'd known. How had she forgotten?

She took the yearbook to Mama's room and found a pair of scissors in her writing desk. After taking a deep breath, she cut into the page, carefully removing her picture. She held it up next to her childhood portrait. Same eyes but without the light. Same hair but without the weight. Sadness grew from hope as innocence became accountability. Heart and soul the same, only broken. And now, though she carried the memories of the older girl, she knew she was closer in spirit to the younger. The two were bound together, and as witness, she tucked the yearbook photo into the corner of the frame. Someday, Mama would see that too.

It was full dark outside, but the revelers continued by the light of torches and lanterns. They were singing "Take Me Out to the Ballgame" for at least the tenth time, and now car horns and an impromptu band made up of Thomas Jefferson High School students joined in to torture whatever jazz tune they could.

Somehow, through all the noise, she heard a knocking on the door and realized the sound had been going on for a while. Somebody must have seen her through the window. One of the old crowd. She cinched her robe tighter and ran her fingers through her hair before opening the door.

And there he was.

She couldn't speak, not at first. The sight alone threw her. His clothing was caked with mud, his hair a wild mop on top of his head. His face—even with the familiar scars—was pale and drawn. But his eyes. They shone with light like she'd never seen.

"Lilly? I've come to take you home."

"Moonsie!"

Mud and damp and all, when he opened his arms she ran into them.

He held her, and when she lifted her face to his, he kissed her. She couldn't begin to count the number of boys—and men—who had held her and kissed her on this very porch. Like seasons they came and went with sweet talk and presents and promises. But Moonsie alone was all of these, and more. And none.

The crowd outside burst into new cheers, and the band launched into a passable rendition of "Ain't We Got Fun."

Lilly grabbed Cullen's hand. "Come inside before they turn us into a parade." Once inside, she looked him over in the light. "You're a mess."

"You're lovely."

She looked down at her dowdy brown robe. "You're lying."

He glanced sideways out the window. "Quite a welcoming party you're throwing me. I thought I'd surprise you."

"In case you didn't know, today was a very important baseball game."

"I know."

"We won."

"Did we? I didn't stay to find out."

"I heard everything. On the radio. It was like I was there."

"You—you were."

"So, was she right? Betty Ruth, about your being healed?"

He smiled and held his twisted hand up to his face. "Do I look any better to you?"

His shirt was open at the collar. She stepped away and, with one tentative finger, traced the mass of scarred tissue from his shoulder to his throat. She laid her palm against his face and pulled him to her, pressing her lips against his.

"Moonsie, you're the best thing I've seen all day."

"I love you, Lilly."

"I thought you might." She let him squirm for just a minute. "I love you too."

She led him to the narrow sofa and had him sit down.

"My clothes— " he protested.

"It's all right. Mama loves to clean."

"I meant what I said about taking you home. I want to marry you, Lilly Margolis. Come with me tonight. We'll find someplace and make our honeymoon the drive home."

"But what about Betty Ruth? What you said— ?"

He grabbed her by her arms. "No more rain checks. Go get your bag."

She giggled. "I'm in my pajamas."

He blushed. "Get dressed, then. It's time to play."

She had no idea what he meant by *"rain checks,"* but she understood *"play."* Quickly, she threw her suitcase on top of her bed and opened it, somehow managing to shove in two wool sweaters, a handful of knit berets, and her red silk pajamas with the pagodas stitched along the hem of both the pants and the jacket. With trembling fingers she buttoned a pink oxford shirt and tucked it into the waistband of her favorite chevron-striped skirt, donning a bright red cardigan over all.

Smiling, she hummed *"Here comes the bride..."* while she wrapped a scarf around her neck and slung her gray peacoat over her arm. Brown brogue shoes and galoshes, and she was a woman fit and ready for romance. Since the door was incapable of being flung open, she settled for tugging it and burst into the main room, then stopped in her tracks.

"Well, that didn't take long."

"Hello, Mama. I see you've met—"

"Not one evening left to yourself, and you've got a man here defiling my house."

Even in this state, he looked positively regal standing next to her mother. "I apologize, Mrs. Margolis. I'll pay for the cleaning."

"There's some dirt nothing can clean." Mama hung her overcoat and hat on the brass rack by the door. "So you're off again, are you?"

"It's different this time, Mama. I'm a different girl. This is the man who—who found me. Who wrote to you. He's a good man, a Christian man. And we're going to get married."

At that Mama softened. Nothing any passing stranger would notice, just the tiniest slacking of the lips, a deep exhalation, but to Lilly it felt akin to a transformation before her eyes.

"Well, must be God's will, then."

Lilly thought she might join the puddles on the floor as she melted into joy. "It is, Mama. It is. And there's a whole grand story. I'll write it all down for you and send it."

"Or she can read the *Saturday Evening Post,*" Cullen said. "In February."

Mama did not look amused.

Lilly gave her suitcase to Cullen and shooed him out the door before wrapping her arms around Mama's shoulders in a stiff embrace. "I love you, Mama." She waited two, three breaths for her mother to say the same, and after that, she walked out into the night. She was leaving. But this time it was different.

Cullen was waiting in the car, lights on, engine running. She climbed in beside him and immediately scooted across the seat, tucking herself under his arm.

"So, that was my mother."

"Yes." He maneuvered slowly through the crowd of people, though the throng had somewhat dispersed.

"I didn't want you to meet her."

"I'm glad I did. And now, it's your turn to meet mine."

Lilly laughed and snuggled closer. "Silly, I've already met your mother."

"True. But she hasn't met you."

"Do you think she'll like me?"

"She'll love you, darling. She already does."

Soon the rain-slicked tire mountain was behind them, and though it was too cold to ride in an open car, they rolled the windows down enough to let in the sweet smell of the world after a rain. If it were daylight, there would be rainbows, but as it was, the beauty came in the moonlight reflected in the leaves of the trees lining the road.

They sped by like so many shooting stars, and Lilly spoke a wish on every one. The same wishes over and over, really—that she would grow old by Moonsie's side. That her heart would relive the joy of this moment if she ever doubted God's mercy, like Mama. That her mind would recall this very scene if her memory ever failed her, like Betty Ruth.

She pictured this moment, flickering in black and white on a silver screen. Indeed, there was no color to be found. But there would be tomorrow. If they drove all night they'd see it, the pink and orange of sunrise, the gold and green surrounding.

And like a good matinée, she would come back to see it, over and over again. Together they'd trade moonlight for dawn.

Readers Guide

1. As a flapper, Lilly represents a major shift in the way women were viewed and treated. What aspects of this "new" woman represented a change for the better? for the worse?
2. Would you describe Lilly's leaving home as an act of rebellion or escape?
3. In 2 Corinthians Paul wrote of the importance of being impressed not by what is seen but rather what is in the heart. He wrote: "If we are out of our mind, it is for the sake of God; if we are in our right mind, it is for you" (2 Corinthians 5:13, NIV). How does this verse relate to Betty Ruth? to Cullen? to Lilly?
4. The Tutwiler Hotel and the Knockabout Campsite represent two extremes of lodging for a family road trip. Which of the two would you prefer? Why?
5. The tent revival saw a huge upsurge in popularity during the 1920s. Why do you think that is? What does such a service offer that an ordinary Sunday worship service in a church does not?
6. If he were alive, how do you think Davis Burnside, Cullen's father, would have reacted to Lilly?
7. Dave Voyant makes an appearance in this story. In both *Stealing Home* and *The Bridegrooms,* we see him as a sports reporter more interested in the personal lives of athletes than their scores and statistics. How important is the human-interest aspect of professional sports figures? Do we care about the story behind the statistic?
8. Lilly grew up in a Christian home, yet she had to leave it to find a true relationship with Jesus. How can we strike a balance between upholding high moral standards and affording grace?

9. *Lilies in Moonlight* touches on the theme of healing. How is Cullen healed? Lilly? Betty Ruth?
10. What will it take to heal the relationship between Lilly and her mother? If you were Lilly's friend, would you encourage her to pursue reconciliation?

Author's Note

It's official: flappers are fun. What an amazing time in our history, seeing women liberated from corsets and petticoats and hair that measured by the yard. As a writer of historical fiction, I felt a sense of liberation myself while writing this book. The fashion, the cars, the brazen independence. Still, I don't exactly envy my Jazz Age sisters. What a tightrope it must have been to balance mode and morality.

Lilies in Moonlight marks the third of my "baseball" books, and I must say, they've been so much fun to write! I became intrigued with Dave Voyant in *Stealing Home,* developed a mad crush on him in *The Bridegrooms,* and am quite satisfied with the man he became in *Lilies in Moonlight.* I never thought I could have so much fun with a minor character.

A heartfelt thanks to all the wonderful folks at Multnomah. I so appreciate all your talent and support. You were a miracle in my life with my very first book, and I thank God every day for bringing me to your house.

And, Bill, agent of the ages! I told you: *Gatsby* is everything!

Finally, to all of you who so graciously go on this road trip with me every few months, driving through the pages of my imagination—what wonderful travel companions you are! I hope you were blessed by the ride.

And if you want to continue this journey, please visit my Web site: www.allisonpittman.com. I'll meet you at the crossroads!